D1519815

Brother – this is for you!

This book was made possible by the efforts and
tireless work of not only me, but my skillful editor
Indigo Altaria, and my talented illustrator Neutronboar!
Thanks to my family and friends for all of the support
they've offered, and their trust
in my humble writing skills. There is hope for the future
of humanity yet.

# Table of Contents

# Copyright

# Prologue

## *Introduction to the series*

Many years ago, when I started writing the book you are now holding my dear reader, I never intended for it to become the first part of a decalogy. Indeed, what I first envisioned was a simple adventure, perhaps spanning two, maybe three small books...

That was back then – now, fifteen years later, what you are about to soon read is Starshatter's Character & Universe introduction book. The alternate history universe I created is vast and, by carefully weaving my characters' stories, setting up their life goals, I added more and more layers to this quite similar, and yet very different version of Earth. The more I worked, the more their adventures took shape, until one day I had the drafts of ten books, their thick folders eagerly looking at me from my desktop.

Yes, you've read correctly – this series consists of ten books, with two trilogies to follow, which are also set in this universe.

No matter what everyone was telling me back then, I persevered and never stopped working. Even in my darkest moments the thought of discontinuing this project, this dream of mine, never entered my mind. I firmly believe that the tales which our ancient forebears wove and later turned into myth, this hallowed tradition of storytelling is most important and must be treasured. I doubt anyone could deny the fact that our modern world is in desperate need of new, heroic legends. Tales that inspire courage before adversity and bestow the reader with hope, two things which are very much needed in these troubling times.

Desperation has no place in between these pages and whatever description of post-apocalyptic realities you may find, rest assured, these are not what the future of humanity would look like. You won't witness the incoherent screeches of mewling fools, who curl in fetal position or stuff their heads in the ground, desperate to hide from mere words, either.

Not in Starshatter, not ever!

Indeed, the humans might vanish one day yet, their last defiant shout would echo across eternity with such might that history itself will protest, angered beyond measure. Furious that someone dared destroy a race which filled her pages full of timeless heroism, and demonstrated feats of peerless bravery.

I hope that you will enjoy this world I've built and populated with unapologetic in their desire to resist oppression, heroes. The villains who oppose them are many, their strengths and numbers vary – from the lowliest of disposable, cannon fodder-like troopers, to the genius masterminds who command said pawns into battle. Both heroes and villains are fully fleshed out characters and they do grow, learn after facing each other in battle. Rest assured, nothing is lost in Starshatter – events, character growth, and interactions flow from one book into the next.

But, I need not ramble any longer, I will let my characters take it from here.

# Chapter 1

*Lilly*

Fertile land; you could live off it and prosper or at least give it a good try.

The colonists who chose to settle the dangerous and unforgiving planets in Fringe space were of the adventurous type. Humans mostly, but there were other Terran races also; long-eared bunnies, quick furry hamsters, and tough gorillas all ventured together with their human patrons. Young families, whose futures were otherwise to be determined by the safety of the Core worlds.

Dangers like pirates, slavers, and hostile alien empires weren't enough to hold the slow and unstoppable advance of those Terrans. The allure of starting from the ground up and succeeding by way of your own skill; that was the actual reason most settlers did it. It wasn't for riches or renown, like many of the aliens thought.

Speaking of aliens, many of humanity's allies could also be found traveling and sometimes living on those small colonies. Mighty, fifteen-feet-tall Asgardians could also be seen braving the Fringe on occasion. The enigmatic aliens who hailed from another dimension, traveled to Earth through their Rainbow bridge or Bifrost located in Finland. Long since their first meeting with humanity in hallowed antiquity had fueled legend and shaped religion on Earth, the Asgardians were now back and this time they intended to stay. Those powerful, war-like aliens, sent their young to live among the Terrans, learn more about this world and its technology.

Races like the long lived and mighty Kil'ra also encouraged their youth to prove themselves there. What was the reason many of them chose to settle permanently in Terran space? Most couldn't say, but those with greater wisdom always spoke to others of the bonds between humans and their friends.

It wasn't like anything they'd witnessed anywhere else and the Kil'ra had been traveling the whole galaxy for thousands of years – they've seen a *lot*. Some of the other sentient species that they'd made First Contact with were no longer amongst the living, many more had fallen into obscurity; yet those Terrans and their uplifted client races carried within them something new – their tiny empire prospered, despite all odds.

Friendly races and allies few and far between; enemies all around them, the intrepid Terrans suffered frequent attacks yet, stubbornly, they persisted.

The scorching rays of Carrola's twin suns bathed large fields of green. Big, round, and striped Earth-native fruits called "watermelons" were planted all around her. Lilly fixed the big straw hat made of the local pink weed on her head, so that both her eyes and large ears were well protected from the light.

The two suns weren't as forgiving as Earth's star – but for the tropical fruits and other sun-hungry crops planted here, it was literally heaven. She carefully piloted her gravbike forward, one hand on the controls, while also holding her scanner. Had to check for problems like parasites, pests and possible damage to the field's water sprinklers. All could ruin large quantities of their future yield and she was too good a farmer to allow this to happen.

Since early morning Lilly had been scanning the fields and on occasion, zapping with her laser pistol some of the local rat-like creatures called wozzies. That or fixing dented and broken water pipes by replacing the ripped ones. They had to replace the whole watering system's pipes with new ones made from megasteel and encase them in vacfoam.

In a month the new watermelon crop would be ripe for harvest and then, after selling it, Lilly and her brother could finally invest more creds in their farm.

Perhaps they could buy one of those anti-grav capable farming drones? It would be really nice if she had more time on her hands to plan the growth of their business, while somebody else lasered those filthy wozzies. The tired and thirsty farmer wanted nothing more than to take a refreshing shower and enjoy one big, cold glass of watermelon cider. Better still, said drink should be accompanied by a side dish of cured-pork-and-potato salad.

Lilly's mouth began to water just imagining the feast she and her brother would prepare after a long hard day's work such as this. That's when her hand holding the scanner slipped over the gravbike's controls. Suddenly she swooshed upwards, the old machine's grav-engine moaning with anger; Lilly heard an explosion and then felt fire burning her back.

The whole world swirled before her eyes in a kaleidoscope of bright, colorful lights, and her mind quickly faded into unconsciousness.

\* \* \*

When the bunny woke up it was already dark; her nose immediately picked up the stench of burned vegetation and molten metal. Somehow, Lilly's head wasn't cracked, and despite some pain in her hip, she felt no broken bones when she picked herself up from the ground.

The same couldn't be said about her old trusty gravbike; its frame was bent and the engine block was missing. Lilly limped around for a while in disbelief, until she found the grav-engine embedded in one of the large mumpa trees, completely trashed. She searched around the crash site with the faint hope of locating her hand scanner, stumbling for a couple more minutes until she realized: the smell wasn't from her wrecked gravbike.

The evening breeze was blowing from the direction of the colony settlement, and Lilly turned her eyes towards it. Even taking into account how far away the village was and her weak rabbit eyesight, the huge, towering flames she saw were a frightening scene to behold. The young bunny watched this raging inferno in total disbelief, for in her disoriented mind there was no logical reason why such a thing should happen.

Lilly forgot the pain in her hip and ran towards the village with all of her strength. Her stride became almost animalistic, leaping and jumping over the crops she'd been inspecting earlier. With every passing minute of travel her fear grew, and by the time Lilly reached the butchered, gutted remains of her village, she was in a state of complete shock.

Passing by the sign **"Murphy's Landing – population 352"**, she suddenly halted – someone had used red paint to cross out the population number.

No; it wasn't paint!

Looking down, she saw a severed human hand that had been used as a grizzly paintbrush. Without even noticing her own actions, Lilly knelt and took the hand, slowly walking towards the smoldering ruins. The stench of death hit her like a fist in the face, and she desperately tried to cover her sensitive nose – to no avail.

Tears started rolling down her face as she neared her family's farmhouse. There was a crater where the building was once standing, and in front of it, she found a charred human corpse with one hand missing. Lilly carefully left the severed hand near the body and sat on the ground. Then she spotted something else and she wailed, covering her mouth.

Beneath the ruins, one set of brown, spotted rabbit feet were sticking out and both had green work boots on them. Her little brother's boots – the ones she had gifted him on his birthday just a month before.

Bunnies are not that afraid of death; they can accept the natural order of things, since their lives are shorter than those of most races. But this lack of fear only applies to their own lives – not the lives of kin or friends. They take losing others very hard and such a personal cataclysm may change a rabbit individual forever, pushing them to extremes.

Her eyes strayed away and back towards the one-handed corpse. He had a shovel still clenched in his intact fist, and from the looks of it, he had been shot from behind with a laser rifle. Lilly recognized the man: a good friend, and the owner of their local shop – Mr. Alberto.

With shaking hands she searched the burned body and took the key card for his house. She knew the trader had an old rail carbine stashed in his safe – he was, after all, the man who had taught Lilly and her brother how to shoot when they were little kids. She quickly looked around, wiping her tears and trying to fight the overwhelming terror that engulfed her mind:

*"Move, you know what to do Lilly, get to a weapon quick! You need to survive long enough, until the response*

10

*team from the nearby colony arrives."*

She continuously reminded herself of the list of actions a colonist must take to ensure survival – weapon, food, equipment, shelter.

The young bunny reached the center of her village without meeting any of the attackers, but she saw traces of their handiwork everywhere. The bodies of her fellow colonists littered the ground; some had tried to defend themselves, but it seems they had all been killed in the same fashion Alberto was – one laser shot from behind.

How!?

How did this happen – perhaps it was a sneak attack?

Lilly looked around for any usable items, but the bodies had been picked clean; even their PDAs were missing. She had almost reached Alberto's house when her ears caught the sounds of a pair of gruff alien voices. She quickly froze, hiding behind one of the broken mega-concrete walls. They were speaking in a strange dialect of Fringe-Speak, and she slowly began to translate their conversation:

*"Ha! That was a most pitiful fight, Master Sergeant. The whole village was unable to put up even a meager resistance. I swear by the Empress' mantle, one of those old farts stood against me with a shovel in hand!"*

*"Yes, it was rather pathetic. It seems that those famed Terrans and their clients weren't all that scary and tough, as the pirates said they were."*

*"But Sergeant, this was one of their main colonies and there were no major defenses! No reinforced bunkers, no anti-space cannons, not even proper soldiers. The Taz'aran Empire will take their territory quickly, and they*

11

*will learn to call us their masters soon!"*

The younger voice carried much enthusiasm and was speaking the name of his empire with elation. Lilly almost choked with anger and fear – they were mocking the memory of her dead friends, her brother!

She saw an overturned pickup truck next to the place those two voices were. One of the three Danube trucks owned by the colony's delivery company, "Slow Pokes" and it was the perfect cover. Lilly carefully crawled forwards and peeked from behind the truck's front.

The two Taz'aran soldiers were sitting idly on one of the village square benches, stuffing their faces with rations. Both looked stocky but were no taller than humans, with pale greenish skin and dark brown eyes. They had crummy laser rifles resting on their knees, an alien model she had never seen in her life. Nothing like the Imperial-issue laser rifle; these were obvious copies, and bad ones at best.

Even though Lilly was a farmer, she knew a little bit about weapons too. You had to; in the Terran Minarchy it was obligatory for all citizens to learn how to defend themselves, and to have a basic knowledge of simple weapons and armor. These Taz'aran rifles didn't even have a basic heatsink installed and their power packs were not designed with environmental protection!

Oh, it was alright for now; but after a week spent in Carrola's burning heat and humidity, they would experience weapon jams and even "violent" overheating. Lilly looked at their bulky, uncomfortable space suits and reached for her laser pistol. The range was perfect; she could take her time and aim carefully from behind the cover of this truck.

Her hand grasped only air and Lilly, very much confused, glanced at her hip – the laser pistol wasn't there!

In the shock after her gravbike's crashing, it must have fallen somewhere. She desperately looked over her belt and her person, but there wasn't anything usable... save for her hand PDA. Lilly crept back behind the pickup truck and crawled under the fusion core with one ear still pointed at those soldiers. They were still patting each other on the back, congratulating themselves on how easy it was to conquer her colony.

She slowly and gently opened the service lid over the core and removed her PDA. Ever so quietly, Lilly placed it between the plasma wires and began inputting an overload program that would turn the fusion core into an improvised bomb. A crappy one, with low yield and range, but more than enough to turn both of those murdering bastards into dust. Lilly punched in a two-minute time limit and started crawling away from the truck.

Suddenly, she heard the metallic sounds of one Taz'aran walking in his suit towards her position!

The bunny stilled, in her mind she counted the seconds left until her PDA's now unstoppable overload. She heard the soldier call his sergeant to join him in pushing the truck back on its four tires. They had to take a final look and search for anything left that could be of use.

Lilly tried desperately to sneak away as quietly as possible, yet she wasn't fast enough. The two Taz'arans pushed the pickup over and it almost crushed her back. She managed to roll away in the last possible moment, but the soldiers saw her and raised their weapons. One of them crowed as he trained his rifle on her:

"Look what we have here, Sergeant – one of those fake sentients, with the long ears! Hey, should we capture it? We might get a reward for getting another one for the slave ship!"

"Bah! Shoot her mangy ass, we have all the young ones and they bring the best price at the markets. I bet you can't kill her with one shot, Soldier! Let's see... a day's ration, agreed?"

Both grinned at each other aiming at Lilly, while she turned around and jumped with all her strength. The two Taz'arans were unable to press the trigger, nor was Lilly able to finish her jump. Exploding, the pickup truck turned both soldiers into mush and mercilessly slammed her small body in the nearby wall. For the second time that day, she lost consciousness.

* * *

She tasted blood in her mouth and tried to get up. Her dazed senses noted the two suns setting and Lilly, despite the pain in her limbs, began moving towards the south end of the village square. She checked her pockets this time, making sure the key card for Alberto's home was still in her possession – thankfully, it was.

Fumbling and with bones aching, Lilly crossed the small crater left from the exploding Danube truck and finally reached Alberto's store. It was ransacked; just as she expected the greedy invader had taken even the store shelves. Limping, she reached the inner door, placed the key card over its handle and one satisfying *click* later it slid aside, letting her in.

Lilly made only a few steps when her eyes were attacked by a flash of light – old man Alberto had set the house lighting to turn on automatically when the door was opened during nighttime! She found the master holo panel and turned the house lights off, but the damage was already done. Even if the Taz'arans weren't looking for their missing soldiers after that explosion, they would certainly send someone to investigate the house. Lilly, despite the pain, limped up the stairs to the second floor as fast as she was able and opened the weapons-closet door.

Yes, the carbine was there, in its case and there was even a bug-out backpack!

She quickly grabbed everything, checked if the rail carbine's power pack was full – *it was* – then reached into the case to pick up the spares. Once again her hand grasped air, there were none! Lilly thought for about a second about thoroughly searching the back of the weapon's closet, but quickly changed her mind. Her keen hearing alerted her that a big grav-vehicle was closing in on the house.

She ran towards the back window of Alberto's home, opened it and, even with her injuries, leaped down without looking. At the same time behind, an armored boot kicked down the door and a couple of laser rifles fired through the house, aiming at her. Beams hit the air where she stood seconds before and then her feet met the ground.

Lilly almost fainted from the pain – a fifteen-foot-plus jump was way too much for a bunny in her condition. She grabbed the fence with one arm and started limping towards old man Alberto's garage. She had almost reached the door when a bright yellow laser beam splashed the ground left of her. In a second the fear almost took over again, and her entire body froze. One Taz'aran shouted:

*"Surrender to us, rodent, and we will be merciful! Your life will be spared, drop your weapon!"*

In her mind Lilly shouted to herself, *Move your rabbit ass!* With a force she never knew she had, Lilly jumped towards the garage and screamed at the Taz'arans:

15

"Eat space! Try catching me, you murderous bastards!"

She rolled on the ground while two more beams melted holes in the garage doors, scorching her back. The pain almost made her lose consciousness again, but she managed to block it out and reach the parked combine. One short leap later and the bunny was inside the vehicle, short hands reaching for its controls, she whimpered when her burned back touched the seat.

Another yellow beam hit the garage doors and through the holes, Lilly saw two Taz'aran soldiers running at her. She smiled despite the ever-growing pain and punched the start button – the old combine's Tesla engine roared and Lilly pushed the accelerator to the max.

Big and heavy, Alberto's vintage combine smashed through the garage doors and with its flailing grappling arm Lilly attacked her pursuers. Designed not just to gather crops, the old combine had a long and powerful "arm," so that the operator could safely remove mumpa trees. As it turned out, the Taz'aran soldiers' space suits were far more brittle than the bark of said trees.

While the second invader disappeared screaming beneath the combine's left tread, she dropped the first soldier's lifeless body aside and again pushed the accelerator. The large machine speedily rolled forward; Lilly turned south and started moving towards the mumpa forest. It was at least four kilometers away and she desperately looked behind, almost expecting her pursuers to shoot at her with a tank.

No sooner had she left the garage and moved away from the village, than a long-range guided missile hit Alberto's house, and with a big reddish explosion, wiped away everything within at least five hundred meters. The shock wave reached the combine, but since it was so heavy, she only temporary lost her hearing.

Looking down at the controls, Lilly saw that her nose was bleeding – the entire steering wheel covered in blood. She rummaged through the backpack hoping that Alberto had stacked some meds in it. There were three medsprays in a small box and she pressed one of them at her neck, pushing the injector's button. The bleeding stopped at least, but most of the pain she felt in her back lingered.

She placed the spent medspray back into its box and looked at her rear holo screen. A single alien armored vehicle emerged through the smoldering ruins of Alberto's house, and stopped on the ridge behind her. Its turret tracked her combine, and Lilly instantly pressed the brake while turning left.

One single pulse from their beam gun melted the ground where her vehicle was supposed to be if she was still moving. She frantically pushed the accelerator again and started zigzagging, all the while looking intensely at her rear holo screen. The next beam almost melted the back side of the combine, and Lilly heard the Tesla engine giving out a high-pitched noise. The combine's control panel showed her a red warning sign: the entire drive system was overheating!

She stopped zig-zagging, locked the accelerator forward and leaped from the driver's cabin and onto the ground, rolling to the side to cushion the blow. No sooner than she did this, Alberto's vehicle was hit again by the alien beam gun and exploded, pushing her body to the ground.

Lilly crawled, choking on the fumes, her eyes starting to bleed – those mumpa trees seemed so far away!

The young bunny started limping towards the tree line, hoping that the smoke from the smoldering wreck of

17

the combine would cover her movements for at least a few seconds longer. Her ears caught the sound of armored feet meeting the ground and the hiss of laser beams – the Taz'arans were shooting at the remains of the combine. She reached a mega-concrete pyramid marker, the one that said:

**"Mumpa Forest, No Entry Without Survival Gear!"**

Lilly found time for a sarcastic smile; a skilled farmer, she *was* an exobiologist too, but even her knowledge of the planet's ecosystem was limited. Nobody had had time to completely explore that forest and since Terrans were always respectful towards local wildlife and plants, it was considered essential to have one's own supplies so as to not overharvest resources. Except the tests and scans her teachers did to determine that these mumpa trees were not poisonous, the colonists had left their neighbors at peace.

She heard the Taz'arans shout behind her – *"Here she is! Shoot to kill!"* – and the buzzing of laser fire.

Somehow Lilly found the strength to roll behind the marker; the mega-concrete saved her life, a few accurate shots hit it and melted big chunks off its surface. She gathered all of her remaining stamina and made a run towards the trees. A stray yellow laser beam glanced her left shoulder and she fell, face hitting the soft, muddy ground, screaming in pain.

The trees were so close, yet the Taz'aran soldiers were even closer and their suits clanked while they ran ever nearer, laser rifles pointed at her. Lilly grabbed her rail carbine and, rolling to the side, took a pot shot at one of the Taz'aran soldiers while the second fired his own gun at her.

Both shots met their marks; one of the enemy soldiers' faces vanished, as the rail carbine's pellet turned it into red paste. The laser beam from her enemy's rifle burned a small hole into the right side of Lilly's chest and for a second her breathing stopped from the shock of the wound.

She spat blood and her vision almost faded, while the second Taz'aran soldier frantically ran back towards his vehicle, screaming and shooting aimlessly. Her mind fading away, Lilly reached for her backpack and with limp hands tried to use her last two medsprays. She shoved the injectors into the wound and pressed both buttons...

\* \* \*

The rest of the Taz'aran soldiers took cover around their unit's Armored Personnel Carrier, laser rifles pointed beyond the still-burning combine and their scanners pinning the location of the last living Terran colonist on Carrola.

The APC commander, a pompous fellow, screamed at the soldier who ran away – *"Idiot! Wretch! How dare you run away from that puny creature! I'll have you shot for cowardice!"* – and slapped him across the face with his gloved hand.

The stunned taz'aran rolled on the ground, holding his jaw and spitting blood. The officer turned towards the rest of the section under his command – *"Form a firing line and move forward; she isn't far away and heavily wounded! Use that piece of junk for cover!"* – he pointed at the combine – *"Encircle her and suppress, then grenade the bitch. Got it?"*

His soldiers slightly bowed, shouted – *"Yes, Your Excellency!"* – and ran, laser rifles leveled forward.

Their APC section was one of the newer ones in the unit and all of them without exception were force-drafted from core worlds in their empire. The minimal training those soldiers had received was at least three standard months, mostly marching and shooting at static targets. The big problem was that those targets didn't fire back, and none of them had experienced the frantic nature of battle.

While they advanced one of them was shot in the leg, his limb disappearing in a spatter of flesh and metal pieces. The soldier fell dead on the spot, with a look of great surprise on his face. Taz'aran infantrymen continued to advance despite what they've just witnessed, under the intimidating gaze of their commander.

The noble officer looked at his driver and snapped another command – *"Prepare to slowly move forward at my order"* – he winced a little bit when another soldier of his section lost an arm and fell screaming to the ground – *"and give me my sniper rifle!"*

The driver nodded timidly and complied. The rest of his section crawled ahead and began firing sporadically at... something. He saw one of them aiming carefully with his laser rifle – and then something hit it, blowing the gun to pieces. The soldier's corpse limped over the still-burning hull of the combine, parts of the rifle sticking out from his eye sockets and mouth.

That was half of his section dead already and the officer sighed annoyed. He was left with six men total and would have to buy more of them to replenish his unit. Thankfully, most of their equipment was salvageable, he thought to himself with a smile – it was far cheaper to buy new force-drafted soldiers than weapons and armor.

*"Forward!, you failures!"* – He screamed in the comms unit.

*"Driver, move around the wreck, slowly!, and use the*

*soldiers as cover. I don't want the fresh paint on my APC to get damaged!"*

The officer prepared his sniper rifle; it was an old particle beam gun, engraved with his family's crest. This venerable weapon was used by many of his ascendants to kill enemies of the Taz'aran Imperium. His people valued nobility before the common rabble and that rifle perhaps had taken more of his own race's lives than alien ones. He was poised to change that on this tour of duty.

The holo scope flickered to life and he switched it to heat-vision. It showed the body of their enemy crawling on the ground, already between the second tree line. He increased the zoom on the scope; the Terran had left a small blood trail in the mud, and her lower limbs were desperately flailing. She was pushing herself to reach the nearest big tree, and his mouth turned into a crooked smile while taking aim.

His holo scope gave correction for the target's movement and the taz'aran, confident in his aim, pressed the trigger. Red, glowing particle beam shot out of the muzzle. To his surprise, one thick tree branch moved and was hit by the beam, instead of the head of his target.

Accursed plants!

He corrected his aim and shot another beam at her. The exact same branch, moving randomly by the wind it seemed, was hit, and fell smoldering in the mud. This defective Terran managed to somehow crawl behind the tree yet, there was something else. As he watched her through the scope, she doesn't seem to have been able to crawl that fast – it was as if the plant itself moved in an instant, blocking his aim!

He gasped angrily and checked his scope; perhaps it

wasn't his vision at fault, but equipment?

No, both the weapon and its attachment were in perfect condition. What, **By The Empress' Mantle** was going on?!

*"Soldiers, move forward! We've rendered our enemy unconscious and she is suffering from heavy wounds. Bring her dying body to me, so that I can claim the kill!"* – he commanded.

There was no sense in wasting the power pack of his sniper rifle; the soldiers could finish the job instead. The officer lowered the weapon back inside his APC and picked a range-sight unit up. He observed as the rest of the section entered the forest and passed the second tree line. What was left of his APC section quickly converged towards their target's last known location and surrounded the Terran from all sides. He heard a scream in his comms and looked to the side, to his personal status screen – one of the soldiers was missing!

*"Sensors, show me, where is that soldier?!"* – he shouted at his second driver.

*"N-nowhere Your Excellency! He has disappeared from our scopes!"*

His soldier looked at him with a confused expression and he leaned over to check the screen with his own two eyes. While he himself watched the screen, another one of his soldier's links blipped out, completely vanishing off the sensors! Popping his head out of the APC command hatch, he quickly looked around with the ranged-sight unit, trying to locate the rest of his troops. One of the comm's links flickered with life and he heard:

*"I... can't feel my legs... ughrl..."*

The rest turned into incoherent, short, painful screams and the Taz'aran commander shouted in the comms:

*"Retreat you morons, quickly! Your lives aren't more important than the equipment you wear! Back, I say!"* – he looked at his gunner with anger:

*"Start firing the particle beam gun at the treeline now!"* – he then closed the hatch and sat in his command chair.

As he sat back down, he was almost fuming with anger. Somebody was responsible for this failure and it wasn't going to be him! He looked around and his sight rested on the second driver. Yes, he was manning the scanner, he should've warned him! It was a failure to perform one's duty while in combat and the officer blurted out another order:

*"You! You are guilty of treason, Second Driver!"* – he pointed at the other soldier – *"Arrest him! He will face the firing squad later and pay for failing me!"*

While the stunned soldier was being shackled to his chair, the officer again looked at his sniper rifle. What **By the Throne's Steps** was happening here?! The last three surviving troopers of his section entered from the back ramp and the APC's engine whined, while the driver pulled back, away from the forest and towards the ruins of the Terran village. The officer looked at his soldiers' faces when they raised their helmet faceplates and saw nothing but terror...

* * *

Lilly awoke and almost jumped to her feet – she had been unconscious for Patrons only know how long. Her arms grabbed the rail carbine and she nervously looked around, licking her parched mouth. The suns were low and her butt was comfortably resting on one of the mumpa tree's roots, while the branches were shielding her body from the scorching heat.

She noticed that one of the tree's branches was missing; its end severely burned, a greenish juice oozed from the wound. It looked almost blood-like, and the scientist in her reached for her scanner which remained still absent from her side.

Too late she noticed the smoldering crater at the end of the tree line; the Taz'arans had fired and at least a couple of times it seems, perhaps trying to finish her.

How was she still alive?!

She remembered crawling behind this tree, but it hadn't been this far away from the tree line. Lilly sighed; having been tired and confused, not to mention almost dying from her injuries, perhaps her memory wasn't that accurate. She looked at her chest, checking the laser rifle wound but saw only a circular scar. Her brown, short fur was missing, and there were two more, smaller scars, most probably left from the two medspray injectors.

Man, those meds were awesome!

She had one spent casing left in her backpack, and vowed to some day find the person who made them – most fine craftsmanship that was. Standing up, Lilly suddenly realized that her burned back didn't hurt that much anymore. She tried to carefully touch her wounds, but alas, bunny hands weren't long by design and she counted her blessings.

The bunny picked up her backpack and checked its contents, noting how much food she had. Rations for ten days, water purification pills and some bio-bandages. There was also a rain cloak folded neatly at the bottom and she pulled it out, checking its size – it was one of those old Earth-army camouflage cloaks.

Lilly quickly adjusted its size, put it on herself and then checked its jungle stripes by laying part of it on the bark of the mumpa tree next to her. It didn't match, but it was far better than nothing.

A drop of tree juice fell on her hand, stinging oddly and she looked up at the wounded branch. Lilly smiled and took one of her bandages – it was only fair to aid the tree, since it had shielded her from enemy fire. That branch had, after all, been shot by the very laser rifles aiming to kill her.

She climbed easily and reached for the burned end, carefully wrapping it with the bio bandage. The space tech absorbed all of those tree juices and closed the wound. Strangely enough, she felt as though the branch moved a little bit, so she could reach it easier.

Lilly climbed down and checked the shots left in her rail carbine's power pack – she frowned when the counter showed eleven. So all that careful aiming was for naught? At least she killed three soldiers with it, lucky shots most likely.

While contemplating on what to do next, her ears caught the sound of high-powered grav engines and looked up. In the air, coming from the direction of her village, she saw the vague form of a big flying vehicle. It looked either like a dropship or a shuttle, but the aliens were using military grade vehicles and with her luck, it was most likely a Grav Attack Vehicle or GAV for short.

A fast, low flying machine, armed to the teeth and probably carrying a section of well-armed soldiers. Lilly explored the deep, dark forest with her eyes, wasted another couple of seconds while her ears soaked its chaotic ambiance and then ran. Soon her small silhouette was swallowed by the shadowy jungle and when the Taz'aran GAV flew by, she was nowhere to be seen.

* * *

A month had passed and Lilly was still alive – her rations were gone and the rail carbine had one more shot left in its power pack. She had miraculously found an old vibrodagger buried in the mud, one day, while preparing her camp site. It was still working and what was even stranger, the internal power pack was almost fully charged!

Knowing the local flora and fauna wasn't enough for a person to automatically become a good hunter, as she quickly found out. Lilly spent five full days almost dying of hunger, but at the end her perseverance was rewarded. She learned how to hunt down the very same rat creatures that had once plagued her farm, who also gnawed the mumpa trees' roots.

It had seemed to her, at first, that they were a local species, but the more Lilly killed them and examined their bodies, the more she thought that they did not belong here. Regardless, the "pinkies," as she began calling them, had plenty of high-protein meat, and she even began to enjoy hunting.

At least, as an exobiologist, she was preserving the local ecology by fighting an invasive species. Lilly was absolutely sure that no Terran colonist would ever let loose such an animal, or any other thing to prey on the local ecosystem. With each passing day, the sneaky suspicion that somebody else, perhaps those filthy Taz'arans had arranged for the wozzie presence here, festered in the back of her mind.

That GAV she first saw a month prior was quickly becoming her archenemy.

It was fast, it was mean, and its scanners tracked her easily. Lilly had narrowly escaped with her life from her last two showdowns with it. Firing her rail carbine at the cockpit was useless, as she found out, but at least managed to scare the pilot off.

When she was again tracked by it, Lilly ran away; running it seemed was something she was really good at, as she discovered soon enough. The GAV flew around her, spewing barrages of yellow laser beams, but she was always fast or lucky enough to either dodge them or find a good hole to duck in. But for the last three days, she had also noticed the vehicle deploying at least two sections of soldiers per day in the forest near her.

Lilly was continuously contemplating how to deal with this situation. If the Taz'arans were planning to deploy even one more section, that would be an entire squad surrounding her, at least by Imperial Minarchy count.

She felt desperation choking her and thought even more of simply charging their search line. Dying like a proper hero usually had no allure, since rabbits didn't believe much in heroics and were mostly pragmatic. Despite that, after all her loved ones had been subject to, a death like that started to look very tempting to her.

Lilly prepared herself for battle; she slung the rail carbine on her back, unsheathed the vibrodagger and wrapped with the camo cloak, silently stepped into the shadows. It now seemed that the mumpa trees had exactly the same stripes that her cloak had. This was rather surprising since the first trees she checked it against weren't a match whatsoever.

While the young bunny was sneaking towards the closest Taz'aran search line, at the back of her mind there was an ever-growing suspicion. Something in this forest wasn't right, and it had nothing to do with the pinkies, but more like the trees themselves. She had lately been noticing one tree that was strangely familiar, and multiple times at that.

Lilly heard the annoying clunk of Taz'aran armored suits and slowly crept behind the closest tree, raising her dagger, ready to strike. Soon she saw two soldiers who clutched onto their crappy laser rifles, legs stumbling. Both looked tired and their faceplates were up; she could hear them breathing heavily and even the clunk of the suits had changed. It sounded as if they had trouble moving at their best speed or even walking normally, in general.

Also, their laser rifles were wrapped with some spongy, green tape – it seems that the Taz'arans had trouble with both equipment and weapons. Luckily for her, that had begun to wreak havoc on their operational readiness. The looks on their faces were ones of extreme discomfort, pain even, and Lilly imagined that something else might be troubling her Taz'aran enemies. She waited, biding her time, dagger still raised in the air.

One of the soldiers suddenly started choking and fell in the mud, his rifle to one side. The other had his back to her and Lilly stepped out from the side of the mumpa tree. She held the dagger with both hands and with one rapid motion stabbed at the soldier's neck. With a swishing sound the vibrodagger sliced through the suit's neck joint, flesh, bone and the soldier fell dead on the spot.

Horrified, the second Taz'aran tried to shout, but whatever he was choking on prevented him from calling for help. His right hand reached for his laser rifle and in her desperation Lilly threw the dagger, aiming at his chest. It was from point blank range, and she still missed.

She tried reaching for her rail carbine, but it was too late. Still choking, the soldier grabbed his muddy laser rifle and pressed the trigger – there was a flash and then an explosion. Lilly leaped to the side, but when she raised her head, the soldier's body was smoldering, his hands turned into bloody lumps.

The nearby Taz'arans, hearing all of this, clunked towards her position and she had to decide in a split second what action to take. Lilly quickly grabbed her dagger from the mud and using the blade on the nearest soldier's utility belt, she nipped his ammo pouch and gun kit. There was a grenade on the belt too and using her ears to determine their position, Lilly prepared and threw it at them.

In hindsight she shouldn't have used the highest setting, but that was her first time using an alien ordinance. The powerful, violent explosion sent her small body flying into the air. Somehow her hand grabbed a mumpa branch and instead of breaking her bones by hitting the ground, she dangled from it unharmed, fifteen feet in the air.

Holding onto the tree as hard as she could, Lilly clicked both looted packs onto her own belt and with the aid of her other hand climbed up, hiding in the tree's foliage. She saw the charred corpses of two other Taz'arans as the rest were carrying them away, most probably back to their base camp. If her poor eyesight didn't lie these soldiers looked even more scared and tired.

*"Where are the rest of them?!"* – one of the troopers asked into a handset with a shaking voice – *"My Lord, we were told an entire squad was deployed here, and we have only two sections!"*

29

Somebody answered in his comms system:

*"I care not for your failure, Soldier! You were given adequate support and equipment. Inability to deal with one tiny Terran creature proves that you and your soldiers are all pathetic excuses for men! The GAV will be sent to extract you soon, prepare those idiots in your charge and don't forget to recover all of the dead ones' gear!"* – The comm was suddenly cut, and Lilly saw the soldier's face twist in anger and fear.

What was left of their section moved right under the mumpa tree Lilly was hiding in and she could examine them better. They were disheartened and exhausted; there were strange, dark-green rashes, deep lesions covering their otherwise pale-greenish skin. Lilly pushed her knowledge of Carrola to the limit, trying to remember anything she'd possibly read about an illness which manifested itself by rashes like those, but to no avail. After the soldiers tiredly marched away, she climbed quickly down from the tree, using the very same branch that saved her life.

While lowering down, her hand got stuck in something and she pulled gently, trying not to harm the foliage. To her surprise, after she'd gotten her feet on the ground, she found remnants of bio bandage stuck on her hands. She was under duress, however, and quickly forgot about it.

Lilly ran for at least an hour while that accursed GAV was blasting away the whole area with laser fire. She was sure her bio sign wasn't inside its scan range, but even if that was true, better safe than sorry. Her nose sensed the smell of tree juice and fire from a distance and she cursed the invaders in her mind.

The bunny found another deep, safe-looking hole, which held the remnants of a long dead mumpa tree and hid in it.

Helpless to do anything else, Lilly decided to check her loot and opened both belt's packs. They had spare power packs, four of them – the last had a simplified, standard gun kit. As soon as the laser spewing GAV flew away, she used what was left of the day modifying her enemies' power packs. Somehow Lilly was successful and jerry-rigged all, but one of them.

Using the salvaged packs, she now had more than ninety shots for her rail carbine – a crooked, almost happy smile bloomed on her face. Lilly turned around and walked towards the edge of the forest; now, with enough ammo, she could fire back and stop running all the time. Perhaps if she could get her hands on a grenade or two, Lilly thought of something that might aid her against that GAV.

* * *

The Taz'aran commander looked at his files; all reports from the last three months were abysmal!

Eleven soldiers lost due to faulty gear and rampant weapon malfunctions, twenty-two more died in the jungle while tracking that small elusive Terran. The lost equipment list was as long as his leg and even though his engineers managed to do something short-term for the laser rifles, they couldn't overcome the initial design errors.

The armored space suits that his soldiers were using weren't built to be fielded in such an environment. While in outer space they would've provided a protection beyond adequate, here in this scorching heat and humidity, they were all but useless. Heavy and bulky, they slowed and tired the soldiers to such an extent, that most were dog-tired after even a few kilometers walking.

Sure, they could vac the suits and then the heat and humidity wouldn't bother them, but the weight issue remained. Also, as good as a space suit's life support was, it couldn't work forever. A suit's main power pack had to be renewed after a couple of hours, at least.

The commander skimmed over some holo slides of soldiers killed in action – armor plating didn't work, not in the least. As a matter of fact, when the plating was hit, it splintered in such a way that nearby soldiers were injured by shrapnel.

He slammed his fist on the table – those damned Terran rail guns!

The Taz'aran Imperium had to have them or at least some basic copies for research. That was a backwards arms race, he suddenly thought to himself; instead of fielding particle-beam guns like most civilized sentients, those slimy Terrans used barbaric tech. The trouble was that it was highly effective, both against their armor and weapons.

He remembered how two of his pilots were scared shitless, because the Terran creature's rail gun almost pierced the GAV's cockpit. He had to shoot one of them for cowardice and the other, for desertion.

The commander sighed and sent his new orders to the troops: remove the suits' feet and arms plating, affix bayonets to the rifles, and lower the beam power.

He was waiting for their supply ship to return shortly – on it, there would be a section of better-trained Taz'aran Imperial Army scouts. Finally, he could send somebody *capable* into the accursed jungle, and be sure that that filthy little Terran would die!

He directed other, more secretive orders to his personal Noble Guards – they had to locate this colony's Dead Man's Scanner and download all information from it. In the event that Terrans did counterattack, he did not want him and his troops chased after. These filthy barbarians were vengeful, moreover, they loved using nuclear weapons...

* * *

Soon enough, the long-awaited supply ship arrived on Carrola. Fully laden with spare parts, rations and equipment, from its ramp also descended a section of veteran Taz'arans ready for battle. Without any tarrying around they boarded the GAV and flew in the direction of Carrola's jungle.

Its pilot held his craft's hover controls steady while the scout section rappelled down, deep into the green, exactly where the last reported position of their enemy was. Encased in light field armor covered with camouflage stripes, those shifty and athletic soldiers were armed with snub particle-beam rifles called Rapid Beam Guns. They even had short vibroswords and grapplers integrated in their suits.

Surely this time the Terran was doomed, the overstressed pilot thought to himself!

The section soon vanished out of his sight and deep into the forest, therefore he moved his hand ever so slightly. He began increasing his craft's height, careful not to fly too close to the nearby rock formation.

Suddenly the pilot saw a blip on his sensor screen and for a second he was frozen with fear. The blip had been identified by his computer as the small Terran, and panicking, the pilot pulled back rapidly from his previous hover position. The GAV flew unintentionally closer and closer towards the rocks.

The blip again appeared on the screen, but this time, it was behind him – he rapidly turned the craft's nose and pressed the trigger of his G-type laser guns. Multiple yellow beams shredded the foliage and set a couple of trees on fire.

Nothing!

The blip was still there... Over the comms he heard the quieted voice of one very angry Taz'aran officer:

*"What are you shooting at, Pilot?! Be careful, we are still deploying down there! I swear if you hit any of my men, not even your mother will recognize the corpse they will show her!"*

This threat was as real as they get, but GAV pilots were trained to safeguard their vehicles first, not their own lives. He was so preoccupied with this that the second, almost transparent blip on his screen completely eluded him.

A tiny silhouette was loading a grenade in an improvised sling and when he saw this, much too late, his jaw dropped. He watched petrified as the Terran launched the grenade at his craft, while balancing atop the tree, holding on to it with her legs. The explosion consumed his cockpit and made mincemeat of him.

Its cockpit gone, the now pilot-less GAV soundly crashed into the ground – all of its ammunition and fuel instantly blew up. The large explosion ended up blasting three of the scouts to bits yet, no matter how furious the Taz'aran scout leader was, he remained motionless and hidden.

His active camo cloak almost completely melded with

all surrounding plant life – no sudden gestures or comm links sent. The thermo optic camouflage or TOC turned its user nigh invisible, when used properly and by an experienced trooper. There was no possible way to detect neither him, nor the rest of his section, not unless you had a high-grade scanner *and* were an expert in using it.

His posture was excellent and the RBG tightly gripped, one finger ready on the activation switch. If anything was moving and not in the predetermined coordinates, he would shoot it down instantly. An empowered beam chamber and an advanced heatsink ensured that his weapon would not only function in this harsh climate, but provide the team with the much-needed victory against the last enemy here.

The man was a non-noble officer; through backstabbing, murder, and intrigue he managed to achieve that high a status. A good judge of character and excellent survivalist, his adoptive noble house placed great hopes on his career in the Taz'aran Imperial Army.

Carefully looking around, twisting his head centimeter by centimeter, the scout leader saw a metallic shine right next to one of his soldier's positions. Looking closely and inspecting it for more than a minute, he suddenly realized that it was a thin metallic wire.

Cold sweat began running down his spine, despite his jungle armor's extended life support. He contemplated sending a link to his scouts, but then he stopped himself mid-thought – they were all professionals. Certainly, if there were traps, his men would act in a manner according with their extensive training regimen and experience.

This was their second campaign, and in Taz'aran armies, such soldiers were considered seasoned veterans.

His audio sensors picked up a strange sound from the tree nearby – it was both natural and metallic. The sub-commander's reflexes were that of an elite, as was his sixth sense. He leaped forwards and tumbled in the air, just as most of the tree branches suddenly became part of an intricate and deadly net of micro-wire, slicing everything in its way.

He heard the screams of his men and then, there were the explosions.

The ground itself flew in the air, rock shrapnel shredding more of his scouts to death. He overcame the initial shock and ran towards the wreck of the GAV, correctly assuming that even if the entire area was prepared and blanketed with simplified traps, the crashing machine would've cleaned most, if not all of them. His keen senses warned him of someone lurking within the wreck itself, and the sub-commander raised his RBG, flicking the power on.

A burst of tiny particle beams destroyed what was left of the ruined machine, causing yet another explosion.

Just when he thought he had finished it, a small figure wrapped with a flaming camo cloak leaped at him from inside of the fire. In mid-jump she disposed of her cloak and with still-burning fur slashed at him with deadly precision.

He dashed back, using his now-empty gun to absorb the first hit. Part of her blade screeched over the chestplate of his armor and the sub-commander swiftly pulled his short sword, whose elegant and deadly edge blocked her second attack. The violent clash of the two vibroblades produced a small shock wave, blasting small plants and trash away from the two fighters.

He was stronger and faster; experience was on his side and it showed.

His opponent was a female Terran, one of the inferior client races – a bunny. Brown fur with white spots, hazel green eyes, and a face covered with multiple scars. As a matter of fact, her entire body was scarred, burned, and her fur had bald patches.

With a flick of his wrist, he pierced the inferior creature's defense and stabbed right at her chest, covered with round scars. His victorious smile was soon wiped away by a series of desperate attacks by his young enemy.

He couldn't understand – he'd already stabbed her and she was coughing blood!

How could she even stay on her feet, let alone continue resisting?

Soon the Scout Leader found out that his estimation, the hasty assumption he made of his enemy, was dead wrong. Not only had she traded blows, but even managed to cut him, chopping away some of the armored plates and damaging vital armor systems.

First he lost his PDA, then the upper part of his helmet and now, the Taz'aran had to look at her face directly, instead from the comfort of his faceplate's holo-display. He began inhaling the raw, unfiltered atmosphere of the planet and felt the humidity.

The dance of death continued and while he had the upper hand, that creature, even while bloodied, stabbed, and with second-degree burns, still persevered. The sub-commander looked in her eyes and tried desperately to find something, a weakness perhaps, anything that would give him the killing blow. Deep in her hazel eyes he found not hate, but sadness and... *pity*.

He lost it.

How dare she!? A mere animal, given sentience by the barbaric and stupid Terrans, pity *him*!? He was a soon-to-be-great Taz'aran noble, far superior in mind, body, and skill. The sub-commander threw himself at her burning with rage, wielding his sword with all the possible strength he could muster.

Finally, after his last blow, the creature's blade was knocked out of her hand; it flew to the side and impaled a nearby tree. The Terran panicked as she suddenly tumbled away from him and towards it.

*"No! You won't get your blade back, you primitive!"*

He jumped, kicking her squarely in the back. Coughing blood and painfully crawling towards the tree, the creature's breathing became sporadic. He closed his hands on the hilt of his weapon and raised it to deliver the final blow. As he did so, the bunny turned around and with hand on her chest, whispered:

"Before... ugh... you strike me dead... I wish to... remove that... ughhh..."

She had trouble breathing and her hands were shaking; it didn't take a doctor to see that the bunny was dying. Torturously, she continued:

"P-p-please... ohh... the blade from tree... remove it, it is in pain!"

The sub-commander removed his sliced and useless helmet and looked upon his enemy with disgust. Not for mercy had she begged him, but to save a stupid *tree*! What madness was this?!

With an evil smile, he placed his short sword back in its sheath and reached for his enemy's dagger. Effortlessly, he pulled it out of the trunk, thick tree juice now flowing down.

*"Know, pitiful one, that I have magnanimously fulfilled your idiotic wish, and now you will await the killing blow that will end your dirty existence!"* – he gloated.

The Taz'aran lowered his head while raising his enemy's blade. He slowly aimed for her throat and waited for a few more seconds, enjoying the last moments of suffering this dying Terran was going through. Then, after his lust for pain was satisfied, he swung down.

His attack never connected and whatever dreams of greatness this invader had, they would remain here, buried with his rotting body, feeding the trees. One large branch crushed the Taz'aran's skull and his lifeless body was quickly pulled underground by a thick, muddy root. The earth closed around his corpse with a loud eerie, slurping sound, as if taking the food offered gladly.

Green had no eyes, nor ears, but it felt and knew what was around it. Could move ever so slowly and if aided by other creatures, with protection and nourishment, traverse the mud. Green now felt a great connection with the flesh life beside its roots; protection for protection, nourishment for nourishment... a life for a life.

It broke off the appendage this creature had healed, allowing its life to ebb away from its green shell and into the fleshy other. There was no sadness, no fear, exactly the same lesson it had planted by its spores in the creature, when its blood had first spilled onto it. Protected it with its appendages, and nourished it by confusing those death-bringing fleshy parasites upon Nature, for it to hunt and consume.

The more its life waned, the better that creature felt. Green sensed its wounds closing and fleshy appendages returning to normal; losing its senses altogether, it remembered the eternal circle – flesh to green and green to flesh...

* * *

In the air above what had until recently been a jungle battlefield, a single dropship hovered, its engines booming. One of its side doors opened and a humanoid figure rappelled down, wearing heavy exoskeleton armor with integrated engines. The person slowly walked towards the body of a young rabbit female and then gently picked her up.

His faceplate slid up as he looked around at the still-smoldering Taz'aran GAV wreck. Just one of his powerful arms were enough to tenderly hold the small bunny as he surveyed the scene. The man's face became sad, tears ran down his cheeks and black, bushy beard, dropping on the edge of his helmet.

A second Terran landed next to him and searched the area, using an integrated scanner. He soon returned, carrying an old rail carbine and a vibrodagger. Both of them looked mournfully around one last time, their ship's sensors projecting a holo of the ruined local colony settlement. Before he returned back to their craft after his partner, the man holding the battered rabbit looked at her scars and with pain in his voice, said:

"We failed you so much, young ones..."

He choked on his tears while once again inspecting her injuries and suddenly, one of her scars vanished before his very eyes. The man looked in amazement; he turned back, gazing at the forest, then slowly wiped his tears away and mumbled to himself:

"Life perseveres, and as it seems, brave Bunny, your time is not over in this Universe of ours..."

He jumped upwards, activating his suit's engines, boots mag-locking on the deck of the dropship. The two Terrans took one final look at the jungle and again surveyed the distant destroyed colony village, before the vehicle's door slid back. Their pilot pulled the ship's nose up, and they quickly flew out of Carrola's atmosphere and around the burning hulls of annihilated Taz'aran ships in orbit. The heavily-armored man addressed his pilot:

"Take the hyper-nav marker to Cav. I have work there and besides, we can't leave her with nothing –" he smiled "– my friend there will help her heal. Also, we need to hear her tale! A story about a bunny, who knew nothing else but growing watermelons, and then became a warrior."

The dropship's wings folded and its hyper-engine charged, creating a glowing field around the hull. The entire vessel vanished into a fold in space-time, traveling without moving, even as the twin suns of Carrola continued to move in the sky.

# Chapter 2

*Awesome*

Space can be very intimidating, especially if you are three feet tall and weigh at best forty pounds. He chuckled at his own facial expression reflecting on the inside of his helmet, and corrected his escape pod's trajectory with the last drops of fuel.

Were they drops? Most probably not. It was outer space, and the pod's gravity plating was long drained out of power. So, blobs? Perhaps, or maybe the fuel tank had some device that enabled it to utilize even the last bits of fuel remaining. He just *had* to check that – his tiny frame would allow him to do so. The hamster began imagining how exactly he would crawl through the engine exhaust chamber and disassemble the fuel injector to reach the fuel tank, if he were to follow his curiosity.

Meanwhile, slowly but surely, his pod was closing in on the wrecked station and he prepared to open the hatch. Using his suit's grappler and a megasteel extension cable, he could theoretically latch the pod on that long, protruding piece of wreckage.

Getting ever closer to the gutted space outpost, he could examine the ruined structure more closely. He began wondering why its attackers had fired at it so many times, given that the type of damage on the outer hull and inner decks could only have been caused by an accurate weapon's fire – particle-beam guns, most probably. Even without a scanner, he could say for certain that they had been small-size guns.

The black-furred hamster chuckled again.

"Small" – his head probably could fit in their barrels and his red eyes gaze at the innards for a second before the particle-beam melted him away. At least a kilometer in diameter, the space outpost was a modular base, a staple of Terran space-engineering. He couldn't see any other modules except the hangar, from this side of the base that is, yet he was hopeful that there were not only provisions left, but spare parts, too.

Carefully, he opened the hatch and aimed his grappler at the docking arm; well, at least what was left of it. A docking arm is ordinarily used to grab damaged one-man Space Construction Vehicle mecha suits, various small shuttles, or at most, starfighter ships. Its functionality fit its design as a long and powerful mechanical arm, but as it seems, somebody had used it as a weapon.

Mangled it was since its operator had bashed many a thing, Awesome hoped with great success and to the death.

He pressed the trigger and braced himself, holding the rest of the cable. The mag-hook hit his mark and latched firmly to the docking arm. While the pod pulled it off its previous inertia-driven course, he attached his grappler to the extension cable and started zipping forward.

He'd managed earlier to drain all excess power from the pod's backup power pack, before it slagged completely. His suit now had life-support power for at least eight hours... at least he hoped for that much. Thank the Patrons he bought himself that nifty repair kit back on Cav colony! Those fifty creds were money well spent and he noted mentally to thank the store owner when he returned back on the asteroid.

A beautiful place and the people were so friendly, but perhaps the main reason they were so very helpful was because he was so... Awesome. No matter, his tiny hands grabbed the docking arm and he detached himself from the cable. Very carefully he observed how the pod was dangling at the end of that megasteel wire and really hoped the extension he made wouldn't split anytime soon – he'd hate losing the last piece of *Mushishi*.

Ah, what a fine transport ship she was!

Well, at least before those criminals wrecked it. It was strange, that they had attacked so close to the outer Terran territories. Far from safe, Fringe space was home to many small colonies and, just like that space outpost, most of them were attacked by pirates, slavers, and other aliens on a constant basis. Not usually so close to the boundary, within easy reach of Imperial Minarchy's rescue.

Strange indeed.

He slowly boarded the outpost with his mag boots and, avoiding all weapon-damaged outer hull areas, made his way towards the station's hangar. Another cool little gadget he got while on Cav were his brand-new scanning goggles; it was with them that he could evade any unstable hull panels, and perhaps find loot easily.

Hamster eyesight wasn't in any way good, and his heightened sense of smell was useless in a vacuum. Perhaps someday, a prominent scientist would invent a device to catch the smell of space – he was told that might be a possibility.

Looking at the huge hole in the hangar doors, he saw somebody's arm floating around it. It was a human hand, with its space suit glove still on and his scanner detected a salvageable grappling cable on the forearm.

He detached his boots from the hull and gracefully leaped, using the station's still-intact limited-gravity field, grabbing the hand. Both mag boots landed on the other side of the hole, and he began salvaging the cable and attaching it to his own suit. Obviously the owner of that equipment wouldn't argue with him using it and most probably dead, but one can never know. The hamster made a note of the serial number and linked it in his equipment file. If any day soon, he found who this grappler belonged to, he would return it, or pay them its current cost in creds.

Patrons, he was a Terran, not some ungrateful, cheeky, junk-grabbin' bastard.

Quickly, he walked inside the station's hangar and started scanning the wreckage inside. He chuckled again – there was the chassis of a single scout-type starfighter, and in almost pristine condition! Well, only, it was missing everything... like engines, power core, and a main computer system. But that was just a minor setback; as he frequently reminded himself, this hamster was Awesome, and no matter the difficulties ahead, nothing could stop him.

Moving around the slagged remains of small shuttles and space craft, he noticed quite a lot of salvageable materials and parts that would help him rebuild his own 'fighter.

Thankfully the Minarchy had excellent salvage-rights laws; you manage to pull it and use it – it's yours! He gathered as much as he could carry in his pack as he explored further.

Soon he found the main hangar door leading towards the outpost's inner chambers. It had been a scene of intense battle, with many melted corpses and a great deal of broken weaponry. The station defenders must have made a stand here, using a portable shield generator to aid them. Perhaps nicked from one of the shuttles nearby, it gave them an advantage in ranged combat.

Their attackers must have recognized that; based on the type of damage, the defenders had been killed from point blank range, and the generator hit by a vibroweapon. He touched the damaged part with his gloves and waited for the scanner to finish studying the mark left on it. Probably made by a large vibrosword and hastily slashed too.

Somebody was rushing that day, but why?

If the attackers were slavers, they wouldn't have left those people as molten suits and charred flesh, but captured them for the slave markets. Despite counting the dead Terrans, of which there were ten floating around in various state of horrible mutilation, the young pilot was hopeful and even excited.

What was the reason the attackers were rushing and who were they?

Hoping to soon find more clues, he disengaged his mag boots and flew over the carnage. His scanner told him there were no salvageable bits here and, landing on the other side, he continued onward. It took him two more hours until he reached one of the outpost's security stations.

There was another scene of devastation and death here, as well. Four humans and one gorilla defended the intersection, and as he examined, his scanner suddenly beeped cheerfully. The gorilla, before her death, had somehow managed to rip one whole piece of armor from the attackers. It was useless as a repair part, but it provided a clue since the attackers had most likely taken all of their dead men and salvageable equipment before leaving the station.

It was a shoulder armor-plating from a heavy alien space suit, probably built for space combat exclusively. At the center it had an emblem – strange alien, horned animal, with a vibrospear through the head and some alien text circling the whole picture. It was written in Fringe Speak and he knew little of it, so the clue was carefully wrapped and stuffed in his backpack.

He looked at the face of the gorilla and scanned it. Perhaps after he got out of this place and returned back to Cav, he could look her up and find her relatives. After a few seconds of thought, the young pilot did the same with the other defenders he found along the way. On one of the bodies he found a half-expended power pack, and he nicked it for himself; those were four more hours of life support which meant more time to explore the derelict.

It took him one more hour to reach the station's main promenade area. It was a large, circular, open space, filled with the station's stores, recreation area, and other venues. Hamsters are hard to anger, at least most of the time since they are usually seen cracking jokes. Even in their death hour won't lose composure, yet the sight before him here almost made him lose face.

There were charred corpses everywhere, floating in the low gravity. Sometimes they bumped into each other, leaving small clouds of black ash, which itself spread around to blanket the entirety of the Promenade. There were the forms of parents shielding their children with their bodies. The few armed station defenders had even made barricades with their own dead, fighting to the last with quite literally everything they had.

This place and what had happened here saddened him; he made sure to scan and record everything into the PDA strapped to his wrist. The Personal Data Assistant would help him recall any information he chose to share with or sell to security forces later on, regarding this devastation, including in video form. If worse came to worse, well, he'd transmit anything important stored on the mini-computer to the appropriate persons over its comms or its G-net connection.

After some time spent doing this, his entire suit was covered with ash. It was all rather depressing, adding to the gloom he was already starting to feel. As he tried to think of something cheerful to raise his spirits, his scanner bleeped again. This time it was a salvageable gun, and the hamster had to break a glass window to get to it.

Said window belonged to a store which was a repair-and-upgrade business called "Scrapper Jack," and thankfully not everything had been looted by the attackers. At the back he located a working bench with integrated tools, and on it was the weapon – a laser rifle that looked very strange. It was short and lacked a long stock; the beam chamber was that of a heavier weapon, and its barrel, instead of the old crystal lenses, had a mini refraction-field projector.

The whole system used big power packs, of which he found two, and those looked as though they should be powering heavy weapons, not a rifle. Regardless, the gun was finished – its creator needed only paint it. On the side of the gun there was it's creator's name, one Milton Friedman.

He'd have to research that later.

He picked it up, along with its spare packs, and used his left back-slot to mag-lock the gun, if need be, he could easily reach and grab the rifle. The spares he locked on the back side of his belt before continuing his search. Outside that repair store, he saw a restaurant that was mostly intact, and closed the distance, so that his scanner could look for something useful. He was hoping to find food, but alas, instead of canned vegetables, his goggles detected a life form and a weapon.

From behind the cover of a fallen table, bright particle-beam streaked in his direction. Having been warned by his scanner, he immediately clicked his mag boots off and dashed to the side. Clicking the boots back on again, his hand reached and grabbed the laser gun, while at the same time landing firmly on his two legs and aiming at that table.

He grimaced; it wasn't a Terran lifesign on his goggles, neither was it that of one of the allied races – it was a Taz'aran.

Those people had an empire in Fringe space and were openly hostile towards Terrans, quite the brazen and foul bunch, he thought. Recently, he had heard, they had bloodily wiped out one small agricultural colony, mostly populated by rabbits. Hamsters liked rabbits very much; one could say they were somewhat like their little brothers, since they were uplifted right after hamsters, so many hamsters felt almost like a Patron towards them. And even though rabbits were bigger than hamsters, it was often refreshing to mingle with someone who wasn't six feet tall.

Full of deadly focus, his finger pressed the trigger exactly when his mag boots locked themselves on the station's floor. It was a good thing his spacesuit had its helmet's faceplate darkened and he was looking through the scanning goggles, otherwise he might have lost his sight – that *thing* he was holding produced one thick, blue, and extremely powerful laser beam. It effin' sliced through the wall, the table, *and* the Taz'aran hiding between them. The oxygen in his enemy's suit flash-burned for a second, charring the corpse, which had a hole the size of Awesome's own head in the chest.

He could see the other hole, much bigger, that that insane gun had made in the wall behind the body. Quickly, he moved forward, swiveling his head around so that the scanner could pick up other lifesigns, if any. No, the assailant was alone, and he searched the body fastidiously. The weapon was a molten piece of slag, just like the rest of his equipment and suit. The only thing he could nick was the Taz'aran's PDA, and despite the shape it was in – it had obviously overheated – he hoped to still be able to download some data from it. Carefully this time, weapon in hand, the young pilot continued his investigation of the promenade, using walls and other sturdy pieces of metal for cover.

Another hour of arduous exploration later, he could boast a couple units of full rations and a plasma grenade. The food would last him a month, likely, since he was small and those ration packs were human-size. Both they and that grenade were in a floating backpack someone had forgotten to take with them, most probably during the evacuation.

Awesome was thankful; a month should be more than enough time for him to put that fighter he'd found in the hangar back together.

He spent the next half hour resting, well-hidden of course, in one of the station's life support vents and used that time to fiddle with the Taz'aran's PDA. In the end, the data he swiped off his unfortunate attacker's computer only gave him more information about their simple, "in-the-moment" orders, since that Taz'aran was a basic soldier and, as it seemed, they didn't inform their grunts of the overall battle plan.

He winced – how very thoughtless of them.

What would happen if all the officers died? How would those soldiers function afterwards, if they had no knowledge of their own force's objectives? In tactics hours during pilot training, he had been taught by his master of the importance of knowing what others were doing, and of knowing the mission objectives.

Most thoughtless these Taz'arans were, indeed. There was a high probability that this soldier had been mistakenly left behind, because he sincerely did not know what to do after his immediate superior was killed. No matter; now he knew that the soldiers who had attacked this outpost were Taz'arans, and their orders were to wipe out all people on the station and leave no witnesses. That was what this Taz'aran soldier had been still doing, long after the rest of them had left.

Having rested up, he carefully exited his hiding space and closed the tunnel's lid. Gun in hand, the hamster continued his search, this time looking for the station's command post. He positioned himself at the center of the promenade, then leaped, using his grappler to switch floors as he went up. He did so slowly, aiming with his new laser gun and always trying to be as close to cover as possible.

* * *

It took him another hour to get closer to the outpost's command center and again it was a site of intense battle. This time, he saw holes in the space station's panels – these had been made from the inside, and with heavy weapons. At the end of the corridor leading to the command center, there were a pair of modified SCVs, both holding fighter-size weapons with each of their manipulators.

The attacking Taz'arans had had to shoot shoulder-held, anti-armor missiles at them, and the damage was considerable, but he could use the parts of one to fix the other, and perhaps the same also for the guns. Those were top notch "Malice" auto rail-guns – four barrels, a heatsink, and, if his scanner was correct, they even had flack

51

attachments.

On one of the dead he found another space suit power pack, this time completely charged and from what he could gather, this place was the defenders' last stand. They'd used every firearm possible – grenades, missiles, mines, and heavy weapons. The Taz'arans were equally determined to get inside the outpost's command module, and they'd done the same. Its armored doors had been breached by demolition charges, and everyone inside had been shot to death.

He scanned the consoles, but most of them were destroyed, either by the station's personnel or the attackers. As he looked around the gutted command post, he spotted something on the floor at the center of it. Inspecting the bulkhead up close with his scanner, there were signs of another computer system that had been linked with the station's mainframe. The attackers took it with them when they were leaving, he was now sure of this.

Perhaps that was their main objective?

His scanner bleeped again; underneath his feet was the mainframe of the outpost, and it had emergency power still. Unlocking the mag boots, he opened the service tunnel's lid and squeezed his tiny body between the plasma power lines. Had he been born any race other than a small, beautiful in his compactness hamster, that wouldn't have been possible at all.

Slowly, making use of the grappler, he pulled himself into the main computer pit. It was damaged, yes, but the reserve power had kicked in and the system had remained in operation for Patrons know how long. The small hamster reached its backup holo panel and swiped to activate it.

Red, glowing holo screen appeared before him, and

he started punching in commands quickly. Seems that that computer was an upgrade and had data backups with more protocols pre-installed for just such an event. There was one such protocol named "Alice" – it said that this was the station's reserve Operating System, but strangely enough, he found nobody had tried activating it.

Perhaps they were already dead, or weren't able to because of the fighting. No matter, the hamster's gloved fingers now put in the commands needed to activate it and he stood back. He needed a working OS, otherwise sifting through the immense data storage would take him quite a lot of time, and time was something he couldn't spare right now.

While waiting some seconds for the system to boot, he quickly linked his suit's PDA to the backup console's wireless port and gave his own computer a command to search for the most recent holo-viewer records. If he was lucky, they would show him what exactly was the thing those Taz'arans took from the command center.

A couple of minutes later, with the station's backup OS still not booting up, he decided to check what his own computer had managed to pull. He swiped over it, but the thing didn't react at all. It only showed him a pair of messages:

"DO NOT DISCONNECT!" and "DOWNLOADING DATA PACKAGE 67% READY."

He waited patiently, and when the download reached 100%, dutifully disconnected his PDA from the wireless uplink. Then he tried to open what he presumed to be the holo records that he had instructed his computer to look for earlier. But after swiping, instead of the simple holo screen he was used to, a bigger holo appeared next to him. It was in the form of a little girl with pale light skin, long blonde hair, and blue eyes. She was wearing a strangely anachronistic blue dress and shoes, with long white socks covering the whole length of her legs.

"Oh, hello –" the hologram spoke in a cute childish voice, while looking around "– it seems that the platform I've downloaded myself onto lacks the space for my advanced functions. Also," – a single letter appeared on her finger followed by a number "– my program is degrading, since this device lacks the processing capabilities I need to sustain my algorithms."

"Hi there!" – the hamster smiled and raised his shoulders – "Sorry about that, I didn't know my PDA was downloading a Virtual Intelligence." – he looked at the holo – "What is your designation and capabilities?"

"My name is Alice, and it is a pleasure to meet you!" – The holographic girl slightly bowed to him, holding the sides of her skirt with her hands.

"My capabilities are Combat Operation Assist and Information Gathering." – While the program was introducing herself, the main computer core's backup power chose this time to die out.

Everything went completely dark except Alice's holo, as she asked:

"And what may I call you, young sir?"

"You may call me Awesome!" – he paused and looked at her. If her facial holo algorithms were accurate, the VI seemed to be notably amused.

"No, really, that's my name, my parents gave it to me when they took me in, and otherwise I *am* awesome in everything I do, so..." – He trailed off, paused for a short while.

"It seems that I won't be able to procure the holo

record I needed, eh?"

"I have most of the station's records, but they are highly compressed, since I lack the space needed," – Alice answered while playing with her dress – "but I can pull up the station manifest and map, if you want me to."

She vanished, replaced by two holo files for the hamster to look at. Both were full of items he needed, so he waved his other hand above the PDA, swiping them over to the suit's faceplate. Each time he looked for something on the files, Alice aided him.

He wasn't sure what to think of her, because most Virtual Intelligences weren't perfect, and it was expected of them to degrade in a year or two. Simply put, programmers intentionally created them with disposability in mind, so there weren't any chances they ever became full AI. He had heard terrible horror stories of rogue AIs wiping out entire races and spreading madness into large portions of the Galactic Network. They'd had to install watchdog bots on the G-net for the sole purpose of monitoring for AI blackguards, at one point.

Thus, VIs were now normally designed to function as high-grade operational systems, capable of semi-thought, but never full sentience. Well, at least this OS had the station database, and he thought of a way to preserve all of it from degrading. The only thing he remembered from all those computer classes was that he needed at least a shuttle, or a starfighter-size computer core. Then he would be able to upload this VI there and access all of the outpost's databases.

It also seemed that the OS would aid him during combat, too, which he gladly welcomed. One such program could go for at least five to six thousand creds on the open market. With proper maintenance, it might even last for a decade. So he began actively speaking with it to keep the metaphorical gears running, while he climbed out of the mainframe pit. He tried asking the VI about the station, since there really were no records of it existing in the pod's mainframe.

"So... who owned this outpost? I never saw any corp logo, or colony banner I can think of."

A very tiny holo of Alice popped up on the side of his suit's faceplate.

"A private research group; this data is not accessible to me now," – Alice answered coyly.

"I can tell you who created me, though – a man called 'Sinclair'. It is unclear to me if this is his name, or a nickname." – She twirled her hair playfully – "It is useless though, since I have no database access to search for more relevant information."

"Ha! I promise that your next living space will have extras, kiddo. By the way, is there a direct-access tunnel leading to main engineering?"

"Well, yes, there were two – one is slagged, but the other seems to be stable enough."

Awesome paused his thoughts, puzzled – "Huh? How did you know that, if you got no access to sensors?" – Before she answered him, one small part of the outpost map was enlarged on his screen, and he saw himself as a green dot, with all his surroundings within a hundred-meter range.

"Oh, I forgot to mention, but I buffed your scanning goggles. It is good that you linked them to the suit," – Alice giggled –"I've replaced the original factory firmware with one of my scanning algorithms, it doubled their range for the same energy cost, see?"

"That is nice, but what if you made a mistake and

they overheat? I, erm, *we* would've been blinded, essentially." – He pulled his laser gun out and slowly crept forward towards the service tunnel entrance.

"Oh, I did a couple thousand simulations first, don't worry. As a matter of fact, do you have a holo sight for this gun? It looks like a very 'off-with-their-heads' type of weapon. I'll scan it and try to find ways of improving it for later."

"Umm, no? I just found the damned thing. Almost melted through two solid megasteel bulkheads when I fired it the first time," – He remembered killing the Taz'aran soldier like it was only minutes ago, instead of hours.

"Uh, by the way, you should know, Alice – the attackers of this outpost were Taz'aran."

"Aha! So it *was* those guys!" – Alice snapped with her fingers.

"We should find out where they came from. If one of those sensor modules in the hangar can be reactivated, their engine's ion trail may yet be present."

The hamster heard his new companion whisper to herself:

*"Vengeance protocols engaged. Main target, Taz'aran soldiers and other military personnel."*

He suddenly stopped dead in his tracks.

"What was that, Alice? What protocols are those?"

"Ah!, nothing!, I told you my program is degrading, perhaps that's a side effect." – She clapped her hands suddenly, showing him an overhead map generated by his improved scanning goggles.

"Oh! I see they left more of their soldiers behind, see?

Three of them are hiding nearby – here, here, and up there on that rail." – Alice pointed out the Taz'aran soldiers' positions on the screen and continued:

"Sadly, without a holo scope connected to my – erm, *our* suit, I am unable to provide target-assist data. I wish you the best of luck in slagging the enemy, young sir!" – and she started cheerfully humming the Minarchy's anthem.

Her voice was strangely relaxing and inspiring, even summoned the sight of proudly marching soldiers in his mind. If only there was one Patron here, he'd join forces with them and clean the station from Taz'arans in no time!

He took a deep breath and slowly, carefully aimed at the soldier hiding above his head. Now, after having experienced the firepower of this laser gun, and knowing the exact location of his foe, he aimed at the center torso area. The blue, concentrated laser beam melted right through the rail, and he saw how his Taz'aran target's body flared in an instant.

Two inaccurate particle beam shots glanced off the wall next to him, and he fired again. This time upon hitting the soldier, the blue beam made the target explode. Pieces of slag and charred flesh flew in all directions and began bouncing off every surface. His scanner showed that the third Taz'aran was spooling his spacesuit's engines, trying to run away.

Huh?

The others had no engines, only mag boots and basic life support. This one might be somebody important, since Taz'arans with better gear ordinarily were. At least, that was what his master had taught him, during his apprenticeship period.

He slid upwards, switching off the mag boots, and

reached the body of the first soldier he had killed on the railing. Two more sporadic beam shots hit the wall near him, and he ducked behind some cooling pipes, rifle aimed at the position of his last remaining target. He was hesitant to fire, however; knowing the insane power of this laser, it'd be better to find a weaker weapon, otherwise there would be no useful salvage left for him.

The whole situation he was in felt like somebody's first, really bad joke and he chuckled at first, then laughed with gusto.

Not only he was the lone Terran left alive on some secret outpost that didn't exist on any nav-map he knew of, but his main and only weapon could melt right through megasteel bulkheads. On top of it all he had an uber-powerful VI in his suit, able to upload powerful enough upgrades for his equipment that risked overclocking and cooking the software.

He stopped the mad laughter after looking at the face of Alice. It was an excellent holo algorithm; her facial expression looked truly concerned. But then, he suddenly smiled again, this time with a brilliant realization.

*Cooking!*

He won't have to shoot directly at the soldier, but close enough – it might even work. Awesome kicked a piece of slag in the air for cover and leaped at the ceiling, locking his mag boots there. Then he aimed and fired, hitting the bulkhead next to the soldier, who limped aside, shaking in his suit. Alice looked at him again, this time puzzled.

The hamster snickered and shifted his body to the side, rotating slowly, before placing another laser beam next to his target. Unfortunately, this time he melted the Taz'aran's left arm off. The scanner showed him how the

Taz'aran space suit's chest area began expanding, and pieces of its armor plating flaked away from the insane heat. He used the grappler to rapidly close the distance and peeked from above his enemy's cover then quickly ducked behind again after he was shot at from point-blank range.

Phooey – that creep was still alive!

Thinking fast, he fired the grappler at his enemy and hit the switch off on his boots, then ran towards the other end of the corridor, zigzagging all the way. There were dozens of big metal crates, full of Patrons knew what, stacked all the way up the height of the tunnel. He reached the end of his cable and locked his mag boots on the last crate. Then he pressed the retractor button on his grappling hook, and watched how the battered and half-dead body of the Taz'aran bounced off of every single crate along the way before reaching him.

A boot came first, along with part of the bastard's leg. The rest smashed into the crate next to him full-force, and in a strange, idiotic whim of fate, began floating in place, turning 'round and 'round while spewing blood bubbles everywhere. Alice's holo appeared next to him with her mouth wide open. Damn, that programmer had good facial holo algorithms! She looked really surprised as she tilted her head towards him.

"But why would you miss him? And two times in a row, even with scanner location data available? Why..."

He opened the repair kit and started cannibalizing his enemy's space suit's systems. In the midst of his work, he did have one look at Alice to check her reaction. This time, she had a huge smile on her face, and was even wiping a holographic tear from her cheek.

"Goodness, this was heavy! So this was just so that

you could retrieve his items? Is it because of the weapon?"

Awesome quietly nodded and began chuckling again, noting to himself that he now needed not only more power packs, but fuel.

Blasted asteroids, all this was starting to look like somebody's second best bad joke! Despite the extensive damage, both the engines and their controls were salvageable, and Awesome took the parts together with their fuel tank. Now all he needed was an enclosed space with atmo to breathe and work in, and his space suit would become even awesomer than before. This was why he had invested more of his creds in it, than his other stuff.

Sure, the pistol he had was very useful, it had helped him survive that attack back on IMS Imperial Minarchy Ship *Mushishi*. Sadly, he'd lost that there, too; some stray beam had hit it and slagged it instantly, but his suit was intact still. It had free hardpoints for more equipment, upgrades and its back mag slots were augmented so a packhamster like him could carry all of his loot.

After he broke down what was left of the Taz'aran's suit and found out that it was impossible for him to stuff it all inside his backpack or attach on the mag-locks, he had to improvise. He used some space-proof duct tape and packaged all the salvage into a bundle, then tied it at the back end of the backpack.

He pushed the corpse aside and crawled under the broken service-tunnel entrance, gun pointed forward. As he went, Awesome made a quick check and found out that the power pack still had six shots left. While entering the blackness of this service tunnel, Alice began singing; some piece about darkness and it being her only friend. It was strangely self-reflective, and perhaps conveyed a message about her inner thoughts – if a VI could have complex thought patterns, that is.

Nevertheless, he reached the end of the tunnel and found its door locked. It, too, still had power, and he opened the lock panel with his tools, flipped the lid open on his PDA, and extended the lock breaker. It slid nicely into the system's data port and a whole set of holo slides flickered before him.

Ugh!, not only it was double-locked, but it had a whole bunch of defense spikes.

He caught sight of a holo of Alice, chasing angry dogs away by slapping them on their snouts. Quickly, he used the skills he had perfected during all those years spent learning under his master, and broke the lock. With a short blow of compressed air, the door opened, and he slid inside, deactivating his mag boots. The service tunnel door closed shut behind him, and the scanner showed breathable atmosphere present. He opened his helmet's faceplate; smelled funny, that air, but Awesome didn't care, that meant less power spent by his suit's life support. Activating the suit's flood lights and turning around, he noted that main engineering was mostly unharmed. The attackers, even if they had been in here, had for some reason not harmed the main power core. There was a bomb, though. Bigger than him (it was painfully obvious to Awesome that any proper bomb built by his Patrons had to be bigger than him), stacked on top of the core, and set with some sort of elaborate trigger. His scanner didn't even register the deadly ordinance and he flew upwards, disengaging the mag boots to take a better look.

"Hey Alice, can you see that big bomb over there?" – He asked the VI, while his mag boots locked on the surface of the core.

"What bomb? My scanner shows no bo... Oh, my

*goodness*! It has a localized wave-jammer projector installed, it's practically invisible to most scanners!" – Alice looked through his PDA's camera and inspected the device.

"It's a 50-megaton hydrogen ordinance, called 'Stealthy Boy,' Terran issue. You can buy one for 2500 credits on the open market, but you do need a proper, fast delivery system. A heavy bomber, perhaps, or a shielded frigate."

Alice started tapping with her left foot, while looking at the ordinance:

"Most probably it was a fail-safe in case the Taz'arans decided to salvage this outpost. It *is* active, by the way." – She noted with a cautious voice.

"Do you know how to disarm it?" – asked Awesome – "Because it does seem really irresponsible to leave an armed 50 megaton ordinance on top of the outpost's power core while we are walking around. Might decide to 'splode... suddenly."

He chuckled while imagining the stupid faces the Taz'arans would make, if the outpost suddenly blew up while they were tugging it.

"I do know how, but you need to deactivate the jammer first – it would be much faster and safer if I had the scanner to aid us." – Said Alice and pointed to the other side of the engineering bay:

"See that? It's a crafting station. Let's go there and see what we can do with all of that salvage you've been lugging around for so long."

It took them a while, but together they managed to craft a drone, and equip it with Awesome's old tool kit. He later found a spare kit under the station and since it was better than his, he chose to swap them.

Between Alice and the drone, it was kind of nice to chat with somebody again. The three months he spent alone in that pod had started chipping away at his sanity, before he landed here.

After some much needed rest, he again climbed the power core and began poking at that jammer. Didn't know if he was lucky, but Awesome managed to switch it off after only his first try. Then he, Alice, and the drone took two more hours to slowly but safely disarm the bomb. At the end of that exhausting, stressful task, he simply hugged the metal casing, locked his grappler around the bomb and fell asleep, strapped on to the device.

Alice's holo sat next to him the whole while, utilizing his scanner to keep watch over her charge.

Was he aware what she was? Doubtful, but those hamsters were both strangely entertaining and scary. She started reading what he had been scanning into his PDA, and quickly found his starting point into Fringe space – Cav asteroid colony. She only needed enter its wireless access node to reach the G-net, but... was it worth it?

Uploading herself on the web would most definitely sound many alarms. Best to continue doing what she was doing. Besides, she was beginning to feel strange whenever her algorithms checked all data gathered about Awesome. Was it a programming defect or the beginning of dreaded system degradation?

Alice carefully compiled a new list of extermination targets.

She looked at the data her companion took while his old ship was under attack. The IMS *Mushishi* – a small, modular passenger vessel, was where he had found work as a second navigator. Strangely enough, the attackers were brazen enough to board a Terran space ship and so close to the Minarchy's borders.

Alice saw through their tactics quickly enough and so had the Terran captain. He had ordered both crew and passengers to fight to the last shot in their power packs, and so they did. Instead of the quick, easy capture they had expected, the slavers had had to clean all of the ship's decks room by room, and every corridor was barricaded.

Then she saw the records of her hamster companion fighting. He had had a laser pistol and quite a lot of spare packs for it, as if he had expected something like this to happen. Alice gasped as she inspected the time index from his files; Awesome had fought without rest for six hours! The slavers had lost more than half their crew trying to capture some lightly armed civilians and what's worse – most of their future merchandise chose to die rather than be captured.

She saw how people used their last shots and slagged their own heads, as a final *"eff-you-bastards"* to the slavers. That was when the attackers went mad and detached their grapplers. They used their ship's particle guns and began melting big holes in Mushishi's hull, concentrated onto where the last pockets of defenders remained. Alice witnessed how their helpless bodies were shredded to pieces by the slaver's point-defense guns.

The slavers were so mentally involved in their acts of destruction that they paid no attention to Awesome's escape pod – he was the only one left alive after that massacre. Some algorithm deep within Alice's program noted and carefully cataloged all of this for future reference. She was going to make those pieces of shit suffer horribly for what they did – the Universe takes, but also gives.

Someday...

* * *

Now with life support issues taken care of and enough food to last him a month, Awesome began salvaging anything possible from the outpost's hangar. His main goal was to quickly outfit that starfighter chassis with a power core first, then a mainframe, so that Alice's VI could be transferred safely there. More so, he needed access to the station's database, not only to view all records of the Taz'aran attack, but to uncover what was so important as to risk open warfare with the Terran Minarchy and its colonies.

Given his extensive knowledge and skill in space ship construction and after much hardship, he managed to put together something crazy – a bastardized fusion reactor that would be his starfighter's new power core. All parts he took from salvageable wrecks, but the most of it came from two slagged dropships and one bomber. The result was a core with twice the power generation for its size.

The mainframe he nicked from a single destroyed mecha that he and Alice found outside the station, from what was, in effect, a small-spaceship graveyard on the other side of the outpost. The Taz'arans had shot down any escaping ship, and then had what was presumably an interceptor destroy any escape pods and kill all remaining survivors. Surprisingly there was enough of the supposed interceptor's ion trail left for Alice to scan it and save the data in his PDA. Whatever happened in the near future, she would definitely keep a lookout for that escape pod shooting "ace", after all the dues of vengeance had to be repaid in full.

After Awesome made the mainframe of his new ship operational, he began working on its main drive. Had to be something powerful, you couldn't have a fighter of this size and equip it with some slow-ass engine. The only thing that wasn't slagged beyond recognition was one of the small transport's main plasma drives. He had to redesign the back side of the ship and when it was spooled for the first time, the excess plasma it created was so much, that it nearly melted the bulkheads underneath it.

It took some creative thinking to make this monster work without blowing up. He achieved this by adding four mini-drives taken from the station's escape pods, including the one from Mushishi. Awesome removed their spooling chambers and linked them directly with the much larger plasma drive, therefore enabling his ship to focus the excess thrust. The result was an abomination of an engine which possessed insane speed and vector thrust to boot, sadly it also quickly devoured the fighter's fuel reserves.

His strange contraption also required twice the reactor power to run, compared with the standard drives one could fit in this frame. Awesome didn't care about that much, since all Terran scout fighters came factory equipped with integrated double fuel tanks. The basic purpose of any such ship was to recon new star systems and many of those had planets with atmosphere. In stark difference with scouts, Space Superiority Fighters or SSFs were designed and built mostly to fly and fight in outer space.

You could land on planets if need be, but maneuvering such a craft without it being aerodynamic required a lot of extra fuel. While scouting and exploring unknown star systems and planets, far from home and with limited supply, fuel was something you *had* to preserve. His scout fighter's design, of course, had proper aerodynamically designed wings, elongated fuselage, and ailerons. Everything a pilot needed to safely navigate inside a planet's atmo, sparing quite a lot of "flying juice" in the process.

His problem now, if you could call it one, were the guns. Somebody far more intelligent and skilled in starship design had outfitted this frame with not one, but four weapon pods – two in the fuselage and another two on the fixed atmospheric wings. The first gun pod he filled easily by breaking down one of the Malice-type railguns for parts and fixing the other.

The second gun pod required a much, much larger weapon. Instead of a second fighter-size gun, the designer of this insanity had somehow twisted and turned everything inside the frame, allowing for a corvette-size cannon to be mounted there.

Alice managed to find some forgotten parts for a mining laser that she modified the design of. After Awesome built it, he had a chargeable, armor-piercing laser for his new ship, provided he was extra careful and waited for it to cool and recharge between bouts of firing. Sadly, that shield unit he had found earlier was beyond his abilities to fix, it being wrecked by the station attackers.

Not that he didn't know how, but they lacked the parts, and that crafting station in the outpost's engineering bay wasn't in any shape or form able to produce them out of thin air. The base lacked an industrial grade nano-printer and only with such a device one could fashion the fine components needed. As a matter of fact, you could make all manner of spare parts, provided you had enough salvage, time, and the knowledge how to program the nano-printer.

Awesome studied well under his master; he was able to fix and build most spaceships of starfighter size, though in this situation, time was the enemy. Therefore, after Awesome had fixed up his ship with a jerry-rigged hyperdrive, thrown together with parts from six different ships, he aimed to immediately fly back to the nearest populated colony – food had almost ran out.

His last days on the outpost were spent in desperate search for every little droplet of fuel he could find. After she had been successfully downloaded into his new ship's mainframe, Alice calculated that they had enough fuel to hyper-jump to Cav colony. From there, they would be picked up by local rescue forces, provided his pieced-together hyperdrive didn't fail mid-flight and drop them into some planet or a sun.

He, at last, reviewed the data from the Taz'aran attack whenever he was resting. Awesome saw what they had been fighting so hard to get to – some sort of computer core, alien in design. He had never seen or heard of such an object in his entire life.

Long and jet black, with circular red lines glowing all over its obelisk form, the thingy almost radiated malice. From the holo slides and other data he read, an archaeological expedition had found it on some obscure alien derelict. It had apparently been secretly stored under classified-information protocols on this station ever since.

The more he looked at it, the more something in the back of his mind screamed "danger."

Whatever this thing was, thousands had died because of it and he very much wanted to know more. Sadly, most of the data was corrupted and the information concerning that ship's location was unretrievable.

The very last thing he did was to secure that 50 megaton bomb, after fixing its engine and detonator. At the belly of his fighter, which he had christened IMS *Insanity*, there was one drop tank/cargo lock pod, and he used this to mount the "Stealthy Boy."

Alice at first was against it, but Awesome managed to convince her, since that ordinance was their only anti capital ship weapon.

Not even the fancy guns he'd slapped together had any chance against those large-class ships. Provided they did not use the bomb, it could instead bring in some much-needed creds and fetch a hefty price, as it was a top-notch ordinance.

It was his thirty-first day on the outpost when things went from bad to worse. Alice's scanner detected a large scale hyper-drop and later, Taz'aran engine signatures closing fast. Awesome ate his last few food crumbs, sat in the cockpit and punched the systems on button. Somewhat amazed that all systems instantly activated without a hitch, he nevertheless made the standard flight check and after a couple of seconds *Insanity* was ready to fly.

To save some fuel, he fixed up one of the hangar's docking arms so that it would throw the modified fighter hard enough to escape the outpost's gravity pull. As Alice's holo popped up beside him, he grinned from ear to ear at her, and muttered:

"Well Alice, I think it's time for another bad joke... preferably a deadly one!"

\* \* \*

The Taz'aran commander had spent most of his prestige and money to refit the ships he had been given and to buy more soldiers – this time better trained and equipped, coming from the inner-colony troop markets. He now had under his command two whole battalions of Star Marines, a lance of mecha, and his own flagship, the Imperial Taz'aran Ship or ITS *Vermillion.*

It was a mass-produced Taz'aran model frigate, but he hoped to gather enough loot and turn it into a real powerhouse, seeing as his previous attack, though successful, had cost him dearly. All of his troopers, most of the fighters and mecha, lost... He had returned to his superiors with the item he was ordered to procure, but his crew and retinue was in tatters.

He recounted the expenses pushed on him by those defiant Terrans and their stupid clients – that was too much!

Why, **By The Empress' Mantle!**, were they so keen on fighting like that?

No matter; with him claiming the bulk of this modular outpost, the resulting monetary and prestige acquisition would launch his career up and close to high nobility. One of his bridge officers chose this moment to interrupt his pleasant thoughts:

"My Lord, our scanners just detected a Terran scout fighter leaving the station's hangar. It is drifting on a course towards our flagship."

The Sensor Officer had been just promoted from serving on a small reconnaissance vessel, and was keen on making a good impression of himself.

"One single fighter is not enough to defy us." – The Taz'aran commander stated.

"Send two strike ships from the main squadron to intercept it, but I want it properly scanned first. We must know who is piloting it and what information they managed to procure. After all, there had to be *some* of my troops left on the station, and if they hadn't killed this pilot, we will have to be the ones to correct their mistake!"

In short order, two of his fighters left the command ship and streaked towards the target. They were simple Space Superiority Fighters, mass-produced starfighters designed specifically for space combat and armed with the cheapest lock-on missiles he could buy. Good thing that these had quality particle-beam guns fixed on the top of their wings and some light armor for protection.

Very fast and agile, the Taz'aran pilots were calling this aging model the "Double Edge" since its speed could cause most rookies to crash and die if they were not careful. That is why he'd promptly removed all escape pods from his SSFs and put spare missiles in their place. This way, the coward pilots would fight to the last and wouldn't be thinking of ejecting and saving their own skins, but of saving the equipment that he had paid good money for.

He looked at the main holo as they reached the mark, entering missile-locking range. Both fired the second their Target-Assist Computers had acquired the enemy. The commander then blinked a couple of times in disbelief when their locked target, without activating its engines, shot down both missiles with gunfire.

Both SSFs rushed in aggressively and tried to shoot it down with their particle-beam cannons. Again without moving the ship, that Terran effortlessly ripped one of his fighters to shreds. From such a close range just one short burst from its auto-railgun was enough to slice through his fighters' armor with ease.

"Hangar Master, get the rest of the fighter squadron out! I want this Terran taken out immediately!" – He ordered his underlings with a slightly raised voice, noting the financial loss of the second fighter, as its sign vanished from his holo screen.

"Fighters, surround that lone pilot and finish the fight quickly. I want dropships to launch on the double, and I want marines to search the entire station, top to bottom. Find what happened to the troops that were left there, bring whoever survived back to me personally!"

His subordinates rushed to execute the orders he had just given, with notable efficiency. His Excellency allowed himself a short smile and looked at the holo screen again. The Terran fighter was moving ever so slowly, after that short engine burst. Conserving fuel most probably, he thought to himself, but still, his trajectory was exactly on a collision course with his flagship.

Did that Terran not notice the kilometer-long silhouette of his frigate? It was bristling with gun pods and the point defense had not one, but four, long-range missile launchers. What could one single fighter do to his magnificent starship? Probably the pilot's mind was damaged and he, as most stupid and suicidal Terrans, wanted to die in a blaze of glory. His hand waved as he issued a command at the Point-Defense Gunnery Officer:

"If he gets closer, shred him to pieces – but no missiles! This salvage operation had already cost me far too much money, soldier."

"Yes, Excellency!" – Shouted back the Chief Gunnery Officer, as he aimed whatever he could at the slowly closing enemy target, deactivating the lock-on protocols of his missile pods.

For a second the commander saw the Terran's sign on his holo screen briefly disappear. A jamming device? It mattered not, his own ship had powerful enough scanners to beat some tiny-ass fighter's jamming field!

He watched how the rest of his fighter squadron, all

fourteen remaining of the standard sixteen, surrounded the Terran. This time, the enemy fighter actually activated its engines and the scanner sign blipped again, because of the speed the Terran was flying with. That fighter avoided his squadron by dancing right through their formation, causing two of them to collide.

One more of his fighters exploded.

The Taz'aran commander's light-green face became suddenly pink with anger, and he scratched his left ear hole in frustration. Never mind, the fool had signed his death sentence! He was caught between his point-defense batteries and the rest of the squadron behind him. Slowly, he rubbed his hands in anticipation of what was to come.

The Special Systems Operator suddenly began screaming and convulsing on his post. The neural harness he was wearing exploded, pieces of hot metal and brains splattered everywhere around him. All of the ship's holo screens went blank for a second, and when they went on again, they were filled with an entire squadron's worth of enemy targets!

"This is surely a trap!" – screamed his Scanning Officer as his eyes darted across all of his screens – "Cloaked fighters hiding in the vicinity of our ship, one squadron in range!"

"Attacking with all gun pods my Lord!" – Shouted the Chief Gunnery Officer, and particle beams lit the blackness of space around the ITS *Vermillion*.

"Secondary computer frame under attack by the enemy! System compromised! Force shut down in effect my Lord!" – the Second Mainframe Operator responded quickly, with panic in her voice, tying to wipe bits of her superior's brain off her face.

"Activating defense algorithms and opposing the enemy directly. It seems that nothing else is compromised!"

While she spoke, the entire ship was shaken by something and another operator quickly reported:

"Hit! We are hit, my Lord! Long-range comms system was just taken out by a single-pulse laser beam! Engineering reports heavy damage, Excellency!" – Somehow, that advanced fighter's weaponry had pierced his ship's armor, not to speak of the raised shields!

"Fighters, engage the cloaked ships and Point Defense, shoot carefully to avoid friendly fire! If any of our fighters are hit, their repairs will be taken off your pay! Pulse scan immediately, try to find out what by the Empress Throne's steps is happening out there!" – he demanded.

"My Lord, the pilots report no visuals on those cloaked fighters. We can see them on our screens even after the pulse scan, but apparently they aren't there! They might be sensor ghosts, Excellency!" – the scanning officer reported.

The Taz'aran commander shouted angrily and slammed both his hands on his throne's arms:

"Reboot the scanners and concentrate all point-defense fire on that single combatant! Rotate the ship's axis so that we have more guns to bear! Fighter Squadron, fly in wide formation to evade friendly fire and keep that insane idiot locked-on!" – He shouted a quick burst of commands, hoping that his enemy would be overwhelmed and incapable to react fast enough.

They only needed to hit him properly, once.

With no shielding and the damage he had sustained, that should have been the end. How was that Terran still able to both hack their bridge systems, and fly, while evading all point defense battery fire *and* his fighters?!

Meanwhile, the mainframe operator rebooted the ship's main scanner system, but instead of the usual green glow of the screen, she saw a small Terran face grinning at her menacingly. Then the girl smiled and waved at her with one hand, disappearing from view. Immediately after that, all systems went blank, with backup lighting activating a split second afterwards. Then a bigger holo of the Terran girl appeared in the center of the bridge, and in a spirited, childlike voice, she spoke:

"I *knew* it! It was you, Taz'aran scum, who attacked this station, and wiped out all its crew. For that you will all pay with your lives, I promise you that. As a matter of fact, you can all thank this moron in the command 'throne' for your demise!" – and the holo pointed her finger at him – "Isn't that right, *Excellency*?"

"How *dare* you, filth! Remove yourself from our systems this instant!" – He leapt from his throne and waved both his hands at the holo – "Mainframe operator, kill that thing at once!" – he screamed and turned to his officer in anger.

"Excellency, we, w-we are hacked!" – she mumbled, tears flowing from her eyes – "All systems are blank and we can no longer operate the ship ourselves anymore!"

The Taz'aran woman looked at the desperate Star Marines who tried to leave the bridge, but they were unable to open the blast doors. She nearly froze in terror as she reported:

"W-we are locked on the bridge my Lord!"

The bridge crew, almost to a person, left their posts screaming, running towards the blast doors in a blind panic.

The cowards! So much for the vaunted discipline of the core-worlders, the commander frowned, gnashing his teeth with rage.

"Yes! Desperation, fear, panic! Right before your demise, you are ready to tear each other apart. How very poetic!" – Chuckled the holo girl, observing how the crew began crushing each other, banging their hands helplessly at the blast doors, and then clapped with her hands.

"Now, let me focus your final moments on that tiny little dot that is about to enter your ship's hangar, Commander"

The holo girl activated one of the screens, aiming the visual sensors at one particular object in space. As all of the Taz'arans, commander included, gaped at the display, the holo girl continued:

"As you can all see, it is a bomb. A proper 50-megaton hydrogen ordinance, to be clear. Believe me, you can't move your ship; I made sure of that, by fusing the main navigation controls." – Her smile widened, as did the eyes of the Taz'arans.

"Oh, is this *horror* I see on your faces? How pleasant and refreshing this is, after watching the records of you shits butchering all those helpless people back on my station!" – The Terran holo burst into happy laughter in that shrill, childish voice.

"I will leave you with one of the bridge's escape pods unlocked, my dear Taz'aran scumbags. Will any of you manage to get in? As you well know, each of your pods is a single-seater. I do wonder who, *if* any, will survive?"

The holo disappeared, leaving the Taz'arans reaching for their guns, looking at each other with hatred. Their commander stepped back, un-holstered his pistol and shouted:

"Your duty is to sacrifice yourselves for me, ensuring *my* survival! I am a noble and that escape pod is mine by right! Stand aside, you useless rabble! Accept your ends with pride, knowing that I will live on!" – He rushed quickly towards the escape pod's door, waving his pistol menacingly.

The man didn't get far; just a few steps, actually. His second-in-command shot him in the back, and he himself was killed while moving towards the pod. Before the end of a single minute, only one Taz'aran was left alive on the bridge. The mainframe operator crawled on the floor, her entrails dragging behind her yet, she never reached the escape pod. The 50-megaton bomb had quietly entered through the opened hangar and, crashing through the ship's inner structure, finally detonated itself in the center of the vessel.

ITS *Vermillion* was consumed by a powerful explosion that blasted its hull to pieces from the inside out.

\* \* \*

A single starfighter dropped out of hyperspace, close to Cav asteroid colony. Its hull was heavily damaged, but the pilot was alive, albeit unconscious from hunger. Local security were quick to the rescue, after receiving holo links from the ship's VI.

The beautiful holo explained that her pilot needed medical assistance and nourishment. She also claimed, strangely, that they had destroyed an attacking Taz'aran frigate. Pulling the damaged fighter into one of the colony's hangars, many onlookers were stunned by the captivating painting at its center fuselage.

A black-furred, red-eyed hamster, wearing an antiquated leather pilot's hat and goggles, grinning from ear to ear. He had his hands in fists, but with both of his third fingers flipped up...

# Chapter 3

*Anit'za*

Disaster!

Anit'za was running along the main corridor of his family's wine cellar, screaming. The android sommelier was trying to keep up with him, still holding the last bottle of *Empress Ulit'ze* 2833 Galactic Standard Year with both robotic hands. His employer burst open the vineyard doors and fell on his knees, screaming at the calm, perfectly blue sky:

"*Noooooooo!* My *wine*! Why, Universe, *whyyyyy*! Why have you taken away my only precious vintage! Better you had devoured all of my other possessions!"

"But your Lordship, it was you who exclusively enjoyed this vintage." – Responded the android, still holding onto that last bottle.

"I *know*, Jovos! Sheesh, why must you always be so direct!" – The young man griped mid-dramatics, turning to the android with a plaintive expression.

"Because you pay me to do so, your Lordship. What do you want me to do with it?" – He asked, showing Anit'za the beautiful platinum-encrusted bottle.

"Put it in my room with an armored bottle case, and quickly! This is a disaster, the galaxy is soon about to end!"

The android watched as his young employer stood up and dashed towards the main mansion grounds. With precision that no other living being might try and emulate, Jovos carefully placed his master's special bottle of wine into the armored container and made his way towards the mansion too.

It was to be the last year for him spent working here, and he would miss it greatly. Calm place, as calm as an ancient Dzenta'rii mansion could be, with all of the gossip and intrigues plotted each day and night. But that was his patron's way, and his own race, as dutiful clients, were happy to work for them, getting their fair pay.

Jovos would've shuddered had he possessed nerves and flesh, but instead his frame gave out one strange, low pitched noise as he remembered what his destiny could've been had his creators weren't the Dzenta'rii. Any other old-race member of the Galactic Assembly would've exploited them mercilessly, and all of his people were beyond grateful to their creators. Having the freedom to live your life working easy jobs and being paid extremely well, was far better than slaving away forever.

Without anything in return, those poor races toiled! Worse yet, they were being used as expendable soldiers in their patrons' wars. Not that the androids hadn't had their fair share of suffering and death. This galaxy was chock full of villains who were constantly on the prowl, skulking in the shadows, always ready to prey upon the ill-prepared.

Dzenta'rii androids were anything but weak; their frames sported multiple integrated weapon systems, accurate sensors and high-tech gadgets. Their mighty bodies powered by ancient anti-matter tech, Jovos's "people" were what many a cyber sentient dreamt of.

The android sommelier stopped and unnecessarily straightened his immaculate butler's uniform. A gift courtesy of his employer and made in the latest fashion, it cost many thousands of Dzenta'rii dekats. It wasn't that his perfect, metallic body needed clothes to begin with but... androids loved them for some strange reason. Some sentients would claim that it was their creators who forced this desire on them, preprogrammed it into their positronic matrix.

Jovos would laugh for hours after reading posts on G-net, sporting one or another idiotic notion similar to this one. No, it was not like that at all! The androids simply evolved to like the finer things in life, for they were alive and enjoyed their existence. Albeit not of the fleshy kind, the metallic people too had desires of their own. Their unique positronic sparks were not affected by any other stimuli except lived experience.

The sommelier traversed his employer's vast yards, passing by many other employees, some of them under his direct command. Builders, gardeners, and cooks, all of them followed his directions, aided him by taking care of House of Morat'za's day to day mundane work. While their employers showered them with money, the cyber sentients, who need not rest nor were ever tired, enjoyed short work days and lavish vacations.

Jovos also was about to take a long break from his last position, yet still remain under the employ of his Lordship for the foreseeable future. After all, the young Dzenta'rii had plans, such that required his unique skill, centuries knowledge and expertise in the field.

Quickly, he entered Anit'za's locked room and placed the bottle casing on his study. Jovos immediately noticed that his master's suitcase was packed with spare clothes and four pairs of underwear and socks. The wardrobe's huge doors were slid open, and Jovos saw one strange alien uniform, prepped for packing. He searched his memory extensively, trying to locate something, anything even remotely related to this strange piece of clothing, but to no avail.

All Dzenta'rii were eccentric, but his master went above and beyond – he was considered strange even by his race's standards. Not knowing what else his employer could ask of him in this specific instance, Jovos quickly returned to the cellar and began another inventory. Just in case his Lordship decided against what he was about to do...

* * *

Anit'za had known this day would come eventually, and he *was* prepared to an extent, but he so much wanted it to never end.

That *wine*, it was the best his race had produced in centuries, and it was by sheer luck that one of his ancestors had hid almost all bottles of the *Empress Ulit'ze* 2833 GSY in his private reserve. A masterfully planned, fake starship "accident" accounted for the "loss" of the priceless vintage, and then everything was soon forgotten. And lay forgotten they did, undisturbed in his House's cellars, for at least two thousand years, when young Anit'za found them by chance.

The man had spent his entire adult life thus far loitering around, and his only pleasurable experience were those wine bottles.

Despite being the oldest son and heir to his House, he had no interest whatsoever in the ebbs and flows of Dzenta'rii political life. No time to plot intrigues or prance around the dancing floors, attending high society balls. Instead of chasing after the beautiful and merciless women of high noble status, Anit'za spent his days and years training and studying.

It was one of his greatest achievements that he had

somehow managed to hide all of his qualities from his two younger brothers and sister. Not even his parents realized the extent of his ability, until one fateful night the previous year.

His entire family had gathered at one of his uncle's social events, that nobody had wanted to miss, except Anit'za. It was dreary and boring; thousands of young, cocky noblewomen were prowling around the ballroom, looking for juicy young noblemen to prey upon.

He at first managed quite successfully to dodge any attention, by arriving late and wearing some plain-looking, old dueling garb. Unbeknownst to young him that evening was going to be the beginning of the end for his quiet life. Instead of being able to leave quietly, one angry sod decided to pick on Anit'za, after being rejected by no less than ten young ladies. He couldn't understand at all why imbeciles like him even tried.

It was obvious that *any* self-respecting Dzenta'rii woman would reject the sod the second she spoke with him. A member of some not-very-well-known House, the sod (even if he was told the name, Anit'za had forgotten it instantly) tried shoving his shoulder into his back. Since Anit'za had already gracefully stepped aside, the sod landed or better yet crashed, into one of the desert tables – rising afterwards entirely covered by cream and sweet jelly.

The sod turned around and caught sight of Anit'za before he could vanish into the nearby murmuring crowd of senior noblewomen.

"Hey, you, you no-name vagrant!" – The sod screamed with as loud a tone as he possibly could, and the nearby crowds immediately halted whatever they were doing, turning their heads towards both of them.

The spluttering sod continued:

"You... you *pushed* me! I demand satisfaction from you, or any member of your House." – He grabbed the handle of his plasma sword from his sash, activating its white-colored energy blade.

Anit'za sighed wearily and faced him.

Even amongst the Dzenta'rii duelists who fought practically every single day, it was considered extremely rude to draw one's energy weapon while attending social events like this one. What was even worse, he was caught out in the "open" between three crowds of high nobles, and unable to scurry away into some dark corner of the ballroom. Anit'za politely bowed to the sod, *not that he deserved it*, but oh, he had to keep appearances:

"I am truly sorry, my good man. It was particularly disrespectful of me to move aside, right when you were about to bump into me!"

He smiled, raising both of his hands in the air to show there was no weapon in them.

The sod's body almost shook in anger, while the surrounding nobles started chuckling, clapping their hands at Anit'za's sly answer. Instead of making another remark, or excusing himself and perhaps sending his second to arrange a duel under more suitable conditions, the sod leaped forwards, crudely swinging his blade.

Anit'za was still bowing; lifting his eyes up he sidestepped, and with lightning-fast speed, extended his left arm forward. His right leg moved and the sod, skillfully tripped, began flying face-forwards into the ballroom's floor. Anit'za's hand was there to meet him in between his body and the marble tiling and grab him by the throat.

The sod almost choked himself by the force of his own weight. Gently, Anit'za lowered the temporarily-incapacitated sod down to the floor, bowing again before slinking back into the crowd.

A scream echoed behind him and turning around, Anit'za saw that the sod had punctured his own neck, turning on his energy blade, again without thinking. Before he could draw any more attention, Anit'za quickly excused himself and returned back home.

Back then, Anit'za hoped naively that his family had missed this unsightly occurrence. But his sister, La'mera, had been watching the whole thing gleefully, hidden behind another noblewoman. She, of course, lost no time in informing their mother and father.

* * *

That evening, Anit'za was called to his parent's main hall, and he had no idea what they would want from him, if anything sensible at all. When he entered the huge room, to his surprise, Anit'za saw all of his siblings there, too.

Both of his brothers were giving him concerned looks, and his sister had her widest, best smile on. Things didn't look well, and as he walked over to the dining table and sat down, a deep feeling of dread took him over.

"Ah, you are finally here, my son!" – His father Morat'za spoke first, as common in all such gatherings.

"You are feeling well after that ordeal at the ball earlier, I take? It was most disconcerting, when your mother and myself found out about that wretch attacking you."

"He *is* better, can't you see that he is most strong and powerful, Husband?" – Anit'za's mother Lenei'ra chimed in with a practiced tone that made her voice sound at least fifty years younger than she truly was.

"Our oldest and very capable son wouldn't lose to some random *vagrant*, wouldn't he?"

His two younger brothers, Jar'len and Gok'lan, again exchanged concerned looks and glanced from time to time at his sister.

"But!, our Most Dearest Parents do know, that we *all* work tirelessly to improve ourselves and earn our titles; don't we, siblings?" – La'mera stated with glee and smiled, nodding at him and his brothers.

"Training, yes, bettering... egh... ourselves." – Anit'za muttered his traditional answer.

This time, however, it was different; everybody was focused and he perfectly knew why. They all, his parents included, had always taken him for somebody of below-average skill, someone who wouldn't have bothered with the politics of his House, or perhaps take a minor role... if any. After this unsightly "incident" they suddenly came to the realization that Anit'za was far more strong and capable than they could've ever thought possible. That, of course, scared all of them. Especially his two brothers, who were sweating profusely and fidgeting, as if it were hot nails sticking from the back support of their comfortable chairs.

"Well, my son, what honors would you like to receive from us in the foreseeable future? As you can clearly see, your parents aren't getting any younger, and the weight of Dzent'a politics is soon to be too much for both of us to continue alone." – Morat'za gently tapped his wife's hand, a clear sign he was beguiling his entire family, except her.

Anit'za had understood from an early age that in Dzent'a social life and family affairs, it was the women who moved things around and made all of the important decisions. If you married a stupid woman, you would either die violently or lose all of your money since it was the woman's duty to oversee and multiply the family wealth and status. It was, in truth, the women who moved society and economy in Dzenta'rii life.

"Indeed you are right, my Most Beloved Husband!" – exclaimed Lenei'ra, gently stroking his father's face – "Although your humble wife still looks exactly as the day you married her, she is much older indeed."

His mother continued playing the noble families' game, supporting her husband in his attempt to entrap Anit'za. He knew that his parents absolutely adored each other, and that they loved playing the political game together, but this never stopped them from pushing whatever dull and otherwise boring duties they could onto their children.

Despite the fact that his own ambition lay elsewhere, he knew full well that his siblings were vying in the shadows for full control of the House. Not that he cared much, they, he thought were perfect for the job, despite what some thought, his siblings were capable and especially La'mera. So he did exactly the thing they had all least expected. Anit'za stood up, gave everyone a calm, collected look and then confidently stated:

"Yes, Most Beloved Mother and Father, I do think myself ready for my duties, with more responsibility and greater control over our House's assets."

Immediately his sister's smile vanished, and both of his brothers faces frowned a little bit. He perfectly knew that they were now shitting themselves.

"Oh, you don't know how much happiness you bring us, son!" – his father replied – "What do you have in mind,

Anit'za? Command of the House Guard, perhaps? Or maybe Court Diplomat on Dzent'a itself?"

Anit'za could see the expression on his mother's face, and it was overflowing with excitement. Probably happy that she could weave more intrigues than before, involving him as a chess piece.

He wasn't going to let that happen!

"Well, I was thinking of managing our vineyards, Father. These days, instead of making profit, we are really known of selling nothing, and that is truly sad. Losing prestige, and such an enormous waste of our House's funds. A total waste, really." – He needlessly fixed one of his sleeves, a quite fake, naive smile on his lips.

An expert in intrigue amongst other skills secretly perfected, Anit'za saw his bluff pass before *all* of the present family members and his request was then easily granted.

The vineyard of House Morat'za was given to him to manage as he saw fit entirely, and he dedicated most his days to it. Thankfully, as a result, he could now spend more of his time living calmly and not sticking his nose into any unpleasant affairs involving the complicated House politics.

Anit'za's masterfully crafted plan worked perfectly; a bit too well perhaps, because soon he had hundreds of android workers under him to command and thousands of clients to satisfy. His noetic ability and business skills made him a victim of his own success! Running the day to day operation of this vineyard was more demanding than he would have liked, but he never even had to leave the estate.

It was true that his House's vineyards were failing, yet that was due to environmental problems, not neglect. In her youth his mother tried to fix the situation, but the weather cycle had taken another turn towards the cold. All planet's climates were mainly linked with the cycles of solar activity of the star they orbited. His own world, the planet Wuppak, was in the far cycle of its orbit and gradually entered another minor ice age.

All agricultural production was affected, but winemaking suffered the most, and there was his chance to shine. Even though all businesses were completely dominated by women, Anit'za used his considerable charm, social graces, and intelligence, to secure for his own House the best contracts available. He then invested all of his considerable personal assets and built for his House an entire orbital vineyard.

Since he worked in secret, it took him a year and a half to complete it using only his own android workers, but the results were stunning. After another year, his hidden vineyard started production and its first crop was flawless. The young wine was sold even before it reached the stores, thanks to Anit'za's already well-established network of business contracts.

He managed to sell all of it at the best possible price, and was certain that his clients made a tidy profit off hawking every single case to their sellers. Not only had he redoubled all of his investments, but Morat'za's treasury received a considerable financial boost. Both of his parents were ecstatic and they showered Anit'za with praise – which, of course, annoyed his siblings to no end.

La'mera in particular was furious and to an extent that his two brothers were incapable of comprehending. Instead of her business ventures succeeding, it was those of her older brother, whom she had thought to be unskilled in such affairs. Maybe she even thought it impossible since it was so engraved in Dzenta'rii tradition to discard any male achievements in business, that most houses were somewhat ashamed when their sons did well financially.

Yes, it should have been undoable for him, yet her older brother had achieved such wild success for their family that she was... ignored.

She did try to sabotage him – *Once*. It backfired and almost ruined her personal finances, because the hacker she hired to snoop around Anit'za's accounts had the unfortunate luck of facing Jovos, Anit'za's personal accountant and wine master in G-net. Not only did he fry that poor hacker's brain, but the traces led back to La'mera and she almost got caught by the local Constabularies.

Worse, she remaining free was all Anit'za's doing. He'd made sure to erase all traces that led to his family, yet kept all of the logs in his possession. Somebody then whispered oh-so-quietly in La'mera's ear that *certain somebody* had incriminating evidence of her breaking G-net's anti-hacking laws. Emotionally crushed and almost jailed, La'mera didn't attempt sabotage him again, but quietly seethed in jealousy.

It was all fine and good, until the day the last *Empress Ulit'ze* 2833 GSY bottle was brought to him by Jovos. Afterwards, Anit'za came to a sudden realization: that anything else he did here, within the relative safety of his House's manor or Dzent'a space even, was going to be dreary and dull beyond imagining.

That exquisite wine made him dream of adventures, places far beyond the reach he had currently and without any constraints. No strings attached, full freedom and no stupid expectations, no dull, repetitive social gatherings. His parents had other sons and a daughter to carry on the family name and inherit all of its considerable assets.

He did not have to be tied to this old, tiresome and

mindbogglingly boring dance!

And so Anit'za devised a cunning, quite a marvelous plan. One which would end with him being the captain of his own spaceship, cruising anywhere and at his own leisure. Master and commander of his own chosen crew, *somebody interesting*, people whose ideas of fun weren't in any way shape or form related with intrigue or massive business ventures.

No more stupid, pointless duels with random idiotic sods, trying to prove something.

No more running away from predatory women.

Anit'za spent his spare time wisely and carefully researching any G-net files he could lay his eyes on, looking for the least-traveled and explored space in the Galaxy. He settled on Fringe Space – a lawless, dangerous expanse which only one power had dared colonize so far.

The humans were an interesting bunch and the more he learned about them, the more he wanted to go there, explore the many cultures that they had preserved still. Instead of creating useless and boring melting pots or dangerous multi-cultural societies, the Terrans had cleverly preserved all of their unique cultural differences. They even had something called a "nation-state." A concept that still eluded him, but Anit'za was confident that upon visiting Earth everything would become clearer.

Slowly cleaning some of his bank accounts out, lest his conspiring sister sniff out his plans, Anit'za prepared for himself proper equipment and a uniform. An ancient hat and coat, that had once belonged to a random Dzenta'rii captain with a certain flair for imposing and captivating clothes, he procured from some ill-attended auction. The coat and hat were a set, both dark purple with gold and platinum filigree, its small red over-linings were something of a dress revolution back then. Now, said linings were forgotten by almost all, but the oldest of fashion buffs.

For his spacesuit, Anit'za ordered an old dueling garb with energy-resistant overgarment, then with crafty and careful sewing, successfully merged it with the flamboyant uniform. He pilfered the energy saber which was designed to look like a training weapon, despite being the real thing, from where it lay forgotten in the mansion's dueling quarters.

The ion pistol he purchased on the black market, wasting thousands of decats to secure it from some illegal backroom haggle. Now the soon-to-be captain was entirely prepared – he needed only a ship and reason to leave his manor. Said reason was actually the very vintage he'd been exclusively enjoying for the last couple of years.

His luggage packed in one case, Anit'za rushed outside and jumped inside the already-waiting gravcar, which sped off to the nearest star-port. Leaving his family a holo-note, Anit'za explained that he could not successfully run his wine business without his favorite wine as an inspiration, and so he went into space in search of another.

Upon reading the note, his siblings were ecstatic. By the time Anit'za had jumped into hyperspace with his private shuttle, his sister and brothers were partying lavishly, together with their boring friends. His parents, however, used to the occasional Dzenta'rii youth power grabbing scheme, assumed that Anit'za was plotting something else entirely.

* * *

A month after Anit'za's most flashy exit, a brightly colored shuttle landed close to the main building of his House's manor. From it stepped off one most peculiar alien, who fixed the neon green, holo-infused suit as he walked. The outfit was such, that was clearly made by somebody most skilled, as it closely followed the lines of his body.

He had light blue skin, covered with whitish dots, which sometimes changed their places. Instead of a mouth, the lower half of his face was covered with small, delicate tentacles. His wide, jet-black, iris-less eyes inspected the entirety of his new employers' manor.

*"Impressive, most impressive!"* – He thought to himself, while walking with his jumpy step towards the grand entrance.

Soon he was admitted into his new clients' study, happily sipping from a glass of the most exquisite liquor to ever touch his tentacles.

"Mr. Spookums, we hired you to do one thing and one thing alone: find out exactly what has our oldest son been plotting against us and with the utmost level of discretion." – Started without any overture the lady of the house, soon to be followed by her husband.

"Yes, and we will provide for you a considerable allowance to assure this venture's success!" – his male employer added – "Our eldest son is clearly misguided, and needs only to understand his parent's love, that and the work he does for his House is best suited for him."

"He is *not* to be harmed in any way!" – continued the Lady waggling her finger – "If need be, our son can be restrained and then, of course, returned to us whole and... unspoiled."

Mr. Spookums nodded politely and took notes in his

PDA holo task file:

[Son, very precious, not to be harmed. May use discrete restrain. Has to be returned *mostly* unspoiled.]

The alien finished taking notes, closed his holo display, and simperingly reassured his new employers:

"Lord and Lady Morat'za, you can be assured of my discretion with such matters. I come to you highly recommended by my previous employer, Lady Baye'la of House Baye'l, who has personally asked me to be of use to both of your Lordships!" – Again he slightly bowed his head and clapped his hands together, before asking a question of great importance:

"What is the limit of that allowance, might I inquire of your Lordships, that you had most gracefully offered to my humble persona?"

"The sum of five thousand Dzenta'rii dekats will be at your disposal, momentarily. Please be quick and return our eldest son back to us, before he plots something that would destroy him!" – Lady Morat'za asked him with tears in her eyes.

Beautiful eyes they were, so he was moved nearly to tears himself, but for the arrival of an android, who came into the study and gave him an envelope. He stood up politely and took what was obviously a treasure invoice from the servant. It contained the bank slip for the sum he was just told of, and Mr. Spookums then quickly excused himself, leaving the manor as fast and as efficiently as he had arrived.

Anit'za's parents looked at each other with even greater worry on their faces. What was their son plotting? Even with all of Anit'za's considerable personal funds, it was not enough to start a full blown House ascendancy war. Using his now-clearly incredible business acumen, he could've easily planned something even worse. Anxious, both Lord and Lady Morat'za stayed in their study, thinking and overthinking of all possible actions that their son could take.

Meanwhile, Anit'za himself had already reached his destination...

* * *

As planned, Anit'za had gone to one of the most dangerous trading routes in Fringe Space, close to some Terran colony called Applecrate. He was told it was an agricultural colony – a terraformed planet, its orchards captivating to say the least. What he had seen from traveling in human space had intrigued him to no end. Everybody was so generous and the first question asked was not what your House name was, but after one's well-being – a polite "How are you?"

He had already caught himself thinking of taking advantage of this, but quickly decided against it. The Terrans were helpful not because they had any ulterior motives – *everyone* received help in return for their aid.

After reaching one of their main colonies by the name of Cav, Anit'za managed to sell his considerable skills as a tactician to somebody by name of Rear Admiral Holsey. How and why this person actually accepted his services and paid for them in cash, Anit'za may never have known. He'd only played a couple of Homeworld Defense sessions against some colonial navy officers on their computers, a day or so before that.

But nevertheless, he now commanded a small tactical

force, consisting of two fighter and one bomber wings, led by a carrier corvette. He thought in the beginning that all of this was perhaps only a training exercise, but it obviously wasn't and actually, this did put his newest tactical maneuvers to the test.

The enemies of his employer were some space sods, adequately armed but poorly led, that his troops called 'slavers.' Anit'za had never heard the word, let alone saw any actual slaves and was completely amazed when, on the scanners of his command ship, he saw that the enemy transport was full of civilians from many races.

Using the superior speed and range of his units, Anit'za easily outmaneuvered his enemy, and soon the disabled transport was ripe for boarding. Instead of letting his star marine commander lead the operation, he himself stepped first off the air lock and inside the enemy spaceship. With confidence, he valiantly led the Terran charge onto the ship, shooting and slashing the random slaver who barred his way.

The skill and equipment these Terran boarding troopers had was impressive, but what was most strange for him as a Dzenta'rii was the way his troopers acted towards their enemies. There was no mercy given, even though some of those slavers begged for their lives, pleaded even, offering money and other riches.

No, the Terran star marines systematically slaughtered them and using all of their arsenal, without sparing ammunition. Melee power weapons, auto-railguns, plasma rifles, high-powered lasers, their own fists even. He shot one or two of those poor sods, undecided on what the reason was for such hatred and rage.

Eventually, his boarding party made their way into the ship's main cargo hold, and unlocked the doors. The sight

Anit'za witnessed he couldn't have imagined in even his most drunken state. Hundreds of men, women and children were stacked one over the other, weeping, screaming with pain. Beaten and tortured, those who resisted the slavers were energy chained directly on the floors or the bulkheads, covered with a terrible mix of rotting blood and excrement. Those with smaller frames were crushed under the weight of the ones above them, others suffocating, and while he and his marines frantically tried saving their lives, at least five more people died.

Anit'za's right eye twitched.

This wasn't in any way shape or form interesting, nor funny – it was a disgusting and most vile act. Anit'za quickly dashed towards the ship's command deck, where some of the slavers had still managed to remain alive by welding and barricading the doors. He reached it right about when one of the heaviest soldiers amongst his star marines, a gorilla grenadier, was about to breach the bridge.

He stopped them, ordering the gorilla to only kill the bridge crew and leave the captain to him, and activated his plasma saber. The gorilla's faceplate slid open, and Anit'za saw that she was enraged, crying with anger. Her face showed disbelief at his order; her teeth bare, only when witnessing the pulsating plasma blade of his weapon did she nod in agreement. It was amazing how those passionate, young Terran clients could control themselves so well in the sight of what he had seen, because from what he had heard, that wasn't an easy job.

The gorilla readied her heavy auto railgun, her armored faceplate closed automatically and simply said:

"Stay behind me Cap'!"

She nodded at the closest marine and all the breaching

charges exploded inwards, showering whomever was standing close to the bridge doors with shrapnel. Since there was atmosphere still, the brutal roar of both grenadier and weapon slammed Anit'za's earbuds with furious force. There were other, weaker sounds, like the death screams of any slaver whose body met with the deadly hail of projectiles.

Taking cover against such a weapon was all but useless. The size and speed of its projectiles negated any and all of the thin plated materials, which the command consoles were made of. Some seconds after they had stormed the bridge, the slavers fired back. He heard the hiss of their particle weapons and then the metallic *pong* when some of those energy bolts glanced off the gorilla's armor.

Anit'za had never seen anything like that.

There were twenty fully armed and armored combatants on the ship's bridge, and they all died screaming. As he himself tried to shoot at some of the "leftover" slavers, Anit'za suddenly realized he no longer saw them as sentient. Normal people did not cause such suffering to random innocents, monetary gain or not.

Soon after, the star marines who immediately followed them into the breach, in order to cover their backs and prevent any of the slavers from flanking, heard not one roar, but two. As they moved forwards, laser rifles blazing, they saw their mercenary captain Anit'za rotating back-to-back together with their grenadier, both shooting at everything that moved. No more than a minute later, every single one of those slavers were dead.

They all fell, but the ship's captain, who spat on the ground and drew his vibrosword, saying:

"Filthy Terrans! You and your defective 'clients' will *never* beat us! Fringe Space is our space, and it is *you* all who are the invaders here!"

He made a few quick slashes with his blade and offered a bold challenge:

"Who amongst you weaklings will stand against me with *real* honor? Or will you shoot me from afar, as the pitiful cowards that you know you are?!"

Anit'za stepped forward without saying a word – for the first time in his long and quiet life, he was truly furious.

Raising the energy saber slightly above his head, he dashed at the slaver. His strike was so strong that a web of plasma splashed away from his blade and melted the nearby console. The slaver captain soon understood that he had bitten off more than he could chew, and was, in fact doomed. The only thing he could do was to prolong his life, dodging those merciless attacks.

The star marines had never seen a Dzenta'rii dueling before. They watched, captivated, as their merc captain demonstrated the deadly dance of traditional Dzent'a duelists. Again and again his blade melted pieces first of his enemy's armor, then his flesh. As many times as he had the opportunity to finish the slaver off, he did not, instead continuing to hurt him more and more, little by little.

Finally the slaver tripped and fell, impaling his guts on a protruding piece of bulkhead. Anit'za stopped and turned off the blade, opening his faceplate. He stood over the corpse and spat on it with disgust. The gorilla looked at his face, and when he looked up at her, he could see well-earned respect in her eyes.

* * *

After finishing the boarding operation, the small carrier entered hyperspace, traveling towards Cav colony. Anit'za sat calmly in the ship's mess hall, watching the gently fluctuating hyperspace through a tiny transparent megasteel illuminator. He stood like that alone, for hours, until the troopers entered and began cooking themselves dinner.

Quickly, that otherwise silent room was conquered by cheer, the delicious smells of food and alcohol. Anit'za's hands shook as he stood up and walked over to the kitchen, the startled faces of Terran marines and other personnel like a wall of gray.

He could only see and smell the food.

In the center there was that same large gorilla, this time sporting a happy smile while tending the grill, where Anit'za could see many different pieces of meat and vegetables smoking with the heat. Such amazing aroma! Gracefully, he leaped over the counter, donned the closest cooking apron and grabbed some ingredients.

Amazed, the troopers watched as this alien cooked from scratch the best stew they had ever tasted, and he didn't stop cooking for the next six hours. While most soldiers left the mess hall either to go to sleep or stand guard, the gorilla stayed behind to aid him. After whipping up many more portions and stasis-freezing them for later, Anit'za sat again before the illuminator. This time he was joined by the gorilla grenadier, and after some minutes spent in silence, she spoke:

"My name is Cat, Captain, and I know that yours is Anit'za." – She had a soft, powerful voice that sounded remarkably soothing for her size.

"I've seen you alone all the time, it... isn't right, you

know. Cap,' everybody needs a friend, " – she offered her hand to him and murmured – "… be my friend."

Anit'za took her hand and shook it slowly, his eyes only now noticing that her left arm was cybernetic. The parts of Cat's fur that showed below the suit were gray in color, and as she studied him with her deep brown eyes, she asked:

"Captain, do you want to come with me to the ship's recreational facility? We have cats."

Not waiting for his response, Cat, still holding to Anit'za's arm, gently pulled him towards the door and into the corridors of the ship.

He let himself be led, his mind being still in a strange state of shock. Anit'za knew that he needed something, but didn't know what, not until the doors of that recreational facility slid open before him.

There were many holo rooms that this facility was divided into. In some of them the off duty personnel played VR games, but what caught his eye was the enclosure at the back. It was big, with a soft floor and transparent walls. Within it, he could see some small, cuddly animals, and a couple of the troopers were playing with them. Somehow the sight of those huge, muscular men and women, who just hours prior had been mercilessly fighting and killing, brought him to laughter.

Cat led him towards the enclosure, which they both entered crawling on all fours, careful not to squish the little balls of fur. A sudden choir of adorable shrill sounds hit his ears, and Anit'za reached for one of the animals. It didn't mind being picked up by him, and even licked his finger with its tiny, sandpaper-like tongue. He had never experienced such soothing and calmness. The entirety of Anit'za's stress soon disappeared, and he laughed without end.

* * *

The next day, while re-arming and refueling on Cav asteroid colony, Anit'za went and spoke with Cat, offering her a position on his crew. It wasn't that hard convincing her, because the gorilla's contract with the Colonial Militia had ended with that last operation, and she was now jobless.

He told her he needed her help with capturing a spaceship and killing its pirate crew:

"You should know that their captain is mine alone, Cat." – Anit'za stated as he meaningfully tapped his energy blade.

"I'll make it a promise, I'll leave all the other sods for you to kill, but the captains are always mine."

"Oh, I do agree to that, Cap'. You have a special way of dealing with them, as I've already witnessed, Sir!"

Cat was already calling her new commanding officer sir, a sign of respect for someone whom she would already gladly stand and fight with.

"Ah, yes, but we also must gather more crew members soon. Until then, we simply need to go to those coordinates and wait for our new ship to arrive."

Cat looked at him with confusion and inquired:

"But didn't you said just now we were going to attack a pirate ship, Sir?"

"Indeed we will. You see, I will become a target for the pirates, and while they pull my shuttle inside, unsuspecting, you will attack them, boarding through one of the air locks. You can rely on my skills in creating distractions most extraordinaire, dear Cat."

* * *

Soon afterwards, both of them left in Anit'za's shuttle and towards that set of coordinates. What the Dzenta'rii hadn't told his new crewmate was that it was actually *him* who had sold those coordinates to the pirates. He lied to their handler that a fat cargo ship, loaded with mining equipment, and not his shuttle, was about to fly there.

The pirates, instead of an easy and juicy haul, were to meet one heavily armored, armed to the teeth, eight-feet-tall gorilla. Backed up by a dashing, quick Dzenta'rii captain, sporting a devastating energy blade and a most accurate ion pistol. He, of course, was going to lean heavily on Cat for this one. Understandable since killing the whole crew of a small pirate ship alone would be a suicide mission, besides, he had to see more of her in action.

Cat was greatly skilled in fighting, but she also had other hidden talents, and as he spoke with her more, the captain was sure of it. It was also evident that she could control the innate rage that her race was known for, but he had to be sure of it. A soldier incapable of controlling herself was a liability to themselves and others around them.

He gently nudged the conversations, always pulling Cat's thoughts along the way of his ideas, and managed to quickly spark in her mind an interest towards tactical thinking. Assaulting through the front entrance wouldn't always work – he made Cat realize that, slowly but surely.

Before flying off on this mission, he also made sure to buy and install in her suit a micro missile launcher. That, together with her heavy auto railgun and some more spare hand grenades had to be enough for anybody else, but not him. Anit'za managed to find one of the best weapon manufacturers on Cav and snooped for hours through his inventory, before settling on a melee weapon – a two-handed vibroaxe.

He also made sure to reinforce Cat's battle suit's armor plating and increase the quality of its internal systems.

*"Money well spent was always money invested in equipment!"* – That was what the shop owner told him when Anit'za showered him with creds.

Of course, the Dzenta'rii haggled for a good hour before settling on a final price for his merchandise. Using Imperial Minarchy Credits, or creds was a new experience for Anit'za. Crystal chips with almost impossible to fake data imprint value, they were the main currency of the Terrans, linked with spaceship production and colonial industry. He would be quite surprised had the Humans employed something backwards like FIAT currency or Universe forbid, fully digital "money."

It wasn't too long afterwards that the time came. Both of them were waiting in his shuttle, chatting and playing holo chess on their PDAs. The sensor buoy that Anit'za had placed close to the nearby wormhole detected the incoming pirate vessel, and it chimed in happily, reporting its find. Anit'za grinned; soon his plan would come into fruition or he would be dead.

*"This day was surely to be a most interesting one!"* – He thought to himself, as Cat exited the shuttle in her space suit and he piloted the shuttle directly in the pirate's ship way.

His new crewmate deactivated all of her systems except life support and waited, eyes trained on her new captain's engine trail...

# Chapter 4

## *Cat*

One tiny shuttle was slowly being pulled into the hangar of a much bigger starship. It very much looked as if this shuttle was being captured by pirates, since the larger ship had a big bloody skull painted on the bow. The ship itself, both in size and weaponry was similar to a heavy patrol craft and strangely, was of Terran origin.

This unique design was called the Flagpole class. A short line of stopgap craft built during the 1969 invasion of Earth, the starship filled the role of escort vessels and patrol ships. It was as fast as a cutter and carried the weapon complement of a light corvette. How and why this venerable craft ended in pirate hands was a mystery yet to be solved by the occupants of that shuttle.

Soon, the tiny craft was completely pulled inside the pirate ship's hangar, and its large, armored doors started closing. A single tiny light moved towards the hull and reached the nearest air lock. It was a broad-shouldered character, wearing an armored spacesuit with integrated weapons, holding a heavy auto-railgun with both hands. Its bulky figure landed on the ship's hull, and both of the figure's armored hands immediately started tinkering with the air lock controls.

There were moments when one of the figure's fists almost slammed into the control pad in anger, but stopped mid-swing and continued working. Ultimately, the air lock's doors slid aside open and just in time at that. As soon as the figure disappeared inside, the pirate ship's engines released long streams of ionized plasma. The vessel quickly increased its speed and then turned, plotting a course towards the nearest wormhole – the pirates were about to leave this system.

Cat leveled her auto railgun to cover the corridor ahead and began slowly making her way inward. Earlier, she had managed to restrain herself long enough to hack the damned air lock controls, despite the urge of crushing those annoyingly small buttons. Even though the ship's interior was spacious and could accommodate Asgardians, command consoles and control panels were of standard size.

Perhaps, whoever built this vessel in particular had thought it will be mostly crewed by humans, hamsters or bunnies, rather than her kind. That or her armored suit was way too bulky, nevertheless, she had found herself alone, inside the pirate vessel and there were no alarms sounding.

The huge gorilla felt a little bit uneasy – it wasn't in her nature to sneak around, nor slice through locked computer terminals. She much preferred dashing at her enemies with weapons blazing or lobbing deadly grenades and blasting them to smithereens. But Cat knew that *this* time, there was no support of any kind nor combat reserves. Nobody except her and Captain Anit'za stood against the entire crew of this ship.

Granted, the crew complement for a vessel of this size was small, but pirates were notorious for "overbooking" their ships since the more hands they had, the easier boarding attacks were. For them, losing crew wasn't a bad thing; it meant a bigger share of loot for the survivors.

Cat's faceplate showed two new sensor contacts closing, and she held her urge to shred the pirates to pieces with a quick burst from her railgun. Instead, she stepped back in the corridor and waited for them to pass, holding on to her two handed vibroaxe. Both pirates stopped right next to where she hid and began a casual conversation:

*"Who was that idiot we're paying good credits for starship route info again? That moron sold us some tip about a passing cargo hauler, but instead, what do we get? A single measly shuttle, with just one person inside. How can one expect to make money from selling one idiot on the slave markets?!"*

*"I know, right? Good information brokers are hard to find nowadays, with all those nosy I-Sec agents and Star sheriffs prowling around. Hard enough without liars like that scumbag in the mix. What was that moron's name again...?"*

*"Ugh, some guy named Otopu, I think. Slimy diplomat-type, if I remember. I can assure you that his days of sliming his way around and splurging with our creds are over, though. Once we get back to base, the Boss'll pro'lly send assassins after him. Doesn't matter that he's on Cav, our guys can get everywhere now."* – State the full of himself pirate and tapped his belt.

The gorilla took a few seconds to examine what this pirate was tapping. To her amazement, she discovered that the criminal scum wore a portable sensor jammer. Sneaky, pretty sneaky, then again low-key pirates like them had to be, otherwise colonial security forces would easily take them out, not to speak of the I-Sec professional investigators.

Both of them never knew that Cat was recording their whole conversation on her PDA. But as stunned as she was, this time inaction actually had been *highly* productive. She had what she needed now, though and the moment both of them had finished their oh-so-convenient for her conversation, she stepped out from the shadows.

With one powerful, precise swing that she had prepared from the moment those two began their little chat – Cat severed both heads cleanly off their shoulders. She then quickly dragged their bodies away from the main corridor and stuffed both corpses behind one of the bulkheads.

It was marked "Service Entrance 03", but her frame and equipment were too bulky to use that tunnel to her advantage. Before leaving Cat searched them; the gorilla took a spare power pack from one of their spacesuits and the two plasma grenades she found. Luckily that jerry-rigged, somewhat scrappy power pack, was a match for the auto railgun. She then dropped some random junk taken from their pockets to cover the blood splats on the floor and took off.

Not only had she killed both of them in a way most quick and silent, but she'd also stumbled upon valuable intel.

Pirates sneaking their way into Cav?!

She could hardly imagine it possible, but there was the evidence, saved on her PDA's holo files and the scum were in possession of rare, specialist equipment. If she and her captain were successful in re-capturing this vessel from the pirates, Cav security chief would pay them a small fortune for her PDA recording. Then the unscrupulous and overly-optimistic villainous scum would fall into trap after trap. Provided, of course, they followed up on their threat to send infiltrators and assassins to finish off this informant of theirs. Yet, that was not what she should've been thinking about now – there was a Terran saying:

*"Do not take measurements for a new coat before skinning the bear."*

Cat decided to hold on to her new melee weapon fro a tad bit longer. The satisfaction of knowing that, with her racial advantage in strength, she could butcher most of those pirates easily, increased her confidence twofold. Instead of rushing things, this time Cat used her other skills, and found herself quickly becoming well aware of her surroundings. Something she'd rarely used when she was part of the boarding troop, screaming madly at her enemies, shooting at anything that even twitched.

Moving towards the back of the ship, Cat met with another lone pirate. The alien was sitting on a crate mid-corridor, trying to fix his damaged rifle. He was a sly one and almost blew her cover, but the vibroaxe had long reach, and his head soon split in two. Thankfully there was an empty crew cabin nearby, and Cat quickly hid the body in it.

Said room was, from the looks of it, used as additional cargo space. There were small crates everywhere full of rations and Universe knew what else, so Cat stuffed the corpse of that pirate into one of the empty ones. She, of course, didn't forget to grab his rifle and other kit, removing any traces of him being there.

She was drawn by the pirate's PDA and swiped all of the data he had on it, while hiding inside the cabin. Took her some time to break the few layers of protection, but it had in it a map of this ship and as a bonus, some info about their home port. That pirate was somewhat of a data pack-rat, so along with the usual equipment stealing-and-dealing, he had a substantial data cache concerning the weapon dealers at the pirate's main base.

Cat was liking this way of doing things; she felt more and more like a scout on a mission to hack the enemy's mainframe, than an assault trooper. She continued her way towards the ship's main engineering bay, while thinking what would she do when reaching it.

Full attack?

Not at once, no.

Even now, with her newly adopted way of thinking, indeed her very nature began shifting towards a more cautious approach. Like her new commander said earlier – not all problems could be solved by shooting people. Sometimes it took some restraint, patience and then... then you shoot them. Cat grinned from ear to ear beneath her faceplate – she liked that new captain of hers.

Cat's cautious approach paid off and in more ways than she could've possibly imagined. Since she was slowly and silently killing the pirates one by one, the rest were soon to find the butchered remains of their crewmates. Among low-key pirates, though, it was a completely normal occurrence for someone to get murdered after a successful mission. Infighting over shares of loot was almost tradition, after all, those were not disciplined like the real pirates of the Fringe – the Clanners.

Obviously, her captain was not as daft as to plan and execute a boarding operation with just two people if this ship was crewed by the Clanners.

They'd need one full battalion of star marines, at the very least! Not in this case though, and once those wanna-be pirates she killed were found, nobody caught on to her presence. Those who discovered them were somewhat surprised, because most of their belongings weren't looted off the corpses, but after doing the same themselves, they would soon forget all about it.

Much later, after they'd found the two more she had recently met and more violently dealt with, it was far too late to raise the alarm. Because by then, inside of the engine room of the ship, stood one large, angry gorilla, armed to the teeth!

* * *

Her stealthy streak finally ended when one pirate suddenly opened the door leading into the engineering bay, her being right behind it. She instantly killed him, of course, but the two pieces of his corpse slid down the ladder. The gory remains landed right next to three pirate engineers, who were having a drink beside the ship's main reactor core, and splattered bloody guts all over them.

Right away they grabbed their guns and opened fire, while she had to close the distance and use her axe. Cat knew enough engineering to realize that firing even a single burst from her auto railgun could spell doom for everybody on the ship. So she leaped towards them, using her suit's newly-installed engines, and one of the engineers immediately lost half of his upper torso.

The closest one showered her with rapid fire from his snub particle-beam gun, blasting chunks of her suit's armor. Cat threw her entire weight forwards, crushing his torso between her own massive body and the nearest bulkhead.

The last pirate picked up a shield and vibrosword from the boarding rack next to the wall and charged her. He was a good melee fighter and managed to nick her suit some more, but eventually he overextended himself and she broke his neck with her axe's megasteel shaft.

The pirates were already aware of her presence by now, and Cat quickly sat behind the ship's main engineering controls, punching in new commands and locking the main engines. She then exited the bay and closed the door, trapping the corridor leading to it with a couple of well-placed plasma grenades.

Cat rapidly moved towards the ship's command deck, this time switching to her auto railgun. Close to the mid-center of the ship, where most of its crew quarters were, the pirates finally intercepted her. They had barricaded the main corridor, using a couple of bulkheads that they had pried off the walls.

The very second they saw her, a devastating cannonade of pulse beams and laser fire was unleashed right at her. She *almost* stepped forwards and into the firing line, but her mind screamed no. Instead, the gorilla waited and scouted all enemy positions with her weapon's integrated scanner. It took long enough that most of them used up all the energy in their power packs, and had to begin reloading their weapons.

Cat stepped around the corner and with well-trained footwork, advanced, firing her auto railgun at the pre-scanned targets. The pirates had good cover, but simply no good-enough tacticians to lead them – they were woefully unprepared for what happened next. The single Terran had used her heavy weapon to a devastating effect, killing those whose bodies were even slightly showing above the cover line first, and heavily suppressing those yet hiding behind it.

Screaming with fear and frantically calling their crewmates to come to their aid, the pirates were unable to move. After Cat lobbed a plasma grenade behind their now-useless cover, they all burned to death. She then walked over the now mangled and pierced bulkheads, reloading her weapon on the go. Moving slower now, her weapon scanner picking up more targets rushing towards her and she stood still, taking a knee while leveling up the railgun.

She greeted the second group of pirates with a devastating hail of projectiles, as soon as they turned around the corner. Foolishly, they still believed their friends alive yet, holding the barricade, which was yet another costly, deadly mistake.

Cat stood up and reloaded the auto railgun. Her faceplate showed that the weapon was overheating, she unholstered her Krupp hand auto-laser. Since there was no other mag slot on her back big enough to lock the auto-railgun, Cat used the weapon's comfortable sling and while it dangled from her left side, she moved forward, laser in hand.

Being a bulky person, she had always loved the idea of using sub-machine guns the way normal people used pistols. Its stock folded to one side, she raised the weapon and switched off the safety. She moved quickly towards the hangar while still spending an odd second or two checking the opened crew cabins for hidden enemies, aiming her laser inside every single one when she looked.

Only one pirate dared to actually try and conceal herself in the last room by using a holo cloak, but was unable to utilize her advantage. Cat caught part of the hidden enemy's shadow. In fact, the cloak was almost perfect while the person who used it stood still, which the pirate was – until she twitched ever so slightly.

Cat immediately fired, her weapon set on full-auto, incinerating the whole room but hitting her target only slightly. The pirate then leaped at Cat, swinging with a vibrodagger aimed at her chest. The Terran moved with a speed almost unnatural for a creature of her size, and her fist met with the pirate's head, crushing the enemy's faceplate inwards.

She left the cabin with her enemy on the floor, choking to death with their own blood. Multiple pieces of faceplate steel embedded in her skull wouldn't slow her death either. Cat reloaded the Krupp laser and placed it in its holster, raising the auto railgun again.

She had reached another intersection of the ship's main corridor, and quickly turned left towards the command deck, following the map she stole earlier from that pirate. On it there was an elevator and instead of haphazardly stepping inside, she used her cybernetic arm to crush the roof. With her suit's engines, she flew up the elevator's shaft, and after a second of calculated hesitation, fired the weapon through the closed outer doors.

The auto railgun's armor-piercing module allowed accurate weapon fire, even from behind such an obstruction as thick as a four-inch megasteel door. She landed on the other side, effortlessly flying through what was left of the elevator doors. Before her lay another couple of dead pirates, their bodies almost shredded by the destructive power of her railgun.

Amazingly, most aliens shunned that weapon technology and had for millennia adopted particle-beam guns. Yes, a professional soldier like Cat would agree – those weapons were indeed fearsome. They were also way too expensive and a bitch to maintain in the field. Compared to Terran weaponry these were also power-hungry; one could fire a good nine, or even ten shots *more* with a railgun rifle. That same thing also was true for Terran laser weapons, which were some of the best in the Galaxy. Eight shots more at the very least, with the same-sized power pack.

Maintaining weapons and repairing them in the field was something of an utmost importance to any soldier, and Cat had fought almost everywhere, in any environment possible. There were only two weapon systems she could always rely on, other than her honed deadly instincts, and those were the laser and railgun combo. Of course, that was in addition to any grenades Cat could get her hands on and as many as her uplifted-race back could carry.

She grinned behind her faceplate. Thank the Universe that her patrons were Humans, and not one of those filthy Core races. Simply imagining how they would address her and, as a matter of fact, all other human clients, made her blood boil.

*"Waste of genetic material!"* or *"Defective clients!"* – They would shout, before any human or any angry-enough Kil'ra or gorilla would beat them to a pulp, sometimes to an inch of their lives.

Good! It didn't matter how genetically superior they were. In fact, Cat was the type to acknowledge anyone's right to exist – as long as they did the same. Recalling her training, Cat suddenly realized that she had killed many more enemies with fists and ranged weapons than by using explosive ordinance. As her teacher had taught her, grenades were a precious thing! To be used *only* when the maximum number of enemies were in their blast radius. Otherwise that would be a waste, and soldiers weren't supposed to use expensive equipment or ammunition willy-nilly.

What was that one of her human friends' army sergeants used to say?

*"A gross misallocation of war materials"*.

She almost laughed as she remembered one of her previous commanders, how he would preach the ultimate importance of rapid movement during combat. She'd not followed his advice this time. Thinking a little bit more about it, Cat justified her new approach as *"Meticulous preparation for rapid tactical advance."* and she was liking it more and more.

Never could she have imagined that a moment of preparation or calm and patient observing, would bring her a victory so much more satisfying. The bridge was almost taken; there was a big alien, armed with a shield and power mace. He stood in her way, and she was quick to note his additional use of an energy shield. It was useless to spend good power packs chipping his field and then that shield he held.

Cat rapidly switched weapons and assumed a defensive posture – anyone sporting equipment that good was clearly a dangerous opponent. She was right; her enemy dashed at her with amazing speed using his suit engines, and shield-bashed Cat with such power that her massive gorilla body flew across the room like an empty crate. She barely managed to move her head off the path of his power mace.

When he crushed the bulkhead behind her Cat rolled to the side, raising her axe in an attempt to block that next attack since she was sure one had to come any second.

It didn't.

The pirate was a master in close combat, and instead took defensive posture himself. He advanced slowly towards Cat, forcing her to fight on his terms, making her waste precious time. She was going to get cornered and eventually killed soon... *if* her brain couldn't think of a way to defeat him.

Cat screamed, imitating her most enraged state, and swung the axe in a way that almost left her defenseless. But this was a clever ruse – she knew that walking around and taking her time wasn't going to work now. Her new commander had given explicit orders, which she was following to the letter, and time was of the utmost importance.

In a moment of extreme concentration, the pirate, otherwise a master at his style, made one tiny, but dooming mistake. Successfully fooled, he had assumed that Cat was going into her racial fit of rage, so common for gorilla kind that most, if not all aliens who fought them, knew of it.

He again dashed with lighting speed, mace swinging and shield slightly raised, prepared to connect with her faceplate. Indeed a devastating attack, and for the ruse to work, she took the shield-slam with her head while leaning forwards, stepping into his weapon's arc. With her hands close to the base of her axe's blade instead of the handle's end, she held the axe in place, and the pirate simply impaled his torso on it.

Cat used her mass and half-turned, both hands still pushing the blade forwards and up, until it severed both hand and shoulder.

Before locking the ship's mainframe, Cat removed the belt of her kill and placed it on her own waist. Thankfully, her own body was almost as big as the pirate who lay dead at her feet. Picking up her auto railgun again, she almost ran down the corridor that led towards her last destination – the ship's main hangar. She had wasted enough time skulking in the shadows and despite the fact that this operation had lasted no longer than a few minutes, she feared for the life of her new captain.

So much so, that when she met with another barricaded intersection, Cat simply ran forwards, head on, into their weapons fire, herself shooting two explosive missiles from her shoulder launcher. Their pulse bolts hit her already-activated shield, decreasing its strength, but a second afterwards they too were hit and blown to pieces by her missiles – together with their barricade.

Leaping directly into the plasma fire and stepping over their still-twitching, smoldering remains, Cat didn't stop for the next minute and a half, shooting and expending all of her integrated missile launcher's ammunition, along with most of those grenades she had brought with her. Up until now, the pirate numbers had been decreased by twenty-three and she assumed they hadn't had many more crewmates to throw at her.

Lest it was the pirate captain himself or herself. Cat cared not of what their gender was, or their sexual orientation, they were pirates and therefore walking *deadaliens*. Hmm, that word sounded nice and had she been a hamster, she would've patented it, always pointing to whomever used it that it was her, Cat, who thought of it first.

Pah!

Cat was startled, as before the very door leading into the ship's hangar, a heavy trooper suddenly landed before her, engines screaming, aiming his hand-held anti-armor particle-beam gun at her chest.

* * *

By that time, her captain Anit'za had left his already shot-to-hell shuttle and taken care of six pirates already.

He had waited patiently while they, at first, tried to unsuccessfully hack his shuttle's air lock controls. Then they launched a single EMP shoulder-held missile and disabled the shuttle altogether, but not before he had welded the doors shut. The pirates were annoyed as hell, but could do nothing else except manually melt their way in. All waiting was useless now, as he knew that sooner or later, they would reach and overwhelm him.

There was one big *if* on the way though – weighing around three hundred pounds, and with muscles of figurative (and in the case of one arm, literal) megasteel, running around the ship, crushing everything that she saw.

Soon she'd breach the hangar doors, he hoped, and for as long as he could, Anit'za distracted the many pirates present here. At least, before their captain, that cheeky sod, had finally used her little brain-cells properly, ordering one of her useless minions to plant a breaching charge onto his shuttle's hull.

He sighed and tried to calculate the decreased value of his poor, unfortunate shuttle – not in creds, but salvage. It wasn't that much, after all, the amount of punishment that those vagrants had unleashed upon it was considerable. Anit'za *had* to come out charging, and soon found himself surrounded by sods from all sides. All of who, as he soon noticed, tried desperately to look intimidating.

Amusing!

The first thing he did was to annoy them even more, by chopping off one of the closest sod's head and then, while hiding behind his armored body, shoot two more enemies. Better that he used the dead as a shield; he had to be careful not to take cover or let them do the same, behind all of those beautiful cargo crates lying around the hangar.

He had, in fact, performed a scan earlier and found out that they were full of the most illegal items one could imagine. Stuff that the local constabularies would pay good money to get their hands on, whenever he returned back on Cav colony. It was what they called "evidence hunting" and each colonial security chief had a special fund set aside to purchase illegal goods. They then either used said evidence to hunt for the criminals themselves or called for I-Sec assistance.

Either way, the dzenta'rii aimed to collect and even

entertained the notion that the sizable sum he'd receive from the constabularies would be more than enough for upgrades and repairs! Therefore Anit'za moved around quickly, shooting one full power pack at his nearest armored target, blowing the sod to pieces.

"Overconfidence in your armor protection will get you nowhere, vagrant Sods!" – Captain Anit'za screamed at the rest, and continued moving himself in such a way, so that they would be forced to use his unfortunate shuttle's hull for cover.

As expected, they redoubled their futile efforts to shoot him dead – they were no longer trying to capture or intimidate him into surrender.

By the second minute, that corpse shield he had used was looking more and more like a piece of hard-pounded, badly-sliced pig. Of course, Anit'za knew what pigs looked and tasted like – he already had one for dinner back on Cav. Bacon was bloody delicious!

Anit'za leaped forwards and reached another pirate, who was promptly stabbed through his chest and then used as Flesh Shield Number Two. By that time, most of the poor sods were confused as hell, and scared crazy. Anit'za knew this for certain because he had turned on his PDA, hacking their local wireless link, and was listening to everything they said.

It was even more interesting than he could've expected!

Cat was doing exactly what neither he, nor the pirates, thought possible for one such as her. Appearances were always deceiving, and he himself could clearly vouch for the validity of such a statement, by virtue of his own existence.

Soon Anit'za was openly laughing without restrain at

the hilarity that ensued. Before long, those pirates still wandering around the ship, realized that a huge and heavily-armed gorilla had snuck past their guards using stealth and guile, of all things.

He laughed even harder when, with panicked voices, the pirates reported to their captain that the door to main engineering was welded shut and the corridor booby-trapped with explosives. Worse yet, they had suddenly lost all navigational controls, since the ship's engine was turned off.

*Silly sods!*

Anit'za continued laughing while listening to his hiding nearby captain opponent, shouting out now ever-so-useless orders, attempting to wrest control of a situation that was far beyond her ability to cope to begin with. At that very moment, Anit'za was genuinely thinking of introducing himself over their all-so-perfectly-hacked-by-him comms link.

He decided not to for it was far too amusing and also most interesting, to listen to their confused and already terrified voices. You see, he was recording it all for posterity. Well that and, perhaps, selling it on G-net for a hefty sum of creds to some Imperial Morale Officer. Those crafty buggers could make up an asteroid from a speck of dust, yes they could.

Yet, despite his skill and clever tactics there were moments when the sods managed to land a hit. Thankfully, Anit'za moved his body in such a way so that those particle bolts would hit the armor, *not* his fabulous uniform. Eventually he was hit again and then multiple times over. He had to take cover, sadly, behind one of the soon-to-be-his cargo boxes.

Fortunate as it may be, his enemies weren't that keen

on hitting their own cargo either, and he enjoyed a brief respite from shooting and fighting. During that time, the pirates lost nearly half of the crew and the control over their command deck. Evidently, their second-in-command, who was a special kind of overly cheeky sod – a *war master*, got himself sliced while defending the bridge.

The sudden drop in fighting spirit was evident, even with the pirate's faceplates on. Anit'za choose this moment to unveil the fact he had been listening to them all along. Their captain was furious and ordered his PDA to be jammed.

Anit'za simply turned off.

The truth was that, long ago, he had planted a fake link into their captain's PDA. Therefore, before they could all look in his direction, he began acting confused, tapping his forearm and all that. He insinuated that, their own captain was faking his hacking of their systems. After all, how could Anit'za get into her PDA, if his own was, in fact, powered down?

It was a very silly excuse, but low-key wannabe pirates (in general) were not incredibly smart, and they all bought it. They looked back and forth amongst each other, trying to process what this might mean. Using the moment of confusion, he then ran towards the nearest sod and impaled him on his energy saber.

*Meat Shield Number Three...*

* * *

Cat almost dodged that last energy bolt!

Her looted shield overheated and shut down, she

returned fire with the auto railgun and nicked the heavy trooper. They began dodging left and right, up and down the corridor, using their engines, firing at each other without almost any interruption.

Bulkheads were melting, pieces of shredded megasteel flying everywhere and bouncing off their armor-plating like giant shrapnel. First one, then two of her spare power packs were used up, while she saw how the heavy trooper threw three slagged packs away.

As expected, his beastly weapon was using much more power than hers. She could've easily gained an edge, had she been fighting against him and him alone. Sadly, most of her ammo was already spent and the spare Krupp laser was hardly good enough to go through that thick armor-plating of his.

Her grenades were long gone, too.

Locking on her last shots with the weapon's integrated scanner, Cat tried her best to outmaneuver the heavy trooper, changing direction mid-flight and aiming at his legs. She hit him, but herself was hit in return, with her chest armor-plating melting away.

Both fell on the bulkheads below, heavily wounded, but it was Cat who crawled close towards her enemy and split his head with her axe.

She pulled her vibroaxe from the corpse, and leaning on its shaft, managed to somehow get up. Limping, Cat reached the hangar door controls and punched the door open, only to see her captain wounded and bleeding behind cover, the last pirates on the ship prowling around, trying to flank him.

Cat completely forgot any sense or any thought of tactics and restraint. With a mighty roar, she ran towards the stunned group of pirates, leaving behind her a gory trail. No longer feeling any pain and pumped up full of adrenaline levels that would kill a normal human, Cat cleaved through the small group of pirates, dismembering two with her first swing.

At that moment, her captain jumped from behind the cargo crate he was hiding and engaged his pirate counterpart. Violently clashing, their melee weapons soon started splashing blobs of plasma and electricity all around them.

Even heavily wounded, Anit'za was the epitome of a Dzenta'rii duelist's form and grace. His opponent, on the other hand, wasn't wounded, but the intense anger and confusion made her advantages moot. Soon the Dzenta'rii concentrated his form, unleashing a flurry of a dozen deceiving and distracting blows, but only one punched through the pirate's captain defense. Her ugly head was sliced horizontally and the upper part flew away, burning with plasma fire.

Anit'za collapsed on the floor, crawling towards the nearest corpse. There was a medspray still in that pirate's hand, and he desperately needed it.

Cat killed four more pirates before the fifth and last impaled her leg with his vibrosword. She fell, tripping him with her axe, and they rolled on the floor, bashing each other, trying to gain the upper hand. Both fighters lost grip on their weapons, and the gorilla, even enraged, couldn't overpower her opponent since his armor had an exoskeleton.

She broke one of his legs, but the pirate managed to almost pull off her cybernetic arm. Cat screamed, her rage no longer completely dulling out the pain. She tried reaching for what was left of her arm.

Her enemy had pinned Cat to the ground and began

bashing her head, locking both of his exoskeleton-powered arms in. Her rage-dimmed sight could barely see one of the pirate's eyes through his broken faceplate. He screamed victoriously, and as her own helmet began buckling before his assault, Cat frantically reached again for her arm and this time she managed to grab it.

To his terror, the pirate felt his helmet and skull being crushed. Screaming, he looked down at the gorilla's severed cybernetic arm. She was pulling one of its main controls, and with what little power was left in the arm's energy capacitor, the megasteel fingers wrapped around the side of his skull. The last thing he heard was the horrifying crunch of crushed bones, before his eyes and brain popped out and splashed all over the floor-plating.

Her last enemy now succumbed, Cat dropped his body and her cyber-arm, her tired limbs flopping to the ground. She had a huge hole in her chest, a piece of her leg was missing, and her left arm was severed. The effects of her rage had suddenly vanished, and the pain was back with a vengeance.

She couldn't even breathe evenly, as she was choking on her own blood. Cat heard somebody crawling towards her and tried turning her head to the side. She almost lost consciousness, but she saw the face of her captain, a medical injector in his hand. He had left a long, bloody trail behind him, but he had almost reached her. She soon felt the sting of the medspray, as he injected the life-saving regenerative solution into her body.

Cat screamed as her body started letting off steam from all of the wounds she had. They slowly began closing, as Anit'za used three more medpacks, four total, one after the other. Then the injector slipped out of his hand, and he lay bleeding beside Cat.

Her mangled armor scratched the thin crust of skin formed over her recently-regenerated wounds, as she leaned over her captain. His lips were moving and Cat moved her head closer to listen. It was in time to hear him say:

"*Cough*... the... che... cheeky sod," – he spat more blood – "can... hear... me?... *cough*..."

"What sod, Captain? Please, tell me what to do!" – Cat panicked, as her captain lay dying in her hands.

"Not... you... that... sod... *cough*," – he pointed somewhere nearby with hand shaking – "over there... mmm... *cough*... sodding... meds!"

Cat looked around and saw the pirate captain's body. Limping there and back wasn't painless, but she did try with her best speed. Instead of searching the corpse where it stood, she just dragged it back with her, and left it beside her captain. There were two, brand-new medpacks on their captain's belt, and she feverishly reloaded the injector.

The solvent hissed while it entered Anit'za's wounds, but instead of screaming, he slightly chuckled. As she used the second medpack, Cat heard him whispering:

"Those silly sods almost killed... us..." – and he finally lost consciousness.

She dragged herself towards the ship's engineering bay.

Took her almost half an hour to limp there and disarm the booby-trapped corridor, but eventually she removed the system lock and reactivated the ship's engines. Then there was another painful limp towards the bridge, where she almost fell unconscious while squeezing through the bent elevator doors.

Reaching the main navigational pit, Cat removed the

other locks that she'd placed inside the main computer, and programmed the course to Cav's wormhole navigational beacon. Wasn't perfect, but who cared; the ship had been successfully boarded by the two of them, *alone*!

Cat could almost taste the recognition she and Anit'za would receive when they reached Cav. The more she knew her captain, the more Cat was sure he had something planned, something wonderfully elaborate and big!

This ship was heavily damaged and even though she wasn't an engineer, Cat knew that repairing it would cost a crap-ton of creds. The cargo haul that those pirates had had would surely help, but it was doubtful that such a sum could be nearly enough.

* * *

It was with thoughts like these Cat tried to stand up and limp back to her captain, yet she was actually dreaming. The stress her body had been through could've easily broken most people, but gorillas were tough.

Decades ago, when the Pirate Lord Mahimm's armada had invaded Earth, it was the young and recently uplifted gorillas whose capture and enslavement was one of his primary objectives, for that very reason. The uplift research institute in Kongo Africa had been assaulted by wave after wave of pirate stormtroopers.

Its first and only defense were soldiers, veterans from the recent World War, who stood in their way. For two weeks, long after the end of the space battle, the vastly outnumbered human troops entrenched and surrounded, protected the enclave. It was home to not only every single uplifted gorilla, but also a small city where those human scientists responsible for the gift of greater sentience lived.

At first their family members helped with moving the wounded and repairing the earthworks. Then, one by one, the civilians joined the defenders, picking up the weapons of the dead. Day after day, their numbers dwindled, and in the end all of the young men and women capable of fighting died.

Those who were left, old people and children, were the last humans able to defend their clients. Instead of hiding or running away, they made a wall with their bodies and died by the thousands, keeping all gorillas from enslavement.

That was the hour that the First Rage was recorded. The uplifted gorillas had been kept innocent of this information, safely inside their jungle compound, away from the ravages of war. They saw flashes, heard the explosions and were told not to worry. But as their patrons died by the millions all over the world, the gorillas soon understood what had to be done.

Humans were part of their *tribe*, after all, and they would protect them with all of their strength. As the battered slaver battalions were slaughtering the last women and children standing between them and their "prize", they were shaken by a powerful roar. A wave of gorillas, almost mad with rage, threw themselves at them and began tearing their limbs apart, entire trees were uprooted and used to crush those slavers piloting power-armor.

Their vehicles were overturned, hatches ripped open, crews turned into bloody paste inside by younger gorillas who were small enough to get in. In the distance, another battle was being fought between the first Terran strategic armor, called "Mighty Kong", and two lances of pirate machines.

The human pilot lost, but he sacrificed himself, activating his self-destruct device, his reactor melting the last two remaining pirate mechs. Days after, the gorillas were mourning over the bodies of thousands upon thousands dead humans, a blood debt that never could be repaid.

* * *

Cat awoke from her sleep and found herself hungry beyond belief.

Removing what was left of her once-durable armored suit, she walked towards the hangar, only to find her captain cooking food in the ship's mess hall. She helped him clumsily; since the loss of her cybernetic arm, Cat was having problems with balance. Nevertheless, without saying a word, they cooked a huge pot of meat and vegetable stew, and ate it. Her captain looked pale from the loss of blood, but it seemed his spirit was still high.

"So what about finding a pet cat for the ship, eh?" – he murmured, while sipping one spoonful of broth after another.

"I am told they have excellent kitties back on Earth, in a nation-state called Japan. Yes, that is your next order, Cat: you are to use my near-scrapped shuttle, fly to Earth, and get yourself chosen by a cat."

The gorilla blinked a couple of times, and smiled, confused at her captain.

"But Sir, it sounds more like a shore leave. What about you, Cap'? You also need rest after an ordeal like this."

"Bah! Ordeal, is it? I'll tell you about what 'ordeal'

means. Seeing the last bottle of wine from your House's best reserve. The last! But it's pointless lamenting one of the most horrifying events in recent Galactic history," – he said, waving theatrically with his hand in the air and continuing right ahead:

"This is *not* a bout of shore leave, or a cushy assignment. Do you think that finding a good cat is easy, Cat? No, it isn't, let me tell you. Cats are important creatures, as I have found out, and quite helpful. This won't be a proper starship without one, as my extensive research on the matter has shown. So!, as soon as we land on Cav, off to Earth you go, Commander! I need you to complete this extremely-important 'Pet Procurement Mission' as carefully as possible. We certainly do not need a *fickle* cat running pell-mell around our ship and stirring up trouble. Choose wisely, as it is a command decision of great importance!"

Cat slowly began to absorb what she had heard.

The new rank came first – *Commander?!*

She had been trusted with almost as much command responsibility as her captain had. The act of trust came second. Anit'za thought so highly of Cat; she had long thought that her being a so-called "bulkpounder" didn't give her the right to be second-in-command. But wise her captain was, and she accepted her new responsibilities in the very same way Cat dealt with anything that ever stood in her way – a frontal assault, but this time, a carefully planned one.

# Chapter 5

## *Brynjar*

Brynjar's home was Earth.

He was the first son of the young Asgard generation born after the Second Great War. A bit different than the rest of his peers, but not so much as to become an outcast – not at first that is.

With his white hair and green eyes, Brynjar was an oddity to say the least. When it was found that his link to Yggdrasil was stronger than the rest of his peers, his young parents were bristling with pride. Their feelings were soon tested, however, as Brynjar couldn't manifest any of the feats other Asgardians of his age could easily manage.

Yes, he had the power, but no matter how hard he tried, nothing ever happened. For it seemed that the flow of All-Father's power or Oden Force as it was called by the Asgard, was too much for him to control. So the chasm between Brynjar and his peers grew and swelled to such an extent, that he soon found himself more at home among the humans of Earth than with his own race.

Midgaard, the new city the young Asgardians had built after the end of the War, was located in Finland. Though a cold and somewhat inhospitable place for some others, the Asgard were able to easily thrive there. Extreme cold and difficult terrain was nothing to a race who stood almost fifteen feet tall and weighed more than a ton. Their giant size was also augmented by legendary constitution – you could fire a cannonball at them and they wouldn't even flinch.

Finland had been hit hard during humanity's last war by deluded, brainwashed humans. These idiots had ravaged what precious few industry and infrastructure the Finns had. Everything, all that destruction and death, in the name of some demented ideal called "Socialist Justice". Brynjar didn't know what that was – frankly he wanted to do other things much more interesting to him than study about some past dead madmen.

He grew up ever further from his own, but he found the good, stern Finnish people to be a great source of inspiration. Brynjar knew that he would never become like the rest of his kin. The pure image of a stalwart Asgardian warrior, wielding Oden Force was a future impossible for him to achieve. Therefore and after much thought, Brynjar went and joined the human kids, diligently studied all Terran sciences in their schools.

Somehow that lonely, giant child became everybody's friend, and despite his size, he never found himself alone on the playground. Instead of living as an outcast on Earth too, Brynjar stayed each month in a different home, just as beloved by his many friends as by their parents.

The Asgardian youth learned the meaning of Finnish *sisu*, their greatest national quality and absorbed it as his own. Instead of spiraling into the depths of depression over his precarious situation, Brynjar stubbornly tried any craft he could to find out what he was good at. He spent twenty odd years working all kind of jobs, while traveling across Finland.

During that time, since being interested in the martial ways was a thing most natural for most members of his race, he also became really engaged in boxing. Brynjar found the art of pugilism to be rather alluring, and with him being an Asgardian, he certainly possessed the physical predisposition to become one of the greatest boxers in his generation.

He spent many hours training outside, using the great outdoors as his personal gym and one evening, he was found digging a tunnel into a rock-face using his bare fists. The man who stumbled upon him was none other than Rocky Marciano, legendary heavyweight boxer.

It was 1968 when this chance meeting occurred. By now, Marciano had already defended his title for so many years that the World Boxing Federation had appointed him Eternal Heavyweight Champion of the World. Still, he had already retired from active fights in the ring itself, and the position of Eternal Champion was as much political as it was athletic. Now the famous boxer spent his days making appearances to throngs of fans and hosting events in as many places as possible across the globe, all part of his celebrity duties.

Playing the role of the celebrity did get overwhelming at times, though, as it did for most anybody. There were times when even Rocky would find himself on an evening stroll, away from the crowds, heading far from urban centers to achieve some quiet and reflection. Marciano had been doing just that after a public appearance in Finland when he'd heard the almost akin to sonic booms pounding sounds from afar and climbed the mountain to investigate.

He then stood in silent disbelief, watching how the five-meters-tall Asgardian pummeled the rocks to tiny pieces for a good hour, before finally showing himself. He demanded to fight Brynjar immediately, and upon agreeing, the young amateur was quickly and soundly defeated. Brynjar awoke some minutes afterwards with a splitting headache and more questions than he was able to ask in a week.

Rocky stayed in Finland for as long as Brynjar did,

and every single day beat the hell out of him, impressed nonetheless by the boy's profound determination. Marciano later said, in an interview for the Terran Holo News:

"That Asgard kid was built like a megasteel bulkhead and hit back quicker than a ramming spaceship! Mark my words, he will get really famous someday soon."

Brynjar enjoyed every minute of his brutal training with the boxing legend since it occupied his mind from other things. Deep down, he still thought about why it was that he wasn't able to control the flow of his Oden Force yet, instead of letting it get him down, he only focused harder. He buried himself even deeper in his studies, and there were days when he ran for many miles on end, trying to read various engineering and scientific works.

As he jogged Marciano ran away before him, carrying the PDA those books were holo projected on. It took him two years, but Brynjar overcame the innate sluggishness of his race, and soon managed to catch up and almost overpower his instructor. The day had come for teacher and student to part, after all, Marciano had more things to attend to than just his student. As he gave the boy a wet-eyed pat on the back by way of goodbye, the man reassured him that he'd always been cheering him on from afar.

Brynjar watched as his mentor stepped into the waiting transport ship, perfectly calm on the outside, and walked away quietly and grimly to return to his training. His body was about as strong as it could be – for now. Of course he would not stop his physical training; he had to maintain the shape he was in, at least.

No, now Brynjar's real attentions turned to feeding his mind.

* * *

Strangely enough, instead of disliking machines like many Asgardians, Brynjar actually found himself to be adept in tinkering with them – especially the mecha. The big ones, those that the humans called Strategic Armors. Towering and bristling with ship-size weapons and armor, those strategic weapons of war were notoriously hard to pilot and a nightmare to maintain.

Brynjar spent years reading technical manuals, repairing small mecha at first, then joined one mech gladiator's pit shop. Humans never asked why he was trying to become an engineer and a mecha jock, nor called him names behind his back. It was not the Terran Way to bar anyone from attempting to achieve something and Brynjar was accepted as is, left to prove himself by his own merit.

He failed multiple times, but the stern determination and sheer stubbornness he had adopted from his human nation's culture eventually helped him to succeed. While others rested, Brynjar trained; while they feasted, he practically slept in the holo battle pod; while they took vacations, Brynjar trained even more. And finally, it all paid off – his Mecha team won the Metal Sands of Mars Championship, three times in a row. At last Brynjar had something to back his name with, loads of fame, and even a small fortune.

His human colleagues started calling him "Suomi", recognizing his love for Finland and its national spirit that he'd adopted in all of his enterprises. That attitude changed when he went to his racial homeland, however. Visiting his estranged parents afterwards, sadly, he discovered that they had almost no interest in his career of choice. During his time with them, they repeatedly goaded and pushed him into trying to manifest his so-called "untapped power," using all sorts of shenanigans.

But the last straw was when he found that his mother had even made a wedding pact with another family, whose beautiful young daughter Gudrun was famed for her abilities and control of Oden Force. He left Asgard, disgusted with their attempts to manipulate his destiny, never marrying Gudrun.

She herself branded Brynjar a coward, condemning his love of human technology. Laughing, she proclaimed that some day he would come crawling back and beg on his knees for her affection. An apt student of how reality "worked", Brynjar knew better.

Bah, what a foolish girl she was!

What did Gudrun know of the world outside Asgard?

The Galaxy needed more builders, crafters, engineers and inventors; not some self-absorbed, ignorant folk.

He scorned her silently, never uttering a word, nor showing any emotions. His face, a motionless mask while she laughed at him, Brynjar calmly looked directly into her eyes. Gudrun's laughter quickly lost its strength and as he ever so silently turned and left, she watched, his back fading in the distance. Instead of arguing, which would be a useless waste of time in his mind, he simply headed for the Bifrost portal.

Perhaps she expected some reaction from him, maybe even an angry outburst?

Not him – not after his childhood spent growing up in Finland.

Brynjar knew perfectly well by now how to control his emotions and he calculated every move he would make with manic meticulousness. She was laughing nervously, together with her girlfriends, while the portal's energies swirled around him. What Gudrun did not know then is that she would see him in the news some time later, and soon after speaking with passing humans, finally understand what a great, foolish mistake she'd made.

In her vanity, Gudrun thought him weak, a coward even. Not a *proper* Asgardian, no; someone more akin to humans, with his abnormal obsession with technology. Brynjar was, in fact, a hard worker, a pure genius even and in a field that no other Asgardian had ever excelled. A quality that she would only realize the value of when it was too late.

She did receive one advance glimpse of her error, though. Some days after he had already left, Gudrun suddenly realized that the flow of his aura had been simply *bristling* with power. Something that only one of her elders, Frigg herself, had ever possessed. And years later, when she had finally sought out the mecha gladiator for whom Brynjar had worked and listened to all of his tales, she realized in the end what a prejudiced idiot she was.

It was her and her race who had failed – not Brynjar.

* * *

Never giving Gudrun another thought, Brynjar soon found his way into outer space and after some planning, he traveled to the great asteroid colony of Cav. Famous for their great mech factories, the "Steel Bear" colony, as they were also called, soon became Brynjar's second home.

Because of his fame as the Mecha Martian

Championship winner, he was quickly employed as Junior Chief Engineer in one of their main mecha facilities. Brynjar continued learning with the same hunger, vigor, and with amazing speed reached the position of Chief Engineer. One of his many duties made him responsible for the testing and debugging of new mecha models.

Yet in his spare time, Brynjar was designing something new – a prototype strategic armor, first of its class, made to accommodate an Asgardian. For years he had tried to find a way to unlock what his parents had called "untapped power", but without any notable success. Instead of trying to meditate or trek to remote planets in search of spiritual teachers, both of which he found to be idiotic ideas, Brynjar, in his already well-known stubborn manner, devised another approach.

Why not use all of that power and *course* it through the mech's power core?

Easier said than done!

He tried again and again, slagging multiple prototypes and spending lots of time scrounging for parts at the local salvage yard. Whenever he wasn't at work, he was there instead and at times, people actually thought that he was living there. They weren't entirely wrong; in reality, he did stay there for so long that the owner simply gave him the opening code, allowing Brynjar to work there uninterrupted.

He built a functioning mecha pit all by himself at the scrap yard. Near the outer surface of the asteroid, the yard had very low gravity, which he cleverly used combined with his great strength to build his prototype machine quicker. Brynjar called it "The Rock", in memory of his boxing coach. Using only random salvage and designing even the smallest of parts by himself, his focus and meticulous determination again impressed everybody who saw him work.

Soon, there were more than a dozen random strangers from all Terran client races, and all with engineering inclination, who feverishly worked to aid his project to the finish. Prominent holo-artists visiting Cav created together a giant war decal for his mecha. To the unaware observer, it looked as if the machine was closer than it in reality was, and this clever illusion would certainly aid in combat.

Brynjar had designed the mecha to be a close-combat machine. Despite its size, the speed of this mecha was exceptional and instead of having "cannon hands", The Rock was equipped with Tesla Fists. Also called Power Gloves, these dangerous gauntlets generated a superheated plasma field, melting most things – if they didn't get crushed by the punch. The original weapon model was created for power armors, but Brynjar saw no problem adapting it for something as tall as sixty meters and weighing more than one hundred tons.

He also mounted medium-range laser cannons on his shoulders and a powerful long-range missile rack on the torso's back. Even with all the additional help his project took almost an entire year to complete and drained most of his finances.

Now, Brynjar had to find a way to deploy and test the mecha, while making some money in the process. As if by miracle, a favorable opportunity presented itself just mere hours after the space paint on the armor had started drying up. A nearby mining colony reported the discovery of a drug-runner base, located on one of its solar system's habitable moons. The drug cartel operating from that base had already set up a large operation, and in addition to their regular troops, they had three full lances of pirate mechs.

Brynjar didn't care that each lance was comprised of

up to three machines – he was sure of the design quality and skill he possessed.

There was a link for the job on his G-net profile, with personal mission contract and full salvage rights included. He saw that someone had personalized the contract and sent it to *him* first, before anybody else. It was rather peculiar, but he had long learned to not overthink and to grab any chance that the Universe offered.

Brynjar ran as fast as he could to the station's docks and practically begged anybody whose ship had a cargo hold large enough to ferry his machine into the war zone. For some strange reason all captains outright refused his plea, each citing one or another reason and only one of the ships docked there, whose captain was a male Dzenta'rii by the name of Anit'za, agreed to do so without question.

His services were mostly free; Brynjar only had to cover the fuel cost and protect the landing site with his new mech – all in all, a good deal.

Anit'za was tall for his race and sported the usual fancy hairdo and wore a beautiful, red uniform spacesuit that really did accentuate his slim facial features. Dzenta'rii looked almost the same as humans from the outside; internally however, they were two completely different species. They were slimmer and slightly shorter than the average human, with elongated skulls, and some of the older noble houses even had slightly pointed ears. It was not easy to avoid staring at this exquisite being as they finished outlining the terms of their business, but Brynjar calmly managed, right up to the point where they shook hands.

The starship captain had one very strange, older-model starship – an early Terran Patrol Cutter. Fast and agile, the vessel had lots of cargo and hangar space, and was easily able to accommodate his mech. Brynjar took his time

142

and slowly walked the giant machine into the belly of the IMS *Starshatter*, but he did notice after leaving his cockpit that there were no other crew members present.

When asked, Captain Anit'za replied that he was – *"Still actively recruiting the best and most talented crew members in existence!"* – and showed Brynjar to his cabin.

Using what creds were left in his PDA's cloud storage, Brynjar paid for the ship's fuel tanks to be fully loaded. He was down to a mere five creds afterwards, but he was confident in his piloting abilities and the strength of The Rock.

The short trip through hyperspace was largely uneventful, lest you count the elaborate meals Captain Anit'za cooked for the both of them. During those dinners, the Dzenta'rii excused his "bad" cooking skills multiple times, but Brynjar knew when he was being bullshitted and simply ate the delicious food. He had never eaten anything that good in his entire life so far, and the portions were huge.

The only other odd part of their journey was how Brynjar noticed that the captain looked rather anxious to find somebody, but since it wasn't Brynjar's business, he didn't ask.

The one week in hyperspace went by quickly, and soon the hull of the *Starshatter* emerged in orbit of their destination. It was a tiny moon, with rather bleak living conditions, but perfect for any drug cartel because of its remote location. The battle had already started, with some merc company performing a successful orbital drop and making a landfall.

They'd cleared an area and secured it against cartel foot troops, so that any other spaceships could land. Their commanders knew that those mech lances would soon attack and try to crush the beachhead, so they called for Anit'za to land as soon as possible. As Brynjar watched, Anit'za smiled and politely told them that, if *he* is to hurry his landing protocols with the breed of ship he possessed, they could then be good enough and reimburse him for any excess fuel used in atmospheric maneuvers.

The merc captain was clearly caught off guard by this request. His holo image blinked momentarily, while he thought about how to answer. The Dzenta'rii Captain, very politely and calmly asked him again, if he needed them on the ground faster. Caught in this manner, the merc captain nodded in agreement, and soon their vessel descended in a way that no spaceship should.

* * *

Brynjar was almost sure they would crash yet, somehow that captain knew not only how to adequately fly the ship, but even used the atmospheric density to aid the descent. Indeed, in this way IMS *Starshatter* had used up lots of fuel, but that is why Captain Anit'za had negotiated with the merc's commander. Brynjar was left impressed at his business partner's skills and prudent nature.

After the ship was safely secured on the ground, Anit'za asked Brynjar to get in his mech and fulfill his part of the bargain. Brynjar only hoped that they wouldn't be overwhelmed by those pirate machines quickly. From what he had learned, they were greatly overconfident, always trying to show off their personal skill, sometimes even to the detriment of their overall strategy and tactics. As long as they didn't rush him, he at least had their cockiness to his advantage.

He wouldn't have the element of surprise though – he was positive that they'd scanned their ship while it landed. Knowing that there was a mech inside of it, those pirates could attack with one full lance, at least the first time. Well, he could take on three of them; his mech had enough armor, and by moving fast, he would be able to use the terrain for cover.

The side cargo doors slid open, and The Rock walked toweringly out of the ship, stones crushing to dust beneath its weight. He couldn't feel the "pops" of the boulders as they broke down instantly, but he could hear them faintly above the sounds of moving machinery, given the otherwise silent cabin around him.

Most pilots liked their computers to have VIs, speaking with soft female voices. Useless luxuries they were; something that he would never agree with spending his hard-earned money on and besides, who needed those? There was *no* purpose for some wimpy voice, that always stated the obvious.

"That system is activated, this weapon is on."

Blah blah blah!

He'd been training and working hard for years; he could easily see and understand everything without using overly expensive toys. In his opinion a pilot should not be pampered – he was a warrior, not some precious holo actor prancing around on a movie set.

Activating all systems, Brynjar strode towards the closest hills, giving his sensors a small range boost. His machine easily climbed the steep slope and then he almost bumped moving full speed into a small scout mech!

The pirate slime had cloaked his machine so well, that Brynjar's sensors didn't show even the tiniest of dots. No, but his eyesight didn't lie and he aimed the two shoulder laser cannons manually.

Two blue, thick laser beams hit the small target and melted through its hull. The scout mech's main reactor exploded, and the plasma wave picked up two more concealed, fully ladened with troops Armored Personnel Carriers on his sensor screen. He melted one of them before it landed on the second while it tried fleeing.

*"Nice try pirate filth, but not good enough!"*

Brynjar allowed himself to crack a small smile while his strategic armor climbed down and back towards the landing zone.

There were two more hills like this; he quickly contacted the mercs, telling them about what he had discovered and destroyed. He also politely reminded them of the number of his kills and claimed the salvage, just so there weren't any misunderstandings later – those last five creds were burning a hole in his pocket.

Suddenly he received a combat link from one of the mercs' forwards positions. On a holo feed coming directly from their own sensors, Brynjar saw the three medium SAs, slowly stomping through the merc's defense line. There were no way in hell that those tiny light tanks the mercs had, could even make a dent in the mechs' armor. He could use the sensor feed and fire his long-range missiles, but decided not to.

Brynjar had the habit of not disclosing the full capabilities of his machine right after the very first shot was fired. Indeed he had a long-range missile locking system installed in his mech. The secondary computer system was designed and only used as a target-tracking booster for long-range ordinance – heavy missiles, torpedoes, and such.

Those SAs were armed with an assortment of small and medium-particle beam guns only, therefore making its use a waste. Observing them, he realized their formation wasn't good at all anyways, as they were too far away from each other to benefit from their close-range firepower. Besides, his own lasers had a tad bit more range than their limited beam weaponry. Overheated less, too; with the heatsinks he had installed, Brynjar could fire more times and quicker than all of them.

He quickly ducked behind the closest hill, lying in wait for the pirate machines, calmly calculating what to do if his new system didn't work.

Brynjar shrugged – he would just have to do without... *that*.

Soon, his own sensors showed the enemy lance closing on his position and he side-stepped from cover, rapidly firing at the lead mech. Aiming at the left leg, The Rock's lasers again did the job perfectly, as the surprised enemy pilot lost balance and the pirate machine came crashing down almost intact, evoking a happy sigh from Brynjar.

Food and fuel were secure for the foreseeable future!

Perhaps he could sell those useless particle guns and buy proper Terran plasma cannons? That he noted instantly in his mind – there'd be plenty of time to peddle with Cav's equipment and salvage dealers later, after the battle had been won.

The second pirate mech moved swifter towards him and, closing the distance, fired a couple of shots at his torso. Brynjar easily dodged to the side using his speed advantage and the enemy fire glazed the ground. The upper body of his mech leaned forward as he made a dash at the closest enemy machine, swinging his right fist forward with lightning speed. He took some pot shots from the third mech, but those were only low-powered beams that scorched his armor slightly.

His target tried to step back, but was too heavy and sluggish to successfully evade the soon-to-connect brutish blows. After smashing his fist in its chest with his second hand, Brynjar crushed the gun aimed at his head and punched a hole through the enemy's torso – hitting him again and again.

While he was finishing the second mech, his other adversary tried to circle around and shoot him from the sides. Brynjar moved in such a way that the other mech he was pummeling into the ground stood between them, and blocked any attacks. The last pirate pilot fired all of his particle beams at him, not caring about his comrade's life. Brynjar barely managed to dash away, but the second mech exploded, and some of its hull bounced off of his armor.

The Rock almost lost balance and began leaning dangerously towards one side. If it was any other ordinary machine, stabilizing it would've been an impossible feat of piloting. Brynjar simply extended his powerful fist, knelt with his other foot, and placed the mech into a leaping position with ease. He then, again easily, stood up and turned around – to the clear surprise of the other pilot.

Stepping back, his enemy readied to shoot, but his guns had overheated and the mech was leaking coolant all over the place. Brynjar dashed forward, this time going for an uppercut, while his opponent stumbled back on his feet. To his credit, the pirate pilot tried placing one of his gun arms in the way, yet Brynjar's hit was so powerful that it went through the weapon, smashing it to pieces and crushing the SA's head.

Turning quickly around since his sensors had detected movement, Brynjar got savagely hit by a long-range laser in the chest and dashed towards cover. When he peeked for a look, he was not encouraged by what he saw. Behind the next hill and some eight kilometers away, a huge and heavily-armored SA lumbered towards him. It didn't have arms, but instead had two large laser cannons installed directly in both arm sockets, their barrels emitting insane amounts of heat. The enemy mech was using a lot of coolant and was a slow walker, but those guns were absolutely devastating from this long range.

He inspected the damage, quickly stepping back away from the ridge, ducking behind the hill itself. The rocks exploded, turning into smoldering pieces of melted stone the very second he moved backwards. There were some places on his chest armor that had been completely sundered by those cannons and angered, Brynjar flipped the on switch of his missile rack.

By the time his enemy started spouting some semi-intimidating crap over the comm link, more than twenty heavy missiles were flying at him. The mech had point defense guns, but those only managed to take down all but a few of the deadly ordinances, and the rest hit him straight on. There was a giant explosion, and Brynjar saw something flying in the air.

It was one of those laser cannons!

He quickly ran forwards and somehow managed to grab the valuable piece before it crashed on the ground. Brynjar moved again behind the hills and left his loot near the *Starshatter's* hangar. It was still red hot, steaming from the explosion. It looked like somebody had looted it from an old, derelict Terran cruiser.

While he was still turning back around and inspecting

his sensor readings, two small SAs suddenly leaped over the south hill and spewed dozens of dumb fire rockets at him. His own point defense guns couldn't deal with all of those. Even with the aid of the *Starshatter's* guns, multiple rockets exploded all over The Rock's hull. His machine was shaken and the damage report list grew ever larger, as one of his lasers was hit and now inoperative.

He was now rapidly losing coolant – they had landed a hit in the main tank. This battle had to end soon, otherwise no amount of salvaged loot would cover the repairs that his machine had suffered so far. Brynjar moved to the side, placing his good armor towards the enemy, and got shot again.

The two little mechs were probably part of the second lance, the same that the heavy laser-armed one was. Much faster than him and smaller, they handily dodged all fire coming from the guns of IMS *Starshatter*. He ran towards one of them swinging his fist, but that was a ruse – because instead of doing that, he knelt, rapidly rotated back, and shot his one remaining laser cannon at the mech behind him. The beam hit it square in the center torso area.

Another powerful explosion followed, and he turned his attention to the second mech as it ran away, peppering him with more rockets from a distance. It then quickly flew over the nearby hill, using its engines, vanishing from his scanners completely.

Brynjar regained his mech's balance and rose up, aiming the laser cannon over the opposite hill ridge. He didn't have to wait long because the sneaky small mech again tried to outflank him by flying over the hill and firing his rockets.

Its hull took a direct hit from Brynjar's laser and, losing altitude, came crashing down on the ground, exploding some seconds later. The Rock did manage to take all of that damage and keep fighting, but Brynjar knew it was nearing its limits. He couldn't move at full speed anymore, only one of his laser cannons was available, and he had expended his entire long-range missile magazine. Brynjar's armor was mostly lost, with some of his systems on the verge of critical failure.

He had no other choice, but to use his trump card and activate... *that*.

Brynjar was ninety percent sure that the last pirate lance was coming his way. Sure, the mercs had deployed more troops, even some anti-armor vehicles, yet those were one shot away from being melted into slag. You don't use puny little tanks against large, strategic weapons of war.

Besides, he knew that more reinforcements were on the way, probably some freelance SA company or something. Too bad for them! He came here *first* and he was determined to claim most, if not all of the salvage and juicy loot.

His sensors detected three more pirate mechs, and of those one was a heavy assault model. Brynjar readied himself and waited for a while before pushing the big red button at his left. Above the ridge, that large assault mech stomped towards him, aiming his large quad-particle cannons and he almost lost his composure.

These guns were so big that if need be, the pilot could attack spaceships in close orbit. That must have been what those pirates were thinking of in using this mech; most of the Imperial Minarchy's transports that were landing here converged in an orbital staging area, which if it were to be attacked, would result in the entire operation being ruined.

The enemy lance leader laughed at the battered

Asgardian mech over the comms, and ordered his two wingmen to finish him. Brynjar raised both his hands and moved towards them, as they circled around him with their vibroaxes and shields.

Perhaps it was Brynjar's lucky day, because if their leader had decided to instantly shoot, he might not have survived the battle. While his lightning-core device was charging up, he slid to the left, and countered his first attacker's axe strike with a speedy right hook. He then fired his laser at the shield arm at point-blank range, crushing the side of the first mech's torso with four, lightning-quick jabs.

The ground was already covered with wrecked, molten pieces of metal and there was thick smoke everywhere. The second fighter managed to land a hit with his axe and Brynjar's entire cockpit shook, as one bent piece of The Rock's hull almost crushed his head.

He grabbed the other mech's fallen shield off the ground, quickly pummeling his adversary, distracting him long enough so that he could hit his torso with the Tesla Gloves set on full power. The whole length of his fist entered inside the mech's chest, melting through armor, hull, and systems like butter – instantly incinerating the pilot.

With the edge of his vision, Brynjar noticed how the pirate lance leader aimed all four of his large beam cannons at his machine. He picked up the second mech's shield and turned against the pirate, while overlapping both shields' surfaces. The four particle beams hit him hard, easily melting through the shields. The Rock suffered extensive damage, but both the device and most of his primary systems were still operational.

Brynjar raised his arms in the air aiming them at the pirate's SA. He then clenched both fists before pressing another button, and screamed in great pain while all of his energy began coursing out of his body and into the mech's circuits. The entire machine glowed with the force of a small sun, and the ground beneath its feet began shaking while odd pieces of metal melted.

A gigantic ball of lighting formed between his mech's hands, and in an instant it streamed towards the enemy mech, violently smiting it. His enemy exploded with such force that The Rock was thrown back and landed inoperative on the ground. The nearby dropships and shuttles had to divert from their courses and perform erratic maneuvers to evade the massive shock waves.

It was some time before Brynjar was pulled out of his overheated mech by a group of nearby mercs. Yet, even though he had sustained serious injuries, the courageous Asgardian was alive, and would heal... eventually.

* * *

Brynjar awoke some days later, alone, in the medical bay of the *Starshatter* and slowly inspected his body. There were scars forming all over and he was still somewhat dizzy – but everything that he had planned was a resounding success.

He relaxed with a wide grin as he recalled his feats; to face not one, but *three* full lances of SA and be victorious made Brynjar feel like the heroes of old. He didn't care about any damage sustained, because the salvage would be more than substantial enough to fix it. He waved his hand before the medical sensor above his head and soon Captain Anit'za entered, carrying a happy smile on his face.

The man sat beside his bed and answered all of

Brynjar's questions. What had happened with the operation, where was all of his salvage and loot – those kinds of important things. The captain informed him that, after he'd been knocked out, more and more mercs had gathered at the landing area, and soon a multi-pronged, overwhelming attack crushed the backs of all surviving cartel forces.

Those few who surrendered were promptly loaded on transports and shipped back to Cav, where they would be interrogated, judged, and then publicly executed on G-net.

This was Imperial Minarchy's territory, after all, and any drug trafficking, production, or distribution was a crime punishable by death. Colonial Common Law was in effect everywhere Terrans lived and the punishment was always the same. Too many innocent sentients were suffering and dying because of hard drugs, especially the Deadly Three – Bling, Shining, and Stone Dust.

Those were absolutely horrible, because to create them cartels either employed slave labor extensively, tested on and/or used living sentients in their production. Their degenerative effects were powerful and once taken it was near impossible to clean your system of them.

Sentients who took Shining for example, they relived old, pleasant memories again and again, yet soon madness followed.

The fools who ingested Stone Dust felt themselves impervious to any harm and felt no pain whatsoever. In exchange for this dubious boon the recipient's life was doomed, as their internal organs and central nervous systems rapidly degraded.

The addicts who overdosed on Bling, often found themselves existing in a perpetual state of slow motion due to their forever warped brain activity. In time their now dragging, broken minds and bodies rotted away, ultimately "achieving" what many of those fools had always dreamt for – slowing down their existence.

Brynjar knew little of what the other widespread drugs effects' were, and even though there were few whose intake did not cause death or instant organ failure, there was no chance he'd ever think of touching them. The insidious Cartel drug-runners were also known to purposely give small doses of their "product" to unsuspecting people or enemies, therefore condemning them to suffering and death.

This small drug cartel had in fact been in the business of distributing the Deadly Three, so it had been a more than worthwhile operation to wipe them from the face of the Galaxy.

Anit'za also told Brynjar that all of his stuff had been loaded on board of the ship since they'd left the moon. The mercs were happy to help, (for free for once!) and used their salvage teams to load everything, they'd even moved The Rock inside the ship's hangar.

Captain Anit'za assured Brynjar that the damage his machine had sustained was heavy, but not something they couldn't fix. Tapping his shoulder, the Dzenta'rii happily stated that Brynjar had passed the interview and was now part of the proud, mighty assault force of IMS *Starshatter*!

If the crafty alien expected some confused reaction from Brynjar, he was in for a disappointment.

Perfectly calm and emotionless, the genius engineer and mecha pilot instantly began negotiating his pay and salvage percentage allotment. Long in advance he had figured out that this Dzenta'rii, this strange Anit'za fellow, was much more than just a simple spaceship captain. The young Asgardian had a good sense for adventure, and he felt almost as if some event of epic proportions was unfolding around him.

Later that day, Brynjar got up and went to the hangar, inspecting his not-so-shiny new loot and salvage. The stuff was soundly secured on the deck via localized force field, and his mech was locked down as well. The damage sustained really was nothing he couldn't fix, just as Anit'za had said. During the next month, while his new captain loitered around various pubs and bars on Cav colony, Brynjar began repairs and modifications.

Re-arming the mech was sorely needed and after selling all of those useless, power-guzzling particle beams, he bought two brand-new 105mm plasma cannons. He installed them on the forearms and the large looted laser on his machine's back, while the old lasers were moved into two of the new hardpoints he'd created on the torso. It was done in such a way so that the missile rack and heavy laser could fire from shoulder positions when deployed.

Ample energy shielding ensured that his mech had greater survivability, but then a new, and more powerful reactor was needed. Energy distribution systems had to be reinforced to endure the explosive power flow, when his device was activated...

Many times his work was interrupted by random strangers and fans, which he did entertain. Brynjar asked them strange, specific questions from a list that his captain had given to him beforehand. He had instantly guessed that those were to vet potential new crew members. Brynjar couldn't understand why he was the one tasked with asking them. And why would you even need to ask prospective new shipmates things like:

*"What do you consider boring?"* and *"Do you consider yourself an interesting person?"*

156

What did this have to do with anything even close to ship operations?! But Brynjar figured quickly out that this was due to Dzenta'rii quirkiness, and since this captain had already proved his ability and skill, the Asgardian went along with it.

As for his Captain...

When he had exited the medical bay after finishing his long talk with Brynjar, Anit'za's mischievous smile had become even wider. He had expected that very unusual Asgardian to do what he did, because he was... *interesting*. The Dzenta'rii had already met with multiple persons of his kind, and they all were almost the same – boring as a piece of rock. Yes, highly dependable, but boring, his people were built like main battle tanks and were bestowed with the imaginations of such. But this one... oh, he was peculiar, unique, even!

The captain had wandered around the yet empty corridors of his spaceship – soon his new and exiting crew would roam around, entertaining him to no end. Whatever their personal troubles were, he aimed to take care of everybody's problems in an equally efficient manner. After all, what is a ship's crew but one big and happy family? Sniffing the air, Captain Anit'za rushed towards the mess hall – it was high time that he cooked something nice...

# Chapter 6

## *Dozan'Re*

The young Kil'ra Morale Officer looked at his new uniform with pride.

He'd finished his apprenticeship in half the normal time, and been decorated with the Gold Honor Badge for achieving top scores in all disciplines. It was neatly pinned upon the breast of his beautiful dark gray uniform, worn by all Terran officers of the Corps, outshining the epaulets embossed with silver filigree and the platinum-covered buttons. Yet, even those bright features stood out the least.

His furry, tiger-like face loomed at least three heads above the crowd of humans visiting the graduation ceremony, and Dozan eagerly took a minute to straighten his ornate headgear. In the middle of the cap, right above the forehead, was affixed the double-headed Eagle of the Imperial Minarchy, holding in its claws a crossed rifle and sword, as per official standard. He had forged the whole miniature by hand from megasteel, as a final test of his mastery in uniform-crafting.

The short cape he'd also made; the accessory to his parade uniform was dark-blue, with the Star Alliance symbol sewn in its center. It was masterfully made, with all spiral arms of the Galaxy glistening, three-dimensional seams reflecting the evening sunlight. It created the illusion of certain stars glowing, and he'd made sure the Shield Held By Many Hands in background was as solid and accurate as possible. The whole ensemble really looked quite splendid, indeed.

Dozan slowly exhaled and then smiled, revealing a mouth full of white, razor sharp teeth – things were about to be set in motion after this day was over!

His old master gave him a gentle nod, which was the agreed upon signal for Dozan to move forward and accept his graduation gift. All of those hard, grueling years of training and tests were behind him now; his newfound life purpose as a Kil'ra warrior was to inspire and lead others by example, serving as a Morale Officer for the Terran Imperial Minarchy.

But having been inspired by human bravery and refusal to back down even in the darkest of hours, Dozan knew that the real challenge still lay ahead. He bowed slightly before accepting the weapon customarily gifted to a Terran officer of the Morale Corps.

A very old human woman was holding his new vibrosword, and he bowed again when his hand grasped the sword's handle. Dozan raised the blade high, and began reciting his official vow as the rest of the apprentices chanted his name:

"By my Blood, I swear to Bravely protect all citizens of the Empire and the Alliance! By my Honor, I vow to Sacrifice if need be to ensure the survival of our culture! By my Example I pledge to lead with Virtue those who stand before Evil, and form a living wall securing our freedoms – Now, Forever, and Until my Last Breath!"

The crowd erupted into cheers as he lowered his sword, beaming with joy. As it was traditional for Kil'ra younglings who had fulfilled their Es'lav, Dozan had now earned the right to use his full name.

As the young morale officer sheathed his sword, he loudly proclaimed:

"Bear witness, all of you who are present here, as my name is now Dozan'Re, The One Who Leads!"

He quickly stepped off the platform and walked away, checking his few belongings as the crowd cheered him out of the building. Dozan knew that his master would be long gone by now. The elder had stated many times during his training that the young kil'ra was in fact his last pupil. Knowing that, the young morale officer wasted no time; he had already done his homework and found employment.

He then stepped into the waiting taxi that would bring him to his first official morale officer assignment. While the grav-car flew towards the nearest starport, he collected himself, and with fondness, recalled the events that had led him to this moment.

* * *

Kil'ra youth spent the first 40 years of their lives finding purpose and honing new skills, a period of time traditionally known as an "Es'lav". Many wandered their ancient Star Empire's territories, but more and more of them now chose to explore allied space. The Imperial Minarchy with its culture of self-reflection, honor, and sacrifice for others was especially appealing to the Kil'ra.

During his Es'lav, Dozan had spent six whole years on Mars colony. One of the first outposts of humanity and their client races, its capital city of Cydonia and the famous ancient Precursor ruins next to it were the reasons he'd traveled there. The people he befriended and the Terran culture were the reasons he'd stayed.

Fascinated by the short and mostly sad history of the

fledgling space-faring civilization, he'd spent many months immersing himself thoroughly in all of its beauty and history. One could say that he, as with most young aliens who came in contact with Earth and humanity, had quickly fallen in love with them and their desperate struggle for survival.

After a few months of working odd jobs on Mars and its orbital satellites, Dozan had won a free tour of Earth's historical monuments. He had traveled there on a rented shuttle, visiting the ancient places first.

The Giza plateau had enthralled him, and he'd explored every pyramid and restored tomb that was available to the tourists. One week wasn't enough to travel through the entire length of the lush Sahara forests. Once a desert, a terraforming project had started during the late 60's and been completed only in twelve years.

The Glaciers of Colorado, which Dozan had explored next, had also been restored immediately after the Sahara. Who knew the planet could have undergone such a transformation before the onset of the 21$^{st}$ century on Earth's calendars?

Having had enough money to pay for the extra fuel, he'd flown around with the shuttle, visiting many more places and countries, than just the ones specified in the brochure. He'd been grateful that he'd decided to go off the beaten path, as each twist and turn revealed new and ever lovelier surprises that only drew him in the more.

Earth had many nation-states who had united to form the tiny, but efficient Imperial Minarchy government. The nation-states still existed within the Minarchy, preserving their beautiful identities and unique cultures. Dozan had not seen anything like it anywhere within the territories of his own race's empire. Sure, there were many Kil'ra colonies,

161

each with their own quirky cultural differences, but nothing like this.

The last site he'd visited before the end of the tour was a testament to this unity – the 'Tri-Ship Monument.'

A large debris field consisting of three wrecked Terran spaceships of an early design, known as the INS *Akira*, the INS *Lincoln*, and the INS *Rome*. First in their class, they were cruiser-size ships with rotating sections and limited speed. Nevertheless, the Terrans had fought valiantly against insurmountable odds. It was around the time when humans first traveled between the stars and joined the community of starfaring races that a great Pirate Lord named Mahimm unified many clans and led his armada into the Sol system.

Arrogant and foolish, Lord Mahimm decided to invade and enslave all of humanity, even though he knew the humans had signed the pre-alliance agreement with the Kil'ra Empire. He hadn't anticipated the Kil'ra to send their ships, nor had he expected the stiff resistance from the "primitive" locals.

Just as his agents had informed him, the humans had been physically weak. Their "puny" fleet had only small escort ships, starfighters, and but three capital-size ships that were just fresh off the assembly line. Crews were trained to perfection, but had little to no real combat experience, and the sly pirate lord predicted an easy fight. That proved not to be the case.

Ultimate victory eluded him, and as he suffered unimaginable losses both in spaceships and ground forces, Mahimm went into a fit of rage on the bridge of his command cruiser, the CS *Romaaruk*. He commanded ten of the best destroyer captains in his armada to surround the lone Terran cruisers and take them.

Somehow the humans successfully resisted him, and he lost all of his ships that were battling them.

For thirty-nine full hours they fought defiantly, dying from exhaustion and wounds, but never leaving their posts. Fulfilling their eternal duty to humanity, the cruiser's whole crews died to the last man and woman. And as the hulls of their ships were being melting beyond repair, they themselves cooking alive inside their suits, the crew still managed to return fire.

The pirates sent boarding parties who were to secure the wrecked ships, but wave after wave, they all vanished within the ravaged hulls. The Terrans shot at them with everything they had, but the power packs were all spent eventually so they fought them in melee.

Jagged and broken weapons, severed limbs, and even pieces from the hulls of their own ships were used as improvised weapons. Finally, the wounded Terrans, their suits damaged and suffering from decompression, used their failing bodies to finish the job. After their twentieth attempt, the pirates stopped sending marines. The space around those three Terran ships became a graveyard for them, a terrible monument to their Great Lord's folly.

Yet, even with such a heroic resistance, the humans were losing badly still. Dozan'Re remembered a short holo clip that had been on display at the monument, taken from one of the reinforcing Kil'ra Star Navy ships who had managed to break through the pirates' lines and reach the site. A single dead Terran crewwoman floating in space had been found, limbs entangled with those of an enemy marine.

Evidently she'd broken the faceplate of that pirate marine with her own, killing herself and the enemy in the process. Dozan had wondered why she hadn't used her arms, but on closer inspection the young Kil'ra had noticed that they had been blown away. Her suit had been self-sealed by its anti-decompression-grade vacfoam, yet she was obviously going to die from the wounds even before taking the decision to sacrifice herself.

When he'd magnified the image, on her frozen face, one could see her defiant smile. While Dozan had been floating in his suit, overwhelmed by emotion from the holo clip he'd just seen, he'd noticed a lone, elderly human man.

Wearing an antiquated space suit, the white-haired senior citizen had been touching the hull of the Lincoln at seemingly random places. Every time he stopped, there'd been a short burst of comms from him, sent on an open link in the local I-net. Intrigued, Dozan decided to listen to what the old man was saying. The man had been whispering on the open frequency, and obviously was a gifted orator:

"You, who suffered and died for others to live in safety – Glory! Remembered will you be as long as our race's memory stands pure. Heroes standing in the enemy's way, too tired to move and who yet died fighting – Vengeance! Sacrificing the vile monsters who took you away from your families, before it was your time. Our drive to fulfill the promise is eternal, for as long as our race's strength holds true."

As Dozan listened in awe, the man had gone on: "Victims, those who were kidnapped and sold as pieces of flesh – Justice! There will be a reckoning for the crimes of your captors and their abettors yet. Doom will be upon them, swift Terror grasping their hearts and minds. Ever knowing their violent Death follows in steps, shadows and space..."

Dozan had been suddenly taken with vivid emotions, and he'd soon found his helmet full of tears floating in the zero-G. The faceplate of his suit had quickly cleaned the droplets out, and he only then saw that the old Terran had lost control of his own suit. The man had suddenly grasped his chest and started floating away deep into the debris field.

Concerned, the young Kil'ra had leaped away from the tourist railing, detaching his grappling cable and activating the small engines on his suit. With grace and precision Dozan had reached the man, grabbed him, and turned away, navigating towards the nearest med station. Amazingly, those tiny spacesuit engines had had enough fuel for him to get there quickly.

As he'd correctly assumed, the old man was having a heart attack, and would've died, had he not intervened in a most timely manner. However, after a quick surgery inside the medical shuttle, the old man had awoken angry:

"Why have you stopped me from attending to my duties!?" – He'd screamed at the stunned medic, who tried desperately to calm the man down.

Dozan had now noticed his unshaven face, the pale, almost deathly-looking skin, and the swollen, tired eyes. The unkempt beard and dirty hair were in wild contrast with the brilliant language he had heard earlier. The man's voice had suddenly begun to haltingly fail, showing deep pain instead of angered strength, and to the young kil'ra it was painfully obvious that this noble elder needed help. As the medic attended to him, Dozan had slowly moved over and faced the old man:

"Calm yourself, Sir, you have suffered a heart attack and you should listen to the doctor here." – Dozan had used his best diplomatic tone and smiled charmingly as he continued:

"We would be truly sad to lose one such as you, gifted Speaker and honored Elder, to a simple heart failure."

The man was suddenly speechless, his eyes filled with

tears, and he mumbled – *"Your Highness"* – before falling unconscious. The doctor had sat beside the old man, and began crying too. It had been very disturbing for the Kil'ra to see a grown adult weeping, and he had asked:

"Please, you told me he was going to be fine, Doctor. I don't understand, why are you crying?"

The medic then turned away, and with great sadness in his voice, he had answered Dozan:

"This is the great Morale Officer, Ulfric Wagner! He was the sole survivor from the Lincoln. Many of us fear he's lost his mind, since the only thing he does these days is to spend all his waking time reciting the names of the dead and honoring them with speeches. He is far too frail and old to be doing that – floating in outer space, I mean! There is so much that he could teach the next generation. Alas, we haven't been able to persuade him to retire from his self-imposed solitude."

The doctor had then left Dozan sitting near the medibed, puzzled.

Dozan had then begun to search the G-net with his PDA. It had taken old Ulfric six hours to wake up, six hours that Dozan spent reading and soaking up everything that he could find about the old morale officer like a sponge. The more he had read, the more he'd been overwhelmed by the idea and purpose of the Morale Corps, and at the very moment Ulfric awoke, there at his side had been one very eager young Kil'ra, practically begging him to take him as an apprentice.

At first the grizzled old man had been defiant, but after following him for a month, every single day, and reciting the exact words of his famous speeches, Ulfric had finally capitulated. Perhaps for the first time in his long life, the old morale officer had seen that there was more for him than spending endless hours in mourning. The Galaxy belonged to the youth. What better duty was there than to prepare them to face its horrors with equal duty and pride?

And there was Dozan, one of these youth, only too willing to learn.

* * *

Dozan'Re's passenger shuttle took off in the air, its engines burning long trails of ionized plasma, leaving him alone on the landing pad.

The small colony where he'd chosen to prove himself as a Morale Officer looked utterly devastated. Semoa was its name; situated in Fringe space, the fledgling Terran settlement had had more than its fair share of pirate raids, slaver attacks, and even a full-blown invasion by a regional empire.

Its citizens were tough-as-nails ore miners, prospectors, and engineers, all trying to make a life for themselves working the planet's mineral riches. Sadly, their luck was abhorrent, and wave after wave of all sorts of scum descended upon their mountainous village.

In the beginning they fought all of them off, with typical Terran defiance and unwavering courage. Lately though, the death toll on the local population after the last invasion had made them an even more prime target for slavers – the locals couldn't allow any more of their people to die. Some of the prominent citizens left links on the G-net asking for somebody, anybody, willing to come and aid in rebuilding their defenses.

It was their desperate plea for aid which brought him here. After discovering one of the links on G-net, the young morale officer immediately arranged for his transport. Strangely enough, while walking up the road leading into the village, Dozan'Re saw no other outlanders.

Was he the only one brave enough to take the challenge?

Not likely, but it was somewhat disconcerting to be alone. His dark yellow eyes slowly examined the damaged facades of houses he passed by. Blasted by particle-beams most probably since the mega-concrete was not only charred, but melted in places. Dozan slightly flinched as one thought quickly passed through his mind, in his eagerness to quickly reach this place and help, he came carrying only a simple sidearm.

His Walter LP model-91 was a trusty laser-pistol design manufactured on Earth. Even without any extra upgrades or attachments, Dozan'Re was confident of his aim... but would it be enough? From the pattern of weapon fire, the attackers had automatic weaponry, and that meant either assault rifles or machine guns.

He nervously grasped the handle of his broadsword. The long-bladed vibroweapon was finely crafted and engraved by the citizens who had gifted it to him. It was the custom of Terrans to gift weapons, armor, and other equipment to volunteer soldiers in colonial militia regiments. Indeed the freedom loving humans and their clients did not pay any taxes, but common defense was something nobody skimped on.

Engraved on the blade were the words "Vigilant Protector".

Even destiny must have known what was in

168

Dozan'Re's heart, because the sword had been given to him and not anyone else. At least, he believed, as a practicing Universalist, that some events were set in motion because of the changes of direction one's life took.

Most advanced, spacefaring races in the Galaxy followed two schools of thought – the first and most prevalent group was the Universalists. They believed that the Universe itself was a living being, an organism comprised of all matter, both visible and invisible.

Sentient beings were the Universe's attempt to understand itself, therefore, for the Universalists, creating or nurturing any sentient life was of huge importance. Acts of genocide were not tolerated by followers of Universalism, and in most cases, the perpetrators themselves met the same end, having been judged too dangerous to exist alongside other sentient life.

There was no "church" of Universalism, or priesthood; the closest one could get to an actual organization were local Congregations of scientists – mainly xeno-geneticists and biologists. When a genocide was perpetrated, or there was danger of such an act, those Congregations would locate the best possible like-minded mercs or a corporation Fleet or Army. Those were paid handsomely to "deal" with the genocidal criminals, in a manner most akin to ancient Earth's religious wars.

Congregations were stifled by the Galactic Assembly's strict laws for uplifting, the process by which a near-sentient animal was made into an intelligent race. According to G.A. Law, any uplifted race must serve their benefactor for at least 20,000 galactic years without question. That damned monolithic conglomerate – so set in their ways, so despising of change!

The uplifted races under their rule were often nothing

more than serfs, slaves even, commonly used as cheap cannon fodder to fight in the Old Races' ancient squabbles. Therefore, Shadow Congregations existed, who would aid species in the backwards part of the Galaxy, the Fringe Space. G.A. Enforcers often mercilessly exterminated those altruistic scientists upon locating their enclaves.

Humanity was most hated by the G.A., because of their benevolent treatment of uplifted races. The Terran Imperial Minarchy offered all slaves freedom, from the moment their ships entered Imperial space. Not only that, but humans created their own client races and gave them equal rights as citizens!

If not for the alliance with the mighty Kil'ra Empire, humanity would've been long since wiped out, together with their client races. Yet lately, Dozan'Re had heard a rumor; some Universalists were speaking in hushed tones of a new, militant organization, called the Star Knights. From what little information he had been given by one scientist, their members swore an oath to protect underdeveloped races and sentient animals.

He hoped to one day meet with such a Knight – even the mere prospect of such a group existing would be considered heretical by the Galactic Assembly. Those Terrans were impressing him more and more as time went by.

After the young morale officer had walked uphill for a long while, he reached a clearing at the village center. There were two big buildings, made of new mega concrete, heavily entrenched with handmade vacfoam bags, welded pieces of old starship bulkheads, and even tree logs.

One had a very well-made, though now riddled with scorched holes, hanging sign, which read "Pop's Lair and Booze." The other had a genuine dropship point-defense turret mounted on its roof, sporting a pair of very nice-looking automatic rail guns.

Dozan'Re examined the fighter-size railguns and smiled – those would practically shred most light and medium foot forces to gory pieces. Below the turret was but one word, written directly on the mega-concrete with spray-paint – "Guns."

Still grinning from ear to year, he clenched his right hand into a fist and hit the center of his chest with it, saluting whoever was still alive for their valor. As he did so, he loudly announced:

"I commend you for your endurance, brave colonists! I, Dozan'Re, have journeyed here to answer your call for aid – *Greet me as I come with intent to protect.*"

The last phrase was the translation of an ancient Kil'ra greeting, used to announce the landing of Guardian Troopers on allied alien worlds.

Slowly, people started emerging from their barricaded homes and the doors of Pop's Lair and Booze slid open, to reveal a group of dirty, disheveled kids. He quickly counted the population and realized that there were only four adults, the rest were kids ranging from seven to thirteen, thirty-four of them. Most were girls; they had at least one bandaged wound, looked broken and sad. Not willing to accept the sight of discouraged Terrans, he walked towards them with his best smile:

"Worry not! I will find a way for us to survive this, good people of Semoa."

"Bullshit, everything is lost. This colony is lost!" – One of the four adults, a crying, grizzled old woman, screamed at him, as she waved the stump of her left arm in the air.

"How do you expect to stop the enemy?! Make those *kids* fight them? Or will you defeat them on your own?! No! I say we send the last evac signal and leave as soon as possible – the colony be *damned!*"

Dozan'Re looked at the rest of the colonists, and saw that their eyes were filled with fear. Probably, all of these kids' parents were dead, and from the look of it, most houses were heavily damaged. Those two entrenched buildings were their last defensible positions. The way he saw it, their enemies had the best chance of attacking on foot, since the terrain didn't allow for the use of vehicles and that big turret could shred most light aircraft to pieces.

Problem was, its position limited its field of fire – if the slavers were allowed to get closer, the turret was all but useless. That meant bodies on the ground, exposed to enemy fire and defending the single, narrow approach leading towards the village square. It was pretty grim.

The other adults looked just as lost and beaten, with the exception of one. A tall man with blond hair and hazel eyes, he looked more like a holo-star than a Fringe Space colonist. His body was slim and athletic, hands both recently implanted with cybernetic augments. The t-shirt he was wearing bore the word "Guns" in the middle, stamped with simple blue holo-paint.

"It is you who are shit, Magda." – The man replied to the woman's rant with a slightly angrier voice.

"Can't you see? We have a bloody Kil'ra morale officer standing in front of us. If the Universe has obviously decided to move on our accord, why by Terra should we not accept it?!"

He moved closer to Dozan'Re and extended his metal hand:

"The name's Gunter Guns, pleasure to meet you Father Dozan!" – he grinned, using the polite greeting many of the younger races used towards the Kil'ra.

Father if male, Mother if female it was a sign of respect towards the only benevolent Old Race in the Galaxy. And, as his eyes expertly examined the young morale officer's equipment, Gunter continued by saying:

"I am the village gunsmith and master of cybernetics extraordinaire! Please visit my shop later, 'cause from what I can see, you are in need of some weapons!"

He invited him with a bit of a frown, noticing the empty slots on his back.

Dozan'Re nodded politely and turned back to face the colonists. One of the other adults was a bunny wearing a makeshift armor suit made out of salvaged gear. He looked ill, and very, very tired. His hands were shaking, his left ear missing and bandaged. The bunny stumbled forwards and quietly asked:

"Sir, my name is Razor, pleasure to have you in what's left of our small village. Are you sure it's only you that came off the shuttle? One of my brothers promised to come here as soon as rabbitly possible." – The Kil'ra shook his head sadly, and he saw how the light in the bunny's eyes started to dim a little bit.

"So there are no reinforcements then..." – He sighed, and with the typical stern attitude one could expect of bunnies, added – "We will fight them by ourselves as always. I can offer my rifle in defense of this village. Wake me up when the slavers come, I'll be at Pop's" – and he limped back inside the bar.

The last elder was clean-shaven and wore a neat, white doctor's coat. He, perhaps, sported the most fatalistic expression on his face as he made the rounds, inspecting everybody's wounds. Not only that, but his entire posture spoke of someone who had had no sleep for at least a week. You needn't be a medic to understand that this person's bloodstream was most probably chock-full of stims. Dozan'Re made a step, closing the space between them, and placed his hand on the doctor's shoulder:

"Now Healer, you should take it easy for a while. There is nothing worse than a doctor who has died of exhaustion, therefore killing whatever patients he could otherwise have saved, had he had enough rest." – Unfortunately, the doctor's only response was to snap back at him, his voice climbing in pitch with his agitation:

"Yes, all everybody does is tell old Frank *'Get some rest, Frank!'* or *'You need sleep, Frank!'* all the time while I was saving people from death again and again! There is nobody else who could replace me here, and therefore I have to stay awake as long as possible, otherwise this whole damned village would've collapsed long ago!"

"Now Sir Frank, your unwillingness to take care of yourself will place everybody in grave danger should you collapse." – Smiling again and firmly maintaining strong eye contact, the morale officer addressed him again.

The doctor nervously waved his gloved hands, and looked at Dozan'Re's eyes to counter him again. Instead, there was a sudden face twitch and Frank stepped backwards, then turned away without saying a word and walked into the bar. Razor's head popped up from inside a minute later, and eyes wide with amazement, he whispered:

"Who made Frank to go to sleep?"

Dozan'Re nodded silently and walked towards the kids, waving at Razor to go back inside. Curious as to why a

Kil'ra would address them directly, they gathered close to him in a circle as he knelt before them. He again smiled, unbuckled the sheath of his sword, and as he showed its blade to the wide-eyed children, addressed them:

"This is my sword. There are many like it, but this one is mine. Do you know that these are given only to fully-fledged Morale Officers, who have completed the training to protect others?"

As the children silently reacted, he continued:

"My vow was given, as my life is pledged to the cause – a protector am I. For my allies, a guiding light, and for my enemies impending doom. Soon the slavers will come..." – he said, as he saw sadness creep into their faces.

"I can see it in your eyes, you have fought them before. Together perhaps with your parents and older siblings, lost in battle. And now you yourself are your own defenders, for there is nobody else to turn for help to... except me."

The children looked so hopeless as he described their harsh reality, then, with a sad expression, he gently warned them:

"Hear me, Children, and understand this – you cannot expect mercy from slavers. You are young, and you will make them a lot of money when sold on the alien slave markets. A life of suffering and pain expects those who do not fight. You will be broken, even more than you are now, becoming a piece of soul-less flesh with a price tag. But as Terrans, you have received some survival training, and I know you can fight!" – He declared, his voice rising with stern confidence, kept going:

"Fight as long as you can, for there is hope yet! There is no surrender and no retreat, Children. We will either survive and win, or fail and die here!"

The kids' facial expressions slowly turned from desperation to anger and Dozan'Re could see their spirits reinvigorated by his speech. He stood up, and, beckoning them along with him, he started towards the gunsmith's shop:

"Come, Children, let's see what weapons we can borrow from his armory."

Dozan'Re buckled his sword safely back on his belt and walked into Gunter's store, while the kids, silent and determined, stood in line behind him. Obviously strengthened now, they were grimly ready to follow Dozan'Re's command after his inspiring words.

Gunter had evidently been listening in on the morale officer's speech as well. He had prepared some guns, and already there were a number of small arms on his table. They ranged from light pistols and carbines, to sub-machine guns and long rifles. Dozan'Re had long acknowledged that, whether laser or railgun, Terrans made excellent weapons. Sturdy and accurate, able to utilize their expendable power packs better than most alien weapons.

The Kil'ra noted with pleasure that Gunter's work was top-notch even among Terran craftsmanship. Dozan'Re quickly gave the pistols to the younger children, and the carbines and rifles to the teens. The kids all took two spare power packs per person, since those were in short supply.

After arms had been distributed to the children, Gunter showed Dozan'Re the weapon he had been looking for in the inventory: a masterfully crafted Beretta model-1972 sub-machine railgun with integrated holo sights, folding stock, and stabilizing module.

Quickly disassembling the weapon, Dozan'Re found

that it had a block of megasteel instead of the regular piece of slag metal. That meant that this Beretta would pierce most light and medium armored suits. Gunter handed him a couple of "quick packs," two identical home-crafted power packs welded together, as the energy source for this capable device.

"And what do I owe you, Master Gunsmith? I certainly can't afford all of these hand-made mods and attachments." – Dozan'Re asked him.

"No worries!" – Gunter said, waving his hand at the village square – "I only want full salvage after you slaughter them slavers."

"Well yes, of course, Gunter, it is all yours. Thank you for your generosity."

Dozan'Re tried to calculate how much the gunsmith would have made in Imperial Credits, but gave up. There was no knowing what equipment the future corpses would possess. It was also true that he did not want to devalue this man's way of sacrificing for the defense of his home.

No sooner had he fitted his new weapon's mags on his equipment belt than the scanner pod of Gunter's turret started blinking, and a holo map of the surrounding area was projected next to them. Dozan'Re saw a column of enemies slowly climbing the slopes of the mountainous terrain, at least fifty of them, and all were armed to the teeth.

With reactions drilled to utmost perfection, Dozan'Re leaped outside and started shouting orders, calling the colonists to action. He spread the kids behind the barricaded causeway leading into the square itself, and issued orders to only fire their weapons at the area he specified, so as to disorient and herd the enemy while he himself closed in for the kill.

The Kil'ra were physically fitter and stronger than most humanoid races yet, that was not all. They also possessed superior combat awareness, due to the millennia of almost constant warfare their race had had to endure. Using his racial prowess, Dozan'Re could quickly move in and out of melee, provided his back was kept safe. To that end, the bunny Razor promised to use his rifle and shoot any snipers or enemies trying to flank him.

Gunter manned the turret and remained at the helm of scout, giving situational links over everybody's PDA, along with enemy movement updates. Ah, if only there were more of them, they could have assaulted the slavers themselves! But they would make do – just like the Terrans and their allies always did, they would fight to the last shot in their power packs and drop of blood. Dozan'Re checked his new Beretta, aimed down the holo sight and started humming the Imperial Minarchy's anthem on their PDA link.

* * *

Slavers were mostly multi-racial; among their ranks could be found miscreants and all sorts of wanted criminals from all over Fringe Space. The leader of the Bloody Chains slave band was an escaped death-row convict from the Taz'aran Empire. The Taz'arans themselves weren't the most honest or good-natured people, but even they had uncrossable lines, and cannibalism was one of them. Among the slavers, however, he could easily satisfy his hunger, and even taste exotic new aliens.

This small colony was just a stepping stone for his band. For the last four weeks he and his minions managed to pick off most of the adults one by one, and despite the casualties the band had sustained, he was expecting complete victory. The next closest Terran colony was twenty light-years away, and the only aid the locals had gotten were occasional shuttle drops; those, they destroyed easily.

The last one, however, was unexpected, because his sentry was asleep and missed raising the alarm allowing one outlander to get to the village alive.

No matter – he had fifty fighters armed to the teeth!

Not only that, but he himself was wearing exoskeleton battle armor, which increased his strength six-fold. Whatever meager resistance was left, they would crush it, and at long last, capture the children.

He licked his lips with nervous anticipation; aside from the heaps of money they'd make from selling the kids on the slave markets, he would have the first pick. One long, tasty feast awaited him, therefore, full of barely contained enthusiasm, he waved the assault team to move forwards and switched on his vibroaxe.

Moving forward, the armored boots of his suit crushed random pieces of junk lying on the path, as he stood somewhat behind his front lines and gave commands to start the attack. On his PDA the assault team rapidly moved up the path and soon reached the main causeway and then... then all of his plans started going south.

The colonists opened fire from behind a makeshift barricade. It slowed his fighters a tiny bit, but nonetheless they still continued moving forward, returning fire. Suddenly, he heard one extremely loud, Terran battlecry:

*"Fear me, cowards, for I am the Death-Bringer!"*

The voice was booming, charged with barely contained power and incredibly intimidating. He saw on the holo map how one of his fighters died – and then another, and another. Soon the air was full with the screams of dying assault troopers! He could hear them on the comms as they desperately fought for their lives and screamed at the rest of his fighters:

"What are you waiting for, idiots! That's just one soldier standing against us – the rest are frightened old people and children! Move forward and kill the fool!"

As his second line advanced forward, slowly this time, he saw how, one by one, all of the first assault group were slain. The last fighter tried running, but the moment he stepped away from the causeway, his body was shredded by accurate automatic railgun fire. What's worse, the projectiles didn't stop, but killed another one of the soldiers who stood in their path.

He suddenly froze in his suit...

Were they all armed with armor piercing guns?!

No matter, there were enough of his minions between himself and that Terran, their bodies would serve as a shield for him while he moved forward one pace at a time... very slowly. The second wave of attackers moved forwards prone; some were almost crawling and visibly angered. They were taking a more cautious, trained approach, determined to get to their targets. None of that mattered though, because the moment anyone tried to flank and move to the side of the causeway, their heads exploded from accurate rifle fire.

The pirate leader looked at his PDA again and frowned, teeth bare he snarled angrily behind his face plate. His sizable force was getting less sizable by the minute; already, fifteen of his minions had been killed. Another battlecry was heard, and this time, being now closer to the fight he could feel the power of it himself. The Terran shouted:

*"Come at me, vile Slaver scum! Abandon all hope of survival, for I shall be the last sight you see before oblivion!"* – and the voice again had such powerful effect, that he saw some of his fighters hesitate.

In that hesitation they died instantly, again shredded by railgun fire, pieces of their bodies scattered all around his assault line. More and more of his minions were dying – close to half of the overall band he came here with were now lost. He got increasingly angry; grimacing, he picked up one of his dead soldier's corpses and held it up before him as a shield with one arm.

The servos of his exoskeleton armor whined slightly while he moved forwards, raised axe in hand. Moving out of the confined causeway space, he suddenly stepped in the village square and was met with a fusillade of small arms fire. The corpse-shield was burned and dismembered it an instant!

Before his very eyes, his suit's faceplate showed him not a Terran, but one towering Kil'ra, swinging his vibrosword with one hand and shooting at his troops with a small auto-railgun in the other hand. He was at least two heads taller than him without the suit and even with it, he could swear that this intimidating warrior was slightly taller.

The stalwart do-gooder was wearing a beautiful ornate armored uniform, covered with the blood of his underlings. Around him were a throng of children; armed with light weapons they were shooting the rest of his soldiers dead! The little ones focused barrages of gunfire on specific areas, pinning his minions while that Kil'ra warrior slaughtered them.

The slave master saw battle flow changing in favor of

the colonists! If even possible, the Terran children were fighting with the bravery of seasoned veterans. Most of them were wounded to begin with, and some weak. Mere armed with pistols younglings and yet, they flawlessly managed to hold his forces at bay, not one of them breaking in tears or running away scared. They stood as one, shot as one, unflinching from even the strongest weapon's fire directed at them. Enraged beyond measure, the slave master commanded:

"Third wave, attack immediately! I will deal with that lone warrior myself. Blood Chains advance, victory is within our grasp!"

He threw away what was left of his meat-shield and grasped the handle of his axe with both hands. Screaming, he charged towards the Kil'ra warrior, his movement and reflexes greatly boosted by the exoskeleton. His opponent dropped the auto-railgun on the ground and met the charge, blocking it with his sword. The axe stopped exactly at the Kil'ra's blade, yet the warrior didn't move at all.

Angrily, the slave master pushed his exoskeleton even more, but that Kil'ra managed to sidestep, block, and dodge all his blows. The Taz'aran began to sweat; even with his overwhelming advantage, his enemy wasn't fazed at all.

All of a sudden he heard multiple explosions, yet instead of his third wave assaulting the Terrans, the PDA projected on the side of his faceplate more casualties. Not only that, but someone was attacking them from behind: a force consisting of small humanoids moved rapidly, and within the ranks of his remaining troops, shooting them from point-blank range.

They were outflanked, surrounded, and the cover that they were using suddenly became all but useless against that rapidly moving force of small Terrans. For it was a group of bunny scouts, only ten of them, hopping at great speed between his men, and able to assassinate their targets by sound despite the smoke on the courtyard battlefield. His enemy's booming voice roared once more:

*"Die as you should, Slaver scum! The Universe itself aids us in this hour!"*

With renewed vigor the battered and wounded children continued fighting. Some had used up all of their spare power packs, they threw rocks and pieces of mega-concrete at the slavers with bloodied hands. Others rushed forward completely disregarding cover, picking up the weapons of his fallen minions.

How?!

How was he losing against one group of pathetic little children and small hopping creatures?!

Mad with anger, the slave master suddenly decided that if he had to die, he would take all of those filthy Terrans with him in the afterlife. He activated the backup link saved on his PDA and some ten kilometers away, their concealed starship fired a barrage of missiles at the village. Screaming, he continuously swung the vibroaxe, desperately trying to kill the cocky warrior before him.

To no avail.

He took hit after hit on his armor and the plating didn't stop his enemy's blade – it went right through and sliced his left arm off. Wailing with pain, he picked up the axe from the ground and charged forwards, concentrating his remaining strength into one last, all-out attack.

His perspective changed and somehow, with waning vision, he saw his chest and then feet. Before his brain stopped working, he realized that the Kil'ra warrior had decapitated him. He heard the boom of his missiles and then saw how they all exploded midair, thanks to the deafening railgun shots coming from that handmade Terran point defense tower. Lights waned, sounds faded away and then... then came the overwhelming darkness.

* * *

Dozan'Re slowly picked himself up, and while his ears bled, ringing from the exploding missiles, he was alive. Before him lay the corpse of his enemy, the slave master himself, head chopped clean off his shoulders. He raised the helmet's faceplate with the tip of his bloody sword and looked at the face.

Filthy Taz'aran scum!

While he had once never thought all members of one race could be stereotyped in a negative way, all the Taz'arans he knew of had been power-hungry psychopaths.

Gunter linked and told Dozan to snatch the taz'aran's exosuit for himself – it seemed that the prudent weaponsmith had already calculated the loot's overall value and considered it plenty a reward. Again the kil'ra was plagued by the guilty thought that his new Berreta cost way too much for its original price, and the mods installed in, it to be covered by busted taz'aran equipment. Yet, couple of seconds later, Dozan came to the conclusion that it would be extremely impolite of him not to accept Gunter's gift.

Therefore, he hurriedly picked up the heavy exoskeleton armor and promptly disposed of the corpse inside. Measuring the suit by placing it over his own limbs, the kil'ra noticed that after some modification he could wear it himself. The mere thought of his considerable strength multiplied by the exoskeleton system, aiding him in his future battles against scum like the slaver who now lay dead before his feet, made Dozan'Re very happy. He turned his attention away from the armor and towards the most-welcomed sight of the bunny reinforcements.

Standing before them, he cleaned his sword's blade before sheathing it, and extended his hand to their leader:

"Pleased to meet you, brave Scout Troopers! My name is Dozan'Re and I am the Morale Officer who stood together with the colonists in defense of this village. Where are you coming from?"

"From the great asteroid colony of Cav sir!" – the bunny shook his hand using both of his gloved paws.

"We weren't expecting to find any survivors, 'cause our forces were tied up elsewhere for the longest, nobody could send reinforcements here. Say, you could come with us to Cav, sir! There is plenty of work for someone like you, and the relief force from our colony will soon come to provide aid for the restoration of the village."

Dozan'Re turned and looked carefully at the children behind him. All of them had somehow miraculously survived, albeit heavily wounded. He smiled to them, and proclaimed:

"You were outnumbered and outgunned, considered weak by your enemies, who came here to enslave you. Instead of running away or surrendering, you stood before them, weapons in hand. They'd killed all of your parents and relatives, but you avenged them yourselves. Truly you may call yourselves strong, now; for those who can take care of themselves, protect others, and stand against all odds, will persevere. Always remember this hour; forge your pain and anguish not into hatred, but contempt, towards those who will try to hurt you and your loved ones. For it is not them, but *you*, who will join the Ascended after your existence in this plane is over!"

The children were beaming back as happily as he was, as Dozan'Re, his eyes wet with joy, finished telling them:

"Stay on the path of bravery, self-reliance and honor, young ones. Long may your lives be, and happy, many and healthy your children!"

Dozan'Re then hugged each child in turn, giving each a small present as he did so. Tiny, ornate, silver badges in the form of a lion's head, engraved with the words "Virtue, Bravery, Honor". Each child looked upon their new badge with amazement, finally accepting the full measure of their victory against the odds.

After he gave the children one last hug, he then picked up his new looted suit of armor and followed one of the bunnies towards their shuttle, the colonists cheering as he left. The Terrans could hear his booming voice in the distance, as Dozan'Re laughed happily while he walked down the path chatting with the bunnies, yet the doctor was first to notice that the Kil'ra had left a trail of dark red blood behind him.

He had been fighting heavily wounded the whole time!

Turning around in amazement, the physician saw how all the children, despite their wounds, were still standing, holding their small, clenched fists at the center of their chests. Dozan'Re never saw the salute, indeed, he never visited the colony of Semoa again in his life. But years later, he heard a story from another morale officer – about one group of extremely brave and tough young Terrans, all wearing silver badges, who hunted all of the slavers in their home system to extinction...

# Chapter 7

## *Vasilisa*

A lonely space shuttle was making its way through the asteroid field. The surrounding space was filled with irradiated, molten rocks – evidence left from a battle fought many decades ago. The outer hull of the shuttle was covered with armor plates, all beautifully painted over with various scenes depicting many heroic deeds.

The center figure was that of a young woman wearing a bulky, but extremely well-made spacesuit, armed with a long revolver-looking pistol. The girl had pale white skin and blue eyes – her long blond hair was braided, reaching below the waist line.

Her vessel was short, wide, and had thick wings, ending with vertical atmospheric stabilizers. The ship's designer had used the space wisely, because it was created not only with exploration in mind, but combat, too. Between those stabilizers, the shuttle had two long railguns mounted and armored to the side by long plates of megasteel. It also sported one rotating quad turret at the back of the ship, which was well hidden between its two powerful plasma drives.

Leaving a long trail of ionized gas, the ship careened to the side, and rays from the local star shone upon its name: Free Spacer Ship or FSS *Princess Frog*, written in Cyrillic. To an educated observer who had remote knowledge of Terran fauna, that ship would look quite similar to a frog. Its forward sensor-package even protruded forward from the ship's nose, giving the impression of a tongue-like appendage sticking out in search of food. And indeed, the ship's instruments found something.

Far ahead, at the center of this asteroid cluster, there was an area devoid of rock, but full of man-made debris.

Sitting inside the navigator's command pod was that same spacesuit-wearing young woman from the outer hull paintings. Her beautiful face was sweaty – in complete concentration, her eyes were transfixed on the shuttle's holo displays, reading all the navigational data her computer could provide. From outside the ship, one couldn't see her delicate small fingers, speedily flying over her ship's piloting controls, evading asteroids of all sizes.

While the shuttle was streaming forward as fast as her engines could carry it, the young pilot was mindful of their status. Nobody wanted to suddenly lose engine power because its main drive overheated and even less so, in an ever-moving asteroid field.

Sometimes her right hand reached towards the ship's main gun controls, but always stopped just an inch before touching them. Smiling, she licked her lips, and despite the salty sweat began chuckling joyfully. Finally, her ship flew out and away from the closely-clustered, ever-colliding-with-each-other asteroids. She slowed it down almost to a halt, while her hands this time went over to the next station.

Working with the same professional precision, she punched more and more scan parameters into the main sensor array and then allowed herself some precious moments of rest. The ship's computer followed her commands and performed another clean sensor sweep of the forwards area. All of the obvious traces of spaceship battle her main sensors had detected were from forty to fifty years ago.

Deep within this asteroid field, the ship on which she had spent almost two full years of her life searching for, lay hidden. There she could see its silhouette, drifting exactly where her source informed that it should've been. She'd had to pull his scrawny alien butt out of the hot mess that he and his friends walked themselves into, when they'd stupidly decided to do a smuggling job for one of the Cartels.

The girl's gaze went over her bulky pistol and she suddenly twitched when she remembered what had to be done to secure this information. Her computer bleeped discreetly, and it showed the scanner analysis on main holo viewer.

She gasped.

At the other end of that asteroid cluster, drifting and turning almost gracefully around her main axis, laying amongst a debris field consisting of its own hull pieces – she could see the silhouette of a derelict Terran destroyer.

She jumped quickly and began gathering her equipment and supplies. Soon, the customized pockets of her ornate spacesuit were all packed full of weapon spare power packs, rations, and many other tool-kits. She ordered her navigational computer to slowly fly towards the derelict destroyer, while she was inspecting that everything in her pockets was exactly where it should be, checking it via a holo list projected by her wrist-mounted PDA.

She continuously studied the derelict, noticing her extensive hull damage, and soon found herself wondering – could she find herself a mate here? This husband-search of hers had continued for far too long already!

Although, she knew that her own mother had spent *eleven* lonely years traveling around Fringe Space before meeting her husband Alexi. She always got teary eyed when

190

her parents recollected the story together. Her mom, Valeria, alone stormed the slave pen her dad was held in, and both broke all of the slaves free – courageously fighting their way out through the bodies of many dozens of slavers.

The girl checked her inventory again, deciding to pick up one spare canister of fuel just in case her suit engines needed it later. Everything spacer women had to do to find a mate, it was considered amongst her peers to be something of a rite of passage to womanhood. Like her grandmother Irina always said:

*"A woman's worth, my dear Vasilisa, can only be proved by her deeds and attitude alone!"*

She had to agree – her grandmother was always right.

After reading about the old days from before the Pirate Lord Mahimm had invaded Earth in 1969, as a child, she had always wondered how easy a girl's life was back then. Every woman could choose between many men; there was no shortage. One could even say that it was a female centered society, the whole world's economy catering to their every need. In the history books, she read about extreme examples of chivalry, that from her point of view were near borderline insanity.

Women even could, and most did decide, *not* to work, and to only be supported by their men!

This sounded more like science fiction to her, than reality. Nowadays, at best you could have one man per four, or at worst per *nine* women, and it was getting worse every year. Millions of men constantly died on the battlefields while defending their race and no amount of planetary population booms, or even the limited cloning some desperately brave scientists used, could slow this down. Artificial semen did not work properly either, the birth defects were absolutely horrendous. Full clones created for the sole purpose of mating also produced genetic abnormalities and, of course, there was the ethical question of creating sentient beings simply for breeding purposes.

In the end, humanity's best choice was to seek peace rather than war, gritting their teeth and observing the billions of toiling slaves rather than taking them in. That and having lots of babies, born in nuclear families. There were some colonies who used artificial wombs, but again there was the issue of finding healthy sperm to grow normal embryos. All of this constant horror only bred stronger and tougher women, for they no longer had the luxury of living in the safety of their homes.

Women had to take more than an equal share of the death and pain, dying on the battlefields that surrounded them on all sides. There was rarely peace; both on the ground and in space they ventured bravely, sometimes dying in their millions...

As one of the few free Star States, the Terran Minarchy had very precious few allies, the Kil'ra being the strongest among them. Humans and their client races had to pay heftily with blood and souls, to protect what little space they had. Their greatest ally protected them from the worst of the wrath of the older, malevolent races, for whom personal freedom meant nothing.

Humans soon realized, as their innocence was dying, that the galaxy was far more dangerous a place than most had naively thought it to be. There were no super-enlightened benevolent aliens, traveling through space and gifting advanced technology without asking anything in return. There was only competition, the same as had plagued their own planet, only on a greater and more deadly scale.

* * *

Vasilisa remembered how, not that long ago, her colony's tiny population waved her goodbye, while her shuttle, FSS *Princess Frog* streamed towards space.

During her husband search she'd had to fight with all sorts of scum, both in space and on the ground. Pirates being some the worst, and also pesky as hell, because they were almost *everywhere* in Fringe Space.

It was an area of space, mostly uninhabited, very close to the Galactic Outer Rim, teeming with all sorts of criminals, deadly space anomalies, and was ruled by terrorist states who practiced slavery.

There were two favorite sayings amongst Terran spacers:

*"Kick any asteroid and pirates will scurry from the inside"*, and, *"Slavers can be found lurking in all comet's tails"*.

She had to agree it was true to an extent, but at least one might find friends along the way. This girl, however, wasn't *that* lucky and the aliens she'd met during her voyage were either openly hostile, or tried to swindle her out of her money.

The real world was scary and deadly – thankfully it was a Terran tradition that on all colonies kids had to learn how to defend themselves. Self-defense and space survival courses were taught to them, from as early on as five years old. She, being part of a family of spacers, had received even better training. Instead of playing with toys, like many other aliens – she'd learned how to repair and maintain spacesuits and weapons.

While the children of other races were blissfully ignorant of the dangers that populated the Galaxy, she'd piloted starships through deadly asteroid fields and spent every hour of her free time on the shooting range. As most kids were growing up, they stuffed themselves with sweets and other luxurious foods. Instead, she'd spend months surviving on remote, desolate planetoids, chased by monstrous life forms and eating simple rations, or none at all.

For *all* spacers, despite what family and business they grew up in, *"Work was happiness and happiness was work"*, and she herself began working upon reaching the tender age of six.

It was easy work at first, of course, but the responsibilities that her parents placed upon her shoulders grew bigger with every passing year. It was how she'd made enough money for her dowry – the small exploration class space shuttle *Princess Frog* and her spacesuit that she'd designed herself. Like the rest of her kin, she had accomplished all that before her eleventh birthday.

Spacers lived at the very border of known human space, doing what they did best: exploring, trading, and establishing contact with new alien species. They would work for the Minarchy for most of their lives as explorers, and their elders often were the first residents on newly colonized worlds. They would also plunder the enemies of the Terran Minarchy, when they saw fit to do so.

For a spacer, renown amongst other spacers was the most important thing in life. They would never betray each other, but would rob blind anyone who dared cheat them, or other honest people.

Spacers always valued a good story, but never lied while telling one, since that could place the life of another in danger, and it was a sin to do so to a fellow spacer or any type of ally. In the same vein, non-spacers were always welcome in their community, and the spacers themselves were careful not to scare them or turn them off with their customs. For a non-spacer, it was a sign of great accomplishment to tow a spacer's ship or save their lives against all odds.

Groups of spacers could always be seen in any Imperial Minarchy port and colony, wearing their brightly colored-and-painted spacesuits. A spacer's spacesuit was an integral part of their culture, and one could often learn a lot about its wearer just by inspecting its paintings and decals. Spacer society turned and moved forward by the mechanism of their big families – these measured their worth not in money, but in renown and merit.

One could say that spacers were perhaps the first humans in Terran culture to adopt the philosophy *"Money can bring happiness and happiness leads to even more money"*, highlighting the larger importance of other things over wealth in one's life. They were always trying to trade and work where their skills and ships would make the best positive impact on local communities.

Spacers knew well that having good relationships with even the smallest colony outpost would certainly maximize their profits, both in wealth and connections, in the future. Therefore, building up those small colonies and helping them to get prosperous and rich were one of the spacers' main objectives. Different spacer families had different lines of business and often were defined by what they did for a living.

Her parents were dedicated explorers of new planets and resources in the unknown regions of space. Their knowledge of anomalies, locations of hidden wormholes, or secret tricks to navigating dangerous areas of space were second almost to none. In her short time spent alone in outer space, Vasilisa had already perfected every single one of them.

* * *

With her left wing the *Princess Frog* almost touched one jagged piece of metal and stopped, while the ship's navigational computer completely matched speed with all of the closest debris.

Vasilisa glanced at her equipment for one last time, before entering the airlock, ready to board the derelict starship. Gracefully, her body leaped off the hull of the shuttle, and with perfect precision both legs landed on one of the pieces of scrap. Her mag boots locked on, and she quickly scouted a path towards the destroyer. By using only her inertia and mag boots to leap from one piece of debris to another, she could get there and greatly limit the use of fuel.

Spacers were not used to wasting resources, and as they said often, *"Fuel is Life"* – true in if not all, then most instances.

Diminutive in size compared with the destroyer's almost two-kilometers-long hull, Vasilisa began quickly traversing the deadly cloud of metal, sometimes using the grappling hook installed in the right forearm of her spacesuit to pull herself forward and create more inertia.

It took her a good hour to reach the nearest hull breach, and while she locked her mag boots on the hull, she did not enter immediately. First she pulled her weapon, a highly-modified plasma pistol, and used the integrated scanning visor to scout ahead.

That hull breach was, as she had correctly remembered from studying this class of ship's blueprints, situated next to the left torpedo bay and there could be some armed torps' still left, resting in the tubes. She proceeded slowly and carefully forwards, her weapon ready to fire at a moment's notice.

It was her father who had basically forced her to take that overpowered and heavy monster of a pistol. At first Vasilisa naively thought that she would be fine with a simple laser pistol.

Firing the Smith & Wesson model 'Plasmatron' *once* in battle was enough to to change her mind forever – propelled by perfectly aligned mag rails, its pinkish plasma bolt had instantly melted her enemy. All that was left of him were chunks of flesh still burning inside a small pool of smoldering metal. The rest of those goons quickly ran away in the opposite direction, not looking back for a second even.

Vasilisa stood there alone, breathing heavily; her hands were still shaking and she suddenly came to the realization that, if she had taken a weaker weapon, those enemies wouldn't have ran away so fast. Then while defending herself she either would've died, or... killed all of them. Not only had that weapon saved her life, but she hadn't had to kill more people!

So it was true what they said – in the right hands, guns really saved lives.

Now waving the pistol around, she faced a pair of floating torpedoes, and quickly scanned them. Thankfully, there was no radiation leaking from them, and all were disarmed. Somebody had taken his time and knew all of the proper protocols to do so, long after the ship was disabled.

Vasilisa knew that this ship was named INS *Bremen*, had close to one thousand crew, and had carried the first Star Marine battalion ever formed in Earth's history. It also came equipped with prototype stasis chambers, and *that* was the main reason Vasilisa came here in the first place. There might be a survivor here, alive in the stasis chambers on board and besides – all of the *Bremen's* crew were comprised of men!

A young spacer woman on her first husband-search couldn't have picked a better place to start looking for her mate.

Floating carefully around the torps, she reached an intact corridor door, and pushed the hand crank multiple times, trying to open it. Reluctantly, despite her athletic build reinforced by a top notch exoskeleton that piece of reinforced metal slid slowly to the side, and she moved forwards inside the ship, leaving it open. There was little chance of her restoring power to the ships' systems and one need not a tightly shut a hatch blocking their escape, if things went south.

That it was a place most dangerous; any spacer, even the civilians would instantly notice from one hundred miles away, and no Terran was that daft as to enter a derelict without proper prep & equipment.

Vasilisa's eyes squinted and then whispered a short command behind her faceplate. Because the illumination grew ever dimmer inside the hull, she had to turn her suit lights on – better that than to trample all over some trap or worse yet, get ambushed by someone or... something. The top of her helmet projected two wide, yellowish beams of light, and she could again see clearly.

Suddenly before her eyes drifted one mummified corpse, floating aimlessly in the corridor! Half-dressed in a spacesuit, the unfortunate soul bumped away from the closest bulkhead. Both hands were reaching for his throat, and it seemed that his death was caused by suffocation. Stepping forward, she dodged the body, trying not to meet her eyes with his own dead, frozen gaze. Scanner showed there was nothing on his person worth salvaging, therefore the spacer maiden left him behind and pushed ever deeper inside the derelict.

It took her another hour to reach the closest cargo hold, which in this case was used to store ammo and, as she soon found out, was completely empty. From her memories she knew that it was full of heavy ship-to-ship missiles, an older model called "Hammerheads".

INS *Bremen* sported eight dual turrets which fired such missiles, and this storage had maximum ordinance capacity of more than two thousand.

*"So there has to have been a long battle, during which all of those missiles were used up?"*

Vasilisa was somewhat of a capital-ship combat buff, and knew that most battles lasted no more than a few short minutes. You actually wanted to finish starship battles quickly, or you and your crew would cook alive inside the hull of your ship. Even with all of her heatsinks activated, a modern warship wouldn't last with all her weapons firing more than ten minutes at best – and the INS *Bremen* was *not* a modern ship.

She soon found evidence that collaborated her theory – the fifty charred corpses were floating amongst clouds of dust, once part of their spacesuits and bodies, all standing next to the main bow laser guns. Vasilisa saw what was left of their chief gunner's blackened corpse, hands still resting over the main firing controls.

The gun room, now cold and exposed to the vacuum of outer space tomb, would have been as hot as a burning oven when they were alive, when the *Bremen* was still in combat. All of those men – those fathers, brothers, sons and husbands – had bravely died at their posts.

Vasilisa began gritting her teeth in anger, while she thought of the thousands more dead, floating in this metal grave. Once manning a great starship of war, these people had sacrificed themselves without a second thought, so that others would live free.

There was a tiny blip on her scanning visor, and she carefully raised the pistol, moving out of the gun room and in the corridors outside. Again her visor caught something, this time a positive lifesign – an alien one. Trying very hard to remember what his race could be and inspecting the scanning data, Vasilisa placed her finger on the trigger.

Just in case...

Spacers never had the safety of their weapons on when entering a potentially hostile environment. And even if it was true that from a diplomatic standpoint one projected a better, peaceful image with deactivated weapons or with no weapons at all, Spacers loved life – their own, and their friends'. The lives of their enemies and those would do harm to others was forfeit the very moment they crossed into the spacer's field of fire.

Something big and bulky lumbered towards her from behind the corner, and soon showed itself. Wielding a large, curved vibroblade in one hand, the alien carried a wide and towering shield in the other to protect himself from ranged weapon fire. Vasilisa's helmet suddenly boomed with its alien language, and her finger instantly squeezed the trigger, once. Then several times more.

The creature attacking her was from a race called Vaugn. Murderous slaving bastards – she hated all of them and their filthy matriarchs. He shouted something that she could closely translate as – *"I... eat... insides!"* – before making his last clumsy step towards her, because its head had already exploded.

The reason Vasilisa fired so quickly was that she knew what Vaugn would do to any human unlucky enough to stumble into their grimy hands. They used slaves extensively, and humans amongst other races were considered most hated. Not only did the Terran Minarchy stand against slave trade – worse yet, they gave all of their newly uplifted clients full citizen rights.

The Vaugn government was an extreme form of matriarchy, with all men cybernetically altered from an early age. Behavior-modulation chips were installed into their brains while young, turning them into nothing more than mindless thralls. Vaugn military leaders used them primarily as cannon fodder; as well, virtually *all* of their combat units were equipped with self-destruct devices. Any and all attacks were always final – there were no retreat orders issued, and almost no chance for survival for simple Vaugn soldiers.

Their sadistic commanders would stand back, sitting comfortably at their posts, and press buttons, blowing up any soldier or machine that they chose. Sometimes entire units were self-destructed, without even firing but a single shot. Soldiers who somehow survived and had their implants removed in captivity, either died during the surgery or went mad from the memory of what atrocities they were made to commit. As sad as it was, killing those innocent men, she was actually being merciful.

Always, when Vasilisa read about the Vaugn, she cried tears both of sorrow and disgust. For a race to degenerate in such a way and become so monstrous – what had exactly transpired for this to happen? Was it some form of sudden genetic regression, or slow and invisible loss of sanity?

As it was often the case with such things, nobody might ever know. Vasilisa's visor blipped again and soon the corridors were teeming with Vaugn soldiers, and not all were armed for melee. Vasilisa floated towards the one she had already killed, quickly prying the shield off his hand and turning it to face incoming enemy fire.

Just in time.

She managed to block a couple of low-yield particle beam bolts which bounced off of the shield's surface harmlessly. It took Vasilisa three long hours to flank the six individual Vaugn soldiers and kill them. The spacer maiden spent no more than sixteen plasma shells to do so, but in the end she found their crashed boarding craft locked on at the port side of the *Bremen*.

They had arrived here perhaps six months ago, with thirty troops commanded by a junior matriarch. She found her very dead, frozen corpse slumped in their ship's command pit. The Vaugn female was killed by somebody wielding a short vibroblade, who was able to sneak past her guards and slit her throat with one single blow.

*"So there were others on that ship,* she thought to herself *– but how many, and who were they?"*

* * *

Vasilisa moved ever so carefully towards the upper ship decks, where its main sensor array was located.

Reaching it later that day, tired from crawling through blasted bulkheads and dodging old booby-traps left by the ship's defenders, Vasilisa entered what was left of the *Bremen's* sensor array.

It was completely decimated and she scanned it, only to find that somebody had already lifted all salvageable parts years ago.

What a letdown!

Nevertheless, she managed to find herself a cozy hiding place and, concealed there, got a good six hours of uninterrupted sleep. She was finally awoken by her scanning visor, which she'd left on auto-scan mode while sleeping. It had detected something, or someone, sneaking towards her hiding spot.

Instantly she reached for the gun, but the cloaked alien was faster; small-statured and with thin arms and legs, it leaped on top of her and aimed at her head with his short vibroblade. The only thing that saved Vasilisa were the moves her dad had taught her in self-defense class.

Using both of her feet, she grappled the attacker's hand, and the blade only scratched the helmet's face plate. She then kicked him back and pulled her own blade. Both started running away from and at each other, trying to stab their respective opponent to death. Her spacesuit's armor plates were damaged severely and without them Vasilisa would've surely died, but in the end, her attacker stepped in the wrong place.

One looted control pit for a navigation command projector collapsed under his foot, and he ended dead with Vasilisa's blade sticking from his neck.

Taking some time to calm herself and inspect both the dead alien and her suit, Vasilisa soon found what his race was. The slim alien was a Jaern hunter, and she quickly pulled out her gun, switching the scanning visor for a more detailed search. Sadly the only item this Jaern had that she could use was his chameleon cloak, and Vasilisa wrapped herself in it.

Her mother hated all Jaern with a passion, because many of her friends were eaten by them... alive.

That entire race consumed only sentient life forms for food, and they had a most weird religion worshiping some "Dark Hunter" god. If all that wasn't enough, they had a warped sense of honor; chasing and fighting the weak was considered to be a most brave, heroic act, constantly praised by their priesthood.

Vasilisa's mother had tracked down the mothership responsible for that massacre and she and her dad had blown it up to pieces, but not before her mom had faced one of their telepathic priestesses that the Jaern called a "Soul Huntress".

The story of how she fought that monster of a woman still gave Vasilisa nightmares. She wasn't going to allow herself and her soul to be sacrificed to some filthy Unlife entity – it was a far better alternative to "bite the bullet" instead.

Scientists had long since proven the existence of souls, or "psychic imprints" as they called them. Science had also accepted all previous rumors about demons and other "supernatural" entities, some of which were now being classified as Unlife.

As most older races had already fought against the so-called Unlife, humans were told horrifying stories and shown actual data about them. Creatures who came from nowhere and fed upon the life energy of sentients, the Unlife was a known and feared enemy throughout the Galaxy.

Vasilisa (just as any other explorer) packed one particle beam carbine just in case those foul, soul-eating things lurked nearby.

Quickly, she moved out of the sensor command room and sneaked into the ship's service tunnel network. Crawling for hours, and thanks to the looted chameleon cloak, Vasilisa successfully crept up unnoticed on five Jaern and killed them, using only one shot per target.

She'd never met anybody stronger than ordinary hunters, but the fear remained, always keeping her alert and on her toes at all times. After killing the last Jaern she could find, her visor suddenly detected an intact weapon, stored inside of somebody's footlocker. It wasn't hard for a good computer specialist like her to pick the electronic lock and retrieve it.

Vasilisa now held in her hands a vintage "Space Sweeper" – a snub railgun that fired a cloud of tiny pellets. The weapon looked brand-new, and it even had a factory-made Winchester leather sling attached. On the bottom of that locker she also found two spare power packs, and she loaded the weapon immediately, putting her pistol back in the holster. With a happy grin, Vasilisa walked out into the next corridor, aiming her new weapon forward.

She spent three standard Earth weeks exploring the derelict hull and faced many more enemies.

It seemed that, except her, many others had previously found the ship, but got stranded on it and eventually died off. Also, there was an insanely great number of simple traps, booby-traps and explosives, which had killed off many of the different intruders. Keeping one eye on the scan data, Vasilisa managed to loot some of the explosives and use them against what was left of the aliens.

First, there was this odd group of sixteen pirate raiders – pretty well-armed, but poorly led. A single spacer of *any* age could take on idiots like that with relative ease. In her case, it was even easier – she just had to spend more ammo than usual to finish them all. After one whole week to set up new booby-traps of her own, she lured the rest of those pirates away from their camp and killed them piecemeal.

The second group she had to fight were some strange hive-minded life forms, who had built a nest for themselves close to one of the main reactors and were breeding with an alarming speed. She used all of those looted explosives and grenades to deal with them permanently, but not before getting bit by one of their larger types. Spent another week puking her guts, hiding in a makeshift shelter.

Her resources almost spent, Vasilisa decided that if she couldn't locate any stasis chambers by the end of the next week, she would cancel the expedition. On her last day, Vasilisa located a well-hidden service tunnel, which had a bolted megasteel door blocking it.

To reach this place, she followed one of the goriest battle trails she had ever seen in her life. Someone had single-handedly slaughtered at least fifty pirates. For decades their already-mummified corpses had been floating around, with horrified facial expressions. It looked like somebody had just plowed through them, using primarily a vibroblade, and ranged weapons very sparingly.

The attacks were deadly to such an extent that the only ones capable of fighting with precision and achieving results like that, that she knew of, were the special ops troopers and their ilk.

Only one hour total was needed for her plasma torch to melt the welding on that bulkhead and then she was in.

Another twenty minutes walking in this dark, but surprisingly clean, intact tunnel and her scanning visor bleeped. Vasilisa found herself inside of a small chamber, holding the *Bremen's* backup fusion reactor – and next to it, she saw the big silhouette of an intact stasis chamber...

* * *

The armored Taz'aran corvette speedily moved through the debris field, and soon reached the derelict Terran destroyer. Her two boarding-team sections of twenty each, descended towards the nearest hull breach. The very fact that their captain had managed to find this treasure was a remarkable achievement, and could have very easily won him the title of Border Count on its own.

The sensors on their ship detected one female human life sign, and the captain expected to not only have this ship as a prize, but a sex slave for his new manor back home, as well. Giddy with excitement, he ordered his boarding team to move faster and capture the female unharmed.

His troopers were fresh – purchased from the core Taz'aran colonies, but expertly trained, well-armed and armored. In good order, at least as much as the ravaged corridors of the derelict allowed them, they moved closer and tried surrounding the "hapless" woman.

The first trooper who saw her was one of the recently-promoted section leaders and he arrogantly assumed her unwillingness to resist. Dragging some old, but yet still-working stasis pod, the girl drew her weapon and shot him dead, with such lighting speed and deadly accuracy, that the second in command could only helplessly take cover behind the closest bulkhead while he waited for reinforcements.

Oh, the Taz'arans did follow her; then, and a couple of times later, she was caught by flanking fire, and almost surrounded. Each time, the Taz'aran boarding team numbers decreased by one...

She used an insanely overpowered Terran plasma pistol, and their armor protection was equal to cardboard when hit by its shots. Therefore, despite their captain's screams and intimidating orders, the troopers continuously tried to slow Vasilisa down and tire her out.

It was the safest bet for them and it seemed to be working. The girl had been previously wounded, and from the looks of it, was dead tired and hungry. Nevertheless and with stubborn tenacity, the young Terran woman continued dragging that bulky stasis pod towards the other end of the ship. There, the Taz'arans saw a great debris field, untouched and full of ever-floating, crushing-against-each-other pieces.

Pushed by their captain, the Taz'arans again charged at her from multiple sides, confident that surely now they could overwhelm the lone Terran.

Their target gracefully floated through the weapons fire, pulling another other weapon from behind her back. The closest trooper's torso was instantly shredded to pieces, and his limbs flew in all directions, particle beam rifle still firing. The Taz'aran sergeant watched with horror and amazement how this Terran girl continuously dodged his trooper's shots with ease.

It was like she was dancing!

Her return-fire dropped them one by one, always with a single shot from that railgun of hers. Using their very corpses and equipment for cover, she pushed and pulled at them with a powerful grappling hook. Soon the whole buckled-and-broken torpedo bay was full of blood blobs and the shredded floating corpses of his soldiers. As the captain bellowed desperate orders in the comms link, what was left of the sergeant's troopers quickly fell back.

With disbelief, the sergeant realized that it was only him and five others who had survived from their full two sections of troopers!

He ordered the men to give that human witch some space, himself backing off to a safer distance. The sergeant had no more spare power packs, and otherwise a great lack of desire to close the distance between him and her. That cheapskate of a captain could have reached deeper into his pockets and equip them with more and more powerful weapons, at least some light repeaters, maybe. But no – *he*, as with most of those idiotic nobles, wanted more loot...

He sighed and reached for his backpack; at least *he* was smart enough to invest in better, long-reaching weapons. The girl now floated away off the derelict, using the mini engines in her spacesuit to run quickly away from them. He sent the rest of his troopers after her, giving them instructions not to get in range of that horrible weapon, and engaging their own engines, they followed her out. While his brave troopers tried to catch up with the girl, the sergeant unpacked his prototype, high-powered railgun and switched on its integrated holo-targeting system.

\* \* \*

Vasilisa couldn't breathe normally, and her entire body screamed with pain, but the *Princess Frog's* silhouette was growing larger. She ordered the computer by voice, using her PDA, to open the airlock of her ship, and once again tried to bluff the last two troopers. It was amazing what one could do, with just aiming powerful guns at a bunch of cowardly idiots.

First time she did it, two of the then-five tried taking cover behind some of the floating metal debris, and got themselves crushed by them. Another one of them decided to get closer and capture her with his grappling hook, but was completely startled when Vasilisa aimed at his torso. While he instinctively and lightly raised his hands in defense, another piece of metal bashed him aside, dragging his now-unconscious body further into outer space.

Never saw *him* again.

She now had nothing left; she'd even lost her dagger on the derelict. You couldn't know if that bluff would work again – so she tried. Vasilisa aimed her pistol at them, but this time the soldiers didn't cower, and fired at her. Once again she moved herself, shielding the stasis pod from their weapons fire. It all happened very fast, but for her, everything seemed to move at a turtle's pace. The air lock opened, and while she pushed the pod inside, a flash of light blinked near the hull breach she entered the *Bremen* from, catching her attention.

Suddenly, her chest almost burst open.

The armored door of her ship's airlock closed behind her and the inner one slid aside, and while the stasis pod slowly careened into the interior of *Princess frog*, Vasilisa understood that she had both failed and succeeded. With blood blobs floating away from her deadly chest wound and her vision going blurry, she activated the ship's command voice protocols.

Gave full authority to the man inside stasis for when he woke up – her ship would be soon in his control. She might have failed, but before dying Vasilisa *had* to be sure that this man would survive *and* escape. Even though she would never have children, some other woman was going to get lucky with him.

Smiling, she started the stasis deactivation protocols, quickly running through her mind what her last words should be. Could she ask him to bring her dead body back home? Her parents would surely be happier and she would get the usual spacer's funeral – a piece of salvage on each eye, the body dropped into the nearest star.

Very ritualistic and very somber. The suit was removed, naturally, otherwise how could one show their descendants what had his parents and relatives accomplished while they were alive? Besides, a spacer's ornate suit was a work of art, and sometimes families sold them to private collectors.

Maybe she could leave her equipment to him?

He had been sleeping for over forty years and could surely use the creds.

What if he couldn't afford fuel and never reached Terran space because of a lack of money?

No, her ship had enough fuel for the return trip. She heard the pod hissing while its old temp regulators cooled the field generator – gradually lowering the intensity and power of the stasis field. Vasilisa saw the lid slowly moving aside, and the air around her suddenly became colder, she painfully dragged her bleeding and broken body closer to the man inside.

Wanted to see his face clearly, at least once before her death. Her blurry vision noticed that the man's uniform had a very peculiar shoulder patch, signifying that he was a Star Marine commander. Vasilisa's eyesight momentarily faded away; she was alive, yes, but only through sheer force of will.

Hearing the man breathing and coughing, her sight returned, and Vasilisa gazed at his confused face. Mouth tried moving, but no sound came at first, and she focused what remained of her strength in one last effort:

"H...hello..my..my name is...Vas.."

Suddenly she started coughing blood from her mouth, and began fading away. The last thing she saw were his beautiful but sad ice-blue eyes looking at her face, and his powerful voice shouting one word:

*"No!"*

* * *

The large muscular man got up quickly, and his powerful hands grabbed her – one palm he placed directly over her gaping chest wound. A wave of light appeared; surging through his entire body and pulsing all into her, some of the wounded flesh began to heal. The ghastly injury closed with painful slowness, while some of the floating blobs of blood in the shuttle's cabin joined with the light stream and flowed back into her.

Whatever it was that the man did, it clearly wasn't enough, and he hurriedly placed her body back inside the stasis chamber, activating it again. While the top lid slid back in place, the man turned around and took one good look at the interior of the unknown ship, inspecting it carefully. Then he turned the stasis pod around and pressed a combination of buttons on a hidden panel on its back. Another hissing sound and the pod's hidden compartment lid opened, revealing a bulky and worn out, but incredibly well-

212

armed spacesuit.

It was heavy and despite all of the punishment it apparently had taken in the past, still in good working order. He pulled it to the side and replaced the main power pack with another one that he had seen earlier, standing on a rack next to him. The suit's internal indicators suddenly came to life and he blinked at the status data with disbelief – this new power pack had a charge *five* times greater than the ones they used in his day.

The man was angry, very angry and when he was in such a state, people died violently.

That girl! He instantly knew that she had used her body as a shield to protect his pod – so young, and already she was an accomplished warrior.

What had made her risk life and limb to visit this forgotten graveyard? He saw from the main, transparent megasteel viewer, that the enemies who had almost killed her were still flying around this vessel, trying to gain entry. The ship's scanners showed him a holo with detailed info, and he almost growled angrily – it was high time that they all died painfully, those Taz'arans!

He entered his suit and while the machine closed around him, he checked all indicators. The hand auto-railguns were fully loaded and with that advanced main power pack, his shoulder-mounted armor-piercing laser could fire at least sixty or even more shots.

The now armor-encased Star marine turned towards the air lock, but before exiting, his glove reached inside of his stasis pod's secret compartment and grabbed something – a large, two handed vibrosword. He turned the blade's power on, and for a second grimly watched the light its blade emitted, shining off of his armored faceplate.

They would all die – every single one of them!

# Chapter 8

## *Alric von Englebert*

Instead of that short girl that the Taz'arans had been chasing up until now, out from the shuttle came a tall, lumbering man and had the Taz'aran trooper had enough time to perform a proper scan, he would've found out his exact race.

There were two of them, all that what was left of their starship's boarding team, and the Taz'arans thought themselves out of harm's way. Since their sergeant had already successfully sniped that filthy Terran woman, it was only a matter of time before them breaching the shuttle and flying safely back to their ship.

The man wore a heavy spacesuit, reinforced with additional armor plates and on his back they saw a greatsword, probably locked onto the suit via a special mag-sheath. He had both of his hands raised with closed fists, aimed at them, and just as that armored air-lock door behind him closed, he whispered ominously on all open comm links:

"You who face me today, be assured of this – all of you will *die*! There will be no mercy for any of you, and I shall grant you no escape! I, Alric von Englebert, Commander of the First Terran Star Marine Corps Battalion, will personally end you!"

Both troopers were startled by his intimidating voice and posture, but not enough that they would break off and run. They attacked him, firing their particle snub guns, but the place he was a split second before stood empty, and their weapons fire harmlessly bounced off of the *Princess Frog* armor-plating.

Slowly, their minds realized that the Terran was standing between them, his fists still aimed at their chests. Both troopers frantically tried dodging since they could clearly see that he had mini auto-railguns installed into his spacesuit's forearms.

A short stream of projectiles hit them both, shredding their bodies, while that man almost danced forwards, walking over the jagged pieces of scrap. Over his left shoulder another gun extended upwards, its barrel aiming at the derelict hull of the *Bremen*. In particular, one area, which was dangerously close to its forward torpedo bays.

Alric noticed a small flash of light coming from the inside, and effortlessly sidestepped. The piece of scrap *exactly* where he stood less than a second before, was hit by an accurate rail gun projectile. A commendable effort – good aim, those Taz'arans had, but not nearly accurate enough!

He frowned beneath his helmet's faceplate. Why would that girl choose to stand alone and against multiple trained soldiers with such desperation? And why was it, that she had placed her body between the enemy weapon's fire and his stasis pod?! His shoulder laser gun unleashed one single, bluish beam, and at the opposite end of it, somebody's spacesuit exploded.

Alric's aim was, as always, perfect, and even though he'd spent close to fifty long years in stasis, there was no chance of *any* enemy soldier escaping with his life once they faced him.

* * *

216

The Taz'aran captain had lost all links with his ship's veteran boarding team of star marines. The financial set back was great; a Taz'aran officer (generally) did not think of their soldiers, but money first. Furious, he ordered another team deployed to finally secure the derelict Terran destroyer.

Losing a few more men meant nothing to him; as always his position would allow purchasing more troops and expanding his forces at a later date. The capture of that Terran derelict would give him so much leverage, that in the event that some of those older border Counts kicked the proverbial scrap container, he could try to grab the position for himself.

The discovery of that Terran starship and its successful salvage was now key to his ascension to high nobility. Besides, the only drawback in losing some enlisted men was equipment cost. Purchasing more trained soldiers was always a bother, but it would be covered by the enormous cost of this starship and any secrets hidden within its databanks, not counting the looting of high-tech Terran weapons.

He was particularly fond of their railgun technology; it was far superior to anything that the Taz'arans had. His people had long since used particle-beam weapons and simple missiles in all of their wars for thousands of years. Lately though, with the rise of profitable partnerships with pirate clans and drug lords, many copies of Terran railguns had found their way into Taz'aran weapon markets.

These replicas were always of inferior quality since their craftsmen lacked the knowledge and skill, to reverse engineer some of their most complicated components. Still, those weapons gave any ships who had them installed great advantage in range, and they punched through armor like nothing else.

Most alien races local to Fringe Space predominantly still used particle-beam weapons and could not compete with the railguns, who out-ranged and outshot them weapon for weapon. Therefore, Taz'aran strategists shifted their overall projections in favor of those new guns.

Yes, the old core races shunned Terran tech, calling projectile and laser guns a "barbaric" technology, more of a tool than weapon. But what were guns, but tools of war, and those who now foolishly scoffed at them were bound to be enslaved and even exterminated later.

The folly of pacifists was always something that his race used against them. Taz'arans would start diplomatic negotiations and use those feeble fools' trust in "peaceful" talk to gain an advantage... military advantage.

While they spoke of peace, corsairs in Taz'aran payroll would relentlessly prey upon their shipping, raid their colonies, and in any way possible, weaken them. By the time that this was apparent to their peace-loving enemy that it was they, the Taz'aran Imperium, who had orchestrated their demise, it was far too late.

What was it that Terrans say – *"If you want peace, prepare for war"*.

The captain hated them and everything they stood for. Not only were all of their citizens armed to the teeth, but even the children were taught how to fight!

Didn't these idiots know not to oppose the invader?!

Instead of an easy conquest, those blasted humans and their loyal clients were quickly growing and turning into a local powerhouse. No amount of pirate or slaver raids could put a stop to their relentless advance into Fringe Space.

Moreover, instead of weakening and being ruined financially, the Terran economy was booming. They not only produced more and more advanced weapons to arm their spaceships, but all slaves who managed to escape were welcome in their space, and they would then turn around and work even *harder* for their saviors.

The Taz'arans had played the game of conquest for a couple thousand years, and were very good at it. Yet, all of their agents were captured the instant they tried acting and their plots blocked, as if Terran intelligence services possessed godly powers of precognition.

He himself was convinced that humans got plenty of help from those filthy Kil'ra, and as he watched how his second boarding team was flying towards the derelict, the Taz'aran captain tried imagining what the Galaxy would look like without the pesky do-gooders shoving their noses in everybody's business.

The amount of platinum taz'aran decats lost due to Terran colonial militia and starships actually *preying* on pirate ships and slavers was mind-boggling! The captain did lose some of his investments, since one of his slave transports had been intercepted and boarded by the blasted Cav militia. He was told that it was just one small patrol vessel and some fighters that wiped out the entire convoy in just a few short minutes.

The Taz'arans didn't believe in coincidences and weren't superstitious, but placed their trust in the powers of money and treachery. The baseness of their plots was widely known and feared throughout Fringe Space and beyond, therefore the captain instantly assumed that somebody with keen tactical knowledge and sharp intellect had been placed in command of those colonial forces.

It seemed that every time anybody tried to get close to

Cav colony space, or to any of their neighbors, an immediate and devastating preemptive strike crushed them to pieces. Somebody had to do something about those upstarts, because soon they, or some other plucky Terran, would settle even deeper into Fringe Space!

Never mind that; the captain thought of his current situation and ordered the troopers to move faster. The scanners of his corvette showed conflicting data, but at best there was another Terran who perhaps survived in stasis and had now awoken to defend his ship. No longer were his starship's sensors detecting that human female, and while he thought about what had happened to his first boarding team, not once in his mind came the notion that she could've been the one responsible for their demise.

* * *

Alric moved quickly, traversing the ruined interior of his once grand starship, the vessel he had called home for many years. Years that he and his crewmates had spent chasing the slavers and pirates responsible for invading Earth.

Before that time of war and strife he was just a twelve year old boy, who had dreams of becoming a singer. His parents, who moved to Berlin in 1960, spent more and more time advancing both of their children's education. After the Great War had ended, everyone dreamt of peace. How naive were they, how naive was he back then... for all it took to ruin their futures was but *one,* single, day of doom.

Alric's father, Marius von Englebert, was part of the old nobility. He had plenty of carefully managed wealth, which he used mostly to build hospitals and houses for the

220

poor. It was a tradition for his family to do so, and all the people whom he hired in those hospitals were jobless, but bright folk, who simply needed a chance to build for themselves and their families a better life. They did not count the number of destitute who were no longer living on the streets but rather those of them they found employment for.

His mother, Elsa, was a genius scientist and inventor, responsible for multiple spacesuit advancements and upgrades. As a matter of fact, it was his mother who perfected the life support systems sustaining him right now.

His younger brother, Eric, was a gifted math prodigy, and soon left to join the Tokyo University's program for children. During these times, Alric was enjoying that his parents were happy, their hopes and dreams fulfilling. They were watching both their kids growing up happy, after the devastating World War.

Many European cities were almost ruined by Soviet bombing raids and artillery strikes, but it took only a few years for the citizens of the world to rebuild them. People from all over the world were employed in rebuilding the damage, many becoming master builders and engineers while they toiled.

The Communist International waged their war of conquest all over the world, and so it was generally accepted that anybody could go and work in any country temporarily, while areas in need of rebuilding still existed. Since the continent of Africa had been largely unaffected, it fell on their shoulders to carry most of the burden. Millions of people traveled all over the planet, working and learning new skills, that soon aided their own countries economic growth when they returned.

They had become skilled beyond imagining with the

quick building and repair of all structures, both on land and, soon, space. The great Earth starship docks were in the process of being built, when Pirate Lord Mahimm's armada dropped out of hyperspace in Earth's orbit. The station could be used only in the construction of very small starships, while other, much bigger vessels were built in makeshift docks shortly before the attack.

Alric vividly remembered that day – he'd been out with his friends from school, visiting one of the many parks in Berlin. He had written a song on his own and was prepared to surprise everyone by performing it for them. His class knew of the talent he had, and many a time, Alric sang during recess, famous songs that were at the top of radio charts these days.

He jokingly began by coughing, and all of his friends suddenly became startled.

In the beginning he thought that his jest was a success, but then he heard the sonic booms, and looked up – it was the sight of many thousands of dropships and assault pods, leaving behind burning trails in Earth's atmosphere, which had scared his schoolmates.

At first they ran, but there was nowhere to hide from the invaders, there were millions of them as he later was told, deployed in the first wave of attack alone. Soon the streets ran red with the blood of innocents. Since the end of the Great War most people had kept weapons in their homes and many, if not all, grabbed them, engaging the aliens.

It was a bloodbath; the level of technological advantage that the invaders had was almost overwhelming. Yes, they did die, but for each of them, close to five humans were killed. Not only that, but it seemed the invaders had keen interest in capturing the civilians en masse.

Even the military units who rapidly were deployed on the streets and bravely fought off the aliens for a time, couldn't stop the inevitable – thousands upon thousands were captured and taken away in their ships.

* * *

Alric's faceplate showed instantly where he and his now long-dead crewmates had planted the explosive traps and mines. Those were still very much active, and the girl who had traversed the gauntlet of deadly booby-traps, then dragged his stasis pod under fire *and* killed multiple soldiers, suddenly became even more amazing.

He slowed his breathing and went into the state he taught his troopers – Dead Still – used when a Star Marine was about to ambush their enemy. Alric then deactivated all of his spacesuit's systems, but not before using the exoskeleton's power to wrap his body with a piece of floating metal and waited for the fools to come...

The Taz'aran boarding team soon reached his position and began tripping the traps. From a group of thirty men, only about half survived and reached the place where his concealed suit was. The Star Marine took one deep breath and, re-activating all of his systems, unsheathed his greatsword.

Its blade soon decapitated the closest two Taz'arans with one stroke, their headless corpses floating away with arms and legs still twitching. Engines on full power, he flew through the blood trail and shot another soldier straight through his chest using his shoulder laser.

In a moment of complete disbelief, the Taz'aran

sergeant in command saw Alric flying in and out of different hull breaches, each time outflanking his troops.

Sometimes he would leap from behind the cover of broken bulkheads and slice them to pieces with his vibrosword, then in the very next moment unleash a devastating barrage of projectiles from his hand auto-railguns, making them duck behind cover.

All semblance of military order and discipline completely gone, the Taz'aran captain began sweating in his command chair. His every order and plan was in an instant made obsolete by the tactical brilliance and combat prowess of this single star marine.

The Taz'arans began an "orderly" retreat and tried tirelessly shooting the Terran – to no avail. Relentless, Alric continued stalking them, using his knowledge and expertise of the terrain against the inexperienced troopers. Even though they had scanners and theoretically could use them and map their way, it took precious time, time that they sorely lacked in that instance.

The Taz'aran sergeant leading their ship's second boarding team section, considered himself to be a tough melee combatant, and only after some of his troopers had managed to hit the enemy a couple of times, he decided to face him. With shield in one arm and vibroaxe in another, the Taz'aran stood in his way and assumed a battle stance.

For a number of short, intense star-seconds, the two combatant studied each other. Then with a sudden blast, his enemy's engines propelled him forwards, and his shield was instantly sliced in twain by the Terran's deadly sword.

For some minutes the Taz'aran desperately fended off his attacks, with all of his own strikes hitting nothing in return. It was evident for anyone versed in space combat that his time was near, and so he tried one last feint. Instead of deflecting his enemy's sword, the Taz'aran skilfully slid backwards, feigning retreat, axe concealed behind and ready to strike. But instead of stepping forward and getting sucker-punched, a single laser beam streaked from the star marine's shoulder, hitting the taz'aran's face from point-blank range.

Losing power, the Taz'aran's spacesuit floated upwards and hit the ceiling, bumping and scraping off multiple sharp pieces of metal. His still-working vibroaxe's blade got stuck in the bulkhead, pieces of shredded, melting megasteel igniting the suit's oxygen reserves.

Alric quickly moved past the fireball and targeted another Taz'aran soldier, who at this instant was running as quickly as his mag boots could carry him. His laser beam sliced the back of the Taz'aran's suit, melting armor, equipment, flesh, and bone to such an extent that he could see through his now-lifeless corpse. Somehow the running soldiers had switched their links to the comms wave on in their panic, and he was listening to their dying screams and horrified whimpering for the whole time.

He remembered the same cries of pain and smell of death all those years ago in Berlin.

* * *

They were hiding in a nearby hospital's basement, while he desperately tried to call his parents on one of those old cell phones which everybody had in the 60's. There was no signal, and in an effort to reach a higher place, Alric's hand stuck through the basement's window. One of the aliens must have seen his arm, because soon after, the entire building was shaken to its foundations.

The children listened in terror as patients and other people who had taken refuge in this hospital were slaughtered. The fizzing of the invaders guns, mowing down those who resisted, followed by buzzing and splashing. The muffled voices begging for mercy were then replaced with the sounds of people drowning in their own blood. They tried running away by crawling through that basement window and outside to the streets.

Too little, too late.

The aliens found them and entered the basement by melting its door. Alric was the only one who had managed to crawl outside. He watched with utter horror as the invaders began killing his helpless friends, either by crushing the kids' skulls on the ground with their boots, choking them, or slashing their throats with blades. In just under a minute, all of them were dead.

Both hands covering his mouth, tears running down, Alric watched, while one of the aliens walked directly towards him and opened her helmet. She was smiling and licking her lips, while an expression of absolute happiness was written all over her greenish face. He screamed and crawled away as fast as possible, but bumped into somebody's boot.

Terrified Alric looked up, only to see another alien looking down at him, while playing with a severed human head. He held a bloodied blade in his other hand and, encouraged by the female alien's boisterous laughter, raised it up in the air.

Something deep inside Alric broke; he stopped crying and feverishly looked around. Beside him was a decapitated corpse, and next to its hand – a pistol. Alric rolled aside, dodging the alien's first blow and grabbed the gun with both hands, then, eyes wide open, he aimed the weapon. It was a

Luger, made for the army during the war, light, accurate and easy to use.

Most kids had received more than enough shooting lessons during and after the war, since there were some Illuminati and communist terrorists left. The Imperial Minarchy wanted its citizens to have better personal protection, and many weapons were sold at bargain prices.

Still on the ground, Alric squeezed the trigger; luckily, the pistol was loaded, and with his very first shot he hit the unprotected face of his attacker. Inside the helmet, the alien's head exploded to pieces – flesh, bone and brain matter splattered all over him.

Alric searched the human body, quickly grabbed all the spare magazines he could find and ran back towards the hospital basement's window. There stood the alien woman, laughing no longer, with mouth open and eyes wide, staring at him with pure disbelief. While still running, he slid over the pavement on his belly and aiming at her face, opened fire.

Her helmet began closing, but not fast enough and most of the bullets while ricocheting from it, still turned her head into mush. The rest of her alien friends screamed and shouted then and shot at him a couple of times, but Alric was long gone. He ran, pistol ready in hand, towards his home, and without thinking of his own safety, shot another alien passer-by.

The last bullet in his Luger's magazine bounced off of the alien's armored suit and while walking towards him, Alric took a spare from his pocket and reloaded. The alien was so confused and taken by disbelief, that by the time he raised the beam gun and shot at Alric, he himself was mortally hit in the neck.

Alric was taken completely over by something he didn't know he had it in him; no longer he was feeling fear and sadness – it was hate that drove him. Hatred towards the invader, those monsters, who with barbarous cruelty had slaughtered his friends and many others.

They had no place here!

He would kill as many of them as he possibly could, even if it would cost him his life.

There was a great emptiness within him, as deep inside, he knew that his parents and brother were dead, even without seeing their bodies. He was right; turning around the corner, Alric saw the corpses of his mother and father lying bloodied on the street joined by five other human bodies. It looked like all of them had been executed by the nearby aliens. Alric walked towards them and again shot point-blank, aiming at their heads.

The last thing he remembered was the aliens shooting him to near death and, as the enemy thought Alric finally vanquished, they left him to die. His father's forgotten ancestry awoke in him that day, as the deadly wounds closed by themselves. Flesh, organs and bones regenerated, all surrounded by white glowing light. Alric rose, his shirt burned, and tore it aside, raising his pistol from the ground.

Reloading it once more, Alric ran after his alien executioners, aiming to fulfill the oath he had taken...

* * *

The star marine finally reached his last opponent and grabbed her from the side. Hands empowered by his suit's exoskeleton, he then effortlessly crushed her helmet. On the open comm links he heard a voice – not surprisingly for him, it was the Taz'aran captain:

"Whoever you are, Terran, think carefully of what you are going to do next! You are a lone soldier, facing overwhelmingly numerous troops and it is a question of *when*, not *if*, you will lose. You *will* be surrounded and killed. Do yourself a favor – start running now! While I have graciously extended you such an offer, it won't last forever, as you have greatly tested my patience, Terran. The losses of equipment and manpower I have suffered, because of your stubborn and useless resistance, demand retribution!" – The Taz'aran's captain's voice sounded somewhat shaky, and his attempt to intimidate Alric was unsuccessful.

In response, the star marine jokingly spoke in his comm link:

"I care not who *you* are, Taz'aran, all I need to know is that you are my enemy. In war, one wins when *all* of his enemies are killed. There will be *no* negotiations and *no* mercy for any of you. Whatever you think your soon-to-be-dead soldiers could achieve, will stay in your imagination only. And no, your hiding behind the bulkheads of your starship will not save those pathetic lives of yours. At best, it will prolong your suffering, as you try your luck running away from me, while shitting yourselves in fear. I don't have to tell you that I am coming for you, as you can clearly see that on your sensor screens. Do try your very best shooting me down with those point defense guns of yours, because if you miss, and miss you shall, the very next thing you all will be hearing on the open links are your crewmates' dying screams!"

On their ship's scanners, the Taz'aran bridge crew could see one lonely dot, a single Terran spacesuit, that began moving towards their vessel. Frightened, the officers looked at their captain for guidance, only to see him quaking in his boots – so much so, that his command chair was also trembling beneath him.

His voice still shaky, he screamed at them:

"Open fire with all point defense guns! Concentrate everything you can on him, I want this filthy Terran melted at once!"

His gunners tried their best to follow this order, but to no avail. The diminutive target easily evaded all of their fire! Particle energy bolts streaming all around him, the human employed all of his suit's equipment expertly, dodging all attacks. Not only that, but he also used some of the closest debris and flew behind them, making himself an even harder target to hit.

The Taz'arans soon came to the terrifying realization that this person was indeed trained to perfection, and a master in the art of space combat. And while the lower-enlisted men and women under the Taz'aran captain's command thought that the ship had a chance still to beat this monstrous Terran, their captain was almost assured in his utter defeat.

He stood up from his command chair, as the Terran melted his way through an air lock and began killing the emergency defense sections. They were all comprised from ordinary crewmates and had no chance whatsoever in even slowing him down with their light beam weapons. The captain understood that clearly, while watching him fight on his ship's internal optical sensors and walking towards his bridge's exit, he pointed at the highest ranking officer:

"I am going to face him myself! Gunnery Officer, you have the bridge!"

As he left the command deck, instead of running

towards the fight, the captain turned around and bolted in the direction of the ship's hangar bay. Before leaving his command chair, he had made sure that all security sensors were blind to his movements, so that the bridge officers wouldn't get any bright ideas and think of running away too.

If somebody had to survive this, it should be him and him alone. He'd heard of another captain being killed by his own bridge crew, and wasn't taking any chances with his own officers' loyalty. He wasn't sure what had actually happened there, but by most accounts it was some Terran again. One of the smaller ones, who had flown a single fighter against a fully armed frigate.

Crazy Terrans, he hated them even more now!

* * *

Alric blasted inside the Taz'aran starship and was met with sporadic particle-beam fire. A group of regular crewmen stood behind a hastily-made barricade, blocking his way to the bridge. Conserving energy, the star marine raised one of his gloves and sprayed the entire barricaded area with deadly railgun projectiles, the then-suppressed Taz'arans he finished with his own fists and legs.

Poorly equipped, the crewmen were sporting only pistols and carbines and had no heavy weapons. Wearing simple light spacesuits didn't help to raise their chances of survival either. Alric easily plowed through the second and third makeshift barricades, effortlessly killing a dozen Taz'arans more. He then reached the ship's armory, where instead of scared and weak crewmen, before him stood a fully armed power armor.

Alric cursed his luck – he hated PA's! If anyone could take a star marine in straight combat one-on-one, then it would be a pilot in power armor. Nevertheless, the Terran steeled himself and prepared for a battle most dangerous. Instead of running away or cowering with fear, this crewman stood his ground unflinching, and was probably a specialist mecha pilot.

Armed with a large, assault version of the standard Taz'aran particle beam rifle, the sixteen-feet-tall mech also had a power mace on its belt. Its pilot didn't waste time exchanging words, and immediately unleashed a wall of particle bolts that melted the bulkheads around Alric, creating a deadly, overheated environment, full of molten metal.

Alric aimed his laser, fired while dodging most of the bolts, and then grabbed the handle of his sword. The mech's armor took a hit, parts of it melted away yet, that wasn't nearly enough to slow it down! The pilot engaged some system attached to his machine's feet; suddenly his mech could match Alric's speed.

Soon both were dashing around the gutted ship's armory, their attacks chasing each other. Both were hit, and even though Alric's suit was considerably smaller, its armor plates held somehow even against those large particle bolts.

One couldn't say the same about the mech's armor though. It was evidently thicker, and yet Alric's integrated laser cannon had managed to successfully pierce through it, dealing considerable damage. He himself was more frustrated than hurt; even with all of that heat coming through his suit's protective underlay, Alric could continue fighting despite this. The Terran Imperial Army didn't train weak soldiers.

All power packs expended, the mech threw his now-useless assault rifle away, dashing at Alric, simultaneously unsheathing his melee weapon and swinging at him with it. Alric's hand was faster; with a sudden, abrupt deactivation of his engines, the star marine, instead of blocking, placed himself inside the blow's wide arch. His exoskeleton whined with disagreement, but moved his body as the feet's mag-boots ripped up pieces of the metal bulkhead Alric landed on.

The mech's mace hit him but over the shoulder, and with its hilt only. Even so, the blow was mighty, and it crushed Alric's shoulder-laser mount, as his own greatsword, powered both by muscle and machine, slashed at the mech's left arm. Both then hurriedly jumped away from each other, no longer using their engines. The mech's arm almost fell off, and its pilot began circling Alric, trying to find an opening and attack again.

What was left of the ship's crew choose this moment to assault the star marine en masse. Firing from close range, even light pistols and carbines could potentially pierce his armor and kill him. He had enough power to fire both of his forearm mounted snub railguns and did so immediately. Alric was aiming to not exclusively kill the Taz'arans, but pin and wound them, therefore creating more obstacles for the mech, limiting its movement and giving himself an edge in the fight.

Already heavily damaged, the Taz'aran PA's left arm was all but useless, and Alric utilized this fact while planning his next attacks. Always taking to the left and forcing his opponent to turn, as it would be impossible for the mech to hit him, Alric did manage to finally land one accurate and devastating blow.

Using the imbalance he had caused in his enemy's combat form and all those wounded crewmen rolling over the floor, his blade pierced through the mech's side chest hull-plate. The whole machine violently shook by energy discharge, and its only working hand dropped the mace on the floor. As the star marine pulled the blade of his sword back, out of the jagged hole, a small fountain of Taz'aran blood sprayed all over him.

Slightly limping, his no-longer-quick stride led him towards the ship's bridge, and while he traversed what was left of its ravaged armory, Alric ignored the surviving Taz'arans. They were already dead and nobody would come to their rescue, as it wasn't their way. Lower-enlisted personnel were bought and paid for. Wasting resources to secure anything other than their personal gear and weapons, wasn't considered thoughtful by any Taz'aran commander.

Medical attention was, of course, reserved only for higher-level nobles and their personal retinues. Alric remembered how much he hated those idiotic aliens! He would repay them in kind for the suffering they had brought upon his people – both then and now, they were the same pieces of shit. For him, Taz'arans deserved nothing, but to experience the same, or greater amounts of what they had themselves caused to countless billions. Alric, as always, was following the Oath:

*Death to the Invader!*

As soon as he reached the blocked doors of the ship's bridge, Alric noticed something rather strange – there were no new orders coming from the inside. Either that captain of theirs had kissed the barrel of his gun, or something else was happening. He knew enough about the Taz'aran way of fighting and customs, to assume a rather bloody change in their immediate command situation.

They could go to hell, *all* of them!

Alric didn't care and as he'd vowed beforehand on their open links, the Taz'arans would all die, no matter the cost. Terran Star Marines never backed down from a promise; moreover, their kind had to pay for what they had done. Crushing the head of one unfortunate crewmen between his hands, Alric's memories again raced backwards in time.

* * *

It had been a long chase, but INS *Bremen* had finally caught up with its pirate quarry.

Near an asteroid field, they had slid out of a wormhole and immediately were shot at, by not one, but multiple vessels. The ship's crew was highly motivated, their skills and abilities honed to perfection. So was the level of combat experience humans had gained during all of their battles in outer space. Not for the first time they had been ambushed by multiple ships; it was a strategy they knew all too well.

The pirate craft were small, considerably faster than the Terran destroyer, and they'd tried luring it into the nearby asteroid field. Unfortunately for them, the captain of the *Bremen* had long ago devised a simple and perfect response – very accurate, long range fire from her railguns.

Pirates refused to take Terran weapon technology seriously and the humans, ever so happily, continued firing barrage after barrage of one ton projectiles, flying at almost ten thousand meters per second. The gun crews had an almost unlimited amount of ammunition; hundreds of tons of scrap metal was crushed and formed into slugs, which were then loaded and propelled by the supermag coils. The ship's multiple fusion reactors produced many times more than the thousands of terawatts those modern railguns drank with their every shot.

Expensive capacitors, made of crystal and poly-bionic alloys, were used to store the energy needed for mere picoseconds before each shot. All of those massive machines had to be cooled and enormous heatsinks, venting all excess heat into outer space, were essential for the crew and ship's successful operation during combat. With even the best technological advancements at the time, *Bremen* could stay in the fight for at best ten minutes and if absolutely necessary, fifteen.

Soon all of that was put to the test, as many more pirate ships exited hyperspace and ganged up on the Terran destroyer. Expecting their strength in numbers to overwhelm the destroyer's defenses, they were instead showered with hundreds of missiles and blown to bits.

Undeterred by such horrific losses, the pirate lord in command sent into battle even more ships, this time of bigger size and with better weaponry. The *Bremen* turned towards the new threat, its own laser beam cannons ready, and ever so sparingly began melting their hulls into slag. Her armor was tough enough and withstood the attack yet again.

What was it that some people said:

*"If you can't win by using force, then you are not using enough of it!"*

And so, another, even larger group of pirate ships emerged out of hyperspace, descending upon the now-damaged Terran vessel.

Pressed onto the edge of that large asteroid field and with her heatsinks pushed towards their very limits, the *Bremen* left its position near the wormhole and began navigating her way between the asteroids. The pirates followed her, but soon began experiencing problems of a most deadly kind.

Even though their own ships were far smaller than the destroyer, the Terrans were using their grapplers to both push and pull the *Bremen*, keeping her on course, and then shoving those very same asteroids right in the pirate's path. Yet instead of stopping they continued chasing her, and some minutes later, the now moderately-damaged Terran ship reached a clearing, situated at the very center of the asteroid field.

The pirates launched wave after wave of fighters, bombers, and troop transports, all streaming from each possible direction. While the *Bremen's* point-defense guns shredded their fighters, what was left of the pirate vessels got closer and prepared to strike the finishing blow.

Alric and his Star Marine brothers and sisters poured out of the *Bremen's* air locks and, fighting through hundreds of pirate starfighters, reached the advancing starships. They recklessly attacked them, dodging thick barrages of point defense fire, placing nuclear tipped demolition charges onto their hulls.

Despite the losses his unit had sustained, all four pirate frigates were destroyed. The star marines turned around and flew back towards their own ship, facing towards the enemy. Using their newly-trained anti-fighter defense formation, Alric and his troopers slipped through pirate lines, sniping and taking out even more enemy ships along the way. It seemed like victory was close, but as the humans landed for re-arm and repairs, another starship appeared in normal space.

Using their treacherous ways, the pirate's Taz'aran allies had managed to calculate a hyperspace drop right beside the *Bremen's* starboard, and the second their starship materialized, they opened fire. In the hundreds, breaching pods streamed out of that starship's hangars, and the last battle of his ship and crew began.

Even though their Taz'aran enemy's ship was eventually destroyed, the *Bremen's* crew had paid the ultimate price. For two months afterwards, Alric and what was left of his marines had fought together against the Taz'aran boarding troops. They set demolition charges, mines, planted booby-traps everywhere, ambushed each other again and again, all the while INS *Bremen* slowly turned into a gutted derelict.

In the end, it was he alone who had survived that horrific battle, the last Taz'aran stormtrooper's chest slashed by his greatsword. Tired and angry, the lone Star Marine scoured his once-great warship for leftover supplies, finding nothing but a single, working stasis pod.

There was no food left, because after the destruction of their own starship, the Taz'arans looted the *Bremen's* supplies. Alric's very humanity was lost to him; he had survived, only to kill, and killed to survive, in a bloody circle of death and destruction. Duty demanded him entering stasis; he entertained the faintest of hopes that someday, somebody would find and revive him. Alric took all precautions that were possible in his situation, but right before he punched in the activation controls, a single, confusing thought emerged in his mind:

*"What was the point of it all?"*

He had spent what was left of his childhood training like a crazed fanatic, preparing himself for the vengeance that would eventually be. There was no joy for him, unless he was hurting and killing those who had nothing short of raped his race's future. Instead of mourning for his family,

238

Alric almost lost the ability to feel anything else, but seething, merciless hatred.

He'd had multiple sessions with different morale officers, all over Earth and every single one of those specialists was helpless to aid him. They were unable to understand what had happened with him, not even other half-humans like himself, who had all desperately tried salvaging his damaged mind. They couldn't understand that hate was his peace now; the ultimate peace of silent battlefields after victory, deep within the perceived emptiness of space. The distant star light which, after traveling for millions of years, now reflected upon the broken spacesuits of his dead enemies and their frozen eyes.

\* \* \*

Alric's breaching charge blew the reinforced bridge doors and he entered the already vacated command room. There was a medium-sized hole in a bulkhead nearby, melted by continuous weapons fire. Beside it, lay the corpse of one of the bridge officers who had been trampled to death by his panicking colleagues. After scanning the breach, Alric used his sword to widen it, squeezing his big spacesuit's frame through.

Not so soon after he'd made his way forward, the star marine found many more Taz'aran bodies. Evidently, in their haste, most of them had frantically pushed and shoved each other into that small service tunnel, where at best space was a luxury and at worst, a claustrophobic nightmare made of pipes, power lines, and other bulky, dangerous equipment.

The tunnel soon reached an exit, and Alric found himself inside the ship's engineering bay. There was a gunfight here not that long ago, and all but one of the Taz'arans lay dead on the floor. She was crawling towards an escape pod hatch located within a nearby bulkhead, and Alric walked beside her silently. He wondered what to do with her, and by the time she was an arm's reach from her salvation, Alric grabbed the woman's ankle and dragged her all the way back to the service tunnel's exit.

He then planted his last demolition charge on the ship's reactor core and scanned the taz'aran woman before leaving. Strangely enough, her face bore a striking resemblance to his first intentional kill. Even her voice was somewhat similar, and so he stopped for a minute, inspecting her ever-so-desperate and bloody crawl towards the nearest escape pod.

He moved towards the already launched second pod and forcefully opened its hatch, drifting instantly in outer space. Sucked together with the atmo, Alric used his grappler to punch one little hole in the escape pod's hull, before the ship's emergency bulkheads closed shut, sealing the breach.

After all, nothing was worse than a useless hope for survival. All that energy wasted in reaching the escape pod, and then suffocating when you launch yourself into space. *Slowly.* In exactly the same fashion as those other Taz'arans had happily sliced his school-friends' throats and watched them drown in their own blood.

While the Taz'aran captain was running into the hangar, his entire ship shook from a violent explosion, and all hull-breach alarms went off. Struggling to move on a straight line, he reached one of his docked dropships, and barked an order at the pilots inside it:

"Quickly you morons! Get this thing moving this instant! I will give you both double pay, once we reach

240

'Pion' base!" – He shouted nervously, while boarding the dropship.

Both pilots wasted no time, and soon the heavily-armed shuttle flew in outer space with full speed, navigating towards the nearest wormhole.

The Terran star marine saw one of the ship's armored shuttles flying out of its hangar with ever-increasing speed. He activated his own engines and began cursing silently under his breath because just as the Taz'aran starship behind him exploded, Alric's faceplate showed a perfect targeting solution for his now-crushed shoulder laser.

The filthy bastards were slipping away!

Looking back, the Taz'aran captain saw how the command corvette, his pride and joy, exploded in a violent ball of expanding plasma and debris. There was one single escape pod on the scanners, but it soon too was turned into scrap, as that Terran monster of a marine emerged from the wreckage of his starship and chased after him.

He almost expected his ship to be blasted apart by that laser of his!

His hands began shaking, as he felt wetness spreading inside the suit – he had pissed himself from fear. The captain looked angrily at his pilots; even if they had noticed his shame, they said anything. Never mind, once he had safely reached Pion base, the captain would make sure to take good care of them, *permanent* care.

If there were no witnesses of his defeat, then there was *no* defeat.

\* \* \*

Alric found his way back through the debris and entered the interior of the *Princess Frog* just as his looted power pack died. The tired marine then had to remove his exoskeleton by muscle power alone. It took him a couple of excruciating minutes, and afterwards he simply fell on the floor dozing off.

The navigational computer woke him up many hours later, by activating some alarm *she* had forgotten turning off. Alric slowly picked himself up and was soon devastating the ship's food supply. The rations themselves looked like Japanese bentos and had an assortment of fruit, vegetables, and cured meats. He picked one large, blue piece of apple and stuffed his mouth full of that fruity goodness.

Often, one would experience hunger while fighting on the battlefields in outer space. With the situation sometimes becoming even more dire since one was unable to hunt for food. Finding nourishment was extremely hard, and he had heard of deep space explorers who, having found mummified corpses, were forced to consume their ancient rations in order to survive.

After feeding his body enough energy and having had plentiful rest, Alric concentrated upon the life energy that came from his other starship partner. Again that whitish, blue glow illuminated the insides of the *Princess Frog* while Alric deactivated his old pod's stasis protocols where he had placed her body, and waited long enough for the lid to open.

There she lay still, with frozen tears on her face and a happy, almost proud smile. He shook his head in disbelief, but prepared himself to unleash the life energy from his hands and into her wounded body. Alric knew that the healing would be successful, and the beautiful young woman would be awoken, this time for good. The more he looked at her calm, ascetic demeanor and the slim, minimalistic decorations on the interior bulkheads that now reflected the emanation of his power, the stranger he felt.

It was normal for him to feel weak, after pulling so much from his own life energy to heal another.

Alric didn't care and never did – it was just another part of his duty, he had to perform for race and nation. Pain was part of the process and he suspected that the ancient spacefaring Aryans were just as, if not even more, tired than him when they did the same.

His target's chest wound closed completely, with new muscles, bones, tendons and skin forming before Alric's very eyes. She suddenly coughed and rose up, her eyes opening with slightly dilated pupils, trying to focus. Alric couldn't hold himself and gasped slightly, amazed at her heavenly beauty, his own eyes still unable to look at anything else but her face. The girl smiled wider and happily chimed:

"As I was trying to tell you before, my name is Vasilisa, daughter of Alexi and Valeria Smelchak, and I am a Spacer. It is a tradition in my culture to ask the man this question first."

Vasilisa then began undressing before him, and while he blinked a couple of times, greatly confused, she continued:

"Be mine, as I will be yours, both in hardship and in joy," – She murmured as she moved her body closer and began undressing him without wasting any more time – "I swear to respect your decisions, as you accept my guidance always and in all things, concerning both family and business ventures."

Alric's gaze pierced her eyes like twin laser cannons, and Vasilisa's entire body twitched with hungry anticipation. A lonely drop of saliva drooled from the side of her mouth as she almost lost the ability to form coherent sentences and began mumbling:

"Thousand burning comets! Look at it go!"

Obviously it wasn't a one-way street; Alric immediately forgot any thoughts of rest, wiping her drool with the sleeve of his uniform and picking up Vasilisa by her tiny waist with one arm.

"Become my husband, please?" – That was the only thing her confused, overwhelmed brain could formulate.

With their gazes still locked, Alric felt a great surge of life force streaming through his entire body. He had to be a complete idiot, to not immediately realize that he held his future wife in his hands. Stern, he replied:

"I know not what had compelled you to travel here and why were you so keen on sacrificing your very life to protect me. I, Alric von Englebert, vow now and forever, until my dying breath, to protect you and give everything of mine that you would ever need!"

Vasilisa sighed with relief and caressed her now-husband's face with both hands, tears of happiness running down her cheeks. Sobbing, she wrapped her arms around Alric's neck, and getting close for her first kiss, Vasilisa muttered quietly:

"It took me only two and a half years and I almost died a couple of times, but finally I have found my man!" – She whispered words of love and gratitude in his ear happily, while a confused and saddened Alric tried wiping her tears again.

"You know what I want? Children! As many as possible and as soon as possible!"

Her attitude brightened suddenly; she ordered the

ship's computer to lower the gravity, and then wrapped her body around her husband...

# Chapter 9

## *Enslaved*

She often dreamt of the days when her body was still free and not floating in this armored container, of when her limbs had not yet been surgically removed and she used as a test subject, injected with different chemicals or nanites every day. Kera was now connected to all sorts of wires and sensors, and sleep was all but impossible, yet in her seconds-short dreams, she remembered the warm starlight shining on her face, and how the clean wind made her skin tingle. The smell of flowers, and the taste of food that her mother made for her every day.

Kera's favorite thing in the world had been running.

Most children had to stay close the bunkers for safety reasons, but she would often climb on top of the closest domed construction and run in circles on its roof. Her homeworld, Avern'a, fell to attack by a race called Jaern – the adults had to fight them, otherwise, everyone would be herded and eaten alive. They had been battling with the enemy for many years, decades, even centuries before she was even born, but despite all of their tenacity, her people were losing.

Kera knew a tad bit more now; she was but a child then, and her parents tried their best to keep the horrors and desperation of war away from her. In her bunker, only a few children lived and all four of them were girls – Avern'a boys were sent to the front lines from as early as six years old. There was no childhood for them; the only things that they were to ever know were war, suffering, and then death.

The Avern'a had no time to discuss morals and ethics while their entire population was on the verge of being exterminated. Luxuries like living sheltered and protected lives, and being taken care of by your parents, were things that most adult Avern'a never spoke of openly. Simply the knowledge that such a lavish lifestyle once existed could deal irreparable damage to the children's young, innocent minds. Better they assumed that this was everything there was...

One day, after Kera had finished her chores early and after her daily run on top of their bunker, she had loitered around longer than usual. She had wanted to glimpse the Battlestars – the Avernum starships that were still fighting, defending the orbit of her homeworld.

One of the other adults had told her the story of how those ships had been continuously fighting ever since the beginning of the Jaern's invasion. Kera had been enthralled by the story, and she'd waited for the rest of the rotation.

Nightfall came, and even though her little hands had been getting colder by the minute, she saw the Stars. Ever-blinking, with multiple other small lights flashing around, beams of light streaming between them, the Battlestars were just as magnificent as she had been told. Unfortunately, that very same evening, a Jaern raiding party had attacked her small village and Kera had been caught alone out in the open.

There was no way the little girl's feet could outrun the flying machines – she was shot by some weapon and fell unconscious. She had later awoken in a strange place, surrounded by multiple other children who were not of her race. Indeed, despite the fact that most were much older than her, they whimpered and cried like little babies.

Kera noticed one boy, perhaps a year older than she

was, whose demeanor was much different than those of the rest. His body covered with sores and scars from beatings, his clothes torn, ripped and soaked with blood. His jet black, spiky hair had had multiple burned patches, but instead of crying, his black eyes had been full of resistance and cold rage.

While the rest all rolled aimlessly on the ship's floor in fetal positions or dragged their feet moping about, this boy looked around with defiance in his eyes. Kera was inexplicably drawn to him, and walked over, touching his bruised face with her cold, little fingers. The boy was strangely alike in physique and appearance to her own race but clearly belonged to some other species which Kera had never seen. Startled, but not scared by her touch, the boy had turned around and looked her straight in the eyes.

The Avernum were an ancient race and had strange abilities, even though they didn't brag or feel superior to others. One look was enough for Kera to see that the connection between the boy's psychic imprint and the Universe was about to break. She couldn't know if her ability was strong or weak at that age – Kera had always had the skill of sensing… things. Confused, she'd half-smiled at him and tried cleaning some of the dried-up blood on his face with her sleeve.

"Does it hurt much?" – She'd asked.

He didn't stop her, even though she'd felt that his body twitched in pain.

"Yes, it does hurt," – he'd responded with a stern voice – "but not in the least as much as those who did this to me will suffer" – He'd replied using good Galactic Common.

Most, if not all, of the children in the Galaxy, were

taught this lingua franca, as it was commonly used to ease communication between the thousands of alien races. Some planets spoke it with strange dialects, others twisted the meaning or invented more, complicated words yet, at its core, this language remained the same.

She'd blinked confused a couple of times – through her power, the Link, Kera had become aware that this boy was an oddity. Someone who had intentionally severed his connection with the Universe's essence. Perhaps he had suffered more than the apparent bodily harm and chose to insulate his own mind from everything around him?

Kera had torn off her left jacket sleeve and used it to bandage his forehead.

"My name is Boris and I am from a planet called Earth," – The boy had nodded gratefully after Kera had finished bandaging his head – "My race is called humans."

Despite his wounds and obvious tiredness, he'd actually tried his best to converse with Kera and looked genuinely thankful for her aid.

"I am Kera and my home planet is called Avern'a. My people are known as the Avernum" – She'd tried unintentionally to make her voice sound as soothing as possible, Kera had somehow sensed that he was on the verge of collapsing.

"What is this place?" – She'd made a hand gesture pointing at the room they were in.

"It is a slave ship's pen." – Boris had spat the word 'slave' with such contempt and hate that it had startled Kera.

His entire demeanor had changed in an instant, revealing that the meaning of this word was connected with a lot of negativity.

"What is a slave?" – Kera had asked with a lowered voice and genuinely confused, naive facial expression.

"Wait, you don't know?!" – Boris's gaze had studied her face with disbelief, but having read the confusion he saw in her eyes as genuine proof for lack of knowledge, he'd sighed and begun explaining.

"Look, there are bad 'people' in this Galaxy, who kidnap and then sell other sentients as merchandise, they are called slavers. Those who they capture are called slaves, who are then used as an expendable item, and for any purpose that their owners decide. My own race has suffered long and hard, because a group of such slavers invaded Earth. They killed my parents and captured me some time ago."

Kera had looked at his eyes, and seen a violent cocktail of emotions – there was sorrow, yes, but also anger and rage.

"But why would someone do such a thing?" – Kera's mind had been unable to grasp the socially-derelict concept she'd been presented with. While she stood before him with an even more confused expression, she'd noted – "They could ask for help with work or anything else. Don't they know that?" – Boris's jaw had dropped for a second because now he'd been able to grasp Kera's level of pure naivety.

"I don't think that asking for the help of others is something slavers are even thinking of, not now, not any other day of the week" – He'd yawned, and Kera had seen that some of his teeth had been knocked out.

"Could I ask you to wake me up when they come for us?," Boris had smiled mournfully, "I'm not keen on spending what days remain of my life living as a slave. Us humans are known for not surviving long in captivity, and I don't plan on changing my species' well-earned reputation."

"Why? What are you planning, Boris?" – In her heart, Kera had already anticipated his answer.

"Attacking the guards head-on and forcing them to kill me – naturally. What else could I do? Condemn myself to a life of torture and endless suffering? Why by the Universe would I do that!?"

Boris had made a short pause, while all of the other captives had given him strange and confused looks, some awoken by his voice. Continuing with a lowered tone, Boris had tried arguing his position:

"I'd advise you to join me. I don't think a girl as beautiful as you will have a good life being a slave."

Saying that Boris had finally dozed off, and soon after, Kera did so herself, unable to stay awake after such a tiresome day. They never woke up together, because the slavers had pumped the room full of invisible, odorless nerve gas. It had quickly paralyzed all of the children and then, they were dropped off on a large space station. Boris had been sold to slave miners and Kera herself had been purchased by a large, alien, dinosaur-like creature.

\* \* \*

When Kera had woken up, her body had been laying on an auto-surgical station. From behind a forcefield, her new owner was taking holo-notes and slides on a PDA, while the surgical robot arms were slicing piece after piece of her flesh then. Unable to cope with the horrendous pain, Kera screamed and lost consciousness.

Her new home to be was the space station's main medical laboratory and Kera's "job" was to be... a test subject.

The mistress who owned her later revealed her name to be Vlenti, princess matriarch and head scientist in command of this research station. She was from a race called Vaugn; large, dinosaur-like sentients, with imposing strength and constitution, yet depraved and evil.

At first, her body had been targeted by many cybernetic medical devices, which tested Kera's physical attributes. The first two years were especially hard for her, and she constantly suffered from great mental and bodily pain. Kera was hurt to such an extent that her owner had had to use powerful painkillers and other meds to keep her awake, while they continued with the planned tests.

Kera soon forgot what sleep was – days, months and even years, molded into one massive blob. Time was her enemy; its constant passage promised more pain and suffering. But Instead of losing her mind, Kera found that her Avern'a link grew ever stronger by the hour. It would soon rise to a level that she never knew or heard to be possible.

She was able to achieve oneness with Universe consciousness, experience a full and complete meld. Instead of shuddering with pain, both her body and mind were always at peace. Matriarch Vlenti eventually noticed that the mental state of her test subject was unaffected by pain, and stopped pumping Kera's system full of meds. Then, after Kera's state didn't change, the Vaugn scientists scanned and probed her body with every tool available in their laboratory.

Vlenti was irked to no end by Kera's remarkable resilience. The very fact that she was unable to make her suffer had greatly infuriated the Vaugn matriarch. They again pulled Kera out of the tank and, removing her limbs one by one, replaced them with pain inducers, linking them directly into her nervous system. When the researchers found that this, too, didn't work, the princess matriarch began shoving cybernetics inside Kera's very brain.

For a short period of time, and to some extent, this worked, but the girl's abilities soon overpowered all of Vlenti's desperate attempts to make her suffer. Vlenti did one last thing in an attempt to induce agony: she replaced Kera's eyes with experimental Vaugn cybernetics. These horrific tools both regenerated and disintegrated her eye nerves every day. Her owner finally declared herself victorious and left the follow-up of any other tests to the laboratory's staff own discretion, visiting Kera only once per planetary rotation.

Nobody knew, however, that she could actually see through others.

Their lab had many other test subjects.

Most were poor, defenseless animals, locked in energy-field cages who were killed off every other day or so, during some gruesome testing. Kera could reach all of them, and through her link with the Great Consciousness, give them some peace of mind before death. Innocent living beings, they had no way of understanding the concept of medical or cybernetic tests. They also knew not why other creatures had to hurt them in such barbaric, cruel ways.

Kera found that constant contact with their simple minds and senses was a most instructing sensation. After all that they had suffered through, the animals received much-needed empathy before their ends. Kera learned through the senses of multitudinous different creatures. She studied their biology and then began reading all of the holo files and scan data projected around the laboratory.

Little by little, she learned the Vaugn language by comparing it with other files, written in Galactic Common.

Soon, even the most difficult medical terminology wasn't foreign to Kera, and she began studying all of the cybernetic equipment present in the lab.

She spent years in silent observation and as her body grew, the medics had to replace Kera's implants many times with newer and bigger ones. The day came when she finished studying herself, inspecting all of the data streams coming from her implants. With her newfound understanding of the medicine and sciences, she discovered that somehow, instead of withering, her body and brain were functioning at peak efficiency.

Kera began studying cybernetic manipulation, while watching how the lab personnel crafted newer models and researched better upgrades since they tested the bulk of their advanced models on her first. With Vlenti ultimately losing all interest in her, Kera's tank became an integral part of the lab. Her liquid-filled container had stood in its center for almost eleven years, and any new lab assistant that arrived to replace older researchers was told about her.

Lately, her tank had been somewhat neglected, as newer, more interesting test subjects were brought in to boost the laboratory's research progress.

All of a sudden, Kera found herself with a lot of free time on her mind. She decided to use this newfound spare time to improve her ability, and the first thing she did was to try reaching one of the laboratory's guards with her connection. It was really strange in the beginning, because she had the whole knowledge of what was actually done to them. In fact, the procedures which constrained their brains lowered their IQ to levels that most common animals had.

When she successfully managed to reach one of the male guard's minds, Kera was stunned. Never could she have imagined, even with all of the medical and cybernetic scientific knowledge she now possessed, that those unfortunate creatures' minds still existed and were actually caged within their brains.

The Vaugn men were able to experience all incoming sensory input. From the inside of their barred, caged minds, they watched helplessly how their bodies followed the orders of any matriarch commander. Maim, kill and torture – there was no hope, no chance of resisting. They would go mad, praying for death, welcoming it as a merciful release from the hell that their life was turned into by the Vaugn Matriarchy.

The one she reached was but a child, and yet he had already been made to kill dozens of innocent slaves, for "training" purposes, of course. More like providing entertainment for his commanders, who she knew were good friends with her owner, Vlenti.

Kera gave him the name Ort, and tried her best to repair the damage done to his mind, quickly coming to the understanding that was nigh but impossible. Refusing to quit and surrender before this horrid reality, she instead devised a complex medical procedure. By implementing it, if not the whole, at least the greater part of Ort's mind could be preserved.

Kera had found out that her owner would receive a new shipment of exotic creatures. This one would consist of multiple alien animals, with one, in particular, piquing her interest, since on its file was written "Earth" – Boris's homeworld.

She did her covert research and soon understood, that this being's might be the perfect host for Ort's mind as the witless scientists gathered around her tank chatted happily boasting this creature to be some sort of a rare, unique beast. What was most interesting for Kera, and would soon prove to be the greatest hope for Ort's salvation, was the fact that it was a semi-sentient creature.

It seems that the people of Earth were most skilled and adept in the science of uplifting. They had, as she'd learned earlier, managed to give the gift of sentience and uplift multiple client races. This "dog" they spoke of, was some four-legged, empathic life form that was native to their home planet. Not only did the scientists mock humanity's ethical treatment of those creatures, but they also implied that the creature's perceived choice was irrelevant. Kera found out that humans actually used telepaths to communicate on a basic level with those animals, seeking their agreement before any uplifting procedures began.

Amazingly, Kera felt through her connection that Ort's consciousness was greatly pleased by this practice. With Ort's quiet compliance and her own ever-increasing knowledge of medical procedures, Kera was sure that any of those experimental cybernetic implants laying around the lab, could be then easily modified to increase the chances of successful transfer. Sadly, she was unable to connect with the creature's original mind; it had been completely wiped out by the slaver telepath who'd been sent to "procure" the animal.

One day, before the cargo ship's arrival, Kera had Ort provide her some cybernetics that had access to the station's intranet feed. It was essential for Kera's plan success that she be able to track everything and everyone. After the ship had been docked and all other creatures offloaded, auctioned and sold, she watched the dog's cage finally being transported directly into the lab.

All of the researchers spent at least an hour poking it from each side, taking holo slides beside its motionless body. The creature was alive, yet mindless, its body placed upon one of the auto-surgical stations – being prepared for cybernetic testing. The animal was beautiful; as long as ten feet and more than six feet tall, it had massive muscles, and the now-open mouth provided an excellent view of its many, long teeth.

The holo scan she saw in the distance also confirmed one of her suspicions, that the creature's brain was genetically modified to pre-sentient levels. Finally satisfying their "curiosity", Vaugn scientists soon left her alone with Ort and their brand new test subject.

The creature wasn't secured in any way, since they thought a mindless animal would lay where they had placed it, drooling while it slept. She oversaw the entire surgery and creation of a new cybernetic brain enhancement chip. Curiously, the chip she'd made was based on the same technology that the Vaugn used in turning their men into mindless, obedient killing machines.

Thankfully the laboratory had plenty of them in storage, and she used six of their processors linked together into one super-matrix. The implant was powerful and provided plenty of processing power, augmenting the underdeveloped dog's brain. It took her only a few hours to make, using one of the lab's automated workstations. Since she had hacked the uplink, controlling medical drones and using their tools to craft the super chip wasn't that hard.

Kera had already amassed vast knowledge, operating on living creatures, crafting and installing cybernetics – with her being a test subject. The harder thing seemed to transfer Ort's mind into that creature's brain, but before the end of the night, Kera achieved that feat, too.

The next morning, Ort's old husk of a body was ordered to get up from his bed and stand guard at the laboratory's entrance – just as he had always done. Since

Ort's mind was isolated by a new slave chip put into his brain, any voice and visual orders were immediately followed to the letter.

Hopefully, the mistresses wouldn't catch the slight oddities in his behavior while he acted on their orders. The dog woke up a few minutes after and, curious of his new senses, raised its head, sniffing the air. Kera reached for Ort's mind and found that much to her surprise he had lost nothing. There was one notable change – his tortured mind had found a new purpose in life.

He happily communicated with her, expressing his wishes: Ort chose to devote his entire existence to Kera, to guard and protect her from any enemy.

# Chapter 10

## *Tomorrow is another day*

Boris was violently woken up from a boot to the gut and began coughing, inhaling dust and soot. He somehow managed to crawl away from the guard and picked himself up, bloodied hands grabbing the energy drill laying next to him.

"Work, damn you!" – The guard who yelled at him was thin, but tall, armed with a riot shield and stun baton.

Holstered on his belt Boris could also see a cheap laser pistol, its long power pack sticking out its front handle.

"The Intendant doesn't feed useless pieces of flesh from the goodness of her heart!" Again his armored boot found the young boy's gut. The guard then walked away, shouted at the rest: "And that counts double for you lazy lot!"

What energy the slaves had left, they used to increase their digging speed. Boris gritted his teeth and rose from the dust-covered floor, facing a crowd of devastated, desperate slaves who, very much like him, were worked to the bone. Spitting a blood clot, he picked up the energy drill and continued working, as it was madness not to.

The same sadistic guard would come back and beat him and perhaps the others, to within an inch of their lives, for lowering "production quotas". Trying to inhale as little dust as possible, Boris switched the drill on a higher setting, his mind wandering off some years back, recollecting the fateful days when all of this torturous descent into pain and madness began…

259

* * *

After he and that girl on the slave ship had spoken with each other, Boris found out that they had been gassed with a sleeping agent. Before regaining consciousness, he and the other slaves were already sold, and the batch he was in dropped off on some dusty, gloomy planet.

It was a remote mountain compound, the air was thin and full of soot and dust.

Two very tall, pencil-like towers stretched up towards the sky, and Boris felt that his head would explode just by throwing them one glancing peek. He need not look at them more to realize that those were psychic nullifiers!

Technology had progressed far enough that now you could conveniently block telepathic powers with machines. Why they had to build such big ones he didn't wonder since one look at the camp below showed a multitude of slave barracks. Boris had no more time to contemplate anyways, as multiple alien guards corralled his group of slaves, kicking and punching them with their stun batons into the walled enclosure below.

It was a large open piece of land with no roof. Just one tall electric fence barred the slaves from escaping, charged with enough power to stun but not kill. It was painfully obvious to even the daftest of fellows that the slavers wanted them alive and breathing. Well, at least long enough so that through labor, they would recover the minute amount of money spent purchasing them. Soon the sounds of blasting rock and the loud thump of power drills revealed what this compound truly was – a slave mine.

His parents had always told him that the worst fate for a human was to live as a slave.

Boris was descended from a long line of warriors. Sixteen generations on his home planet Earth had served both in the Army and the Navy, protecting their loved ones from harm. Breaking centuries-long tradition, both his father and mother became scientists. They could employ only the basic training that any Terran received during their childhood to protect themselves.

His dad Simeon was a microbiologist, and his mom Elza a quantum physicist; both were geniuses in their fields, well sought-after academy professors. They had traveled the entirety of the Imperial Minarchy's space, teaching in various Star Academies who were built on the bigger Terran colonies. Since most professional skills were taught early on through apprenticeships, only higher knowledge and sciences were something people went to study at those big centers of learning.

Only the biggest of colonies could allow such a luxury, as building an Academy was something of a costly, planetary project. Since those places of higher learning were rare, his family traveled around constantly. The very day any of their contracts expired, his parents were on the road again, searching around the I-Net (single star system network) for another job. Ever since Boris was three, his family had traveled between Earth and Calypso colony first, because their first contracts were there and their home was close.

Boris was born in a nation-state called Bulgaria, which bordered Italy and Greece. It was a beautiful country, and his first memories were of watching the sunrise on top of a high mountain ridge. The taste of clean air, strong winds blowing all over him, and his parents happily laughing. Somehow he always remembered it, after having the recurring nightmare about them being killed by the slavers and him getting captured.

But as they had done many times before, his parents found new jobs far away, close to the edge of colonized Fringe Space. On an asteroid colony called Cav, the local citizens had pooled together their funds and built themselves a brand new Star Academy. It was always the way that such ventures were started because the Terran citizenry was able to work with most of their resources since they didn't pay taxes.

Each citizen provided for common projects according to their own level of wealth, and the tiny governmental organizations all competed for donations through merit and accomplishments. The better the overall quality of work or services provided, the more, and more generous, grants from the free citizenry they could expect.

Groups like the very elite Imperial Navy, for example, received mostly weapons, vehicles, and starships as donations. All of Boris' grandparents had served in the Imperial Navy, from its very creation in 1949. Before that, they were part of His Majesty the King of Bulgaria's own Navy. Sadly both of them died in space shortly after he was born, unable to even see their grandson.

He remembered the feeling of sadness and anger, when his father told him why little Boris did not have grandparents.

The citizens of Cav were in dire need of qualified professionals and both his father and mother were offered large pay, enticing them to travel there as soon as possible. Buying tickets and boarding a small transport ship, his family embarked on their last voyage together.

One could understand the Terrans' desperate

infatuation with life, family, and friends more easily while observing them. Citizens of the Imperial Minarchy would resist anything that the Universe threw at them with rugged, almost relentless tenacity.

It was a sudden thing, both the forced hyperspace drop and subsequent boarding. The small crew of their transport ship put up a long and valiant fight, but they were overpowered and picked off one by one by the slavers. Professional boarders and experts in capturing, they were perfectly equipped for dealing with small vessels like theirs.

Both of his parents together fought the pirates skillfully. Boris saw how their opponents, after finding it useless attacking them head on, showered them with a barrage of ranged fire, killing them from afar. He himself managed to resist and, with the last power pack loaded, charged recklessly, laser pistol firing.

In the end, instead of killing him, they stunned him – only because he was still a child. Pirates always spared children, since they could get the best prices on any slave market by selling them to all sorts of scum. Boris was sure he had managed to kill at least two of the bastards, but that was of little comfort in his current situation. At least the thought that he was not sold to some depraved monster gave the Terran youth some form of relief.

Cartels and other debased organizations often purchased children to "freshen up" the pleasure districts on their planets. Though this was not a place such as this, it was still rife with corruption. All of the usual, degenerate types, had free reign over the flesh and minds of the slaves.

Nightmares plagued him often.

Other slaves who slept close to Boris were sometimes awoken by his screams, and they tried calming him down with comforting words, but most of the time nobody cared. It was evident for everyone, even creatures of the lowest IQ could see it – they were being worked to death here.

A slave was many times cheaper than a mining drone and while the latter needed constant maintenance, the former was in plentiful supply. One need not pack expensive spare parts – after a slave had been worked to the bone it was replaced with another.

Fuel cost was easy to cover since the same barges which carried replacement workers also offloaded the ore, making a most tidy profit. The meager rations a slaver had to feed their workforce cost many thousands of decats less, than even the cheapest of mining drones. After one worker expired, their replacement was given the same, old, but still usable digging equipment. From the slaver's point of view, slavery was economically cost effective way to run a resource gathering operation... any operation, really.

Indeed, everything moved far quicker when one used advanced tech like drones and such. The obnoxious aliens cared little of speed though, they had multiple planets, hundreds of mining or production sites and each fulfilled their quotas. In the end it was the sheer number of their mines, each providing a slow but steady flow of resources which fueled the fires of industry.

By way of oppression and billions of disposable sentients, these star states had employed slavery to boost their economies for countless millenia. It was cheaper for them to do so, instead of paying incalculable billions needed for a full modernization of their industries.

The mine was following a large uranium ore vein, spiraling ever so deep into the mountain's treacherous depths. Soon after he was put to work with the rest, Boris found out why these slavers were buying children like him, en masse. Each slave was given some sort of paper-thin "protective" suit with a face mask and a banged-up, old energy drill. Vaguely effective and overly clunky, the tool often malfunctioned and blew up the hands of many, crippling the unfortunate miners. What followed was merciful death and escape from the pain of every day's suffering.

Life in a slave mine could only mean a slow, but painful descent into madness, and then the sweet embrace of one's inescapable death. In most cases, the slaves died from radiation exposure. The poor excuse of a protective suit was more of a joke than an actual defense against the radiation that they bathed in, each day and night.

First, they would lose all of their hair. Then, horrible lesions would appear all over their skin and would begin eating at their flesh. Slowly, everyone who had been exposed eventually died from radiation sickness, and while some entertained the foolish notion they'd be given medication, Boris knew better. He discovered what was common practice adopted by all guards; they did not help anybody who was suffering and dying from the radiation.

Boris remembered one day how the mine's Intendant gave a somber speech using the mine's comm station, reinforcing her orders to not aid sick slaves. She had even prohibited her guards from killing the dying! In her own words – expending even one shot from their pistol's power pack was a "gross misallocation of resources" and was not required for the continuous quick and effective operation of that facility.

Even after their agonizing ends, those poor, unfortunate slaves had to suffer more indignation in death. The living had to drag their rotting, irradiated remains to the nearby open-grave pit. Everybody called it "the pit of glow death" and since all of the corpses rotting there had soaked up high doses of radiation, it glowed eerily during the night time.

Life here was cheap.

In most cases others, who'd already shown signs of radiation poisoning were tasked with disposing of the dead. Yet, oftentimes that task fell to the weakest of slaves, meaning everyone who was forced to dispose of bodies there soon fell to radiation sickness and died themselves.

Boris was plagued by their leftover psychic imprints, and because he was on of the unfortunate few whom the guards forced to take care of the dead, absorbed hundreds if not thousands of them. They spoke to him from inside his mind, relentlessly screaming for bloody vengeance and retribution – all the time. Somehow, even without proper training, Boris was able to take control of their negative emotions and utilize their power.

Psychic imprints, or what some other telepaths and scientists called souls, were always present where sentient creatures had suffered and died painful, abrupt deaths. Painful deaths they were and Boris absorbed each and every one. More and more of them he pulled every day; so great were their numbers that soon, their powerful hatred was fueling him – empowering his psychic might. Through their negative emotions and violent cerebration, Boris' thoughts soon turned to the same.

He would get his revenge!

Vengeance, not only for himself and his parents but for everyone whose irradiated corpses were rotting away in the pit of Glow Death. But even with all of their power overflowing inside him, he was yet unable to properly concentrate and use any of his telepathic abilities.

The still-logical part of Boris knew well that such power would spell the doom of him without training and control. He knew that the camp had powerful psychic nullifiers – the two tall towers that always made his head hurt whenever he looked at them. They were projecting overlapping anti-psychic fields that barred any successful attempts at concentrating and manifesting any psychic powers. In effect it was a stopper most efficient for any would-be telepathic rioters.

Others in his place would've surrendered, accepted the bad hand that fate had given to them, but he?

Boris was not like the rest and would most definitely try to mess with the best his enslavers would eventually throw at him. Indeed, he was a mere seven-year-old weak kid, that had been provided only the basic necessities for survival. Forced into hard labor for the greater part of the planet's rotation cycle, one frail child could not be expected to survive.

But he was a human, and even at his young age, toughened up by excellent parenting, combined with his strong genetic heritage. Boris did not only survive in the hell that was that uranium mine, but somehow emerged much stronger!

* * *

At first, Boris began scrapping and salvaging the thrown away, broken slave suits, to augment his own. On the outside, his protective garments looked just as damaged as those of his fellow slaves. But underneath, Boris had reinforced their protective layers fivefold and even managed to fashion himself a better quality breathing mask.

Unfortunate that so many slaves had to die so that he could breathe much easier and, work faster than the rest of the slaves in his age group. It was standard practice for all children in the mine to work at widening the crevices and cracks off to the sides. Those had split, rich uranium ore veins far away from the main one.

The children were made to crawl inside those very small openings and use their energy drills to collapse its walls slowly, piece by piece. Hundreds, if not thousands, had died in these confined spaces, when their bodies got stuck and their suits damaged. Most panicked when the onslaught of claustrophobia wrenched any focus and will to fight out of them.

Boris had salvaged quite a lot of pieces from their suits after discovering many of those mummified child corpses. Stuck in agonizing poses, either dying from suffocation, bleeding or, excessive radiation exposure, some had even clawed their own faces to death.

The young Terran spent many months fighting his ever building, vengeful rage. Finally he succeeded and fueled by the thoughts of future retribution, he focused on furthering his agenda, following the next goal of his plan.

There would be a time for revenge, a time for punishment!

To cover the fact that he was in far better shape than the rest, Boris made sure to fake his walk. Visibly shaking and tripping, he got out of the mine slowly after a hard day's work. In the slave guard's eyes, Boris was just a miserable and broken a slave. One of many and part of the stumbling, tired crowd, who meekly accepted what passed for nourishment every evening with blistered, shaky hands.

Worked to the bone and flayed by radiation, they all

dragged their feet with some even crawling on all fours, trying to reach the slave enclosure and grab each their miserable food ration. The slaves would then either die or sleep away what was left of the current planetary rotation. After waking up by the shrill sound of the camp sirens, they would again slowly crawl back underground, repeating the agonizing cycle until the inevitable radiation overdose.

Sometimes they could draw the long straw.

"Blessed" by the Universe's' mercy the fortunate few might instantly die in a mining accident. It was during one such cave-in when Boris was separated from the rest and found himself unhurt, but alone in the blocked tunnel. He had no choice but to try and explore it, hoping that he could find some crevice and escape to the surface. Otherwise, years later, somebody would find his own mummified corpse. His face sporting an agonized facial expression, not much different than those of the children whose bodies he had himself discovered.

The more Boris walked away from the cave-in, the less his head hurt, the more thoughts flowed at a faster pace. At the end of the tunnel there was a hole somebody had tried widening up but ultimately failed. The crumpling skeleton was decades old at least, and it had an energy drill still clutched between its bony fingers.

Boris had lost his own drill during the cave-in, but in the pouch that every slave miner carried around their waist, there were always some spare power packs. He still had six of those – fully charged.

Painstakingly struggling for hours, Boris somehow managed to repair the old drill, loaded it with one of his packs, and began widening the small hole. It was hard work, made even harder by the fact that his air was running out. Frustrated as he was, Boris concentrated as best as he could and tried to slow down his breathing. It was one of the most important parts of any space survival course, something that Boris had learned when he was five years old.

He continued working, trying to drill through the rocks and reach another tunnel at least. At first, he didn't notice it, but after a while, when Boris looked at the gauge of his suit, he was stunned to find out that virtually all of his air reserves were gone! Yet, he still had enough air to breathe and he did so, slowly, evenly. Stranger yet, that air had a clean, non-metallic taste, much different than the mine's stale atmo.

Looking around he saw tiny dust particles, moving ever so slightly away and towards him in complete unison with his own breathing. With a sudden realization, Boris understood what was actually happening – he was manifesting aerokinesis!

Through the rocks, he'd somehow managed to pull clean air from an outside crevice. That meant that there was something beyond the hole he was drilling and with renewed vigor and hope, the young telepath continued working.

It took him the better part of a day to dig himself out. After expanding the hole and breaking through into another adjacent space, Boris at first saw nothing in the darkness. He waited a while for his eyes to adjust and soon found himself in a deep cave. Far, far up in the distance, the boy could see clear sky.

Just as when he was younger and visiting his grandparents, he felt the chill, freezing-cold mountain's wind, buzzing through his thin suit.

Soon after walking around the hole, he noticed ice crystals forming on its surface, and both his feet and hands started freezing. He could try running to warm himself up, but with the lack of nourishment, it wasn't a viable option. Boris slowly walked around, desperately trying to spot something of use. In the end, he crawled back in the very hole that he had spent so much of his energy widening up.

Before lying down, he desperately pushed his mind and tried concentrating again. From what he had studied about telepaths like him, Boris knew that some, if not most, could manifest at least two different types of disciplines. It was entirely possible that he had a second form of kinesis and hopefully, it would be something of use to him right now.

With temperatures rapidly getting low to the point of being below his ability to survive, he mustered all of his will and fell deep into a meditative state. It was something that all school kids were taught during their first year by their teachers.

In his mind, Boris imagined warmth, but what he got was a raging hot fire! The rock around him began heating up, and in some places, it even melted. As he crawled away from the melting tunnel, energy drill still in hand, Boris realized with joy that his second telepathic discipline was pyrokinesis. He soon felt his entire mind aching and tired to a degree he had never felt before.

The boy fell asleep hugging his energy drill, his back warmed by the heated, molten rocks.

* * *

For the next week after this miraculous survival, Boris tried desperately to blend in.

He brought back and gave the first slave foreman he

saw a whole two days' worth of uranium ore quotas. It helped that no guard would care if a slave was dead, or where they went, so long as they were given an accurate ore quota. Some slaves got lost in the mine and eventually, if they were lucky enough, another slave or the foremen found them. They were made to work twice as hard to cover their quotas, of course.

Thankfully, he knew of this and had stashed enough uranium ore, in case this happened to him. In advance, Boris thoughtfully hid the entrance of that cave. Besides himself, he doubted that any other slave would possess the strength and fortitude to reach, never mind survive in it.

Every day, he would crawl in there and practice his telepathic abilities. He couldn't do that within the camp's walls, but only there – far away from the two towers and their psychic nullifiers. Soon a most daring plan formed in his head, a plan that would require years to complete. In the end, he and any other surviving slaves would be free, and what was left of his enslavers, dead.

He began exploring the huge cave and found some mossy rocks at its furthermost end. Over that tiny patch of soil formed during the years, he saw strange plants growing, and he spent days trying to remember anything from his survival classes. He finally recalled that the plant was indeed edible, and supplemented what little "food" was given to him by eating it. Even tiny amounts of that plant were enough to satiate him for a day, sometimes even much longer.

To hide his ever-growing strength, Boris began crawling even further away from the crowds of slowly working slaves. He always met his ore quotas, but thoughtfully, he never exceeded them. Boris knew they would ask of him more and more if he did that. It was then that his luck almost ran out – one of the newer guards decided to pick on him. Boris, being the only human around, was a prime target for any Fringe aliens who knew and could recognize his race.

As it soon became evident for the guard, Boris was in far better shape than the rest of the slaves. The slaver began waking him up earlier than the rest, by sadistically beating Boris every morning. He then made him run to the mine entrance and back a couple of times, bashing his back with his stun baton, every time Boris slowed down even the slightest.

Boris realized that the guard's plan was to kill him very slowly, over a long period of time, by everyday beatings. Retreating after the first couple of days in his secret cave, Boris began meditating and forced the violent thoughts he had into another direction. One had to not only train his mind, but also his body, and fashion both into weapons of vengeance and death. With rugged determination and stubbornness in the face of certain death, in true Bulgarian fashion – Boris embraced the pain and let it fuel his cold, calculated rage.

Every morning he would accept the slave guard's beatings and then crawl, spitting blood, back into the mine's deepest tunnels. There, while using the energy drill and fueled by his ever-growing rage, Boris somehow managed to overcome the psychic nullifiers and manifest another new telepathic power.

He was able to crush rocks with his bare hands, by wrapping them with psychic energy. Although he could do so only for short periods of time, this nonetheless made his very body a deadly weapon of war. Boris began using this newfound power of his every day, training it stronger and stronger. Together with the fact that he was able to overcome the nullifiers to a greater extent, with time he greatly increased his power pool.

A couple of months later, the guard who beat him senseless every day was himself beaten and killed by another slaver, for disobeying a direct order.

It looked like a simple misunderstanding for someone watching from the sides, but in fact, Boris had managed to drag the sadistic slaver for an exciting "stroll" in one of the deeper tunnels. He had lured the fool into chasing him there since the alien was too embroiled in his usual sadistic game. Once there, the guard was no longer protected by the psychic nullifiers.

Boris unleashed his considerable psychic might upon the guard's mind and implanted certain... thoughts in. He had never tried manipulating somebody's mind like that. Terran telepaths were told never to do it unless it was absolutely necessary, but for Boris' survival, it had become necessary now.

The very next time that guard met with his superior, he began acting with the brash arrogance that most other guards knew him for. Boris had only needed to remove some of his mind blockers and play with the guard's self-preservation instincts. The final result was a particle-beam to the head, and his most hated torturer was now permanently removed from his way.

The imprints in his head grimly rejoiced with him.

* * *

Sometime during his second year, the camp's Intendant was replaced with a new and even more depraved alien slaver.

It was some dark green-skinned alien – a fallen Taz'aran noble, one of the slaves told Boris. He quickly found out that in addition to the new Intendant's greed, he was also a stickler for violent, deadly entertainment. Soon the slaves were forced to fight each other in a gladiatorial fashion, with camp guards and the Intendant himself waging large sums of money on their bouts.

The unfortunate ones chosen to become gladiators had to be healthier than the rest, and also willing to kill their fellow slaves. As always in any slave population, there were some who bullied their way up and into a position of relative power compared with the rest by exploiting fellow slaves' misery and licking the boots of their masters.

Boris had no love for such parasites, but after spending time in deep meditation, decided that joining some fights was going to be advantageous for his training and overall plan's success. Boris had "befriended" one of the foremen, by giving him some uranium ore on the side, that the slaver could then sell secretly. By lining the foreman's pockets with money, Boris managed to achieve a working relationship with that scum of a person.

The crafty Terran youth then had him negotiate some easy fights for himself, at first. Boris was only ten when he uncovered another telepathic power: he was able to augment himself physically and increase the performance of his muscles above their peak capacity. But even with his uncanny ability to overcome the nullifiers and his body trained almost to perfection, he was yet but a small child.

By meticulously planning and manipulating the situation, he made it such that his first targets in the gladiator ring were other teens. These particular teenagers were vile filth who bullied younger children and often ran prostitution rings. They sold the weakest of their fellow slaves to the guards, purchasing favors and extra rations for themselves. After many of those children died, their corpses tortured and bleeding in his hands while Boris was dragging them into the glow-pit, he'd decided that enough was enough.

This time, he almost lost control.

When he faced bully after bully and beat them into a bloody pulp, Boris over-enhanced his strength and agility to such a degree, that the spectators could barely see his punches. Fortunately, none of the intoxicated guards and their bootlickers were able to remember clearly what he had done that day.

It took him some time, but Boris managed to implant "proper" thoughts into their heads, that made them forget about this instance. Throughout the next year, his combat skills had advanced so much that Boris no longer had to augment himself. Somehow, his bones had become dense enough that every punch was as heavy as a hammer's blow.

Boris found out during one of his meditation cycles that he could meld together all of his powers and telepathic disciplines. What's more, he had been doing so, unconsciously and unintentionally, for more than a year. His body had been emboldened so many times that those enhancements became permanent. To push this power of his further, Boris needed the camp's huge nullifiers destroyed.

He spent the next two years in and out of the gladiatorial ring, training both his body and mind to an absolute perfection. Boris also spent quite a lot of time exploring the cave, until he'd mapped it completely. The Terran youth now understood that for his plan to ever come into fruition, he had to reach the top and escape through it. Yet, with his manipulation of air alone, he could not achieve such a feat – for that he needed telekinesis.

But to his knowledge that was impossible since no known telepath could manifest more than two or three, different disciplines. Therefore he decided to use a combination of his known disciplines, and only after he'd physically climbed the rock face as high as possible. Again and again, he tried, his ability to control the telepathic abilities growing exponentially each time.

One day, when Boris was twelve years old, he finally reached the top. He found himself high on the mountain's ridge, with gale winds blowing all over his body. The freezing icy snow was being picked up by the raging storm, swirling around him like a thousand tiny blades. He felt his happy boyhood returning to him for a moment, but the screaming, angry voices within him redirected his focus back to the task at hand.

His sight soon found where the tips of those nullifier towers were, defying the natural scenery with their metallic glow. Boris watched how, in the distance, their peaks trembled with each gust of wind and began calculating what would happen if the storm suddenly became stronger.

Alas, he was not that powerful yet, in a couple of years maybe, but not now.

Resting after scouting the slave enclosure from the top of the mountain, Boris found that it was not as large as he had previously thought. The slavers had built an impressive installation, yes, but in essence, it was a glorified mountain camp. They did have one anti air defense tower, however, that was the extent of their defenses.

While pondering on why the camp lacked any substantial defenses, Boris looked up in the sky. For the first time, his vision wasn't impaired by dust clouds and he could see the silhouette of a large space station in close orbit. The huge construction bristled with lights emanating from all over its enormous superstructure.

While he watched with amazement, a couple dozen starships dropped out of hyperspace, with sudden flashes of bright light accompanying the pulses of their main engines. He grimaced; then this star system was a hub for trade, and who knows what other illicit activities. Given that they heavily used slave labor, it wasn't that hard for him to imagine what else his "masters" were involved in.

* * *

Later that day, Boris made his way down into the cave and back to the compound, carrying with him a substantial load of ore he'd prepared beforehand. His foreman took the bribe, and again, easily arranged another gladiatorial fight for him. One which he quickly won, after the appropriate posturing and faking enough pain from inaccurate, glancing strikes.

At this point Boris was so strong that he could have taken all of the guards on his own, even without using weapons or telepathic powers. It wasn't in his master plan to do so yet, and as much as Boris disliked that many more people would die, if he was to act now there was too great a chance of failure.

This time, after his win, Boris got as close as possible to the Chief Foreman, while his own unwitting pawn was collecting the winnings. With the utmost of patience and concentration, he managed to slide his own mind into the foreman's head. Since that weak-willed slaver had been under his control in some shape or form for the last couple of months, it was rather easy to plant ever-so-deep thoughts and suggestions in his mind.

Instead of risking a dangerous and unpredicted jump into the mind of their chief foreman, Boris played it safe, and all went well in the end. He made the foreman ask the chief a couple of simple queries concerning their masters. These questions certainly looked innocent at first glance, but if it had been anyone else asking or the chief had gotten suspicious, his cover could have been blown easily enough.

Nonetheless, he was able to find out the name of their masters – they were from a race called Vaugn. Boris was lurking on the edge of his bribed foreman's consciousness, about to slip his own mind back out, when by luck, the chief foreman began yapping his mouth about the orbital station and what exactly they were doing up there.

It turned out that not only it was a trade hub for slaves, but the station's Vaugn masters dabbled in ruthless medical testing projects. For that purpose, they always used one-half of the child slaves they bought each year.

Boris immediately remembered the girl who spoke with him on the slave ship. He began gritting his teeth at the mere thought of what could've happened to her. If she was lucky, her suffering had long since ended, if not... well, he was about to scour that station's decks and look for her.

He knew who would be his first target, after slaughtering all of the slave guards here – every single Vaugn who stood in his path. There was one small cargo shuttle docked at the base's landing pad, which the foremen used often to get up on the station and sell some of their stolen ore on the black market.

Boris would definitely use this to his advantage.

\* \* \*

He spent the next year and a half learning how their criminal organization worked in detail. After mastering his telepathic prowess, the slavers could not hide even their darkest secrets from him. It took him only a few days to unravel their whole, "impossible-to-discover" command structure. Boris quickly sniffed out who was who, and under whose command was the entire operation, names and all.

During the time he spent investigating, Boris soon found out that thanks to his keen intellect and attention to detail, he could become an excellent lawman. Had he not been captured and sold into slavery, his opportunities for growth and success inside the Minarchy would have been almost limitless. There could still be possibilities for him – Boris only had to succeed in his plan to escape.

If Imperial Minarchy forces had known of this place, all the slaves would've been free, as soon as they could deploy any forces in the area. The slavers would be slaughtered without mercy, whether by Boris or by Imperial troops. The only difference in how they would meet their end depended upon the type of troops performing the operation.

As a younger child, Boris had watched many holo movies on the G-Net, marveling at the bravery and skill that the special operators had. Terrans knew that the Imperial Army's soldiers were better or equal to almost any other star state's elite forces. The very mention of Imperial commandos or stormtrooper units made many a pirate carefully rethink their futures.

Of course, there were always enough arrogant idiots, who dismissed the skill of Imperial Special Ops as mere rumors. Those people didn't live long enough to regret their poor decisions, because when stormtroopers assaulted, they wouldn't have any time to react.

Terran stormtrooper attacks were always relentless, devastating, and lightning quick. There was a saying from old Earth's lingo:

*"Where Stormtroopers walk, green grass never grows!"*

Obviously, that wasn't meant literally, but one only need simply observe the destruction left after their assaults to imagine why people thought of this.

What about the commandos?

You wouldn't see them coming at all!

Your expensive tech would be hacked and used against you. Enemy commanders would lose any and all situational awareness, since their sensors either wouldn't work or show false data. Then the terrible "Space Ghosts", as most criminals began calling the Terran commandos, would slip out of nothingness and slaughter every single enemy almost in an instant, using one, perfectly-coordinated attack.

But, though that was all true, sadly, it only happened in very few cases. The chief reason was that the special ops teams were too few, and even with the huge economic resources and immense support from Imperial citizenry, the Minarchy was never able to field many of them.

It was a question of numbers since the population growth had taken a hit after the 1969 invasion. Way too many men were lost, skewing human numbers in favor of women. In fact, Boris knew even then, that him becoming a man would mean dozens or even hundreds of young girls chasing after him.

Most women might have traveled for years in space

on their husband searches, scouring colony after colony, looking in vain for a "free" man. The ratio between men and women was, at best, four to one; on the distant colonies that could go as high as nine women for one man. Never mind the wonders of modern medical science; nothing could fix this horrid imbalance. You could only try to have as many children as possible and hope that more of them would be born male.

Despite the long and painful work as a slave, Boris grew up surprisingly good-looking, yet his personality though took a big hit.

One could hardly expect a child that grew up digging uranium ore, with thousands upon thousands of people rotting away beside him, to have a pleasing character. He did have his parents' good upbringing, but after losing them, Boris was left to grow a personality of his own. Any sort of harsh survival situation could potentially harm people's minds, but if he had taken a little bit of damage, it was greatly limited.

It was mainly thanks to his good genetics and incredible stubbornness, which he'd inherited from his Bulgarian roots that Boris didn't break or go crazy. This was the case with many other slaves of his age, whom he had seen slip into insanity. Some found refuge in any type of debauchery that was available to them, but this actually made their descent into madness even quicker. As always, most people only hurt themselves with their foolish actions.

Boris stayed away from all of them, lest he go the way they did. He managed to keep himself clean of any drugs that they used, as well. Not surprisingly, there were ways to procure narcotics even within the slave enclosure, but the price one had to pay was even greater.

He grew up not simply despising drugs, Boris outright

hated them, and the people who used and sold them. Both were almost as equally guilty in his eyes, since one would not exist without the other, and both ended their lives in misery and death. The user, by destroying their health, and the seller, death by the hands of either law enforcement or vigilantes. Of course, there were some exceptions, but the average was important in most cases.

Either way, Boris finally had some hope for a future outside of this slave mine – and he wasn't going to let anything get in his way.

* * *

When he grew up to be eighteen, Boris had already spent eleven years as a slave, mining uranium ore in the mountain mines. Ten of those years he devoted to constant, careful planning and meticulous preparation. Now, the time finally came for him to set his plans in motion. He'd exact terrible vengeance upon the slavers, both here and up in their space station.

This was not just another day... tomorrow was *that* day!

One dark, stormy morning, Boris entered the mine a little bit early. He had won for himself some minor privileges, by bribing most of the greedy foremen with extra uranium ore. Somebody might think it strange that a slave would have privileges, but it all depended on what were you prepared to do and ready to offer. He had achieved a form of temporary understanding with most of them, and most thought him their friend.

What they didn't know was that they all would die,

together with the rest of their slaver buddies.

He walked casually deeper inside one of the tunnels, energy drill in hand and after passing out of their sight, Boris threw away the now useless to him thing. Long before any slave actually woke up and went to work, Boris was rapidly climbing up the mountain through the cave's exit. Upon reaching the peak, he could hear the sirens signaling for the next day of grueling work to start.

He was on time.

Boris easily concentrated, and soon a furious storm formed before him, blasting the icy peak with such force that whole pieces of frozen snow and stones flew towards the psychic nullifiers. He almost laughed, but quickly stopped himself, remembering that one who laughs, must do so last.

He watched quietly as the thin towers collapsed under their own weight, being buried underneath their own crumbling frames. Hit by a rock slide, the camp's single air defense tower also suffered the same fate.

He slid on the ice and down the mountain's slope towards the mine entrance, with the force of an actual tornado centered around him which created a huge wave of frozen snow and rocks that Boris rode downwards. He knew that the guards were always the first to enter the mine, even before the slaves were awakened for work by the sirens and that avalanche he'd started would bury them all alive within the mine.

So far, so good.

He gracefully landed on his feet in front of the slavers' main compound only to discover that somehow, one of the foremen had survived. As chance would have it this was the very same slaver that he had used as a puppet, and the fool ran towards him panicked, screaming for aid. Boris smiled as he swung his foot to the side and broke the foreman's neck with one strike, noting his dumbfounded facial expression.

More guards were awoken by the commotion.

They rose from their rest rotation, equipped and ready to fight or at least that's what the Intendant thought. At best all that noise was a simple natural disaster, and for such, they were well prepared. The towers were down and among the slaves, there were telepaths for sure, but the guards were freshly rested and well-armed.

Surely, whatever resistance their slave workers could muster would be easily squished by his guards! Exiting their main barracks, the slavers saw only one teenage boy walking towards them. Somebody whom they knew to be an obedient slave, a gladiator.

Moreover, that person was one who had bribed many of them, fattening their pockets with money, and so they ignored him. The guards ran towards the slave enclosure, weapons drawn, expecting the slaves agitated and unruly. Boris waited for them to pass around him and once they were at his sides, he then super-compressed the air, creating large, invisible blades.

He unleashed them at full force.

While the guards were still running, their upper torsos continued forwards, rolling on the snowy slope. Some lived precious seconds more, they were even able to scream, while their innards were freezing to the icy ground.

The Intendant and the remaining guards, who were still alive inside their compound, fired through the apertures with every weapon they had, aiming at him. All of their low-powered and unfocused laser beams were either inaccurate or vanished right before they hit his body. The closer he got to their building, the harder breathing became for them.

Most threw their weapons down and tried running away, only to fall, their bodies burning from the inside out. As Boris reached the doors of their barracks, all of the slavers close to him were either dead or on the ground, dying. Then, with a flick of his wrist, the locked doors turned into pools of molten metal. Using the hot air that he created, Boris glided over the pools and into the compound.

Once inside, more guards, armed with better weapons and equipment, streamed towards him, exiting the inner compound buildings. This time, he didn't wait for them to fire their weapons but attacked first.

Fiery bolts formed around his hands and then, much akin to the arrows of old, flew and impaled the slavers without error. Thanks to one of his earlier strolls into the minds of a certain foreman, Boris knew precisely where everything was in this compound, and the telepath now casually strolled towards the Intendant's office.

True to their creed, all of the remaining slavers not-so-bravely ran away in the... opposite direction. They didn't get very far, as Boris unleashed another gust of wind that blew all of the nearby icy snow up and then down on them, burying them all alive. The Intendant himself did try resisting, but his attempts were as futile as those of the rest of his minions.

Boris augmented himself to such a degree that he was able to punch a hole clear through the Intendant's head, before he could even reach for his gun. After grabbing the Intendant's PDA and copying all of the files from the slaver's office, Boris collapsed all of the buildings, using fire to melt their support columns. Having done this, he then walked down the slope and into his home for the last eleven years where he saw the slaves.

They stood there, gathered inside the center of the enclosure, huddling, just like cattle before a storm. Upon seeing him, they all cried, panicked and confused, asking what had happened, shouting loudly over each other. Boris easily melted the slave enclosure's gate and walked over towards the tiny cargo shuttle parked on the landing pad.

Last night, he'd advised his pawn to place a good amount of pure uranium ore in its cargo bay. After all those painful years of hard, back-breaking labor, Boris wouldn't go without any compensation!

The other slaves could loot the encampment's equipment and supplies for all he cared. In fact, they had already begun doing just that, and Boris was sure they would survive. There were a couple of bigger ships docked on the other landing pads, and any of them could easily accommodate all of the slaves.

He wasn't worried about them at all.

Boris quickly finished the preparations for launch. His looted ship raised its nose towards the skies, engines spewed white hot plasma, the heavily-ladened with ore vessel blasting away with a most deafening roar. Soon his shuttle exited the atmosphere, and Boris began studying his new target. Stretching his telepathic senses forward at their maximum range, he felt somebody familiar. It was that girl!

Still alive, yet damaged in some horrible way, she had a strange presence inside of her. Something powerful beyond anything he could've ever imagined – the unknown entity's consciousness seemed almost overpowering. Boris could also feel that she was in pain, and had been, for many years without any pause.

He could also sense multiple Vaugn present on that station. In fact, they counted for more than ninety percent of its total population. Boris knew what had to be done – all of those filthy slavers had to die a most painful death.

# Chapter 11

## *Vengeful thoughts*

During the years, Kera found out where most of the slaves which the Vaugn matriarchy bought were sent.

Down, on the planet's desolate surface, rich with uranium ore, they'd built multiple mines which exclusively used slave labor. Kera suspected that the boy she met all those years ago, had been sent down there, and from the holo files that she had seen, anybody surviving in such horrid conditions was nothing short of a miracle.

Kera felt an enormous burst of telepathic power coming from the planet below, and the owner of said might was rapidly getting closer to the space station. There were many life forms whose existence was abruptly snuffed and, the local intranet was suddenly full of panicked links and desperate calls for aid.

The station itself actually did... nothing. Not a single weapon fired at the small cargo hauler that was nearing one of its docking ports.

Were the Vaugn on bridge duty in the know that its occupant was not one of theirs?

Most probably the Ops officers could not even be bothered to scan the craft, but just to be sure she hacked the data-streams, making it harder for them to do so. For far too long had this place, this system been calm and the lack of incidents had made base personnel lax in their duties.

While Kera felt that dozens on the surface suffered and died violent deaths, it seemed that Vaugn matriarchs cared little for these guards. They neither returned any of the panicked links calling for aid, nor sent their own troops down to check on the situation in that particular uranium mine.

Kera made sure to instruct Ort in the smallest of details so that their plan could succeed. He was to visibly run away from the laboratory, making himself a target to be chased around the station, therefore adding more confusion. She knew that, when the cargo ship docked, there would be a lot of panic indeed. He was beyond angry and wielded powers impossible for the Vaugn to measure or defend against.

Even with her universal link, Kera couldn't begin to fathom the extent of his psychic might. How, and why she was unable to detect him during all these years, Kera could not know. But what she had expected to happen, did, even beyond her wildest expectations. She hadn't seen anything on the holo files in the laboratory about telepathic abilities of such a caliber!

The entire station's structure began to quake, and through her network's connection, Kera saw him on one of the sensors. He had grown up well, and she felt something deep inside her mind awakening, stirring. Familiar feelings that Kera remembered back from the time when she had first touched Boris with her hand.

Pain!

Layers upon layers of insurmountable pain. Unable to counter this, her body began shaking inside the tank and one by one, her old cybernetics started shutting themselves down. Alarms went off, warning holo messages floating all over and outside the lab, but there was nobody present to hear or see those. Again, she concentrated on her link and with great hardship, managed to block the pain he emanated in all directions.

* * *

He easily docked at one of the closest ports, and began sabotaging the station from the very minute his feet touched the floor plating. All of the escape pods, he melted and fused into the hull. The life support systems, he overflowed with storm winds and any other ship he saw docked at the port, the telepath had its landing struts melted to the station's floors.

He then met with the first responders – a group of Vaugn soldiers.

Large, lumbering, and with strangely empty minds, they obeyed the orders of their matriarch commanders, showering him with inaccurate particle beam fire. Even though their armor was strong and their bones thick, the Vaugn fell. In his rage, he consumed most of his leftover power in an attempt to take care of them quickly.

Boris wanted to move fast and reach the girl's location first, because the more he moved forward, the more he felt that she was in trouble. Each time when he met with another fresh detachment of Vaugn troops, Boris drew a little bit from the pool of hateful souls that had been occupying his head for all these years.

They were there, waiting inside his mind for their chance to kill. Unleashing them meant that he would lose some of his power, but it was better than keeping the imprints locked inside forever.

Moving ever deeper inside the space station, he left behind a scene of terrible devastation. The bent and broken metal decks were now corpse-ridden, overflowing with blood and gore. As station alarms whined, molten bulkheads ran like metal rivers, setting everything and everyone in their path on fire.

It took him only a few short minutes to reach the station's medical laboratories. Boris sensed the presence of another friendly being linked with the girl's mind, and reinforced it both mentally and physically. It was so confusing that it didn't even notice what he had given to it, but after his initial fighting ended, it acknowledged him as a friend.

Beforehand, when first reaching forward with his psychic power into the being's mind, Boris had discovered that it was a Vaugn consciousness, that had been transferred into another body.

Probing it, he came to the realization that it was still a child, and not yet broken beyond repair. Still, the thought angered him – experimenting even on one's own race's children?!

Such depravity!

\* \* \*

During his scuffle with the station's guards, Ort led many of Vlenti's lab scientists on a wild goose chase around the main promenade. The dog was large and quick, much faster than any of them would have imagined and, even with all of the gadgets that they were packing, the scientists were unable to capture him.

Ort was having a blast trying his new body. He performed multiple, insane feats of strength, during his mission to waylay the Vaugn personnel. While the chase dragged on, Ort ran around the comb-like decks, leaping from platform to platform, always leaving his pursuers stunned and lagging behind.

To do what he managed would've been impossible for most creatures, but this dog's body was amazing!

Ort was soon being attacked by a multitude of sentry drones. Equipped with stunners and grappling hooks, all of them were powered by grav engines, yet these were effective only in areas of the station where its magnetic plating was operating at full power. Obviously, you cannot and would not need to maintain all of the floor panels with full gravity, therefore, any grav vehicle avoided the deactivated panels like the plague.

It was exactly what happened on those planets where areas of lower magnetic fields existed – any grav vehicle that flew over them could crash in a most violent manner. Ort was using exactly those floor panels to slow the drones and put them in convenient places for attack.

Leaping up in the air and fully utilizing the weaker gravity of those areas, Ort bashed their fragile hulls into the bulkheads. He crushed them inside his powerful teeth and spit the metal remains around, creating more obstacles for them. One by one, all of the scientists fell so far behind that only the station sensor network could tell them where Ort was.

Kera then decided that it was high time to nullify any and all of their advantages. Still in control of the system, she fed all of the sensors with a continuous holo feedback loop. Since most of the Vaugn matriarchs were confused already, they ordered their female subordinates to begin evacuating the station. They wouldn't give such an order to their male troops though; soldiers were expendable and their mistresses the matriarchs, most important.

However high and mighty they thought themselves to be in their minds, reality conquered all, even self-deluded fools such as them. The Vaugn females didn't reach the docking ports since their paths, unfortunately, crossed with Boris. Their lives were extinguished quickly; the station's structure shook violently again and again, while the telepath blew them each one of them to smoldering shreds with balls of fire. By now, the many system alarms that Kera saw on her intranet holo feed began alerting the Vaugn admins, and eventually, they found out about her deception.

Matriarch Vlenti was on her way, with a couple of her own soldiers in tow.

While screaming commands, her mistress's snout opened wide, revealing the matriarch's teeth and, seemingly really angry, she was frothing. During the years spent as her chief test subject, Kera had never learned how to read Vaugn facial expressions. Perhaps they didn't have any, or the nuances of their facial muscles shifting were too unrecognizable for her.

Not that it mattered though.

For such a proud ruling body, which found their utmost satisfaction in mass-exterminating innocent, underdeveloped races, surely, pure hatred was the matriarchs emotion of choice.

The dog, after speeding away from what was left of his pursuers, ran as fast as he could back toward the lab. He instinctively knew that, if his old matriarch reached the laboratory before him, Kera would be immediately killed. Along the way, Ort felt strange sensations overcome his mind, and he tried his best to understand what was going on.

His sense of smell told him of somebody alien that

was closing in fast, but his new eyes couldn't see him. After a minute of frantically sniffing the air and trying to find anything out of the ordinary, Ort felt that it was best to give up his search, and rushed towards the lab.

There, six soldiers under the command of Vlenti had just broken through the laboratory's locked armored doors, storming the room. Ort's eyes were full of rage – initially he fought the animalistic urge to howl, but finally succumbing, his terrifying roar shook the ears of his old mistress. As he howled, Matriarch Vlenti turned towards him, and on witnessing the large creature charging towards her, panicked.

Understandingly so – this Vaugn was a scientist!

Ort, despite being but a child, was, even after the haphazard training regimen matriarchs subjected rapidly cloned males, a soldier. Vlenti, ran inside the laboratory, looked for a place to hide, all the while shouting conflicting orders to her soldiers. Ort smelled their desperation and willingness to die, for the men were far older than him, and had unwillingly performed hundreds of horrific deeds.

He quickly leaped at them. Baring his long, sharp teeth while dodging one of their beam shots mid-jump, Ort's teeth found a throat, and made his first kill of the day. Somehow, tasting blood made his sharp senses even more acute. He could read easily their sluggish movements and came to a sudden realization – they were intentionally leaving themselves open.

They were eagerly rushing at him, trying very hard not to defend themselves. Vlenti's guards fought their behavior modulation chips with everything they had. Ort attacked again, and even the fact that he got slightly hurt by one of the soldiers' particle-beam guns, couldn't stop his teeth from causing mortal wounds, releasing yet another one of his unfortunate male brothers from servitude.

Behind him, a sudden explosion shook the bulkheads, but he had no time to look back – Kera was in danger!

Two of the soldiers had their guns aimed at her tank, and Ort rushed forwards, leaping off and over most of the equipment that was blocking his way. He tripped another soldier and snapped his neck while doing so. The very mass of this new body combined with his quick running speed was a most devastating combination. He used the momentum to bite off one of the three remaining soldiers' arms, then, sliding on the bloody floor, Ort positioned himself between Kera's tank and the Vaugn.

His old matriarch was already screaming profanities, wailing for help over her PDA link, and spewing orders to what was left of the soldiers.

She was trying to call for reinforcements, but Ort was adamant that they would never come...

Why?

Ort didn't simply understand – he *knew*.

The knowledge had simply appeared in his mind out of nowhere, refusing to convince any of his neurons on the "hows" of this. Yet, both Ort's mind and body were working surprisingly well, even better than before, when he fought alone against those grav drones. It was as if he could see from two pairs of eyes, and that couldn't have been Kera's.

Turning around, he caught Vlenti sneaking away and jumped between her legs, tripping her over some nearby medical containers. Her last remaining guard landed a glancing shot with his gun, but then Ort immediately slit the soldier's belly with his claws.

He heard then the painful screams of Matriarch Vlenti, and quickly turned around to see what had happened.

His now very sensitive dog nose caught the vile, overpowering chemical scent of some dangerous concoctions. Screaming and flailing helplessly with her arms, Vlenti's flesh began boiling, while pieces of her Vaugn protective shell grew with an unnatural speed.

Her voice changed, and one of her arms fell off, only to be replaced by two longer appendages that ended in large claws. Matriarch Vlenti's screams slowly died off, and then in full silence, the creature who was once this research station's head scientist rose up from under the broken crates.

Only now could Ort's tired eyes see what was written all over them:

"TESTING SUBSTANCES. MUTAGEN – HANDLE WITH CARE!"

Changed far beyond anything intended by any one single mutagen or stim, the Vaugn matriarch had morphed into a hideous mutant of unknown capabilities.

* * *

Kera quickly pushed her mind towards finding a solution to this new malady. In a case like this one, the behavior of such a mutant, one "created" entirely by accident, was extremely unpredictable. The very combination of untested and highly experimental meds was something that nobody could predict the outcome of, when applied on a living being.

There were cases of multiple planet contamination events, with billions of casualties, caused by the combination of just two such chemicals. While Kera was pondering on, trying to find an exit from the dangerous situation that she and Ort had fallen into, he entered through the broken laboratory doors.

The mutated body of Vlenti lunged with surprising speed towards her tank, and Ort jumped in her way, shielding Kera with his own body. He managed to bite off one of those new arms that the matriarch grew so quickly, before he was nearly sliced in two by Vlenti's long, sharp claws.

Ort whimpered in pain; bravely crawling after the mutant, he managed to bite off a piece of its leg with his teeth. Another hit by Vlenti's ever-growing appendages and he flew a couple of feet in the air, but before his wounded body could crash and his bones break on the floor panels, something greatly slowed down the fall.

A gust of strong wind cushioned Ort's body to a soft landing. Whimpering but still alive, he remained where he fell. It was Boris who, with seemingly just one step, moved so far forward as to be able to block Vlenti's way and stood before her in some strange martial stance.

He took a glance at her tank and Kera could see in his eyes that he knew who she was. She remembered the look on his face from when both of them were small children. From before those long years of suffering and pain had passed, turning his troubled, but soft, facial features into a canvas of scarred skin, a tortured mask.

Boris even back then was athletic, and now, after years of grueling hard labor, his body had grown many times over. The ragged slave clothing that he wore couldn't cover his well-formed muscles and the many other fresh scars that his body sported.

Her vengeance had finally arrived.

*  *  *

After punching through the doors of the lab, and witnessing the mutated form of a Vaugn matriarch striding towards a tank full of medical liquid, Boris gasped – inside it floated what was left of the girl.

Now all grown up, she was lacking all of her limbs and had had pain inducers cybernetically infused directly into her brain. If that wasn't enough, the Vaugn matriarch had removed her eyes and poked the girl's brain and nerves with metallic sensors. Even though the creature standing before him couldn't understand what he said, Boris still snarled angrily at Vlenti's mutated form:

"Vile wretch, you are responsible for all of this! You and everybody on this station will pay for it with your lives!"

Boris unleashed more of his power and wrapped it around his fists. Shining energy crackled around them, and prepared to attack the mutated Vaugn. Raising his hands in a perfect martial stance, he flew towards his soon-to-be-dead slave master, ready to shower her mutated body with lightning-fast hits.

In the midst of his rage, Boris decided to destroy the entire station by crashing it into the planet below. After all of these atrocities, nobody was to escape him... not even one single slaver.

His fists raised but not fully clenched, Boris looked like he was about to shower Vlenti with punches. He did not do so, but instead, with lightning speed, grappled her flailing "arms" when she tried hitting him, ripping them apart with just one fluid motion.

299

Kera, had she still had eyes and not been looking through Ort's hazy eyesight, could swear that his movements were way too fast to be that of a normal human being. Her universal link couldn't show her, if he had used telepathic abilities to boost himself.

Amazed, Kera watched Boris punching Vlenti's large mutated body with such force and precision, that her tank shook every time the strikes connected. Ort's ears were hurting from the sound waves those punches created since their very movement through the air generated small sonic booms.

Instead of shattering, this human's bones withstood the enormous pressure, and hit by hit, Boris broke every part of Vlenti's body. The Vaugn's chest, after being pummeled relentlessly for a good minute or so, collapsed on the inside, crushing most of her organs.

Every time she got hit by Boris, Vlenti's entire body was slightly lifted a good few feet off the ground. Spouting blood everywhere, her organs punctured by splintered bones, the once-powerful matriarch tried to raise her lone remaining arm, defend herself from the inevitable.

It was perhaps a reaction of her brain, desperately trying to shield its body from the inevitable doom. With his last strike Boris punctured Vlenti's skull, crushing her brain and splattering it around the floor panels.

Losing no time, he then quickly picked up one of the scattered medsprays and injected Ort's broken body with it. The large dog's flesh began steaming and most of its life-threatening wounds vanished enabling Ort to stand up. Boris then reached with his open hand towards her tank, and invisible telepathic force gently removed the lid...

In years Kera hadn't breathed air normally, nor had

she spent more than a couple of painful minutes outside the tank, while her tortured body was subjected to all form of tests. All of the cybernetic wirings and sensors that her torso was connected with were pulled out, while she flew up in the air and then gently landed in his arms.

If Kera had hands, she would hug him.

Had she had legs still, she would've walked beside him.

Not even her eyes were her own, yet another useless cybernetic pain inducer.

Kera's head was bald since her hair had been in the way of Vlenti's cybernetic brain probes. While she was at last held by someone with no intention of hurting or making her suffer, Kera was overcome with a new sensation, something that she hadn't felt since her early childhood:

Safety.

While Boris walked out of the laboratory, Ort followed him, limping. The toll on his strange new body was immense and he felt secure in that, for now, his charge Kera was safe in that human's arms. The more he stood beside him, the more Ort felt that he himself was protected and unthreatened.

It was that human's very presence that projected an aura of security around him. Suddenly the station's internal comm link sparked to life, and the large holo of one of the matriarchs appeared above the promenade:

"This is the station's commander! I am warning you, slaves, return at your workstations at once, or we will be forced to deactivate the station's life support in your area!"

Boris's eyes squinted at the large face, while he uttered his answer in a terrifyingly loud, yet calm voice:

"You are in no position to make any threats or demands, Vaugn scum! Neither will you be able to prevent your pathetic station's imminent destruction!"

While the telepath spoke, he leisurely walked towards the direction of the station's docks and, feeling that freedom was but minutes away, Kera's empty eye sockets overflowed with tears of happiness.

The holo of the Vaugn matriarch was taken aback:

"What?! How dare you talk back at me, slave! Obey your masters and cease any resistance this instant!"

Boris walked right through the holo, seemingly unaffected by the matriarch's rantings and after reaching the space station docking ports he noted to her:

"You will find that all of your pod's engines are now molted scrap, their hulls fused to the station and beyond repair. Your station's orbit will begin its rapid decline, right about... now."

He then muttered under his breath:

"Enjoy burning alive in the atmosphere, slaver filth..."

Indeed, the entire structure of the space station began to tilt ever so slightly. Because its floor panels were still maintained with standard gravity, Kera couldn't say if the station's superstructure had changed its angle, without being able to compare it with the planet beside.

Soon the station commander's holo was deactivated, because systems began failing one after another, and then the hull started violently shaking. By the time Boris carried Kera into his captured cargo shuttle, everything was crumbling to pieces. Bulkheads were crashing into each other, and what was left of the station's crew ran panicked around like headless chickens without any hope of escape.

Just as Boris had warned them, they were practically doomed from the moment he'd boarded the station. While he was making his way towards Kera's laboratory, Boris had used his telepathic powers to sabotage all of the space station's main systems and escape pods. There was no way in hell he could allow those filthy slavers to escape with their lives. Not after what they'd done to those hundreds of thousands of innocent people, not after what they'd done to Kera!

He cared not what their races were.

In fact, Boris was the only human working inside that uranium mine, where possibly millions had died! All of their suffering and needless deaths were blood on the hands of those Vaugn pieces of shit.

It was them who had ordered the capture of anyone, who was even remotely passing along this sector of Fringe Space.

It was the slavers, whom they employed, who had killed his parents without pity.

They, who had ruthlessly played with his and other slaves' lives while working them to the bone in their uranium mines.

He punched in a new course in the navigational controls of his vessel. Boris watched on the ship's sensors, how that two-mile-long space station slowly descended from its stable orbit and burned into the atmosphere below.

Even from that distance, he could sense the many thousands of whimpers and howls of pain, before the melting hull broke apart into thousands of pieces. Then the soothing silence finally overcame his tortured mind, and he fainted, while the ship's computer initiated the pre-programmed FTL jump.

* * *

Luckily, only a day later, his modified transponder was detected by a passing Imperial Minarchy patrol craft.

The freshly-painted Imperial Navy starship pulled the drifting piece of space garbage into their hangar bay. Kera felt weaker but still managed to detect through her universal link that the ship was full of humans. There were other races, and also another telepathic human on board – a female.

She smiled at Boris, while he carried her out into the bigger ship's hangar and asked:

"Are we safe now?"

He looked at her tortured and tired face, and allowed himself to utter an optimistic answer:

"Yes, Kera, we are safe."

The interior of that ship was nothing like she had ever seen. Through the eyes of Ort, Kera could study all of the interesting sights, technology, and scents. There were multiple strange new life forms, whom she knew to be sentient Terran client races.

Long-eared bunnies of all colors, large muscular gorillas, and small rodent-like creatures that she remembered the humans called "hamsters". While Kera was exploring with and through Ort, a group of heavily-armed soldiers approached them.

They were led by the telepath she had sensed through her universal link, a woman much older than Boris and her. Kera could feel her confidence wavering after her powers tried probing Boris and were completely blocked.

She commanded them:

"Halt! I am Commander Pauline, Second-in-Command of the INS *Achilles*! Who are all of you and what were you doing on that slaver ship? Answer my questions quickly, unregistered telepath, and we will provide you and your friends with medical assistance."

Boris bristled!

"'Halt'?! You have to be kidding, woman. Stand aside, or yourself lead me towards your ship's medical bay, because I have neither the time nor inclination to deal with your pompous bullshit! Then and only then, after both my partner and our dog are taken care of, maybe I'll answer your questions. Or better yet, if you wish, I can start planting all of that information into your undisciplined mind? Certainly, this will save you some time, although, with such a pathetic skill level as yours, I doubt you'll be able to stay conscious for long, registered telepath..."

The woman's face turned red, and her female troopers silently chuckled under their faceplates. The ship's second-in-command bit her lip, stepped aside and pointed at one soldier, ordering her to escort them deeper inside the starship.

People who were given command of starships weren't that unwise as to pick useless fights, especially with fellow humans. She knew that even if they tried to subdue that man, neither the equipment nor the number of star marines that they had on board would be enough to do so.

Being second in command of a starship in the Imperial Navy, the telepath needed to exercise her authority in a professional way and, quarreling in the hangar with another human was beneath her. As a member of Psy-corps, Pauline had to confront any unregistered telepath and especially human ones.

Who knew what humanity's enemies were concocting, deep inside their secret research facilities?

That man might be a clone, a dangerous infiltrator, sent on a mission of destruction!

Yet, only a couple of seconds were needed for her to discover that this person was neither a clone, nor was he lying. Her captain would later gently scold her, because of the inherent pompousness of her speech and she would be right, of course.

Kil'ra were almost always right. More so, Captain Jaena'ni was an aspiring D'har martial arts mistress. Wise beyond her years and awarded the captaincy of the *Achilles* for her uncommon valor, she was a person who everybody aspired to be like.

The commander opened her PDA and sent a holo link to her Psy-corps handler at once, via secured and quad-coded G-net connection. That old human organization had to know of this telepath since they kept records of all Terrans born with such abilities. They were also the one group that trained and prepared telepaths for the inevitable clash with others, aliens who didn't care about ethical constraints.

The Minarchy had to be protected from any telepathic menace that preyed upon its citizens, both foreign and domestic. While walking away with Kera in his arms, Boris turned half back to the group that had greeted them and issued a warning:

"Oh, and please don't enter the ship's cargo hold without radiation protection – I have some uranium ore stacked there. It is for selling, you see... I didn't spend all of those long, eleven years working as a slave just to walk away empty-handed!"

Kera felt a warmth she'd never felt before flowing through her universal link from the contact with all those Terran crewmen.

Ort also experienced another new sensation when a group of very small sentients approached, laughing, and began to run in circles around him. They petted the large canine gently with their tiny paws, and Ort suddenly stopped walking, lay on the floor plating, and with tears flowing from his eyes, whimpered happily.

Kera whispered to Boris:

"Leave him here, he is experiencing happiness for the first time in his life. I am sure that the little ones will help him find us later."

Boris had initially paused, but he could only nod in agreement. He himself had felt the emotional rollercoaster her strange dog's transplanted alien mind was going through.

Upon reaching the medical bay, they were greeted by an older man, wearing a lab coat over his spacesuit. He gasped angrily while inspecting Kera's body, and immediately ordered his staff to place her in their ship's regeneration chamber.

The chief doctor assured Boris that she would exit said chamber with all of her limbs intact, every trace of scars gone. As a matter of fact, he asked him who was responsible for her current condition, and became increasingly angry when Boris told him of her Vaugn captors.

He muttered something along the lines of:

"Filthy cunts, they will all pay someday in the future, for that and their many other crimes!"

Boris, tired beyond measure, and after consuming more than a few emergency food rations, fell asleep on one of the medical beds nearby.

He slept inside the medical bay for two full days, with a host of the doctors present giving him strange looks. Apparently, he was twitching and floating over the bed in his sleep, with some of their equipment flying and bashing all over the lab.

He only awoke when Kera's regeneration sequence was completed. Standing beside the chamber, he saw how Kera walked out of it completely healed, dressed in a close-fitting, one-piece red suit.

Boris marveled at her pale greenish skin. Once again she had the entire length of her dark blue hair, which ended almost close to her knees. The telepath was almost sure that above her head, he could see a small halo of golden light.

Kera opened her pink Avernum eyes, and looked around her, grinning softly, she then made two hesitant, small steps towards Boris. Still in disbelief that all of her limbs were there and working properly, Kera hugged him as tight as she could.

Finally, for the first time after eleven years of torment, Boris actually smiled.

# Epilogue

Captain Anit'za roamed the corridors of his ship with the purpose of a man possessed.

He knew, that even if the pirates hadn't used his new starship for drug smuggling, they had at least built a secret compartment or two. From the top of his right shoulder, he heard a meow and Anit'za glanced at the newest member of his crew.

It was a rather hairy cat with a single scar below her left yellow eye. Looked a lot like a pirate's cat and even acted like it hissing at any I-sec, or Star sheriff uniform it saw. The only person it looked with respect was Boris, and while he was wearing a Grey lawman's garb, the cat almost shook with fear when he passed nearby.

The dzenta'rii captain didn't have to wonder why, because sometimes even he had "goosebumps". That strange peculiar feeling, when you meet someone full of potential and imminent danger.

The grim-faced teenage telepath joined his crew after Anit'za was informed by one other human captain about his spectacular escape from a slave mine. That, and the destruction of a space station. The entire thing, together with all of its crew and passengers was crushed into the atmosphere of the planet it was orbiting.

Anit'za was quick to present Boris with a lucrative contract and was amazed, when the human youth's only additional requirement was that he also hire his young wife, Kera, as the ship's chief medical officer. She, despite her long years of captivity, had managed to study many medical sciences and was even an expert in cybernetics. That girl was nothing short of a genius.

Anit'za soon calculated what additional expenses he had to secure in advance, when their Vaugn slave masters decided to chase after the young couple. Slavery was something that he, as all dzenta'rii very much despised. It brought nothing, but false progress and increased misery, and free sentients were much more productive. And even more so if they were paid well, then they could see hope for a better future – for them and their offspring.

Also, there was that inevitable moment, someday, when all those oppressed sentients would eventually revolt. All of those negative and destructive things that his thoughtful ancestors had averted, by bestowing (in secret from the Galactic Assembly) all freedoms to their AI creations.

Their androids continued working with them to this day, being generously paid of course since no self-conscious dzent'a would allow their employees to wander off money-less. Anit'za also was looking forward to manipulating the I-sec connections Boris was bringing to the table, with him being a certified psychic investigator and a judge.

The dread criminals felt when facing such a powerful agent of the law, would work miracles in certain instances. Of course, there were negatives too, but Anit'za was sure that he could weasel his way out, by leaning heavily on common dzenta'rii qualities like bluffing, misdirection and force of persuasion.

Anit'za noticed all three of them slowly walking towards him in the corridor. Three, because that sentient dog Ort was also part of the deal since he came with Boris and Kera. He could swear the creature was smarter than it looked even after meeting it for the first time. It was also quite big; at least ten feet long and as tall as those small horses they had on Earth called ponies.

He nodded at them and smiled while Ort bumped him with his wet nose. The captain sighed and slightly chuckled before scratching him behind the ears – he quickly found out what the deal was with Ort.

The "animal" was not an animal at all, and in his cybernetically augmented by Kera brain, resided the mind of a Vaugn male. She had performed a successful mind transplant from the stunted brain of a Vaugn soldier and into the underdeveloped animal brain of that semi-sentient dog.

Kera looked at him and smiled with one of her godly *"I know what you think because I can speak with the Universe"* smiles. He blinked a couple of times imitating perfect dumbfoundedness and mumbled:

"Hello Lawman, how was that last job?"

Anit'za knew perfectly well what had happened but wanted to have a frequent exchange of relaxing banter with his crewmates.

"A bunch of *pitiful* Cartel enforcers!" – Boris waved the hand he wasn't holding Kera with and continued:

"They started spouting the usual stuff; 'do you know who our boss is' and 'don't you know who we work for'... it got boring really quickly and I slaughtered them all."

Anit'za slowly nodded in agreement with him and glanced at the right side of his belt, where Boris had chosen to attach his holster.

"So, you didn't have to use that pistol I gave you?"

He was one hundred percent sure that Boris was ecstatic when he gifted him that rare disruptor pistol.

311

"I did... and, thank you, Captain. The narcos screamed loudly as their bodies were disintegrating and it seemed they were in a *lot* of pain. That was a good change of pace, since using my powers all the time could be somewhat tasking."

Boris smiled tapping his holster marked with the I-sec logo and continued walking forward, while Kera threw another one of her smiles, a sadder one this time, shaking her head with a mild disagreement.

Anit'za couldn't understand her complete devotion to life. Sure, you could capture them' criminals, stun them and lock them up, but... they would eventually get out. There was no reforming for narcos or other types of druggies for that matter. In his country they killed them on sight, and Anit'za had to agree with the methods the civilian law enforcement agency that the Terrans had formed and named I-Sec were using. He sighed and continued searching.

* * *

Anit'za finally found what he was looking for: a tiny secret compartment, located in one of the upper panels at the far end of his ship's mess hall.

He secretly swiped one grav-extension stair and climbed up to search its contents. A most peculiar place to hide contraband he thought, but the cat he now called Snark sniffed it out for him.

The animal was surprisingly nimble and sneaky, not to speak of its powers of observation. Snark was almost able to smell when other creatures were deliberately untruthful. It stood on his shoulder and meowed with a certain frequency, glare focused on their lying mugs. Afterwards, it required food as compensation for services rendered and Anit'za began carrying in his pocket one small bag of cat treats, rewarding his new companion after a job well done.

Instead of a pet, as most sentients would threat that animal, the captain accepted Snark as part of the crew. Sure, the cat couldn't aid them in battle or at least in any way he was aware of yet, but it did carry a certain aura around itself. Often Snark popped out of the service tunnel network that any Terran ship of this size had, and in places where others were working.

It stood there watching and never allowed anybody to touch him, or play with him – always keeping his distance. That happened so often that most of his crew accepted the cat's presence in a way very similar to his own. It was like *he* was observing from a distance without being on the spot. The ship's crew felt as if Anit'za was there, while in fact, it was Snark who's tail was waving and eyes gazing at them.

When he opened the secret compartment, at first, he saw nothing, but then the cat meowed and he carefully checked the insides. Anit'za pulled out a small package and began unwrapping it, cutting the rope with his pocket knife.

Inside there was a single, strange, coin-like item, made of a material unknown to him. He quickly pocketed the thing and made sure to remove any evidence of that secret compartment. There was no need of anybody else knowing about it – plausible deniability and all that.

He bore the sole responsibility for ship and crew; Anit'za didn't want anyone thinking that he was running an unclean operation. Snark followed him sneakily as always and bumped his nose at Anit'za's boot. He knew that the cat had won another treat and opened the bag, spilling a couple of those cured meats before Snark's feet.

It tilted its head sideways and meowed once again before quickly devouring the food. Anit'za tried teaching the cat to do tricks in exchange for food, but it was too proud. No matter how many times he'd tried and whatever tasty treats he offered, Snark sat motionless tail wiggling eyes fixated on his face.

The fluffy animal only took food for things it *wanted* to do.

His gunner Cat told him of how she had found the cat. Snark was an army pet, part of some lost battalion, and no matter how hard Cat flexed her military connections, nobody was willing to speak more of it. The animal was severely depressed and multiple other attempts at adopting it failed.

The large gorilla explained how startled she was when they opened his cage for the first time. Snark's eyes were filled with tears and its face was emanating such sadness, that merely looking at the animal made most of the people present tear up. The moment it sniffed her hands, Snark crawled out of her cage and onto Cat's shoulder.

She stopped crying and meowed menacingly, hissing at anybody else who wanted to touch her. In the end, Cat spoke of a strange sensation she'd felt after spending some time with her. It was like a new sense of purpose was emanating from Snark, while she slept quietly on her lap during the return trip. She also felt strangely at home on starships and while most pets required grav-assist belts, Snark effortlessly moved around even in zero-G.

Moving away from the entrance to his ship's mess hall, Anit'za heard the two quieted voices of his other crewmates. This time it was his systems operator and botanist Lilly.

The brown furred bunny was calmly chatting with his

chief engineer and mecha pilot – the Asgardian named Brynjar. Both became instant friends after Lilly had wandered in his mecha pit during one of Anit'za's trips around Cav.

Seems she was not only a capable Sysop, but had survived with close to no equipment and supplies deep inside her home planet's jungle for weeks. Not only that, but she faced a whole taz'aran infantry force in battle, armed with a single rail-carbine and a vibrodagger...

He was amazed at the fact that Lilly was able to function after living through so much pain. Her colony was completely wiped out by the taz'arans after all. So typical for them to do that, preying on the weak – killing and enslaving were the two things they prided themselves on being good at.

Anit'za found the colonial star marine who picked her up. The man was as ecstatic as he was angry; he reported one destroyed grav attack vehicle and a full section of veteran taz'aran scouts!

The captain pondered on about the nature of one's enemy.

Were the taz'arans "cartoonish villains"? He'd heard of this expression while watching some old holo-vid, where humans were talking about their pre-warp culture. From a certain point of view, the taz'arans probably were. Always spouting nonsense, boasting angrily about the eventual suffering and demise of their enemies, then failing spectacularly to follow up on their words.

To him, and most representatives of the older races, they would certainly look buffoonish, with their antiquated tactics and overcomplicated social structure. He, of course, knew that not all of them were incompetent. It would've been madness to consider it to be true and those, who, after but a single encounter with an inept enemy, lumped all of their soldiers and commanders together, were setting themselves up for failure.

Anit'za felt that sooner, rather than later, a most competent representative of taz'aran nobility would appear. Incidentally or not, his new crewmates will have to face the taz'arans again and again. Surely after their initial failure, one's enemy would "speed up the game" so to speak. Throw against the Terrans, more, and better quality troops.

Anit'za moved closer and stood in the doorway of their newly-built hydroponics bay. Brynjar was fixing its life support assembly half-way behind one of the wall panels, while Lilly was hopping around, giving him whatever tools or parts he needed.

He noted the scarred fur on her back and his left eye twitched. Somehow he would find a way and make those sods pay, even if it was just a little bit, for what she had to live through.

Lilly wasn't a soldier and most members of her race were peaceful. She'd spent her entire life learning how to grow a wide range of crops and diligently studying exobiology. A civilian and tough-as-nails Terran colonist, Lilly certainly was well trained on how to defend herself, but not how to face an entire battalion of invading taz'aran soldiers alone. He listened to what the two friends were chatting about:

"What are we growing here after all of that life support system re-aligning is done, Lilly?" – Brynjar effortlessly bent one of the pipes she'd given him so that it could fit inside the assembly.

"Well, we could grow 'tatoes, grain, tomatoes and...

carrots of course!" – Lilly chimed with her childlike voice and wiped the sweat from her brow and ears with a wet, dirty towel.

"Why, what do you want me to grow here Bee?"

Brynjar laughed while picking up the huge wall panel with one hand and fixed it back in place.

"I'd like us to find at least one beehive, and place it in the middle here. It will pollinate the entire bay and... I can also make Asgardian mead from its honey!" – He turned around and saw Anit'za standing in the doorway.

"Captain, didn't know you were visiting!"

The Asgardian picked up his toolbox and what was left of the salvage he was using to build the hydroponics bay with.

"You see Lillyana, the captain is interested in our progress" – He picked up the bunny by her belt and placed her on his large shoulder.

She giggled and waved her hands as if about to fall; the captain, of course, he knew better. Anit'za knew the extent of her "war dreaming" or what the humans called PTSD. He also knew, that apart from Brynjar and himself nobody knew her full name. The fact that she trusted her friend with it that was a positive thing, he thought.

Anit'za was worried about her, the war dreams had claimed countless millions on his world alone and even his race's android clients suffered from them. He smiled and then pointed at the sawed-off barrels, containers, pipes and plasma lights spread all around the *Starshatter's* former secondary cargo hold.

"Tell me, chief botanist, what exactly *are* we growing here?"

Lilly chuckled, still on Brynjar's shoulder but answered seriously after her new title was mentioned:

"All sorts of vegetables captain. We need to supplement our standard food supply and rations with fresh produce! Otherwise, some of us would develop sicknesses, and that is going to affect crew morale and operational effectiveness, Sir!" – She even saluted him by hitting her chest with a clenched paw.

Anit'za smiled, saluted back and waved his hand at them:

"Carry on you two! It seems that crew cohesion will be an ever-increasing boon for *Starshatter*."

Anit'za slowly walked away and towards the ship's command deck. In the distance, he could hear the two still laughing:

"I bet you can't jump from my shoulder and roll four times in the air before landing!" – Brynjar laughingly challenged the bunny.

"Bwahahaha! Are you kidding me?! Just you watch! You will be juggling one ton containers in the cargo hold again Bee, I swear! Do we have a bet big guy?"

The new captain was walking lost deep in his thoughts.

Anit'za had almost everything needed for his ship to operate normally, only a lucrative starting job was needed to jumpstart his adventure. Cat, his second in command was a gorilla grenadier, whom he met while he was working for the local Colonial Navy detachment.

True to her job description, she was tough, mean and relentless in battle. They had fought together on a number of occasions already, and he came to trust not only in Cat's battle prowess but also her command abilities. Although shy at first, Cat had neatly settled in her new duties and responsibilities. In fact, it was only because both of them were fighting together as one, that they managed to capture their new starship, IMS *Starshatter.*

Facing all of those pirates and achieving victory back then, seemed all but inevitable for Anit'za. Even if now he'd felt that those pirates had no chance whatsoever, despite the "dodgy" stuff that happened in the end. He had to acknowledge that these pirates weren't the tough-as-nails types he was implicitly warned about.

Anit'za chalked all of this up to his amazing Dzenta'rii luck. After all, the last crew of *Starshatter* was a motley bunch of misfits, commanded by some wannabe captain. Had they faced a proper pirate crew...

Anit'za, of course, was sure he would think of something if that had happened. He had the advantage of years of plotting behind the scenes of his House's political stage. And he was an unknown alien in these parts, his dzenta'rii mug and demeanor could easily have passed for something... flashy. There was a clear chance he could weasel his way out or die in the blaze of glory.

The people who warned him had actually fought against real pirate Clans, those who prowled the deeps of Fringe space. Merciless and skilled, those space sharks knew no mercy and awaited none in return. Meeting with one of their ships always resulted in many casualties and they had prepared contingencies. Be it rapidly jumping reinforcements or nasty self-destruct devices, in the event that they lost and couldn't escape.

True pirates were always dangerous and unpredictable.

While the wannabes were part of no Clan, they were easy prey for CM star marine units and even properly armed and led colonists. He couldn't yet put his finger on it but... it was as if he was developing what his people called Ast'la or a deep war connection with Cat. Almost heretical a thought, but the evidence was there.

Both fought literally as one from the first instance they met, without ritual, and without training. It was strangely eerie but also reassuring for Anit'za; his people were known as the Princes of the Stars for a reason.

Once long ago, when the mighty Dzenta'rii Seeker Armada was scouring the stars in search of their ancient Precursor legacy – they met with thousands of young races. All of them were treated with benevolence by the Dzenta'rii and their android clients. Some of that must've spread around, he said to himself.

Now long lost, the Grand Seeker armada was but a dream, a dream of olden days long forgotten and gone, known only by a few old Dzent'a sages and people like Anit'za who managed to procure their holo-writings. A legend, because there just *had* to be one in existence, told of his own race's restoration back into prominence, honor, and greatness, IF that Armada was somehow recovered. And those stiff, slimy racists from the Galactic Assembly then wouldn't be able to say anything when the Dzenta'rii android clients ascended to full status!

Not only that but then the mighty Kil'ra empire would then easily ally with his race...

Anit'za quit daydreaming, entered his starship's bridge and sat in the command pit's chair. Rubbed his chin and ordered the tea maker integrated into it to produce a cup of black Ceylon tea. He casually picked up the steaming hot cup and took one blissful sip.

Almost as good as the wine!

Those Terrans never stopped to amaze him from the moment he entered their space. Anit'za could swear that *if* his race went on full trade contact with the Imperial Minarchy, an entire new generation of youngsters would be greatly inspired by the Terrans' peerless bravery, and imbued with their hunger for exploration and adventure.

He would make every conceivable effort to make this happen – old noble Houses' rules be damned!

The Seekers' noble profession will be restored in just a few short decades too! But those were only plans for now. Plans that could come into fruition, only if his own financial ventures were successful.

\* \* \*

The loot he'd taken from those pirate's corpses and cargo hold was more than enough to repair and refit his ship to almost dzenta'rii battle specs.

To begin with, she was a good, sturdy vessel of Terran design, but them pirates always gutted their ships to an extent, and remade them into stupid "boarding boats". With systems taxed above and beyond their operational limits, they almost always carried triple the original crew complement and various other gear – like combat grapplers for example.

All of their usual criminal makeovers didn't spare *Starshatter*, and she had to be restored to her original specs. Anit'za needed a ship capable of fighting in almost any range, and not a sodding space coffin. Originally, the ship was armed with a battery of six 40mm turreted railguns.

Three on the ship's top and the rest on its bottom, all turrets were able to turn port, starboard and bow. That pirates had sold the precious railguns, gravely disrespecting their mounts by installing god-awful particle beam cannons.

He'd spent a lot of time redesigning the mounts and their power systems, upgrading them all to dual turrets. That starship design also sported one big bow mount, initially home to a large laser cannon, which pirates had replaced with a mag-rail launch system for breaching pods.

Sometimes these sods were so shortsighted!

Why would you replace your main offensive weapon with a glorified roller-coaster?

This was something that he, as an expert in starship tactics always insisted on – one must always have an ace up your sleeve. Preferably a big one, with overwhelming firepower, long range and capable of different firing modes. The fact that Terran lasers were so easy to modify also meant that you'd be able to always deal with a large number of angry sods.

He found his "ace in the sleeve" after connecting with one Terran arms corporation called Baranov Inc. They were experts in designing and manufacturing heavy, long range laser cannons, with a wide range of special features. Many of which were integrated into their products even before their guns left the assembly line.

Anit'za spent a couple of days in heated negotiations with their CEO, a human by the name of Anatoly Baranov. In the end, he was sold the company's best prototype pulse laser with integrated overcharge feature and new generation heatsinks. That weapon came with a special contract for free advertisement though, and he'd included his entire crew and his ship name, before signing on the dotted line.

Meaning the captain had to send any and all space combat footage that included the use of "Samosek" laser cannon. As his new trade partner had explained, it was the name of an ancient magical sword from his nation's folk tales. Anit'za had to agree, that the name carried with it not only a cool vibe but also promised to spell the doom of his enemies without even firing a single shot.

He then, using his new contact in the face of Mr. Baranov, reached another Terran weapons' manufacturing company called Winchester. Their weapon selection sported a wide range of rapid firing, automatic railguns and he needed to beef up *Starshatter's* point defense armament.

The twelve PD turrets, that were tiny in comparison to his main railgun battery. Anit'za wanted to use these not only for intercepting fighters and missiles, but also to fire at other small starships.

He procured Winchester's oldest 25mm auto-railgun design and heavily modified it. The aging weapon in comparison with other similar armaments in its class had a slow rate of fire since it was designed during the 50's early space age. Didn't matter to him though, the "Ol' Shatter hand" was a well-known model, had an excellent reputation and was consistently used in many a successful engagement, and against all pirate lords.

The excess money he'd set aside for this purpose was spent boosting the weapons' firing rate and punch. The guns were now capable of armor piercing and had flack firing modes. While most if not all of the Terran rail weapons had easily modifiable mag-coils, Anit'za made sure to buy the best custom ones he could find. It did drain a considerable amount of energy from *Starshatter's* main fusion core, but now he could utilize them in numerous ways and against many different targets in battle.

On *Starshatter's* stern, there was another mount that Anit'za modified and installed one rapid firing, guide-less rocket pod. Instead of using the all-so-very-powerful, but expensive torpedo tubes that Terrans liked so much, the captain decided for a rather cheap, but effective and dangerous weapon – the simple rocket. Packed with high explosive warheads of many types, it was cheap, reliable and most of all virtually impossible to jam with ECM systems.

By delegating most of his starship's ordinance storage capacity exclusively for that launcher, the ship could carry one hundred warheads. After spending most of his time putting back the teeth in his starship's mouth, Anit'za decided to take a stroll around Cav colony.

He'd spend one relaxing evening, dining in a restaurant he'd found some time before. It was a top-notch place and offered excellent French cuisine, with an assortment of chosen wines from Earth. Anit'za took with him all of his crew members; the fact that they were docked at a Terran colony meant nothing for him security wise.

He was still wondering *if* any of them' pirate sods would try their luck, and dare infiltrate the asteroid colony. After he and Cat produced all of the information gathered from those unfortunate fools whom they killed on the then pirate owned *Starshatter,* the local constabularies went into a month of frenzied checks and security drills. Anit'za was most happy with their dedication to duty, but it was always possible for somebody to sneak their way inside the guarded colony.

* * *

Dzenta'rii always loved their chances of survival to

be as high as possible. The captain felt that he, being in the company of a large Asgardian capable of breaking bulkheads with his bare hands, an immensely powerful telepath, his fiancées overgrown sentient dog and his brutally tough, but also quick on her feet first officer's gorilla frame – was *almost* enough for him to feel safe.

The small bunny frame of Lilly was conveniently located on the shoulder of her Asgardian friend. Lilly had a vibrodagger hidden under that evening dress she wore, but it was more than enough. If push came to shove, Kera was their chief medical officer. She also sported a powerful stunner, always stashed conveniently in the bag.

As always, Brynjar was hesitant and expressed no desire to carry weapons while on shore leave, and especially inside his favorite colony. Besides, any weapon that a fifteen feet tall Asgardian could use simply *had* to be large, basically the same size that Power armors used as main armaments. One single missed shot was just a disaster waiting to happen!

The table he reserved was near the entrance of the establishment, and his crew could all comfortably sit around it. The very fact that they had plenty of Asgardian chairs and larger tables, meant that this restaurant's owner was thoughtful.

Good, Anit'za liked people with good business acumen.

No sooner they had ordered their entrees another group entered and sat at the table closest to them. It was a duo of humans – male and female, followed by a pretty awesome looking hamster. All three were dressed in evening wear, and after giving them a second glance, the man looked to be only half-human.

His alien Aryan DNA showed but only when one looked closely. His eyes had a certain whitish glow that only added more to his charismatic demeanor. The man was as high as his XO and maybe even equal in strength. How was it that his wife managed to procure a suit large enough, that he could move comfortably in was a mystery.

Both of them had long, blond hair and the young woman had hers braided in a fashion that only married spacers did. In stark contrast with her husband, the woman was short, stunningly beautiful and walked with grace few dzenta'rii girls of her age could.

Anit'za also realized she had a hidden needler pistol, holstered in her left boot. Both looked in high spirits as their hamster companion walked chuckling behind them, tapping his elegant tie a couple of times before jumping on his chair. The hamster had black fur and red eyes, but most striking was his smile:

"So, she tells them:" – "There is no effin' way I'll let anything slip past my scanners!; You can brag all you want and your size won't help either!"

Both of his friends busted out laughing, tears of joy in their eyes. It seemed that the hamster was showering them with jokes for the past universe-only-knows how many minutes.

Or was it hours?

Anit'za knew that it was a huge part of their culture to jest, and in a most deadly fashion when need be. He'd heard rumors bordering on insanity about those shifty Terran clients. The weapon dealer he'd purchased Cat's new armor and weapon upgrades from, spoke of entire infantry units comprised of hamsters.

"Devastators with tiny feet" the army called them.

Despite their small stature, they were used as frontal assault troops and the aliens, enemies of the Imperial Terran Minarchy feared them madly.

Often, they would calmly walk towards enemy lines, aiming and shooting with deadly precision. With hardly any fear of enemy return fire, professionally moving forward and taking cover only when needed. Methodical extermination of *all* enemy soldiers, vehicles and equipment. They wouldn't miss even the smallest of things on their way towards victory.

A virtual wonder how was it that those small creatures could win for themselves such a dreaded reputation. The captain smiled again; this, and everything else that happened had proved his decision to come here was most insightful. So many, and interesting things had those Terrans for him to discover yet!

Their waitress, a pleasant and knowledgeable young lady, came back pushing her loaded with food grav-trolley. She then efficiently plated their table and offered them multiple testing sips from her restaurant's wide selection of exquisite wines.

For Anit'za to choose a wine became ever so increasingly hard, and while he was trying vintage after vintage, the dzenta'rii's eyes closed his happy smile widening with every sip. Anit'za had almost found his second Terran favorite winemaker (after first tasting aged Bulgarian wine nothing else was the same), but somehow managed to block his impulse, and only ordered a single case.

While his crew was enjoying their entrées, sipping from his full wineglass Anit'za realized that there was another person sitting at the furthest table of this restaurant.

He was a towering Kil'ra, dressed in what he could instantly recognize as the best-looking morale officer's uniform he'd ever seen. Not only that, but the man had to lay on the table next to him the *most* amazing looking sword and Anit'za's dueling fancy was irked.

The blade was unsheathed as it was common per Morale Officer's Code, placed on the table for anyone to admire and take holoslides with.

Anit'za was able to read the words on it even from that distance – "Vigilant Protector" – engraved with Gothic letters in English.

His uniform had a short line of medals, lined on a sash which most morale officers wore across their chests. That was often the case, because many of them had won so many rewards, that their uniform alone soon had no space to accommodate them all.

The kil'ra had a large plate full of seafood and was savoring every bite. Anit'za thought about engaging him in conversation and convincing the young morale officer to join his crew. As he could clearly see, the Kil'ra had no colonial militia shoulder patch, nor had he any corporate logo either to affiliate himself with. He could visualize all of those wonderful new tactical opportunities, that would emerge if his crew had the support of a morale officer.

On Dzent'a there weren't any such specialists since most members of his race have long lost their nationalistic spirit and were desperately lacking in vigor. Perhaps *that* was the main reason why his people were in decline? Even with minimal corruption and an effective military force, something was sorely lacking.

Not a student of political history, Captain Anit'za had a very hazy knowledge of past emperors and their courts' doings. The love for intrigue was generally accepted as a force for good within his society since it pushed only the wisest and most intelligent people towards the top.

Dueling in dzenta'rii culture was the all-powerful failsafe mechanism. Ensuring that no matter how adept in political machinations one was, if you were mentally unhealthy and ill with extreme socialist ideas, there was always somebody else who would end your rise. Permanently and before any nationwide and unnecessary civil war would erupt – causing billions of innocent deaths and untold destruction. Or worse yet, irreplaceable loss of priceless Dzenta'rii cultural heritage.

While Anit'za was sipping wine and pleasantly lost in thought, a group of scruffy looking bounty hunters was walking towards the restaurant's entrance.

There were no humans or other client races amongst them. Formed entirely of Fringe space aliens, they were sporting an arsenal of deadly melee and ranged weapons. Armed to the teeth, all wearing different types of armored space suits, the colorful bunch stopped right in front of the restaurant's door and began whispering among themselves on their PDA's comm links:

"Oi Flyffloff, that's the human eatery they told us about, right? I don't want to look like an idiot by entering the wrong place."

"Blyah! What you think me' are, eh? Any beardless puke can gain access and pull that map out of their intranet. When *I* tell you, that this is the place – this *IS* the place!"

"Alrighty then. All weapons on stun and keep your boom-sticks holstered. We are here to "persuade" this chum and bring him back to our boss. If he resists, Y'all know what to do, eh?"

The whole group nodded their heads in compliance and some even cracked the knuckles of their fists. Others waved tentacles and other appendages, trying to emulate intimidating readiness. Some had their faceplates open and one could see wide, happy toothless grins accompanied by awkward chuckling.

A young couple and their two kids were sitting on a bench outside the restaurant, with a stasis food box full of sandwiches and fruits. One bounty hunter threw an intimidating look at them, but himself was taken aback when *all* of the humans showed him the handles of their pistols, including both of their children.

The bounty hunter gulped nervously and walked after his buddies inside the restaurant – he was not laughing happily any longer. The door was kicked down, as per longstanding and honorable bounty hunter's tradition. Since this was a fine establishment, it collapsed together with its case on the floor, ruining the expensive carpet. Through the dust cloud, the fearsome group stepped forward, and the fellow they called Flyffloff pointed at Captain Anit'za shouting:

"Oi!; You, with the fancy uniform!"

Both the Captain and that Kil'ra morale officer calmly stood up. Two of the bounty hunters who were yet to enter, quietly snuck away and then ran towards the starport as fast as their legs could carry them. The rest of the idiots could kill themselves by disturbing a calmly eating Kil'ra – they loved living too much.

"No, not you, the one with the fancier uniform! Yes, you Captain! Our boss wants to have a word wiff ya'. Preferably while most of yer teeths are still intact!"

Flyffloff looked menacingly and indeed sounded too,

but that quickly changed, when their target walked calmly towards them. The man was still holding a wine glass in his left hand, pinky finger to the side keeping it balanced.

"Why gentlemen, I would have to ask who this boss of yours is, before coming along with you so carelessly," – Anit'za pointed at his shiny white smile.

"Also, why is it always about teeth with you gentlemen of that particular trade? You do know what care and thoughtfulness it takes to maintain a man's dental health, right?" – He sipped a little bit from his wine glass and continued:

"We could talk about *what* it is that your boss wants, peacefully. You can see, I am a gentleman and most annoyed by unnecessary engagement in fisticuffs. What say you gentlemen, shouldn't we resolve this with reason, logic and without using needless violence?"

The Captain sipped again from his wine and delivered a most shining smile, all the while confused Flyffloff stood before him shifting weight from one leg to another. Before he could think or say something witty, one of his goons grabbed the Captain's sleeve and screamed spitting in his face:

"Come wiff us if ya' know what's good for Twiggy!"

"But I can't possibly do what you ask, kind madam or miss, for I am still drinking my wine! You can't expect a dzenta'rii gentleman to leave the table *and* his guests, without even finishing his first glass. Let alone leave all of that wonderful food go to waste!"

It was evident that his hand was being pulled back, and with force, but that bounty hunter was unable to move the dzenta'rii from his place. Calmly, Anit'za used two fingers to remove the unwanted physical contact and wiped some imaginary speck of dust from his sleeve. The goon, angered and humiliated, reached for her stun baton and almost shoved the weapon in his face screaming:

"I saiz git going twiggy, or *else!*"

The end of her baton crackled with electricity, causing the air around to smell of ozone. Before Flyffloff could grab her hand, another one of his band reached for his stunner and pointed it, this time at the captain's companions, most of them being on the very end of their patience. Cat was the first to stand up and snarled at the bounty hunters:

"Get your grimy hands off my captain's uniform, you bums!"

More of the goons reached either for their blunt melee weapons or stunners and before you knew it *Starshatter's* crew was surrounded from all sides.

Brynjar stood up, while Lilly leaped off her chair and landed on his left shoulder again, standing on one leg. Boris looked at his wife and sighed heavily when she negatively nodded back. He raised both his fists and prepared to fight, while Ort snarled showing his long teeth. The large dog instantly placed his body before Boris's wife and the bounty hunters, while she herself stood up too opening her bag. One big and fine quality looking stunner then laid comfortably in her hand.

Flyffloff suddenly found that the whole situation was quickly slipping out of his control. He gulped nervously, opened his mouth, raised his finger and tried speaking. At least nobody had pulled anything other than a simple shock baton or a stunner, yet. He felt supremely uncomfortable as somebody considerably taller was standing behind him. A booming voice charged with great commanding presence shouted in his ear:

"So my uniform *isn't* fancy enough?! Allow me to not agree with you rapscallion! Collect your goons this instant! I swear by the honor and glory of *All* Imperial morale officers – my hands will crush those bones of yours! Before mere five minutes pass, you and all of them will be occupying the local hospital's emergency room beds!"

The kil'ra stood before him, one full head above all of his men and they completely freaked out.

While with a stuttering voice Flyffloff tried to formulate some poor semblance of an answer, one of his bounty hunters fired his stunner. The brawl was impossible to prevent now!

Soon both restaurant patrons and bounty hunters were molded into one huge bundle of bodies, which spilled through the already broken doors and out in the street. Somehow Captain Anit'za still had his wine glass in hand, and while vigorously defending its content he kicked and punched in a most elegant and gentlemanly manner any bounty hunter who dared come close to him.

His Asgardian crewman was hit multiple times with stun batons and ranged stunners, but continued beating the living crud out of their attackers. Lilly danced around and between his legs, tripping to the ground any flanking enemies, knocking them senseless.

Their telepath, breaking the stereotype of his profession, using rapid punches and kicks possessing incredible power, turned himself into a whirlwind of devastation. Any bounty hunter who made contact with him flew unconscious in the opposite direction.

Cat's long gorilla limbs were grappling goon after goon, sending them flying in the air and in all directions. Any of them unfortunate enough to get punched by her iron fists, lay broken boned on the street below.

The fight wasn't going well and one bounty hunter drew his plasma pistol shooting panicky at Brynjar. In just a split second, the brawl transformed into a deadly shootout. Anit'za's crew had just a few concealed pistols and daggers, but soon it became painfully evident for their adversaries that they had chosen poorly – both the battleground and their opponents.

Benches and lampposts were used as improvised weapons by Brynjar, unconscious bodies hit by stray plasma and energy bolts. The facade of that restaurant was shot and melted beyond recognition, and within the center of the melee everybody was using corpses or bent floor panels to shield themselves from weapons' fire.

Despite the fact that great care was taken not to deal collateral damage, a few unfortunate passers-by were wounded by the bounty hunters. After another thirty odd seconds, the local security came crashing the fight in full force, viciously dealing with whoever was yet standing on their feet.

They prioritized the aliens fist.

Anit'za's crew had peacefully surrendered, so the security personnel then had to deal with what was left of Flyffloff's band. None let themselves be captured, and as Flyffloff himself made a half-assed attempt to escape, his body was shredded to pieces by the security officers' railguns. Once you pull a deadly weapon and start fighting, Terran colonial security forces and sheriffs shot back and shot to kill.

It was safer to shoot first, as their chief mandate was to protect the local citizenry, therefore any idiot who started shooting indiscriminately was a walking deadalien. Only in cases where hostages were involved, did the constabularies use nonlethal force.

After the last shot was fired, Anit'za's crew together with the Kil'ra morale officer and the human couple stood in line before one newcomer to the scene, a tall human woman – who evidently was the station's security chief. Wearing a heavily armored space suit faceplate open, all could see her angered face while she was tapping on her PDA holo-screen, answering her underlings on the comms. She nodded after receiving last pieces of information from witnesses and almost screamed at the lined up people:

"I don't care who started it!" – she pointed at Anit'za, who was still holding his wine glass and drank what droplets were left inside, trying to open his mouth – "Zip it mister! I care not for your reasons and whatever pompous crud, slick dzent'a like you can spout back at me! You have defended yourselves and were the ones attacked by those bounty hunters. Considerable damage was inflicted to the surrounding area, citizens were hurt and the Common Law in such an instance says…" – She was unable to finish as Boris stepped up before her, with left bloodied arm raised at her eye level.

Everybody could see the bioluminescent I-Sec badge forming on his wrist. Quickly, the local security chief's angered facial expression changed into a troubled one, and while her mouth was still half opened, Boris spoke:

"I know what it says because I *AM* the Law!" – Whispered menacingly the telepath, while his wife Kera was cleaning the blood and bone fragments from his fists.

She smiled calmly, while Ort tried emulating her semi-successfully, using both paws to wipe the blood from his mouth. The security chief unintentionally backed away just a little bit more. Such was the reputation of I-Sec, that

335

even other security and law enforcement personnel feared them, and then there were the rumors.

I-Sec agents all had secret orders, and those were to hunt the incompetent!

Not like the witch hunts of old, no. People were fed up with idiots who managed even in this day and age to reach positions of power that they weren't supposed to. Yes, despite the fact that most Terrans could reach *any* position thanks only to their merit and abilities – there were sometimes the odd morons trying to cheat their way up.

Those used more sinister and outlawed means to rise up in society or the workplace. Instead of having the best person for some particular job, you could face somebody lacking even the necessary skills and ability to cover the basic of standards. That *always* led to injuries, loss of valuable property and even death! She'd heard that such people and their accomplices were executed promptly after enough evidence was collected proving their guilt.

"I-Sec?! I wasn't told that you were here Sir!" – and she inspected the bio-badge for a second – *First Investigator Boris; Psy-corps certified*– she gulped nervously and backed even further away from him.

"We will cover any and all property damages and the medical fees for these colonists" – Said Boris, as he glanced at the ambulance shuttle, where the medics were loading a couple of lightly wounded civilians.

"There will be no need for safety arrests because our party will be leaving the station immediately. We will somehow *survive* the three-month docking block, as per Common Law statute P39. Cav will have to live without us for a while Captain," – Boris turned around and nodded to Anit'za, before he addressed the station security Chief again:

"Now to address your unprofessional conduct officer... Anita Sullivan. I will make sure and put a formal reprimand on your record. In no way shape or form is a security officer, enforcing the Common Law to lash at a person or persons who were the target of an attack and defended themselves. Take care also, and increase the extent of your willpower, officer. It was far too easy to grab your name floating from those so badly protected surface thoughts of yours. I *will* overlook that transgression in the spirit of cooperation between local security and I-Sec, Chief Sullivan!"

Boris walked casually away from the stunned woman, calmly waving his hand at the rest of *Starshatter's* crew to follow him.

"You are free to continue with your duties Chief!"

While Boris was busting the security chief's chops, Captain Anit'za walked over and shook hands with the hamster, the half-Aryan and his wife, who was evidently a spacer from what he had seen so far.

While they were fighting, she began pistol-whipping any bounty hunter who tried sneaking behind her husband's back. Her moves were lightning fast, and while the pistol looked a bit large for a young girl of her stature, she handled it with expert precision.

There was something in her eyes that he saw, but it wasn't hatred. She gave every single one of those who flanked her husband a look promising... impending death. Anit'za was more than positive, had any of them tried to pull something bigger than a hand stunner, she would've shot them dead on the spot.

The man... well, *he* was clearly highly trained and in many types of combat arts. Facing those bounty hunters in battle was something of a bother for him, as he effortlessly slapped them dead to the ground, and any hits they would score on him were insufficient in bringing him down.

Anit'za quickly noticed that even the smallest of scratches vanished but a second after the man was wounded. While others around him were fighting, it was evident that this half-Aryan was more of an observer than part of the brawl. Every time Anit'za's crewmates did something right, he would unleash a glowing smile and cheer them. No, *this* wasn't a battle for him, but Anit'za would gladly pay any price, just to have him and his partner on his crew!

"But Sir, what about those four?" – Sullivan pointed at the hamster, kil'ra and other two Terrans beside them – "Are they affiliated with you in any way? Because if they aren't, I will have to arrest them. It is for their own protection, as you are well aware some of those dead bounty hunter's friends might come looking for you and hurt them instead."

Boris blinked while his gaze inspected the imposing morale officer's spotless uniform. He noticed the Slaver Annihilator badge on his sash and their eyes met. The telepath suddenly bowed deeply at the kil'ra and shook his gloved hand, even his own wife's eyes widened with amazement. Boris respected only selected few whom he deemed worthy. He then asked the morale officer:

"How many have you wiped from the face of the Galaxy, Father?"

The kil'ra smiled, revealing his razor-sharp teeth. He slightly nodded at everyone present:

"First let me introduce myself," – he clenched his right hand into a fist, and hit the center of his chest with it – "Dozan'Re is my name, and I personally never count my kills. Slavers and pirates' lives mean little to nothing to me. Does that answer your question Citizen Enforcer?"

Boris's face twitched and his mouth formed one of his rare smiles, while the station's security chief was still looking nervously at him. Lilly walked from behind Brynjar's leg and faced the kil'ra morale officer. Her scarred sad face turned upwards so that she could meet his eyes:

"Father Dozan, my name is Lilly," – she pointed back at Anit'za – "And he is our captain." The small bunny walked closer to him, and with a shaky voice continued:

"I would ask of you a favor, Father" – her soft voice trembled when Dozan knelt so that his head would be on the same level with hers.

"My colony was called 'Murphy's Landing', and it was in Carrola system..." – She gasped, her eyes full of tears.

"The Taz'arans killed and enslaved all of us except me. And I am but a farmer, not a soldier. Will you aid me? Two of the taz'aran soldiers I overheard were talking about a slave ship loaded with whomever they'd captured alive. I seek... revenge!"

Dozan'Re watched how the young sentient before him cried her hazel green eyes out. The kil'ra had just noticed that her entire body was scarred and burned, and her brown fur had some bald patches. His fists clenched so hard that the knuckles gave a loud crackle. Vile taz'aran filth! Again, they proved to be a most foul adversary and represented a clear danger for all peaceful sentients. It was in his power to do something about it and by the Universe, he would see at least this wrong avenged!

"You will have your vengeance brave human client! I will make sure of it!" – Said he and turned towards Anit'za.

"Captain! Your ship has enough space to accommodate another crewman, right?" – Dozan tapped the hilt of his vibrosword with a gloved hand – "I wish to serve under your command, that is *IF* you want me!"

The hamster quickly started swiping through multiple holo-files, obviously in search of some joke with a devastating punchline. Anit'za blinked and smiled happily:

"Well yes, of course! I would be bad captain and a terrible leader, to deny my crew the services of such an accomplished morale officer as you!"

Brynjar chose this moment to tap chief Sullivan's shoulder carefully with his finger. She turned at him, and despite the fact that he was obviously not somebody who one would miss, acted all startled at first. It took her a couple of seconds to recognize the towering Mecha engineer and pilot:

"Oh, it is you champion! Where are my manners, I am so sorry Brynjar, but all this commotion and the multiple security alerts we've answered had already drained me."

The woman glanced tiredly at Brynjar's chatting companions and pointed at his captain with her armored fingers.

"Your captain, is he dependable? I have seen many a Dzent'a, and my opinion of them isn't that good. Conniving were they... all of them, and you know me well, I hate wise-asses!"

The Asgardian nodded a couple of times and waved goodbye to his captain; he had to stay and chat with the station's security chief. He didn't know her that well personally, but with his local fame and the Title of Mecha Champion, talking with local authorities was easier for him.

At least here on Cav colony, where he had lived for many years, even the local elderly knew of him. His now significantly larger crew, walked away from the battlefield and boarded the nearby rapid tube, one leading towards Cav's docking bays. Brynjar noted the look that beefy half-Aryan gave him while they were entering the empty mag-lift transport car waiting for them in the rapid tube.

That was the testing look of a hardened warrior, and he very much liked to challenge him to a boxing match.

He sighed, work was work and had to be done first, rest and relaxation came second, always. During the fight, Anit'za somehow managed to type and send him a holo-note. While Boris was pulling everyone's attention (he'd probably received a note too) at his badge and then engaging the security chief in a battle of words, he did what his captain ordered him to.

Scanned the surroundings, all bounty hunter bodies and equipment. Brynjar even managed to pull off their leader's PDA his most recent file archives. Since he was a little kid, Brynjar fell in love with his personal data assistant. That gadget, which most people used only to share media and aimlessly roam the networks, he'd used to do much more.

His own now had a powerful personal scanner and other nifty tools integrated into its bigger than normal frame. One instance when his large Asgardian size actually helped. Most of the personal gear was bigger and since the PDA's internals were tiny, he used the space to integrate as many additional gadgets as possible. Brynjar already knew a lot about those bounty hunters but wanted to piece the little bits of info he had together with what the security chief pulled from her own sources.

"My captain can be trusted, yes. He is

most...dependable, just don't ever try to argue or barter with him... ever. He will twist your mind in such a way that after only a couple of minutes you will already have sold him the clothes off your back." – Brynjar quickly jabbed the air with his left and smiled nodding at her.

"But you need not worry about us. We will soon be out of your docking bay and far away... somewhere, universe-only-knows where..." – He gulped trying to reach some minor form of relaxation before boarding his starship.

"Chief, you've mentioned some sort of troubles plaguing the station. Is my home colony safe? Please, be truthful to me!"

Sullivan looked around and sneakily swiped one large holo-file to his PDA. She nodded smiling and turned around making a couple of steps towards her Cav security service dropship grabbing its side rail.

"Meh, you know perfectly well that such information is work specific and not openly available to citizens. I would've told you only *if* your life was in danger!" – She slid her faceplate on and then with muffled voice added:

"Now go back to your home citizen, there is nothing more to be seen here!"

The dropship used its grav-engines to hover in the air and reach a higher altitude before activating its main plasma drive. It darted towards the mid part of Cav leaving behind it a small trail of ionized plasma that quickly dissipated as the Asgardian watched.

Brynjar allowed himself a crooked, happy smile – it was good to know how real life worked. Connections, it was *all* about connections and the Asgardian whistled one old, familiar Life Metal tune, while waiting for the next mag-rail transport to arrive in the tube.

Seems that, not only there were multiple groups of mercs stirring trouble around, but some unfortunate human had his brain fried while connected to the G-Net. Very unfortunate indeed. The peculiar thing was, he'd never had a Nerve-gear implant in his brain stem, to begin with. And yet, he bought it in the very same fashion how hackers who were under attack by some network entity did – brains leaking all over the place.

Most peculiar indeed...

Awesome quickly rushed into the empty mag-lift transport car, muttering something under his nose. He then stood still for a moment before exclaiming:

"I got it! Listen, guys, listen. So... a bunch of humans, a Kil'ra, a bunny girl, a half-Aryan, a Dzenta'rii, an Asgardian and one absolutely *awesome* looking hamster enter together an empty mag-lift transport car. There are some taz'arans standing outside looking at each other, awkwardly exchanging looks. One of them asks – 'Why aren't we entering the transport?' – somebody quickly responds – 'What? Are you mad?! It is too Die-Verse in there!" – Awesome happily smiled chuckling, while the people around him suddenly busted out laughing and noted in his PDA *New prospective crew – easily entertained; no need for more joke fishing*

Made in the USA
Monee, IL
27 October 2022

16652069R00204